# The Florentine Trinity

Thomas Crockett

**ISBN 10:** 0692815015
**ISBN 13:** 978-0692815014

To Mary Jo,

*who was with me at San Marco*

*"I like nothing better than to step inside the venerable courts of the ancients, where, solicitously received by them, I nourish myself on that food that alone is mine and for which I was born; where I am unashamed to converse with them and to question them about the motives for their actions, and they, out of their human kindness, answer me. And for many hours at a time I feel no boredom, I forget all my troubles, I do not dread poverty, and I am not terrified by death."*

Niccolo Machiavelli

# Introduction

When I returned home from a trip to Italy in October 2015, I began a period of research that has led me to the writing of this introduction. The impetus for the research was the lingering images I retained from the San Marco monastery in Florence: Fra Angelico's frescoes depicting the Crucifixion, Madonna and Child, and the Annunciation, and a haunting portrait of Girolamo Savonarola in a cell he had once occupied more than five huundred years ago. I knew little of his life other than he had been a renowned preacher and *de facto* leader in Florence until he met a tragic death by hanging and burning in the Piazza della Signoria. I knew little, also, the extent of the Medici influence in restoring, through its patronage, San Marco. I recalled visiting Cosimo de' Medici's private cell, where he often meditated, viewing *The Adoration of the Magi* frescoed on the wall.

Though I read at first to satisfy a hunger to learn more about Savonarola, the Medici, and Italian Renaissance art, my objective quickly changed when I read (I paraphrase) in Paul Strathern's book *Death in Florence*: "Savonarola wanted to destroy man's mind to save his soul." At that moment I no longer read exclusively to learn. I desired to write about what I was reading. I returned to that line, writing it down numerous times in my notebook. Any man with such a beautifully contradictory motive is an ideal man to write about I thought. Soon after, in that same book, I learned that Lorenzo de' Medici (Cosimo's grandson), while on his deathbed, summoned Savonarola to his room to receive the preacher's blessing. The historical references of their meeting remain vague. What is certain is that Savonarola had been Lorenzo's adversary, often referring to the Florentine ruler as a tyrant. How perfect I thought. Lorenzo de' Medici had been one of the leading humanists in Florence, a man who, above all else, valued his mind and the minds of others. Here then was an ideal scenario: a meeting between a preacher and a humanist, representing two potentially polarizing spectrums: the mind and the soul. Questions ran through my head: Why would Lorenzo call to his bed a man who didn't like him? Would he surrender his mind for the sake of his soul? What were the preacher's motives for going to see Lorenzo? Did he have conditions for his blessing? What did he gain to win? What would Lorenzo have to lose to gain? Only by writing a scene between the two could I ever hope to answer these questions. I knew, if nothing else, the preacher would not make it easy for Lorenzo. Thus, I saw in this meeting the basis for an intriguing story.

I checked out many more books from my local library and took voluminous notes, believing I was gathering detail to use in a play. After all, I had three years earlier written a comic play about Henry VIII after having researched early 16th Century England upon returning from a trip to Great Britain. I assumed I would follow a similar path this time as well. I did, in fact, begin a play, writing the first ten pages, beginning with a bedroom scene between Lorenzo and Savonarola. I decided to add a third character, Niccolo Machiavelli, knowing he, who had outlived both Lorenzo and Savonarola, had written a history of Florence. Therefore, I believed he would make an ideal narrator/commentator. His cynical, humorous tone could provide a necessary balance. He could, as well, fill in many blank spaces, historically speaking.

I discontinued the idea of writing a play for this reason: I had, in the intervening period between writing the Henry VIII play and starting this project, been writing a great deal of prose. I had recently finished the second of my memoirs. Thus, my first-person narrative voice was well exercised. One day, in a fit of experimentation, I transferred what I had written in the early pages of the play, writing in first person from Lorenzo's point of view, lying in bed, as he is watching Savonarola enter his room. I wrote one page and liked it. I then wrote in first person from Savonarola's point of view, as he is entering Lorenzo's room, looking at the sick man in his bed. I wrote two pages, including some of the same dialogue I had written in the play's early pages. I followed Savonarola's pages by having Machiavelli, with the benefit of time, distance and detachment, comment in first person. From that point forward, I didn't look back. I had found my creative design for telling this story of late 15th Century Florence. I would write three separate, though intertwining, autobiographies, shifting continuously and non-sequentially throughout the book, allowing me, I believed, greater range in time and movement as well as more freedom to develop the personal identities of the narrators.

Though based on fact, the book is fundamentally transformative in its vision--endowing voice and perspective to dead men, providing them with thoughts, feelings and words beyond what was real—and thus well deserving of its classification as a historical novel.

Machiavelli writes these words in the book: "Though I am not a man given to superstition, I believe the dead have much to tell the living. Thus, I listen to the dead. I would, in fact, not be a writer if I didn't invite the visitation of ghosts." I couldn't agree more. When I am researching and writing about history, I live with the dead and listen to them, and they in return give birth to life. *The Florentine Trinity* is that life, and I am grateful for its birth.

# Lorenzo

It strikes me as he enters that I have never laid eyes on him, though he has occupied my thoughts the way a fever occupies the body. He is large. I do not mean in stature. Of that he is small. I mean his presence, his aura. He stands in the glow of burning candles. A black cape covers his head, bringing heightened attention to his face, which is hard, unmoving and unforgiving: the eyes dark and beady, the nose hooked and long, the lips tight, the jaw locked, the cheeks lined and hollow. Though recognized in Florence as a holy man, he appears as one more in the business of punishment than absolution.

He has only this one look as he stands and stares, as if he is waiting for me to speak first. Does he not see that I am laboring in my breath? I requested him to my bedside to receive his blessing, though at this moment I wonder if he has entered as a priest intent on administering what I desire. His silence and the hardness of his stare tell me he has not come for my soul, of which I give willingly. He has come for something else. What that something is I try to surmise in the darkness of his eyes, which appear impenetrable. Is it my mind he wants? That I will not under any circumstance surrender. I have worked too hard to develop it.

Have I made a mistake in bringing him here? He is, after all, someone who has been critical of me since his arrival in Florence, condemning my acts and behaviors, calling me a tyrant and blaming me for the degradation of the poor. Still, he is a prophet, if one is to believe the word on the street and the many great minds of my age--some of whom are my friends--and a man of significant religious means. Who better than he can save my soul from damnation, if my soul is indeed damned for my having lived my years with humanistic ideals?

1

# Savonarola

I am not surprised to see he looks much older than his years. Illness and impending death can do that to a man. So, too, can a life of debauchery. His long shoulder length hair is thin, unwashed and mostly gray. Eczema riddles his face, which, I assume, even in healthy times, has never been refined or elegant: his high forehead, his long, twisted nose, his jutting jaw, and his firm, thick lips. I notice mostly his eyes, once fierce and intelligent in Florentine reputation, projecting a vigor and determination of a man of the world. They now hold fear as his wasted body lies beneath a heavy quilted blanket. He resembles little the man who has lived in esteem and entitlement, always wanting to win by one means or another, revered throughout the city, if not all of Italy, as Il Magnifico. His title means nothing now, made evident by the stench and sound of his breath, and the feverous vapors hanging about his head like a mock halo sent from the Inferno. He has been reduced, as we all must be reduced in the end, to recognizing the limitations of our human form, understanding that God will judge us not on titles and positions of power but on the righteousness of our ways. In this regard, Lorenzo has reason to fear, for he has lived in the wrong. He knows he has. Why else has he called for me, other than in the hope that I will assuage his fears by telling him everything is all right, that God will receive and comfort him, despite his egregious acts against Christian virtue? I have, however, no intention of making it easy for him. A man cannot simply turn on a dime and renounce his sins.

"Now, in your hour of need, you call on me," I say.

"My need is not for you," he replies. "It is for your blessing."

"Your need is for God."

"Yes," he whispers, laboring between breaths.

"I am his mediator," I declare.

"So I hear," he says, "though self-appointed."

I receive his jest, though I do not laugh, for I am not inclined to behave in a way more befitting a man who drinks in taverns and fornicates with loose women, recklessly casting himself in eternity's shade, never to see the light of God. I, in fact, do not show any face other than the one I wore as I entered. I remain stern, receiving the insult (how dare he say I am God's self-appointed mediator, when clearly God himself has appointed me to do his work on earth?) as if it were yet another mutilation I should suffer, only this time not from my own hands but from another's vitriolic words.

I laugh to myself, where no human eye can see, secure in knowing the truth: he is weak, lying on death's threshold, while I am strong, especially in spirit, where strength counts most. I know the more I use my strength against his weakness, the more I will have my way with him. God himself used his strength against the fallen angel Lucifer, securing that heaven would remain free of sin and deceit. I will do as God and strike a blow to those who follow the selfish ways of Satan. The earth is my domain, and people, such as Lorenzo, need to pay homage to my responsibility as God's chosen messenger.

"Just as you are the self-appointed ruler of Florence," I respond. "Tell me, where is it shown you were elected?"

"I was the most qualified to rule," he answers.

"As I am the most qualified to be God's voice," I state. "Otherwise, why have you called me here?"

"I want my soul received in good faith."

"What are you willing to give in return for the blessing of your soul?"

"So, your blessing is conditional?"

"Yes, even God has conditions."

"You are a friar, not God."

"I am also a politician."

"The politics of man's faith?"

"The politics of God's blessing."

# Machiavelli

Savonarola was not a Florentine. This should be noted from the start. He was an outsider, from Ferrara, and he wanted to make us all outsiders by destroying our minds to save our souls. I cannot, and will not, speak for the soul. I find it of little use living among men who connive and fight for power. I will speak for the prince, however: Lorenzo de' Medici, a lover of pagan art and literature, a renowned leader and diplomat, a self-appointed monarch--though far from being a tyrant, of which I will prove later--out of necessity, for the good of the state, and its citizens. Yes, the ends justify the means. No man should say otherwise. It matters little what the ruler has to do to maintain the peace and stability of the state, to keep its citizens living well and happy, with festivities and tournaments, and ample supply of wool and grain, in a thriving economy. It matters little if he owns and exercises absolute rule, or if he is cunning and deceptive and tells lies. What matters only is the quality of the state and the satisfaction of the people, and during Lorenzo's reign Florence was indeed a stable, thriving city because its leader was decisive, ruling with two purposes: to protect his own wealth, status and familial lineage, and to keep the citizens of Florence content, living in a state of peace of prosperity. Called "the needle of the Italian compass" by Pope Innocent VIII, he was known to all Florentines who knew and loved him as "Lorenzo, Il Magnifico." In 1492, before Columbus set sail to discover a new world, Lorenzo, bedridden from long-suffering gout and fever, at age 43, readied himself for death, toward a country no man in life can discover. Why he had called to his bed the man who had condemned his leadership and way of life is a mystery he took to his grave.

# Lorenzo

His animosity is evident. What have I done to deserve it? Was it not I who brought him to Florence? Does it matter my motive for doing so? He had acquired a reputation in Tuscany for his sermons. I thought his presence would bring greater theological status to the city. Yes, I confess to having desired the advancement of my son's religious ambitions. I did not know then that Savonarola's arrival would serve to advance his own ambitions: one of which was to wage war on my family and me and threaten to take from us our earned position as leading family. I have never understood why he is not grateful to me. It is I who supported San Marco, as my grandfather had, renovating the church, dressing it in art, making sure the monks lived well, with ample food and clothing and private sleeping cells. When the friar arrived, he refused my gifts and the comfort they afforded him and his fellow Dominicans. Worse still, he refused to visit me and pay respects to the man who elected him Prior of the monastery. This, more than anything, offended me. Yet I have extended myself, using every means possible to make peace with him.

His expression remains rigid. A fire burns inside me, causing great pain in my limbs. I struggle to lift myself.

"You have my soul," I say. "That I willingly give. What else is it you desire?"

"That which is most important to you," he answers.

"If it is my mind you wish to have, that I cannot give," I cry out. "That is mine to keep."

"God has no need of your mind and your humanistic ideals."

"I cannot, and will not, surrender those ideals."

"Those ideals have been nurtured in vain."

"I nurtured the gifts that God gave me. Do you not see the beauty of the human soul—the soul of God--in the beauty of man's art and literature?"

"Man's art and literature have nothing to do with the soul of our Christian God. They are a product of a pagan

God. Those who worship a pagan God are doomed to suffer in hell."

"Have you ever doubted what you profess to know?"

"I have never doubted."

"I have doubted."

"It is the curse of Humanism."

"It is a blessing."

"Hypocritical words from a dying man."

"If there is eternal truth, it must come from one's questioning, seeking ... "

"And doubting God?"

"We who live can never know."

"I have sacrificed my body and mind—what you call your gifts--to know."

"Have you ever thought your sacrifice in vain?"

"Never, though, you, like all humanists, in your final hour of need, see your worship of false Gods in vain. Now that death has come to your door, you look on in fright and realize what you should have always known: that you have followed a path of sin, and that, in doing so, you have paid a heavy price, disregarding the righteous path of God. You, Il Magnifico, cannot deny that. Your calling me here for absolution confirms that truth."

# Machiavelli

Savonarola's hatred of humanism was nothing more than vengeance against life, of which he had denied himself. If he had indulged in the pleasures and whims of the flesh, as I have, his ship would have sailed on a different sea. Who knows then how his genius would have manifested itself in so many wondrous ways? He could have been a man of medicine, the profession his father had wanted him to follow. Instead he became a scourge of man's mind and natural gifts. He could have saved lives instead of souls. What good are souls here on earth? I see no evidence of their relevance. Perhaps in the afterlife, if there is such a realm. I, for one, cannot attest to it because it is outside the bounds of the senses and, therefore, remains, for me, senseless and of no consequence. I know what I have learned through living. How could Savonarola know anything shut away in his cloister in silent meditation? What kind of God asks a man to turn away from life?

Though I am guilty of conjecture, I know this: to worship God, as he did, requires a madness of the spirit, a vengeance of the heart, a desecration of the body, a disrespect of everything that makes us human. Whether it is God who gives us the gifts of the body and mind, I cannot say. I do know that religion is nothing more than metaphysics, and I do not believe in metaphysics. I believe in the machinations of man. Call me a cynic, immoral, or unscrupulous. I've been called worse. I live and learn by what I see. I do not dwell in dreams. I prefer to write of history the way it happened, not as men wished it to happen. I hear Savonarola's response to what I say: you, Niccolo Machiavelli, are the finger of Satan. And I shall say to him: you know Satan well since you speak like a man who knows more the knowledge of hell than heaven.

# Savonarola

I see myself as a barking watchdog. Lorenzo is a thief throwing a bone or lump of meat, trying to distract me. But a thief cannot trick me. I will continue to bark, as a watchdog for the poor citizens of Florence. I will not, as other Dominicans before me, be bought by Medici money. When I first came here, I saw friars walking in robes and silk vestments specially tailored by Lorenzo's haberdashers. They lived in private cells, eating olives, fish and fruit and drinking wine. They partook in Lorenzo's entertainments during high days and holy days. I set out to put an end to such foolhardy behavior. I am not impressed with the many entertainments or the large piazzas and palaces crammed with fine art and man-made riches. I see clearly that Medici gifts are not born of generosity. They have always hoped to buy absolution with their money and, thus, their seats in heaven. I have walked the narrow lanes, the backstreet tenement slums, occupied by the dyers and cloth workers who supply the textile industry. I have had my sleeves tugged by both the beggars and the blind. They mistrust us and see us as Lorenzo's spies, for good reason. Their poverty is genuine, while we Dominicans, who took a vow of poverty, live better than them. So, yes, I refuse his gifts because I do not serve sinners, guilty of usury and manipulating the political process, ensuring no one other than themselves can be elected.

"I cannot save your soul," I say. "Only you can."

"How?" he asks.

"By renouncing all that is contrary to it."

"Contrary to *it*--or *to you*?

"Both."

"According to Savonarola."

"According to God."

"Savonarola's God."

"The God according to the Bible."

"Give me the blessing I deserve."

"A tyrant is no more deserving than another."

"I ask only the entitlement of a man who is dying."

"Do you repent your sins?"

"I do."

"And do you believe in one true God?"

"Yes, of course."

"Where are your doubts now?"

"I have cast them aside."

"Because you are dying and in need of absolution?"

"Yes."

His hypocrisy matters little to me at this moment. I am not really interested in saving his soul. Only God can do that, if he is compassionate. The God I know, however, is not compassionate. He is fair and vengeful, when vengeance is deemed necessary. Thus, I leave Lorenzo's fate to God. My concern is more practical, though I rather enjoy his believing his salvation lies with me.

"Do you promise to renounce your ill-gotten wealth and restore to the people of Florence was what wrongly taken for your own means and satisfaction?"

"So it's not my mind you want, after all."

"No, not your mind."

"And yet you said you wanted what was most important to me."

"If you want my blessing you must renounce what I requested."

His back arches, and his muscles tighten. I can see from the way his teeth bite his trembling lip that his pain is great. The blood appearing from his mouth is further testament.

"I will do so, or I will cause my heirs to do so if I cannot," he says.

He lifts his hand, as if waiting for me to receive it in mine. I do not move. I sense in his actions a weakening resolve, a softening of ideals, a fear as palpable as sight, sound, and smell.

"I desire something more," I say.

"I have nothing more to give," he responds.

"I believe you do."

He closes his eyes. Beads of sweat rush down his forehead and temple.

"Water," he whispers hoarsely.

I do not respond or move.

"Water, please," he says. "On the table."

I pour water from a pitcher into a cup and bring it to his lips. He lunges forward to take the water, swallowing small sips. His head falls onto his pillow. His eyes are red and teary.

"Savonarola, what is it you want?"

I return the cup to the table and turn to him.

"Are you willing to restore to the people of Florence their liberty, which can only be guaranteed by a truly republican government?"

He swallows a spittle of blood.

"The citizens of Florence do not desire a republican government."

"Nonsense, they want what is fair and just, such as open elections."

"You are wrong, Savonarola. They want what is best for them."

"And what's best for you and your family is best for them?"

"Florence has thrived under the Medici."

"The Medici has thrived under the Medici."

He turns away, again closing his eyes. His chest rises and falls, as he struggles to breathe, and yet he is determined to talk. I admire his stubbornness to stay alive, though he is clearly torn in body and spirit.

"What you ask is impossible for me to give," he says.

"So you do not need me, after all."

I make a turn to leave.

"My son Piero is heir to all I have," he cries out.

I face him again.

"Including your illegitimate leadership?"

"Including my leadership."

"If you cannot surrender that, I cannot bless you."

"The fortunes of my family are all I have left."

"And these dynastic fortunes are more important than your eternal soul?"

"The legacy of my family is my soul."

"Then your soul is damned."

# Machiavelli

Is not fame and reputation greater than a friar's blessing? Is it not even better than God's holy heaven, if there is such a place? Pardon my skepticism, but I have never heard of anyone's whereabouts in heaven. I do, however, know of men's lives, as they were lived, on earth. I know what Augustus, the first emperor of Rome, accomplished. He punished those who had assassinated his uncle, Julius Caesar. He defeated Marc Anthony and his exotic queen, capturing Egypt, expanding the Roman Empire, as he commanded, through might and power, the respect of every soldier and citizen of Rome. His acts have lived for centuries and will continue to live long after I'm dead. Is not that the very meaning of immortality? Where is the immortality one receives in heaven? I see it not, nor have I had the good fortune to read about it. If it exists in a book, please point my way to it. I suspect I will waste my time waiting for it, for if it exists it is only in a fantasy, and I am not a man given to fantasy. I like history, cold-hard facts about men striving to win on earth: to achieve fame in all its glittering glory.

Is not that what Lorenzo had accomplished? One can argue that Savonarola desired--though he lived with God, through God and for God—fame, as well, in all its glittering glory. Yes, even the holiest of the holy are not immune to the intoxication of power. The truth is all men drink from this cup and become drunk by its effect and no one, from the lowest to the highest on the pole of mortal beings, should be ashamed to admit it. We are men, after all, nothing more, nothing less, regardless of what we believe and what we follow.

But I digress. It is my nature to conjecture. I shall do my best to harness that nature and stick to the story I wish to tell: that being the story of Lorenzo and Savonarola and, in a broader sense, the story of Florence, the city I love more than my own soul, in the final decades of the Fifteenth Century.

# Savonarola

I did not enjoy silly games as a child, with balls and marbles, full of squeals and aimless laughter. I preferred to play priest by myself, erecting altars from scraps of wood, metals, cloths and rocks, where I could commune with the angels above and contemplate the mystery of God. Why else were the clouds and sky given to us but as a staircase to the heavens beyond, far from the silly games and the even sillier pursuits of men, toiling to live in the world, with great sacrifice to their spirits? The streets repelled my sight: the market hawkers, the money lenders, the greedy selling their wares, the grabbing, lustful arms of boys and the senseless chatter of girls.

Yet as the eldest son of a household, it wasn't always my choice where to set my sights. I lived with the eyes my father forced me to have: namely his, which saw not the sky and the heaven beyond, but only the earth, where men, at any and all costs, aim to achieve and succeed, to which they can define their lives with the label of distinction. My father never became such a man as I describe. My grandfather, Michele, had, however, received distinction as a doctor, serving as court physician to Niccolo d'Este, the wealthiest landowner in Ferrara. Far beyond the court, he taught at the university at Padua and wrote a textbook, *Pratica medicinae,* which was widely read and used throughout Tuscany.

My father, a merchant and moneychanger of less than modest means, who struggled to support his family, relying on my grandfather's income and generosity, set me on a path to become my grandfather incarnate. When my grandfather died, I was not yet fourteen years of age and already enrolled in science courses to ensure that I would, as well, serve the duke of Ferrara as court physician and write many treatises, as did my grandfather, on topics such as fevers, purgatives, physiognomy, and pediatrics. I would add distinction to the family name and be able to label myself, among other men of status, as distinguished.

I never believed his seeing his son succeed is what drove my father. He wanted, first and foremost, for me to relieve my family's chronic money problems. In any case, I did as he asked, working studiously to receive my degree, though the practice of medicine, in truth, repelled me, for I did not like its intimacy with flesh and bodily functions. Still, at the age of twenty, I was young and foolhardy enough to believe I could live as others, striving for success, plunging into the world's business, and, of course, marrying and begetting sons to carry on the family name.

I loved a young woman (how foolish that sounds to me now). I attribute that love to youthful infatuation and a conditioned reflex to a pre-ordained belief I had inherited. I had a mother and father, and they had mothers and fathers. Thus it was expected that I, as well, would marry and procreate. Her name was Laodamia. (Why do I, after all the passing years, continue to recall her? Did I not, long ago, kill all my desire for women and their flesh?)

She was the illegitimate daughter of the distinguished Strozzi family--then in exile from Florence--whose house was next to ours. A narrow alleyway separated our houses, making it possible to converse with her from our opened windows. While at the University of Ferrara, I had become educated in humanist studies: reading Plato and classical poetry, writing sonnets in the manner of Petrarch, and learning to play the lute. I used these many arts from my window, wooing and serenading Laodamia.

One night, after I sang to her, her olive-skinned face, with its cat-colored eyes, shone, while the long curls of her golden hair illuminated the darkness, lighting a fire under my skin and through my limbs, making me lose all sense and judgment, as if she had bewitched me.

"Do you love me?" I asked her.

"I love you, Girolamo," she answered.

"How much do you love me?"

"As the lily loves the sun."

"And yet the lily soon dies."

"As the sparrow loves the dawn."

"And yet the sparrow flies away."

"Is it permanence you desire, Girolamo?"

13

"In regards to your love, the answer is yes."

"I shall love you as the cypress loves the earth."

Evidently, I misjudged her verbal flirtations and the attention she gave me on those nights, for when I asked for her hand in marriage soon after, she scornfully rejected my proposal, telling me a Strozzi, however illegitimate, would never stoop to marry a Savonarola.

I vowed never again to be fooled by the deceit of a woman, casting myself as in exile from the Garden of Eden, turning my back forever from love, as that which is ordained between men and women. I, instead, turned to loving what I had always loved: religion and God. For this passion, I thank my grandfather, for he had not only studied and practiced medicine, he had also written moralizing and religious treatises as well, such as *On Penitence, Confession* and *In Praise of John the Baptist,* wherein he discussed the power of meditation and resignation to God's will. It was these treatises, not those on medicine, that shaped my earliest sensibilities, empowering me to duplicate, if not surpass, his spiritual writings, for I believed the study and practice of religion meant one thing: the saving of souls. Yet soon came the realization that those who occupied the Roman curia substituted greed, lust, and deception in place of spiritual emancipation.

I could no longer turn a blind eye to sordidness and sin in a world void of God's virtues. On a May holiday, I left my medical books behind and walked forty miles to Faenza, crossing humid, flat green fields, entering godless streets filled with market wares and street vendors. The sight of loose women and lascivious men crowded my eyes, and sounds of wicked frivolity filled my ears. I sought sanctuary in the Church of Santo Agostino, where a friar was in the middle of delivering the day's sermon from the book of Genesis, which I had memorized as a boy. The friar's voice echoed loudly on the walls and ceilings as he recalled the lines of God, speaking to Abraham: "Get thee out of thy country, and from thy kindred, and from thy father's house."

I received the words as if not the friar but God Himself had spoken them to me. I continued to hear God's voice as I left the church and the noisy, sin-filled streets, and even as I walked back to Ferrara, all forty miles across the dry terrain of the Po delta. When I returned home, I wrote a Canzone I entitled *On the Ruin of the World*, as if possessed with a spirit of freedom and independence I had never before experienced:

*When I see the world turned upside down and every virtue and good practice fallen to the ground, it seems colder than snow. Some deny you. Some say you are sleeping. But I believe you are only waiting, O Eternal King, to deliver greater punishment for the world's sins. For us virtue is finished for all time. Cato goes begging. The hand of the pirate has grasped the scepter. Saint Peter falls to the ground. Oh, look at that catamite and that pimp robed in purple, a clown followed by the rabble, adored by a blind world! Do you not scorn that lascivious pig?*

I told my father I wanted to become a priest.

"Nonsense," he said, "You will take a wife and beget children."

"I do not want a wife."

"You are trained to be a doctor. Do you not feel a monetary responsibility to your parents?"

"My responsibility is to God. I want to follow his son, Jesus Christ."

"Your grandfather was a doctor and followed Christ. You shall do the same, ensuring your success both on earth and in heaven."

"I want to be among the holy that possess only heaven."

"A man can possess heaven as a doctor by administering to those who are sick in body."

"I wish to be a physician of souls."

"You said a thousand times as a boy you would never become a friar."

"I am no longer a boy."

"And yet you talk with so little sense you could as well be one."

"I have never talked with more sense, father."

"Who is it that put these crazy thoughts in your head?"

"God himself put these thoughts in my head."

"Your grandfather, rest his soul, is better off dead than alive to hear you speak like this."

"He would understand, as he himself was a man of God."

"He was a doctor first and a man of God second."

"And I wish to be a man of God first."

"Your genius was given to you for greater good."

"There is no greater good than to cure the spiritual ills of Italy."

"That is a job for the man who sits on the holy seat in Rome."

"The scepter has fallen into the hands of a pirate, father."

"Nonetheless, he is the pope."

"That which God has ordered the pope cannot rule otherwise."

That night I asked God: *When will the day come when I enter your presence, filled with peace, and out of that evil and most wicked world? It sickens me not only to live in it but also to see it. My Lord, I would like to be with you always, to live with you and sweetly to embrace you. Lord, these are the words of the bride inflamed with the love of Jesu.*

He answered, telling me I, too, was made of flesh, and though I found sensuality repugnant, I had to fight cruelly to keep the devil off my back. It wasn't enough to be a virgin. I must expunge all sexual desire. I prayed fervently to Him, hoping He would both rescue me and offer guidance. I fell into a sleep and dreamed (or was it a vision?) that ice-cold water had been poured over me. I awoke with the desires of my flesh checked, the youthful heat that had so often tormented me extinguished. I knew now with certainty that I had the strength to follow Christ and leave behind all worldly glory.

My father stood in my way. In the morning, he appealed to the love I held for my family. I assured him that I held genuine love for him, my mother and my sisters.

I did not wish to replace that love; I wished to inherit another one.

"And yet if you leave, you will destroy us," he said.

"Can you not see any good in my decision?"

"How can the starvation of a family be good?"

"Do not make worse the pain that is already in my heart, father."

"The pain you feel is guilt, as you deserve to feel."

"Can you not understand the exultation I feel for Christ?"

"Can you not understand the love a father has for his son?"

"If you truly love me, then love me all the more for becoming a cavalier of Jesus Christ, his militant knight."

"I do not see the wretchedness and wickedness you see."

I cried out, recalling Virgil's Aeneas, in his struggle to achieve his destiny, leaving Troy for the shores of Italy: "Ah make haste to flee these coasts of avarice, this land of savagery."

My father did not understand the allusion. He became silent.

"We behave like swine and Epicureans, father. Everyone praises vice and ridicules virtue."

"That is nonsense," he said, breaking his silence. "And what of the good? Can you tell me there is none?"

I did not answer his question. I had much to say, which, I confess, I had already written and rehearsed. "We argue over superficial virtues and consider bodily pleasures to be the highest good. If someone is zealous for philosophy and the fine arts, he is a dreamer. If someone lives chastely and modestly, he is unfeeling. If pious, he is called unjust. If he wishes to be just, he is held to be cruel. If he believes and has faith in the greatness of God, he is crass and ingenuous. If he puts his hope in Christ alone, everyone makes fun of him. Those who are corrupt are venerated. Everything is backwards. When will the world move forward?"

"It is not for you to fix the ills of Italy."

"If not me, then who?"

"Others who are not my son and the sole provider of the family."

"You want my body to stay here, but if it did it would do so without my soul, for my soul is already now with God."

"I love your body and your soul, for you are my only son."

"If you love my soul, why then do you not seek what is best for my soul? Rejoice then that I want to join my soul with God and become a physician in the highest realm of the spirit."

"To leave your father and family in time of need is an act of defiance against the very will of God."

"Jesus admonished his disciples, saying, 'He that loveth father or mother more than me, is not worthy of me.'"

"I care not what Jesus said to his disciples, for they are not my children. Why should I hold their emotions in esteem?"

I left the room, understanding that to speak further on the subject would be futile. I possessed little recourse but to follow the path of Saint Francis, whose father had bought him clothes in an attempt to force his son to forget about a life of worship and poverty. In the cathedral square of Assisi the man known to the world as a saint stripped off those very clothes, saying, in effect, to his father, *you cannot stop me from following what rests in my heart and soul. I am one with God, and if it means I should have to surrender my father to fulfill my passion and quest, then that is what I must do.*

With a heavy heart, knowing I had disappointed my father and had caused much suffering to my family, I left my home a short time later and walked thirty miles to Bologna, where I rapped on the door of a Dominican monastery. An old man, wearing a dark, hooded cloak, opened the door. I asked to be taken in as a novitiate monk. He inquired whether I was certain of my decision. I told him I had proposed marriage to God, and He accepted.

The next day, I wrote a letter to my father:

"I thus beg you, my dear father, to put an end to your weeping and spare me any further sadness and pain than I suffer already. However, you must understand that I do not suffer because of regret at what I have done, for I would not undo this even if such a choice would make me greater than Caesar himself, but instead my suffering is because I too am flesh and blood, just like you, and our senses quarrel with our reason. I must constantly battle to prevent the Devil from leaping onto my shoulders, and all the more so when I feel for you."

I wrote also that when a person gets the idea of becoming a friar he could not sleep. On the morning when I took my vows to become a black friar, in the year 1476, I could once again sleep.

# Lorenzo

I inherited gout from my forebears and saw early on its debilitating effects. My grandfather succumbed to it at age seventy-seven, though he had lived mostly strong and vital during his life. My father, however, was never strong. I do not remember a time when he was not crippled in the joints, suffering fevers, organ failure and deep melancholy. He spent most of his time as ruler unable to walk, conducting affairs, as best as possible, from his bed. Leading men in the city--Luca Pitti, Agnolo Acciaiuoli, Dietisalvi Neroni and Niccolo Soderini--once loyal to my grandfather, doubted my father's capacity to rule, believing his ill health and the tender age of his children signaled trouble for the Republic if he should unexpectedly die. Still, despite their misgivings, which my father received loudly, they showed no outward signs that they were conspiring to seize the leadership of the city by violent means. I realize now how naïve I sound, even in recalling the attempted revolution. Even at seventeen years old, I should have known the nature of my fellow citizens: the depth and breadth of their envy and ambition. After all, it was a story Florentine history told repeatedly and one I would experience firsthand more than once in my brief lifetime.

My father, because of his illness, had already begun to turn to me to be the face of the regime. Earlier in the year, he sent me on a lengthy diplomatic mission to Rome and Naples to procure relationships necessary to our preservation, for the continuity of my family's success, as well as Florence's continued stability and survival, depended on alliances with powerful men throughout Italy.

"Put an end to all playing on instruments, or singing or dancing," he said before I departed. "Be old beyond your years, for the times require it."

I, of course, at seventeen years old, paid not attention to his advice. What teenager wants to listen to his father? I would learn all too well of this truth with my own sons, becoming, in a twist of irony, the advice giver. Such is the cruel fate and misfortune of men to carry on the detested traits of their fathers.

I had always desired to visit the Eternal City to relive in my mind the great classical age, which had always fired my imagination: the verse of Horace, Virgil and Cicero, and the antiquity of the Pantheon, Coliseum, and Forum, where Donatello and Brunelleschi had a half century earlier come to study and sketch. To my dismay, I found a city much unlike the one I imagined. I recall the words from a humanist compatriot who had warned I would see a city "stripped of all beauty, lying prostrate like a giant corpse, decayed and everywhere eaten away." The spring and fountainhead of the stink and sin of all iniquities had its root and cause in the papal seat, occupied at the time by Paul II, who fostered little interest in its people's spiritual development. He, instead, pursued a penchant for gold and jewels, as was evident when I first met him, wearing a tiara made for his own use, studded with diamonds, sapphires, emeralds, pearls and sundry other gems. His face, equally costumed, was plastered with dark rouge and powders that gave me the impression he wore a mask. Is it any wonder I held, as all Florentines, a deep cynicism for the Vatican?

I wasn't there, however, to judge his appearance or the nature of his character inherent in that appearance. I was there to procure his signature on a contract naming the Medici bank sole distributors of alum from the papal mines at Tolfa. I knew well how my great-grandfather and grandfather, through their talents, had built a banking empire in Italy and throughout Europe. My father, though infirm, did his best to educate me on banking matters, insisting that for the sake of our success, not only now but also far into the future, I would need to acquire and employ savvy business skills. The truth is I possessed neither the interest nor aptitude for banking. I loved poetry, art and literature--as well as playing on instruments, and singing and dancing!--and much preferred the company of people, regardless of rank, whether in a palace or tavern.

I realized very young my skill for wit and charm, which would become for me, throughout my lifetime, particularly in matters of state affairs, my calling card. I used this talent to win the pope's graces and, more importantly, his signature.

"Your Holiness has such fine taste in jewels," I said.

"You noticed?" he asked.

"Admiringly," I answered.

"You are a smart boy," he said.

"I am honored by your words."

"And how is your magnificent father—still melancholy?"

"If he is melancholy, it is because he does not have the opportunity to stand before Your Holiness as I do."

"You are a humanist, I hear."

"I am a Christian at my core."

"Then we are, indeed, brethren."

"I am your humbled servant."

I learned to conduct business by not conducting business and by doing so received both Pope Paul II's signature and his promise to continue a relationship with the Medici family and bank. Before I left Rome, he confided to me a secret weapon he used in all business dealings to ensure he received what he desired, whether monetary or political:

"I use the threat of excommunication," he said.

"And it works?" I asked.

"Like a charm," he answered.

I received a letter from my father, wherein he expressed much worry concerning the untimely death of the Duke of Milan, Francesco Sforza, who I had met a year earlier on the very first mission I had undertaken. He was someone with whom my grandfather had built a lasting friendship. He had reassured me that he remained well disposed towards our city and the Medici family he had grown to love as his own, saying, in effect, he would continue to be our protector against rival states. My father worried that the Duke's death might weaken our image in the eyes of enemies. I knew that henceforth, without his telling me, I needed to forego playing instruments and singing and dancing, as I would soon enter King Ferrante's venomous web in Naples.

I responded to my father's letter with my own, reassuring him that during my visit to Milan I befriended the Duke's daughter, Ippolita. Three years my senior, she was the most cultured woman I had ever met. Schooled in Greek and Latin, she could recite verse or describe a painting or sculpture with deftness and clarity. We built a connection and promised to always be loyal to each other, whatever our needs. "As long as she holds court," I concluded my letter to my father, "we have a friend in Milan."

King Ferrante's reputation in Naples and throughout Italy preceded him. I had heard much of his regard for torture and murder: that he liked to have his enemies near him, either alive in well-guarded prisons or dead and embalmed, dressed in the costumes they wore during their lifetimes. I did not bring up the subject when we met and neither, fortunately, did he. I knew innately that men of esteem wanted more than anything to be treated with esteem; therefore I communicated with him in the same manner--I will take to my grave my personal prejudice that wit and charm are a man's greatest possessions--as when meeting a king, pope, emperor or duke. I complimented his choice of clothes, his fine furniture, his beautiful wife and children, his vast knowledge and intelligence, his magnanimous personality, while at the same time thanking him for his hospitality and warm welcome for such a one as myself, most humble before his majestic, overpowering presence.

From that time forward, he treated me with graciousness and generosity, repeating often that he bore much love for my father and the legacy of the Medici family. He wanted my father to know that despite the crowing of his enemies in Florence, who had sought Naples support, he remained loyal to him and would fight against any and all who were his adversaries in the Florentine government. On my last evening in Naples, he asked me to play one of his many instruments and afterwards sing and dance. I obliged him, though I made him promise not to tell my father of my foolish behavior.

When I returned to Florence, having in a short time met the most powerful men in Italy, I brought the news my father had been seeking: we now enjoyed the security of alliances with Milan, Rome and Naples.

"And yet security remains in Florence a high-priced commodity," he said, "where it should be least expensive."

Thus, with rumors growing louder about an impending coup, we left Florence for the country villa my grandfather had built decades earlier at Careggi, where I now lay dying. While there, my father received a message from a source in the city that our enemies had begun to lay plans to capture and kill him; whereupon they would seize the city and its rule. Though infirm, he insisted on returning to Florence at once to rally partisans and raise the Medici banner, signaling to the people that our leadership remained as strong as ever. I rode out with a group of five riders ahead of the main party--my father carried in his litter by servants, sheltered by a dozen soldiers on horse and foot--to ensure the road was safe for his passage into Florence, thirty miles to the south.

The moment we left Careggi, I felt unease. The rolling hills, which had always been for me a source of delight, appeared menacing as one thought only consumed me: who lay concealed in the shaded groves and deserted farmhouses? I became acutely aware of every bird that sounded and every branch or leaf or blade of grass that moved. Even the shift of the sun brought new shadows and creeping concerns. We stopped as we viewed the tiny hamlet of Sant'Antonio del Vescovo from which we typically passed on our way to Florence. Its buildings shimmered in the summer's unrelenting heat. I waited in trepidation, watching lizards slither on the road and hawks fly overhead, seeing them as portents. Those who lived in the town--the archbishop, in particular--were associated with the men who wanted to oust my father. We had gone too far, however, to turn around and take a different, longer route. We had little choice but to proceed into the lion's den. I told one of our riders to stay behind. In case of a problem—if we should be stopped—he should turn back and ride as fast as possible to intercept my father's litter to inform his party that passage through Sant'Antonio del Vescovo was not safe. They would need to circumvent it, though it would add time to their journey.

No sooner had we entered the town than men on horseback, more than twice our number, ambushed us from different directions, drawing their swords and crossbows. Why they didn't take me into custody or hold me hostage until my father arrived I cannot answer with certainty. I know only that they were not soldiers. My recent missions, having met with kings, popes and dukes, introduced me to what well-conditioned soldiers looked like. I gathered instantly that those who surrounded us with weapons drawn appeared more like laborers from nearby farms and factories: men unschooled, untrained, bought cheaply for a cheap plan and thus unequipped for the job given them. They had, apparently, not been instructed as to what to do with my companions or me. They, I assume, saw us as mere boys, still toothless, unable to bite the hand that desired power. Suffice it to say I used their incompetence to great advantage.

Their captain--I say that only because he had the grayest of the beards and the longest of the swords--asked, "Are you not Lorenzo de' Medici?"

"I am," I answered.

He wanted to know if my father followed behind. I told him my father should be passing through town in less than an hour.

"What is your business coming through this town in a company of men?"

"We are headed to Florence for pleasure seeking."

"Pleasure seeking?" he queried.

"The taverns, sir."

"I would like a drink myself when this business is done with," he said.

"You must join us then."

Another of their men came forward, a man long in the tooth, in need of a bath and clothing. "How far behind did you say your father was?" he asked.

"Half a mile, at most," I said.

"We have some business with him."

"He will be eager to receive your news," I replied.

The captain said he preferred his time in the tavern, where the women were loose and available for the right price, rather than riding a horse in the heat of a sweltering summer day.

I told him we were like-minded men.

Remarkably the captain put his sword away and ordered the others with him to do the same.

"I don't see the harm in allowing you to pass," he said.

The man long in the tooth questioned the captain's decision, asking if it were not wise to retain us until my father arrived.

The captain insisted that he knew what he was doing.

"They're just kids," he said. "Our business is not with them."

The others in their company, maybe a dozen in all, put down their swords and crossbows.

"We shall stay here and wait for your father while you enjoy your tavern," the captain said. "Save some of the women for us."

I assured him I would do just that.

Once we passed through Sant'Antonio del Vescovo unscathed, we galloped our horses as fast as we could to Florence, and I can say with certainty I did not have pleasure on my mind.

# Machiavelli

Here's the cardinal rule to those who aspire to be conspirators attempting a coup: make sure you have experienced soldiers who are armed and large numbers of them. If you have only one or the other, you will fail. Piero the elder's enemies had none of the two. They had drawn their conspiratorial plans in a parlor room, believing that in his ill health, with his broken body, Lorenzo's father would accede without a fight. They expected a swift and decisive coup against a rabbit. They had not prepared to meet a wolf.

Having been warned by the horseman sent back by Lorenzo of the trap awaiting him at Sant' Antonio del Vescovo, Piero, the elder's party turned off the main road and returned to Florence through obscure country lanes. Once home, he assembled armed men, protecting his palace from attack. In the ensuing days, support came from Milan, Arezzo, Mugello, Pistoia and throngs of loyal Medici citizens, all consumed with vengeance against Medici adversaries.

The coup ended before it began. Luca Pitti, the eldest of the conspirators, cracked first. Meeting privately with Lorenzo, he promised to turn his back on his co-conspirators and thoughts of rebellion in return for safety and the forgiveness and love of the Medici. He rode to the palace on the Via Largo, embraced Piero the elder like a son--he had been loyal to Cosimo, had he not?--and declared himself ready to live or die with the Medici ruler. Though he was granted clemency, receiving as well a government position, he lived his final days in disgrace for having betrayed his soul, his friends, and his principles. He remained cold and alone at home, without old friends and unable to make new ones since none could trust him. He thus suffered the worst kind of self-exile, shut out of the always lively and energetic starts and stops of daily life, which for a Florentine is a living death, revealing the truth of fortune's fickleness: how friends become enemies and enemies become friends as the situation suits the times.

As for the other leaders, Lorenzo's father showed great generosity in meting out his punishments. He banished them from Florence for life. I must confess to not understanding such leniency, for the best way to deal with an enemy is to ensure that he can never again hurt you. Banishment or exile only suspends the time when the ugly head of envy once again rises from the dust of oppression, at which time envy's sister, ambition, wishes to stretch its limbs and become a monster with much to prove.

I digress of course from the main point: that being the failed coup and the reinstitution of the Medici regime. Piero the elder reformed the government, placing himself and his advisors in complete control. Three thousand men, all armed, all Medici loyalists, appeared in the piazza, shouting victory. Lorenzo rode among them, resplendent in full armor, having recently been told he would represent his father in the Council of One Hundred. Though only a teenager, he would become a fixture in the inner circle of the *reggimento*. He received congratulations from the newly elected Signoria, and as he rode back to the palace, all of seventeen years old, the crowd along the streets cheered.

No longer just the son of Florence's first citizen, he became a leader in his own right, his father's right-hand man and the ruler-in-waiting of one of the richest and most powerful states in Italy. King Ferrante had heard of his exploits and wrote: "We loved you on account of your excellent qualities and the services done by your grandfather and father. But as we have lately heard with what prudence and manly courage you behaved in the late revolutions, and how courageously you placed yourself in the foremost ranks, our affection to you has grown remarkably."

Though still a boy, Lorenzo's star rose and would continue to rise as he grew into a man, illuminating the world stage as only one possessed of natural statesmanship could. Is it not then understandable why, even today, the citizens of Florence and throughout Italy still refer to him as Il Magnifico? Is it not also understandable why Piero the elder would defer to him in tight situations when it appeared his life, as well as the lives of others, hung in the balance? Here was a young man who could trade Latin epigrams with scholars and obscenities with laborers in a tavern. Here was a man of the world, unlike Savonarola, who isolated himself from what was real, choosing to terrorize his fellow man with false prophesies.

# Savonarola

I did not ask to be a prophet of doom. I received a revelation at the convent of San Giorgio in 1484. I prayed for five hours and did not move. Such was my ecstasy, my total absorption in the contemplation of God, that my face in its resplendency illuminated the church, as if a thousand candles had been lit. God appeared in that illumination, as he has since appeared: as a supreme light, bright and blinding, veiled in mystery not visible to the human eye. I heard only His voice, and that, in its force and authority, impressed me such that I fell to the floor, on my knees, and wept sweet tears to hear the command of his will: *Girolamo Savonarola, you will speak for Me and through Me; to act as a purveyor of My condemnations; to warn the people of Italy that a scourge of the Church is at hand.*

I have obeyed that will, as any Christian must. I know that any and all who fail to heed the words of warning is doomed to suffer. If I speak harshly, without compassion, it is only because it is the method God wishes me to use. Eternity and salvation are not topics for the weak of heart, and they cannot be achieved on the cheap. They can only be attained through suffering and sacrifice. Yet how many are willing to endure such personal punishment for the sake of their souls? I do not deal in suppositions, though some believe I do. I deal in truth. It is not, as my enemies have said, Savonarola's truth. It is God's truth. I speak it for Him since He does not have time on earth. His affairs are greater.

My revelation clearly showed me the presence of evil shepherds in the Church. The newest pope, Innocent VIII, is the worst of the shepherds. Engaged in the practice of simony, he openly acknowledges his own children and has them live with him, shamefully displaying his dirty laundry for all Italy to see. Such corruption causes me to weep for hours at night and gives further justification for my prophetic warnings.

# Machiavelli

My career as a government official began in the Florence Cathedral, where I was sent to spy on Savonarola. I received this appointment from Ricciardo Becchi, the Florentine ambassador to the Holy See. He did not call it spying. He called it, if I recall correctly, with some paraphrase, a visit to the church, to use my eyes and ears. How discreet of him to couch his words so carefully. I am not a man in his position. I do not need to be discreet. I can call it what it was: spying. The word has a much more tantalizing effect on one's imagination, giving the work more risk and danger, to say nothing of satisfaction.

Savonarola had made an enemy of Pope Alexander VI, calling out and naming his corruption from the pulpit. The pope responded by threatening not only Savonarola but also all of Florence with excommunication unless it found a way to control the mad rages of its leading preacher. To say the cards are stacked in favor of a pope is to state the obvious. He can, whenever he needs, use his trump card, yelling "excommunication," aware that such a word gets the attention of people the way a falling brick on the head does. Becchi wanted a full account in writing of the preacher's words and deeds. I licked my chops, realizing my day of reckoning had come: to employ my skills as a keen observer of men and as a purveyor of truth, knowing the fate of Florence lay in the balance.

I stood among the congregation, watching as the little, hooded friar took his position in the pulpit, standing above the fearful faces of men and women from the poor quarters of the city. He had dark, heavy eyebrows, a hooked nose, and a tight, thin mouth. It didn't seem possible that this small man could create such turmoil in Florence and Rome. His power became evident the moment he opened his mouth and spoke with a voice that cracked like thunder, sending a shudder along the walls and beams of the church. He reproved the people for their sins and denounced those who, like Adam, the weak link in the chain of man, had sinned.

"The wrath of God is upon you. Repent before the sword be unsheathed, while it be yet unstained with blood. Repent!"

Men and women near me convulsed and trembled as the floor beneath me moved. I looked up. Would Brunelleschi's great dome collapse and fall under the weight of so many bricks? A man beside me whispered aloud:

"I shall repent, O Lord. I shall repent."

I understood at once Savonarola's method. He wished to terrorize his congregation from the start, with the crack of thunder, to get its attention. He, unfortunately, did not possess papal authority to use the word excommunication to garner the same effect. Having done so, he regulated his volume and tone, speaking with more calm and control. Taking as his subject the book of Exodus, he told the story of God's chosen people persecuted by a cruel and corrupt ruler. He said the more God's people became oppressed, the more they multiplied and increased. He gestured toward the crowd to make explicit the link between the ancient Hebrews and his own followers. He then proceeded to cast himself in the role of Moses, leading them out of bondage, into the Holy Land.

"But if I am Moses," he said, "who then is going to play the vengeful Pharaoh bent on defying God's will?"

Why was I not surprised when he assigned the villain's role to Rodrigo Borgia, the corrupt and sensual man who now occupied the Throne of St. Peter as Pope Alexander VI? Those around me nodded their heads, as if confirming the choice as a rightful one. Had any of these people, I wondered, ever been hit by a falling brick?

He next referred to the four and twenty elders of the Apocalypse seated around the throne of God, clothed in white raiment, with gold crowns upon their heads. He had a vision that one of these elders rose from his seat to prophesy that the citizens of Italy would fall prey to raging foes. The friar's voice rose once again, as it had earlier, with a crack of thunder, as he proceeded to describe what would happen to all of us: "Soon you shall be washed in rivers of blood in the streets; wives shall be torn from husbands; virgins ravished; children murdered before their mothers' eyes; everywhere terror, fire, and bloodshed. Pope Alexander VI, you shall be the first to burn!"

The man beside me, in mad sweat, cried out for mercy, saying "Save me, O Lord. I repent my sins! I shall never sin again." Others made similar appeals both to the preacher and to God. I stood among them, scribbling on a notepad, making sure to describe in full detail what I heard and witnessed. I, unlike others, viewed his performance and histrionics with detachment, for I, of course, did not believe a word he said. Just the same, I admired his audacity and courage for criticizing and damning the pope without fear of retribution, especially after the pope had threatened excommunication. How beautiful was his disobedience, and yet that very same disobedience spelled trouble for Florence, though the ignorant among the congregation had not a clue. Was I alone in my understanding of what an excommunication meant for the city? Did those crying out for mercy understand the repercussions: the interdict that was sure to follow, resulting in a ban on the city that would jeopardize our worldly goods? Did they not know possessions could be confiscated? Was not the saving of the city more important than the saving of their souls? Still, the congregation swore allegiance to Savonarola, as if he were indeed the incarnation of Moses. I am always amazed at how little discretion people use when receiving information dangerous to themselves and their livelihood. How does one not question the absurdities he hears? Doesn't he want proof of some kind? To a sane and sensible man, the response to such nonsense would be: show me, prove to me; how do I know you are telling the truth? How do I know you are not crazy?

I must admit that Savonarola's sermon nearly demoralized me that night. I almost cancelled my rendezvous with my favorite courtesan. I did no such thing, of course, after having come to my senses. I sent my full account to the ambassador. He thanked me for the report and asked me to observe again the following week, informing me that the Vatican grew increasingly desperate to resolve this problem. I expressed my desire and willingness to be of service to my city in whatever manner it was needed. I discovered that I enjoyed putting pen to paper. Writing would become for me, in ensuing years, an entertainment, a purpose, and a means to an end. And to think: this passion began with those early reports.

I owe much to Fra Girolamo Savonarola.

# Lorenzo

If God should spare me, I will dedicate the rest of my life to writing poetry. I will live in the fields and pasturelands of Agnano and Poggio a Caiano, among shepherds and cowherds, breeding and caring for the horses I love more than men; far from hatred, treachery and political ambition. I will seek some solitary and shaded place or the comfort of a green meadow by the clear and flowing water, and there my pen will write of such simple pleasures as I see and hear, for it is only in the country where I have ever found peace, having spent my happiest days as a boy frolicking outside the Medici villas far from the city.

I did not ask to be a ruler of men. My forebears bestowed the honor on me. I recall returning from a day of reverie in the woods. My grandfather had company. I told the guests of my excitement at seeing hawks in the sky and galloping ponies in the fields. I said clearly, to no one in particular: "I never want to leave." A friend of my grandfather, a man named Gino di Neri Capponi, said, "Honor does not reside in the woods. Worthy men are made in the city; nor indeed can he be called a man whose measure is not taken there." My grandfather, as much as he loved the country, agreed with his friend, for it was in the city where he and his sons, including my father, managed the vast and profitable Medici bank. I did not wish to be a banker, as I believe I have made redundantly clear.

I had, from my earliest remembrance, studied Latin and Greek, reading from the great canon of classical literature: the histories of Plutarch and Tacitus, the sensual verses of Ovid. My grandfather, to his credit, spent much of his fortune on paying agents to find and recover lost manuscripts from the monasteries of Europe. These manuscripts he passed down to me. In them is contained a range of human experience far broader than anything found in the writings of the Church fathers.

"Wonders are many on earth, and the greatest of these is man," wrote Sophocles. "He is lord of all living things; there is nothing beyond his power."

I made those words my living creed and desired more than anything to become a man of letters, like the great masters I had studied, and produce, through honor and desire of glory--is it less than humble of me to say I desire fame, even now?--something admirable. I wanted, especially, to emulate Cato, Cicero and Virgil, all of whom praised country life and worked the land with their own hands.

It is erroneous to believe that I, a ruler and inheritor of vast wealth, shied away from labor. The opposite is true. I always appreciated hard work in the fields surrounding my estates. If one were to visit my library, he would find much more than illuminated manuscripts and rare volumes of Homer, Aristotle and Plato. I have there, as well, modern texts on agronomy, botany and animal husbandry. Like my grandfather, I found great solace in the workaday chores of pruning and planting, and little else gave me as much pleasure as the pungent smell of the stable, where I preferred to groom my horses myself. These simple tasks did much to clear my head after the intrigues and petty squabbles of political life.

If I have a regret it is that affairs of state stole too much of my time that could have been spent living near the woods, writing verses and pursuing both intellectual and spiritual enlightenment. I remember rising early as a young man to write of the rural sunrise:

> *The wolf retreated to its wilderness.*
> *The fox retreated to its den,*
> *For there was now a chance it might be seen,*
> *Now that the moon had come and gone again.*

Why do I remember those lines as vividly as the names of my children and every pope, king, duke and ambassador with whom I met?

> *The busy peasant woman had already*
> *Allowed the sheep and pigs to leave their pens.*
> *Crystalline, clear, and chilly was the air:*
> *The morning pledged the weather would be fair,*

> *When I was roused by jingling bells and by*
> *The calling of the dogs and similar sounds.*

I called that poem "The Partridge Hunt." I had written it when I was a mere teenager, ignorant of politics and the hatred in men's hearts. I knew mostly the world of God and nature, which had been one and the same to me. Perhaps, if I am granted God's mercy in the afterlife to come, I will again live in simple harmony with the natural world given to us by God in all his beneficence.

Savonarola holds no such belief in the harmony of God and nature. He associates with God fire, hell, and apocalyptic vengeance, forgetting that it was God who created the beauty of the earth for man to enjoy the fruits of his labor and to see through it a communion with the divine. Is not this communion the best way to see God, who otherwise makes himself invisible to us? If there is one consoling note to my demise it is that I am here at Careggi, away from the city, closer to God and what is best and honest about life, far from the city where he who lies best is happiest and where a man's friendship is measured by expediency. Did I not write those thoughts, more or less, in verse?

> *Let search who will for pomp and honors high*
> *the plazas, the temples and the great buildings,*
> *the pleasures, the treasures, that accompany*
> *a thousand hard thoughts, a thousand pains.*
> *A green meadow filled with lovely flowers,*
> *a little brook that bathes the grass around,*
> *a little bird pining for his love,*
> *better stills our ardor.*

I preferred my native Tuscan dialect rather than the elevated Latin. I wanted to prove, as Dante did, the dignity of our language, demonstrating that it could easily express any concept of our minds, abstract or literal.

I chose the sonnet form, made famous by Petrarch a century earlier, because honor, according to the philosophers, is attached to that which is difficult, and I know of no other poetic form as challenging. I know now, even in death's grip, I continue to strive for honor, facing my most difficult task yet. Thus, I wish to bear this calamity with as much grace and dignity as I can muster. It is my final act, my final poem to leave for posterity. I want it to be perfect.

# Savonarola

While in San Gimignano, where I honed my preaching skills, I received a letter from my mother, informing me of my father's death. While I felt sadness, I knew implicitly what lay beneath the words "your father has died." She wanted me, as the eldest son, to return home to care for her and my siblings, as if familial obligation and responsibility alone dictate the direction of a man's life. Did she not, as my mother, want more for me than to live a narrow existence, toiling as any other commoner in search of superficial wants and needs? Did she not know (would she ever know?) that God had greater plans for me, which included saving not my family but instead the entire state of Italy and all of Christendom?

I wrote her back, telling her she should no longer regard me as a member of her family. My father was now Jesus Christ and my family the Dominican order. I had much greater concerns than the death of my father and the welfare of my family. The Christian world suffered from ills much greater than those of which she and my siblings suffered, and it was to that alleviation I needed to direct myself with exclusivity. I ended my brief note to her in what I admit is over dramatized emphasis:

"You should consider me dead."

My letter did little to dissuade my mother from writing again. (Why was I not surprised?) Seven months later I received from her another letter, this one informing me that her brother Borso had died. My father had left my mother in debt, and uncle Borso had been her and my younger siblings' sole support. With my uncle's death, she now had no one to turn to in time of need, writing dramatically, as if to match my earlier over dramatization, "We shall not be able to survive without your help."

Did she not know (had she not been paying attention to my life?) that I had nothing material to give, living as I was in poverty, having taken the vows of St. Dominic? I responded to her letter, telling her I could not help her monetarily. I could, instead, guide her spiritually. I offered specific advice on how to become a saint, complete with references ranging from Psalms to Corinthians:

"I want your faith to be such that you could watch your children die and be martyred without shedding a tear for them, as that most holy Hebrew woman did when seven of her saintly children were killed and tortured in front of her and she never cried, but instead comforted them in their death."

Some may read this note and believe my response to my mother heartless. To the contrary, it is a note written with love, for it is a call for her to place her life completely in the hands of God, as is indicative in my letter's final line: "It is better, therefore, to tolerate patiently our brief tribulations so as to have eternal joy and peace and glory everlasting."

As much as I tried to forget my family and look only to my new life with God, the Dominican order made it difficult for me to do so. After teaching for a time at my alma mater, the *Studium generale* in Bologna, my Dominican superiors posted me back to my hometown in Ferrara, where I could no longer avoid my mother's reach and pull. She intercepted me one day outside the monastery, demanding that I share my life with her as much as I did with God. I told her I had a larger destiny to fulfill than that of caring for my family. That destiny required me to travel and live far from home, possibly for always. She reminded me that with the death of my father, I was now the head of the household. Was not my destiny as caretaker to my family as important as any other destiny?

"I do what I do for the good of many souls," I said. "It is God who has asked me to preach, hear confession and counsel others."

"What is to happen to me and your sisters?" she asked. "Are we not your flesh and blood? Are we not as important as the souls you must save?"

"You should take comfort from the fact that one of your children has been chosen by God to undertake such work."

"Your distance from us has created a hole in our lives," she said. "Living inside this hole, we feel no comfort."

"It is only a hole because God does not inhabit it."

"God does not bring food to our mouths."

"He brings something greater: eternal salvation."

"Are we expected to starve on earth in order to receive salvation later?"

"Yes."

"You shame your father and your forebears with such insolence."

"Then is it not best that I take my shame and leave the country of my birth?"

"Only a coward would leave his family to starve."

"Our Savior says in Scripture that a prophet has no honor in his own country. You should be content that I labor in the vineyard of Christ so far from home."

"I do not understand how your God can be so cruel."

I turned from her, retreating to the monastery, wishing to stay inside its walls to avoid seeing her again. To do so would have been contrary to Dominican doctrine. As a teaching order, it was our job, ordained by St. Dominic and God, to go out among the people and preach the Christian word. I prayed to God to help me with the matter of my mother and family. Could he intervene on my behalf and ease both their suffering and mine? A day later, God answered my prayer. I received an order to return to Florence, at the request of Lorenzo de' Medici, to take up residence as a teaching master once again in the monastery at San Marco. I wrote a note to my mother, saying that for her sake, as well as mine, I hoped this appointment would become permanent. She needed to eliminate all thoughts of my supporting her family. She needed, in fact, to surrender her desire to live materially, like a beggar asking for food, and turn instead to the salvation of her soul through the nourishment of God.

In late May 1490, I set out from Bologna on foot. I have never traveled on a mule, like so many of my brethren, for why should this beast carry my burden? St. Dominic traveled wearing only his leather sandals, bringing only water for his thirst. I did the same, carrying no other possessions other than my breviary and the worn Bible I had inherited from my grandfather Michele, beginning the fifty-mile journey south along the Savena valley toward the pass across the high Apennines to Florence. I had walked this same path eight years earlier, without incident, content to be alone, far from the worldliness and wickedness of man, and thus more able to commune with God and understand in the quiet of the days and nights His peace and glory. I know, in fact, that I have never experienced joy as I had on my travels by foot under the moon or sun in the Tuscan hills designed and painted by God. I did not eat and drank only when necessary because, in truth, I felt full, quenched, and satisfied. Many times my joy was such that I stopped and knelt, thanking God for his presence.

As I neared the village of Pianoro, ten miles from Bologna, I could not raise myself from the ground. I lay prostrate, aware that at my age—I was then thirty-seven years old—I could not endure the physical challenge, as I once could, trudging up the long trail into the mountains. At the very least, I needed sustenance to sustain my life. I recall thinking, before I became unconscious, "How did St. Dominic walk such distances without the need for food?"

When I awoke, I found myself lying in the arms of an anonymous traveler, who provided me with food and drink. Steadying me with the strength of his arms, he guided me to a wayside tavern, where I was able to rest for the night. The next day, accompanied by the kind stranger, I continued on my way. In the early evening, we approached Florence, with the dome and towers of the city visible beyond the walls. The traveler walked with me up to the Porta San Gallo, where he took his leave of me, saying these words:

"Go and do the task which God has assigned to you in Florence."

Though I never discovered the name of the Good Samaritan, I know now that it was God Himself who guided me to Florence, in an act of charity and benediction, allowing me to fulfill the destiny he had set out for me years earlier.

# Lorenzo

Christianity for me had always been elastic. I could stretch and pull it as I pleased to fit my thoughts and deeds. I am not ashamed to say I can no longer stretch and pull. While God's blessing escaped me in life, I can say with certainty that I am now ready to receive his blessing. Savonarola calls me a hypocrite, though isn't a man allowed to change? We do not all live so rigid as he in our beliefs. We move in shifting currents and must honor those currents of change.

Why should God's blessing be too late for me because I gravitated toward pagan ideals and nurtured the gifts of my mind? Why can't a man hold simultaneously in his brain humanist ideals and Christian beliefs? Where is it written that the religious composition of one's life must be played by one note only, without variance?

I had been taught at an early age to care for my immortal soul through the Christian faith. I attended mass daily. I belonged to religious brotherhoods, "Acts of Charity" societies, engaged in the patronage of the poor and needy. Did I have ulterior motives for doing so? Of course. No act goes unrecognized, especially the act of a man who wields influence. I have never, in fact, met a man who acted selflessly, and I am certain of the reason: he does not exist. Men are born with ambition to succeed, and none are excluded; men of God just as guilty as others.

I hear the crack and condemnation of Savonarola's voice: *You sought religion for political, not spiritual, purposes, to foster your son's ascendancy in the Church. Is that not the reason you ordered my return to Florence?*

I cannot lie. I did want my son Giovanni to enter the Church to advance the Medici name in a different sphere, and I purchased benefices throughout Europe to see he was on track to be made a cardinal, with the hope some day he will become pope. I believed that Savonarola's strict theological sermons might reshape my son's liberal education, helping to suitably adjust his religious attitude, which had been lax. He had been raised with the humanist teachings of Marsilio Ficino and Angelo Poliziano, learning

Platonism, Virgil and Socrates. To sit on the highest seat of Rome, he required traditional Christian teachings. I wanted someone with the greatest knowledge of those teachings, and I had heard Savonarola was the finest, both in scholarship and preaching. What I knew came from Pico della Mirandola, the gifted philosopher, who knew Savonarola during his residency at San Marco, often visiting him in his cell to discuss Christian and Humanist philosophy. It was Pico, in fact, who recommended I bring Savonarola back to Florence, though in his earlier tenure he existed in relative obscurity, preaching in mostly empty churches, for he had yet to develop his oratorical skills. Pico made a convincing case that Savonarola, during the intervening years, became something of a legend for the honesty and sincerity of his orthodoxy and sermons in surrounding towns, such as San Gimignano, Ferrara and Bologna.

When he arrived, I had little knowledge of his subversive prophesies toward the Church and his animosity for the Medici. In his very first sermon it was reported to me that he spoke of a coming Apocalypse, in which the Church would be scourged and all sinners duly punished, saying, "I am the hailstorm that shall smash the heads of those who do not take cover."

Is it any wonder that those of my age gravitated to new ideas in an attempt to detach ourselves from language such as that, common in a prior age?

I sent word to him through some leading citizens that it would be best in his forthcoming Lenten sermons if he did not speak of future events in such threatening ways. I received messages back that the friar when told of my concerns said he had no intention of altering his sermons.

I was informed he responded as follows:

"It is God's will that I preach the way I do."

# Savonarola

How can one stop God's will? The people, if not the leaders of the city, know this to be true. Within a year of my arrival, I began preaching in Florence's main church, the Cathedral of Santa Maria del Fiore, to accommodate the ever-increasing congregations that came to hear me. Such was the popularity of my sermons and the testament of their truth. I wished to inflict terror, through Scripture, through the crack of the whip God had given my tongue and the fire he had brought to my eyes, for only when terrorized are people willing to change their sinful ways.

"Lo, the sword of the Lord, soon and swiftly! Ye hear it said, 'Blessed the house that owns a fat cure.' But a time will come when rather it will be said, 'Woe to that house.' Ye will feel the edge of the sword upon ye. Affliction shall smite ye. This shall no more be called Florence, but a den of thieves, of turpitude and bloodshed."

I had honed my preaching skills in northern Italy, learning to project my voice so that it resonated in precisely the most effective manner through any church interior large or small. No longer did people laugh at my Ferrarese accent, as they once had, mocking my pronunciation of vowels, ridiculing my pitch, my colloquial diction, and what they called my "comic gesticulations." I have been asked—an insult to the principle of my preaching—if my terrorizing them has anything to do with their former ridicule?

I corrected my flaws through practice, finally learning the accepted Tuscan dialect, which is fast becoming the national language in Italy, replacing the Latin of my youth. I now use language and delivery in my understanding of what moves and shakes people to the foundation of their bones: fear of death, fear of God's wrath, fear of hell-fire and all its torments.

"And I say unto ye: know that unheard-of times are at hand! Ye that are sodomites, murderers, gamblers and blasphemers, know that the hand of God, that mighty hand, shall smite you, and you will burn in hell for your sins. Repent now, for God's vengeance is as mighty as the hand that holds the sword of justice."

The gonfaloniere and his eight-man Signoria at the Palazzo della Signoria invited me to give a private sermon on a Wednesday after Easter. I suspected they wanted to hear for themselves what I preached and how I preached it: to size me up and target me, if necessary, as one who is seditious and invokes the poor to rebel against the wealthy. I did not back down from their invitation, for I had nothing to hide. I had, in fact, only the truth to convey in what I preached. I did not mention names that day, though I blamed those who were tyrants for the city's faults, for in their arrogance tyrants persist to live in sin: listening only to false praise, corrupting voters and paying no attention to the poor whom they oppress with hard labor and low wages. Should they not return to the poor what they have stolen from them in high taxes? I looked into the eyes of these leaders when I addressed the following:

"Ye are guilty of avarice, ye have corrupted the magistrates and their functions. None can persuade ye that it is sinful to lend at usury, but rather ye hold them to be fools that refrain from it."

I still see the outraged faces of my listeners that day. I dared to tell them what they knew to be true. When one of the leaders asked me how I could speak with such authority, I answered, "I am like Jeremiah, who, though mocked and chained, and beaten, felt compelled to preach the word of God in his heart, to prophesy to the princes of Judah and to Jerusalem the terrible destruction that would be visited upon that place. I am like Jonah, who despite all obstacles, fulfilled his mission to prophesy destruction to the great city of Ninevah."

They commended my ability to reference Scripture. Still, they wanted to know why I felt entitled to speak with such criticism against the ruler of Florence. How can any man be so audacious?

"What I say is only what God in Heaven wants me to say," I responded, "for He is the source and the fountain from which my words spring."

# Lorenzo

Though advised to do so, I refused to banish Savonarola, for I had learned three years earlier the consequence of banishing a popular preacher. Fra Bernardino da Feltre had gained a sympathetic following for speaking out against the bankers of Florence for charging high interest on their loans to the poor. He wanted to revolutionize the system of taxation and money lending, creating a bank for the people, which would, in effect, diminish the industry upon which my family had built its fortune. He became a champion among an ever-increasing population that began to look critically upon my regime. Thus I banished him to quell that criticism. My decision, however, only flamed the fires of discontent more. It took great expense and time to remedy the problem. I provided daily entertainments and offered monetary agreements to some of the key people behind the grumblings to once again set the ship right.

I wasn't about to make the same mistake. I had to guard my reputation, for what is a man without it? To banish the friar I had openly courted and invited to Florence would result in my enemies ridiculing me for vacillation and indecisiveness. I could not risk that ridicule. I would need to subdue him another way, using more subtle methods. I consulted with the superior of the Augustinian order, Fra Mariano da Genazzano, for the vast majority of people in Florence heralded him, not Savonarola, as its most renowned preacher. Diverse in learning and current with the time, he loved pagan classical poetry and philosophy and was thus able to reference both Humanist and Christian doctrine in his sermons, which he elucidated with a grace and musicality second to none. I asked him to deliver a sermon that would render Savonarola's claims and prophesies hollow with the hope it would diminish his growing stature He agreed to give such a sermon at the Church of Santo Spirito, the priory church of the San Gallo monastery, on Ascension Day, Thursday 12, May 1491.

# Savonarola

When I heard Fra Mariano was going to attack me in the pulpit of his church (a directive received from Lorenzo, I was certain), I replied to my brethren, "I shall wax, and he shall wane." I had met him once before, earlier that spring, when he visited me at San Marco, assuring me of his friendship. I should have known he couldn't be trusted. Was he not a frequent guest at the Medici country villas? His theology reflected little more than pagan idealism, serving to speak the words Lorenzo and his adherents wished to hear. In return, he and his monks lived lavishly in private cells outside the northern gates of the city.

My colleague Fra Placido Cinozzi, dressed in civilian clothing, attended the church that day, providing me with a detailed account of my rival preacher's sermon. I was not, after all, above playing the religious-political spy game, if it meant my survival. Lorenzo himself sat among the congregation, anxious, certainly, to see and hear how the Augustinian monk would undermine my prophecies. Fra Mariano used as his text Jesus' reply to his disciples, when they asked him to tell them what would come to pass in the future. "It is not for you to know the time, or the seasons." He went on to elaborate how preposterous it was for anyone to have knowledge of future events before they happened. He then attacked me by name, labeling me a false prophet, using lies to generate unrest with the populace against the current regime, with one intent: to gain power and glory for myself. He ridiculed the style and manner of my voice, the way I stood and gesticulated with my hands. He called me a serpent in the Garden of Eden, a serpent that, in the end, would be crushed again as it was under the foot of the Virgin, for the preservation of the Church, though clearly he meant the preservation of the Medici regime. He said, in conclusion, that if I were going to reference Scripture in my sermons, I should first bother to read the Bible (and this coming from someone who read primarily Platonist philosophy!) and learn to conduct a Mass in proper Latin.

How do I describe the joy I felt when I received the news of his sermon, knowing he had undermined his own intelligence and reputation in his cause to diminish mine? Three days later, on the following Sunday, I offered my rebuttal in the Cathedral of Santa Maria del Fiore, choosing to rebuke him not with vitriol or with the crack of my voice and thus fight fire with fire. I, instead, sprinkled cool reason against his unreason, speaking in a gentle manner, hoping that against his circus act my sermon would prove more dignified and thus have greater influence. I reminded him how only weeks earlier he had visited me, congratulating me on my sermons, praising their biblical erudition, assuring me I would do much good in Florence. Having prepared the foundation of my objective, I expressly asked, rhetorically, "Who was it who made you change your mind? Who was it that suggested that you should attack me?" I said no more on the subject. Everyone present knew to whom I alluded. I left the pulpit, knowing I had effectively reduced Fra Mariano's standing in the Florence community, while elevating my own.

Did I not say I shall wax, and he shall wane? Lorenzo and I have this in common: we play to win. I managed, at the same time, to implicate (expose) Lorenzo in an egregious, cowardly act to destroy my reputation among my many followers. Though Lorenzo remained in Florence, Fra Mariano, unable to bear his humiliation in the aftermath of his defeat packed his bags and left for Rome, intent, I was aware, of using his influence in the Vatican-- much as the serpent used its influence in the Garden of Eden--to plan, through cunning and deception, his revenge on me.

My status, meantime, grew exponentially. In less than two months time, the friars at San Marco elected me Prior of the monastery. When my fellow monks told me it was the custom for a newly elected friar to make a courtesy visit to the Palazzo Medici, I asked, "Who made me Prior, God or Lorenzo?"

When they replied, "God," I said, "Thus it is the Lord God I will thank."

# Lorenzo

The monks at San Marco had always been beholden to my family, for good reason. We, the Medici, as their benefactors, supported their livelihood, giving them leisure for theological and charitable pursuits. Why Savonarola chose to divorce himself from our love caused me sleepless nights, as the agitation of my mind increased the pain in my joints and limbs. I desired, above all else, peace. To achieve this objective, I began attending church at San Marco on Sundays. Afterwards I strolled in the garden or in the cloisters, hoping to meet Savonarola and engage him in conversation and thus win his love, as I had won the love of a pope, king, and duke when I was seventeen years old.

Not once, in my many visits, did I see him, though I have no doubt he saw me, peering down from one of the many windows above. What did he think at such times? I wished to be his friend. Did he not know that? What did he have to gain or prove by keeping his distance?

When my gout rendered me unable to walk, I quit my visits to the church and its grounds. I tried to win over his favor with money and gifts I sent to San Marco. Each gift, whether food, clothing or artwork, was returned. I ordered my chancellor, Piero da Bibbiena, to deposit gold coins, valued at 300 florins, in the alms chest of San Marco. I learned later the coins were taken to the brotherhood at St. Martin, where they were distributed to the poor. My chancellor reported back to me, saying, "This is a slippery customer we are dealing with." As he had earlier, he recommended banishment as the only possibly method of effectively punishing the preacher. Again I refused, still believing I could exert my authority in more politically astute ways.

I sent a delegation of leading citizens to visit Savonarola at San Marco, to communicate to the friar that his behavior was putting himself and his monastery in some danger. Francesco Valori, one of the delegates, reported to me that Savonarola did not receive their visit or their words of warning with grace. He cut them off, telling them he was certain they had not come of their own free will; that they had been sent by me. According to Francesco, Savonarola then issued his own advice:

"Tell Lorenzo to do penance for his sins. The Lord does not spare the princes of this earth from his judgment."

The delegates repeated their warning that if the friar continued to behave brazenly and disrespectfully, he was liable to be banished from Florence. Bernardo Rucellai, another of the delegates, recorded Savonarola's response and later gave it to me for my own perusal.

"Only people like you, who have wives and children, are afraid of banishment. I have no such fear, for if I did have to leave, this city would become no more than a speck of dust to me, compared with the rest of the world. I am not frightened; let him do as he pleases. But let him realize this: although I am a mere stranger to the city, and Lorenzo is the most powerful man in Florence, it is I who will remain here, and he who will depart. He will be gone, long before me."

# Machiavelli

I am not a prophet, and yet I could have just as easily prophesied Lorenzo's death. It is, after all, the custom for a gravely ill person, though still young in life, to die. Why should Savonarola have been seen as a seer? Oh, my detractors will say, did he not also prophesy the deaths of Innocent VIII and King Ferrante of Naples? I concede he did, though both were old men. Is it not also the custom for old men to die? For these predictions alone he should not have been lauded. A beggar in the streets, on wits end, could have done as much. As for the Apocalypse said to come, on the heels of these aforementioned deaths, wherein Italy's sins shall be cleansed, I have only this to say: I do not live on the pins and needles of supposition. I need something more tangible, such as a bolt of lightning striking and bringing to ruin my favorite brothel. Anything less than that, I remain a doubting Thomas.

I did, nonetheless, admire the friar's insolence. He cared not a whit whom he insulted in the course of following his own agenda. I do not, as others so inclined, call it a religious agenda. Though I believe he was sincere in wanting to help the poor and reform the Church, he wanted, more than anything, especially as his popularity grew, a power absolute. Thus, more than a man of God, he was a man among men, competing with others to see who could climb higher on the ladder. If he had consulted with me as he climbed the ladder's rungs, I would have said: *if you look below, you will see how far you stand from the ground. Though you think you are in reach of heaven, you will know when you fall that you are closer to hell.*

He had to know he would not fare well if he continued to joust with leaders and popes. Though, Lorenzo, as a humanist, showed respect to men of God, Innocent VIII's successor, Alexander VI, a political mover and shaker, with little respect for religion and even less for a contentious friar, possessed the means and the backbone to eliminate someone who showed him neither allegiance nor love.

# Savonarola

I do not live cloistered and unaware of the world. I am, in fact, insulted that some believe it is the lifestyle of a monk. Here's the truth: I am an astute observer. I make it my business to know the affairs of leaders. My condemnation of Lorenzo does not come from abstract suppositions. It is founded on concrete examples of his abusive power. I point to his appropriation and embezzlement of the *Monte delle Doti*, the Dowry Fund. How do I know this to be true? I have my sources (and resources). The poor have been paying into this account and receiving interest on it since Lorenzo's grandfather, Cosimo, established it in 1424, as a means to provide dowries for girls, who would otherwise not be able to get married. Yet suddenly this fund has become depleted. How did this happen? Look no further than Lorenzo de' Medici.

In debt because he has failed as a banker, he embezzled money from the fund to pay for his son's ascension in the Church. Innocent VIII (can a name be more ironic?) requested 10,000 florins as a final down payment to ensure Giovanni's cardinalate. Lorenzo, with the aid of Antonio Miniati, his henchman in the financial department, appropriated (stole) dowries of poor girls to line his own pockets, and Innocent VIII, for his part, cares little where the money comes from. Lorenzo's son Giovanni has been made cardinal at sixteen years of age. His appointment brought honor to the city, as was evidenced by the parade on the Via Larga, of which I avoided like a plague. It should have brought shame, considering the expense to an already depleted fund. At the Palazzo della Signoria Lorenzo's son received thirty loads of gifts carried by porters, at an estimated cost of 20,000 florins, and where did this money come from? From the pockets of the poor, that's where. I know this: when Lorenzo dies, he goes before God naked, stripped of all titles and entitlements, a man like any other who must toil in eternity to right the wrongs of his failed morality.

# Lorenzo

I spend hours on end shivering in my cloak near a fire, hoping the heat will melt the icy needles of pain in my joints. I avoid my reflection in a looking glass. The leaves that once made my beautiful tree have now fallen. I am little more than bones and barren branches. I see death, though I see it not in my eyes, but in the eyes of those who look upon me: my friends, my doctors, my children, and the foreign dignitaries who pass through. Their shocked faces tell me clearly the state of my health.

I put my trust in a remedy suggested by one of my physicians, Petrus Bonus Avogarius. He recently wrote me the following letter: "To prevent the return of these pains, you must get a stone called sapphire, and have it set in gold, so that it should touch the skin. This must be worn on the third finger of the left hand. If this is done the pain in the joints, or gouty pains, will cease, because that stone has occult virtues, and the specific one of preventing evil humours going to the joints." I did as he asked, and my pain is now worse than ever.

Giovanni had been made a cardinal, and I wanted desperately to share in his ceremonial day. Though I missed the parade and subsequent celebration in the Piazza, I thought to make the banquet in the main hall of our palace. I had invited more than sixty guests, consisting of foreign ambassadors and leading citizens. My crippled body would not cooperate. My servants carried me on a litter to the balcony overlooking the hall. It was there I saw Giovanni dressed in his splendid cardinal robes. I knew then he would become a pope. I knew, as well, I would not live to see that day, though it filled me with pride and hope for the Medici name in future generations.

I realized, also, that once he left the next morning to take up his post in Rome, I would never again see him. I still had much to say to him, for in my final days the only thing that matters is that the Medici legacy should prosper when I'm gone. Though I'm happy for his title, I am worried about his extravagance. No sooner had he left than

I began composing a letter to him, telling him to celebrate less than others on feast days; warning him not to wear too many jewels and fine silks. I reminded him he was from Florence. He should value a few fine antiques and learned books. Given that he is already overweight, I advised him to eat plain food and take regular exercise, for those who wear the habit are prone to illness if they are not mindful of their health.

Yes, I had become what I never thought in my youth I would become: my father, the advice giver!

I told him he must beware of Rome because it is a sink of all iniquities. I wrote, "You will be regarded with great envy by enemies that had striven to prevent your appointment, who will do their best to denigrate little by little your public reputation, attempting to drag you down into the very ditch into which they themselves have fallen."

I knew as I was writing how hard it is to advise a sixteen-year-old. Hadn't I listened only selectively to my father, if at all? Why should Giovanni heed my advice? Still, I continued to write, for what can a father, a dying one, no less, do other than provide his son with the wisdom he had acquired through living?

"As this is your first visit to Rome," I wrote, "I think it would be much better for you to use your ears more than your tongue." I realized I was writing words my father had written to me verbatim when I first went to Rome. Was I not a hypocrite to write these words, for hadn't I used my tongue to great effect with whomever I met?

"Devote yourself entirely to the interests of the Church," I added, "and in doing so you will not find it difficult to aid the cause of Florence and that of our house." I wanted him to know above all else that he was an ambassador, as well as a cardinal. His reason for being there was to enlarge the scope from which the Medici can see greater opportunities, both in business and in the Church.

"Remain close to the pope," I advised, "but ask of him as few favors as possible." Knowing my son has always been prone to laziness, I concluded my letter with a less-than-subtle admonishment:

"One rule above all others I urge you to observe most rigorously: Get up early in the morning."

Two days after writing to my son, my servants carried me on a litter from Florence to the Medici villa at Careggi, thirty miles away. I kept looking back to see one last time the great dome dwarfing the hillside behind it, aware that both my grandfather and father had also been carried to Careggi in their final stages of illness and never again returned to the city they loved. My doctor told me it was for my best that I seek the country air and drink from the clean waters. They, together, would renew my body and spirit. I wanted to believe him, for what does a sick man have other than belief, though it may be vague and irrational?

After having arrived at Careggi, I received news the next day that a thunderbolt struck the lantern on top of the dome of Florence Cathedral, splitting it in two. As a result, one of the marble niches and many other pieces of marble broke off in a miraculous way. I demanded to know from my source which side of the cathedral the shattered marble had fallen. He told me it had fallen on the north side. I found myself succumbing to old superstitions.

"That is the side facing this house," I said. "It means that I shall die."

# Savonarola

A thunderbolt (Lo, the sword of God) appeared in the midst of my sermon at San Lorenzo Church, awakening a revelation, which I described to my congregation. I saw clearly a black cross, which stretched out its arms to cover over the whole of the earth. Upon this cross were inscribed the words *'Crux irae Dei'*. The sky was pitch black, lit by flickers of lightning. Thunder roared and a great storm of wind and hailstorms killed a host of people. The sky now cleared and from the center of Jerusalem there appeared a gold cross, which rose into the sky illuminating the entire world. Upon this cross were inscribed the words *'Crux Misericordae Dei'*, and all nations flocked to adore it.

I felt the power of God surging in me as I spoke, my voice rising to meet the thunder in the sky; sure the lightning was only the beginning of evil auguries to come. That night, in a dream, God verified what I felt and believed. He wants me to build an Ark, similar to Noah's, for soon a great flood will come to submerge the world and all its irredeemable corruption, washing away the stink and sin of centuries. In the aftermath of this deluge, we will begin again, in a New Jerusalem, where only those who survive, those who carry the faith of God in their bosoms, will live in peace and spiritual prosperity.

I understand the dream's meaning. God wants me to do more than preach to a congregation of a thousand. He wants me to lead tens of thousands, beyond the walls of the church, into the very streets of Florence. I told Him I will do as He asks. I now envision the city of Florence as my church. I stand among my congregation. I prophesy that a new Cyrus, whose conquering army will cross the mountains, sweeping all before it, will invade Italy. This invading army, in fulfillment of God's will, shall take cities and fortresses with great ease. As the Lord said in the Book of Isaiah: "I will go before thee and make the crooked places straight: I will break in pieces the gates of brass, and cut in sunder the bars of iron."

Will not this invasion be the great flood (scourge) of which God speaks? The dirt of Italy will be swept away. Popes and tyrants will be cut down and slaughtered. People will quake with fear at the prospect of a vast nothingness. I will be there to fill the void, to lift the banner of a new day.

I have reached a new height in my preaching. I enrapture and hold my congregation, like fish caught in a net. I am both Noah and Moses, at the same time, promising to lead them to a promised land, to return them to the presence of God. They listen in anticipation. They want certainty, and this is what I deliver to them.

"God has placed you in my care. He has made me the bearer of light and faith, through the words I preach. Listen well. Philosophers can tell us what the good life is, but they cannot help us to achieve it. This comes only through the light of faith. O Florence, receive my words as you receive God's lightning: repent and confess and take frequent communion. Shed your old skin and take up another form, and let this form be the blood and suffering of Christ."

# Lorenzo

What else but his legacy does a man have at the end of his life? My forebears, notably my great-grandfather and grandfather, created that legacy before my father and I assumed it. The fortunes of my sons are now the cornerstones of that legacy. What good is power and wealth unless they can be maintained and proliferated? To ensure our continued status as leaders and statesmen, Piero, my eldest, will follow as ruler upon my death. Giovanni, already a cardinal, will some day become pope. The Medici star, I must believe, will rise and shine unimpeded. Not even the damnation of my soul, if it comes to that, can stand in our way. I do not worry about Giovanni. Other than his slovenliness, he is capable. He possesses brains, charm, common sense and a love of culture and art. Those attributes can take a man far. I know, for they are the same skills I possessed and used to great benefit throughout my short lifetime. It is Piero, my eldest, who concerns me most, especially in light of what he stands to inherit.

When he enters my room, I marvel at his handsome features. I, in fact, ask him from where he has received his physical beauty.

"From you, my dear father," he says.

Painful as it is, I laugh, for he is jesting me. He knows, as well as me, that I had not been blessed with physical beauty. I do not refer to the death mask I currently wear on my face. I refer to the features I was given at birth: a long flattened nose, heavy lantern jaw, brooding dark eyes and skin riddled with eczema. My brother Guiliano and my father received the gift of physical beauty. Clearly, Piero has inherited theirs. My beauty, if it can be called that, is more of the mind and soul, if I am allowed such consolation. I inherited personal and diplomatic skills and an appreciation for fine art and literature, much the same characteristics as my grandfather, Cosimo. I have been glad and grateful for these gifts. They served me well as a man and, even more so, as a leader. Sadly, Piero, though handsome, has none of the higher skills a man and leader needs. For this reason, I worry for his future and the future of the Medici legacy. I can only hope he will develop his mind and maturity, though at twenty years of age he has shown little sign he will.

I became a man and a leader at the age of seventeen. Piero, at twenty years of age, continues to persist in immature behavior. Leading citizens and friends alike have reminded me of his arrogance. I blame myself for not having been around him enough as a child. He needed authority, which I failed to give him. He has grown up privileged, acting entitled and ostentatious like a spoiled prince. He must change if he is to have any success as a ruler.

"Come and sit near me," I say.

"Are you comfortable, father?" he asks, continuing to stand.

"As comfortable as a man can be in the throes of terminal sickness."

He asks me if I had drunk the solution of pulverized pearls my doctor had prescribed. I told him I had.

"It should help," he says.

I know the solution holds no benefit. I drank it only to appease my family. My children, in particular, are still young enough to believe in superstitious remedies. My dying body knows the truth. The solution, a crock of black magic, is a last ditch effort to try something, which is better than not trying. It is our nature, after all, to believe that man alone determines his destiny. I think of Pico, writing in his great work, *On the Dignity of Man*: "O great and wonderful happiness of man! It is given to him to have that which he chooses and to be that which he wills." You are right, my friend, but there are limitations to man's will. We are fooled into believing its powers. I am only forty-three years of age. I want and deserve more life, but it is not for me to decide. God above, in the end, controls our final destiny.

"It is my dream that some day the Medici will be the bearers of kings and popes," I say.

"I will do all I can to see that dream realized, father," he responds.

"You must be willing to take advice."

"I am my own man, father, and will rule as such."

"You will need to cultivate friendships with the leading citizens. And you must listen to their advice. You will need them."

"They have more need of me than I of them."

"Do not alienate those who put you in power."

"You speak for yourself, father, for I am not yet in power."

"It is only a matter of time."

"When that time comes, I will act accordingly."

"To have success as a leader, you must follow on the path that I paved."

"Did you follow your father's path?"

"My father was too sick to rule."

"Did you follow anyone's path, father? Weren't you allowed to be your own man in making decisions? And didn't those decisions, though sometimes rash and impetuous, always succeed?"

His face wears a know-it-all grin. I want to wipe it from his face. He stands far beyond my reach, believing, I'm sure, that if he doesn't touch me or breathe my breath, he will be safe from contracting the sickness to which my forebears and I have suffered. I hope he will be spared. At the very least, I hope he lives a longer and healthier life than I have.

"My decisions may have succeeded, but it doesn't mean they were right."

"Do not riddle, father. Speak directly."

"I have regrets."

"Such as?"

"Volterra."

"Why do you speak of Volterra? The war was twenty years ago."

"Two months after your birth."

"And it ended a month later in victory, enhancing your reputation."

"Still, I regret what happened."

"What happened was you quelled the rebellion, and you secured the alum mines for Florence. What is there to regret?"

"The sack of the city and the unnecessary loss of lives."

"Such is the peril of war."

"Those who suffered most were loyal to us."

"They were Volterrans, nonetheless, and brought suffering unto themselves."

"The rebels brought suffering unto themselves; the citizens didn't deserve theirs."

"Is this the reason, to speak of Volterra, that you called me to your room?"

"I bring it up only because I was twenty-three years of age at the time, and you are twenty. If I had known then what I know now, I would have acted differently. I was not then the man I would later become, achieving my goals primarily by persuasion and the delicate balance of opposing interests. I would have negotiated for peace, using the tools of my trade: charm and diplomacy."

"They didn't want peace. It was their intransigence that was to blame. If they had surrendered the alum mines to us in the first place neither death nor destruction would have occurred."

"Violence should always be the last option."

"Sometimes it is the only option."

"All measures of diplomacy and negotiation must first be employed."

"Unless you are dealing with traitors and rebels. They don't deserve diplomacy and negotiation. They deserve death."

# Machiavelli

Volterra, long under the subjugation of Florence, dared to assert its independence, refusing to surrender to Lorenzo the valuable alum mines discovered in its city proper. A most coveted resource, alum was necessary for the dyeing process of textiles, a source of wealth for Florence's blossoming merchant class. If Volterra had acted in accordance with its status, as a Florentine province, subservient to Lorenzo's wishes and whims, the bloodshed and destruction that ensued would have been prevented. Isn't it interesting that it takes the heavy hand of justice--or injustice, if one prefers--rendered violently, for a state to understand who rules and who serves that rule?

When a Volterran mob murdered Lorenzo's agent, Paolo Inghirami, Lorenzo, rightfully so, chose to make an example of the Volterran rebels. Florence declared war on Volterra on April 26, 1472. The Signoria raised money to equip an army, and Lorenzo persuaded Federico da Montefeltro, the most distinguished *condottiere* of his day, to spearhead the assault. He assembled an army of seven thousand mercenary soldiers and cavalry. The Volterrans had one thousand men, mostly peasants and citizens. Montelfaltro's army camped outside the walls of Volterra, hurling insults at their outnumbered enemies inside the walls. Understanding they stood no chance against a superior army, the Volterran priors sent an emissary to the Florentine government to plead for mercy.

On June 4, after five weeks passed, with still no movement from either side, the government of Florence invited the Volterrans to offer their city freely into the hands of Montefeltro's army in return for guarantees that life and property would be protected. The Volterrans accepted the offer and opened the gates to the victorious army. Thus, the Volterrans, who had had the audacity, coupled with stupidity, to rebel against Lorenzo, nearly escaped unscathed. They didn't, though, for it is true as someone once famously wrote—yes, even I borrow from time to time—"that once the dogs of war are unleashed they are difficult to call back."

Never was that more true than at Volterra. The mercenary army had camped more than a month, with little food and even less comfort, having to sleep too many nights on the cold ground. Why had they suffered, if not for the satisfaction of a one-sided confrontation with its vulnerable enemy inside the walls of the city? Once the gates were opened, they expressed what they had been waiting more than a month to express: their pent-up rage at a life lived for the sake of others. To be a hired mercenary, a solider of war, requires a degree of inhumanity, and they possessed plenty of it, as it had grown, like the dirt on their bodies and the emptiness in their stomachs. Hungry like mad dogs, once they were unleashed, they barked loudly and bit eagerly at whatever moved. They tore and rushed wildly, expressing their unrestrained fury, and why wouldn't they? Hadn't they been hired to do just that?

"Sack the city!" they cried. "Sack the city!"

They set fires and razed buildings, attacking and striking down people who defended their homes and businesses, making no distinction between rebels and loyalists. They slaughtered chickens, cows, and mules and destroyed the city's grain and crops. Volterra smouldered with smoke and the smell of blood. If I am unsympathetic to the Volterrans plight it is only because I revile their foolishness, for only those who are fools believe they can rebel against a superior state with impunity. It is utter lunacy to trigger insecurity in a ruler with superior strength. He becomes his most ruthless at such times.

It is equally inadvisable to bark unless you possess the might to bite. The Volterrans did not have enough mad hounds, as the Florentines had in more than seven thousand starved mercenaries. Though many outside of Florence—don't count the Volterrans, for they are biased—viewed the sack of the city a reprehensible act, I felt then, as I've continued to feel, no compunctious visitings to my conscience. Lorenzo had acted decisively in declaring war, understanding that a ruler's first responsibility is to rule, and whatever secures that end can be regarded as just, even if it demands the violation of ethical norms. One can be either a saint or a king, but not both. He subdued the enemy, acting in harmony with the times. So what if the methods were brutal, if cruelty leads to peace and loyalty? I know this to be true: if a ruler's office and life are under threat, virtue and righteousness are useless to him. He must, by any means, hold to power and act accordingly. The middle road for a ruler, to vacillate on a pendulum of moral gymnastics, failing to know how to be completely good or completely bad, is the worst road to take. Lorenzo took the road traveled by kings and emperors for centuries before him. What happened in Volterra is no more than the malice of fate.

If I possess any criticism at all, it is this: If one must do harm to another, it must be such that it will not give rise to a vendetta. Though the Volterrans were subdued, they continue to harbor ill will towards Florence, and in time when the balance of power shifts—and it will shift, if history (see, The Fall of Rome) teaches us anything—they will again rebel, perhaps victoriously, because--I apologize for borrowing yet again--"the seeds of war so hopefully planted in spring, often bear bitter fruit in winter."

I can only hope I am dead and gone by then.

# Lorenzo

I tell Piero that one of my advisors, Tommaso Soderini, an elder statesman, had cautioned me about declaring war with Volterra. "Better a lean peace than a fat victory," he said, referencing an old Tuscan proverb. I had no need of advice then. At twenty-three years of age, I believed I knew the right course to take. I could, as ruler of Florence, stare down our lesser neighbor and, if necessary, make an example of their stubborn act of defiance.

"I am not ruled by Tuscan proverbs," Piero says.

"Neither am I, but I am not so stubborn now, as then, to be immune to their wisdom."

"A man must earn wisdom through his own experiences. Did you not tell me that once?"

"Yes, and now I am telling you that we should also look to others who have earned their wisdom with even greater experiences than our own."

"I prefer not to borrow another man's wisdom. It strikes me as a most dishonorable thing to do."

"I once believed, as you do, that honor was everything to a man."

"And what should replace it?"

"Humility."

He laughs and crosses the room, where he draws the curtains on the darkening sky. When he turns to me, he speaks with condescension.

"That is a word reserved for old age. A young man gets nowhere with it."

"Sometimes you have to sacrifice to win."

"Sacrifice honor?"

I do not respond.

"Never," he says. "Men, such as I—such as you, when you were young and able—live for honor."

"Men also kill and die for honor."

"If that is so, they do it honorably."

"Such honor is sometimes false."

"False or not, honor is the engine that drives men's wills. It is a whiskey that gives a man teeth and a bite.

Humility is little more than a milk that sours the stomach and weakens man."

"You are a poet, after all."

"I am not a poet. I prefer a sword to words."

I close my eyes. The sight of his smug expression is too much to bear. It is the same expression he wore after he returned from Rome on his very first mission. When Innocent VIII became pope, I was too ill to make the trip. I sent Piero in my place, though he was only thirteen years of age. I remembered at the time how my first mission to Rome and Naples had matured me, changing me from a boy to a man while still in my teens. Such was not the case with Piero. He left an insolent boy and returned an even worse one. He entered the gates of Florence, dressed gaudily atop a white horse, running afoul the city's sumptuary laws, in place for more than a hundred years, and respectfully honored by all my forebears. My great-grand father and grandfather had detested ostentatious behavior, believing a wealthy man should always keep out of the public eye. Piero, however, showed little concern for respected codes of conduct. I admit to having been embarrassed by his bold display of princely entitlement. I am still embarrassed at the remembrance, for it is the very kind of display that encourages seditious activity among the populace and leads citizens to oppose our wealth and government.

He believes my closing my eyes is further evidence of my regret about Volterra. He says, "The people of Florence didn't regret your decision. They appreciated your firm leadership. That's what people want when it comes to asserting our dominion over weaker neighbors."

"It was a fat victory—a victory with a price, as was evident in the aftermath, when I visited the besieged city: to see children without clothes, women begging in the streets, people sleeping outdoors, even in the rain, people eating dirt and grass. These were hard working people, our people, loyal to Florence. These were not rebels."

"You did not sack the city. The mercenaries did."

"I paid for their services."

"And the end result?"

I do not respond.

"Volterra remains our subject."

"Out of fear, not love."

"It matters not how they are subjected. The rebels gambled that you didn't have the mettle to punish them; they tempted fate and lost. You quelled a rebellion and in doing so brought pride, honor and victory to Florence. I will guide this great republic in the same such manner."

"All I ask is that you are wise and take counsel."

"I will act first and take counsel second."

"You must do as the times dictate, and the present time requires of you, above all else, diplomacy."

"I am aware of the times, father. I am not a child. I am a man, a Medici."

"As a Medici, you must be patient with the Signoria."

He laughs. I ask him why he behaves in such a rude manner.

"You give me advice, father, that you yourself did not follow."

"Nonetheless, I know what I am saying. If you do not befriend the Signoria, they will become your enemies."

"I will deal with enemies as you always did: with the swift hand of vengeance."

I close my eyes again, briefly. His presence triggers greater pain in my limbs and brings a fever to my senses. I sweat and gasp for air. I drink water from my bedside table. I wish for him to leave, but I must first finish what I need to say, even if my words fall on ears that won't receive them. What else do I have now than the hope that something of which I say will sprinkle cool reason on his hotheaded brain, changing his disposition and manner accordingly?

"A leader needs to know how to stroke the egos and flatter the vanity of potential opponents."

"My sword shall speak for me against all who oppose me."

"The sword is the surest way to invite conspirators into your home."

"They will be too dead to walk into my house."

What had I done to create his behavior? I gave him the best humanist education I could, making sure Angelo Poliziano, among others, tutored him in literature, science and philosophy, and yet he has always acted unschooled and unsophisticated. In truth, there is little about him that is recognizable as a Medici. For years I have heard the whispers and theories: he doesn't behave like a Medici because in blood he isn't a Medici; his flaws are carried in his mother's blood. I believe none of this, for his mother was a shy woman and wholly sweet in nature, humbling herself before most people of status, though she herself came from aristocratic lineage. Yet most Florentines believed she was to blame because as a foreign woman, with links to Rome and Naples, she had bastardized his blood, thus explaining his insolence and haughtiness.

It does not help his position as a future ruler that his wife is despised in Florence. For that I take the blame. When he was sixteen, I married him to Alfonsina Orsini, daughter of the grand constable of Naples, a man whose martial feats of arms earned him the nickname "The Knight Without Fear." She was thirteen years of age and possessed little personal charm. Her limited personality reflected her family. Their brains were of a strange and peculiar nature, capable of instability if not properly checked. While I did not like them personally, it was a necessary transaction if we were to realize the dynastic ambitions I had put in place. It was also advantageous for us to side with Naples. Rome, run by men who know nothing of statesmanship, would always be an unreliable friend, more capable of bringing trouble and ruin to Italy than building constructive, long-term alliances.

I reach for his hand. He gives it, clasping mine tightly.

"Follow that course which appears to be most respectable of the prestige of your inherited name."

"I shall bring to the Medici name greater honor than it has ever known," he says, smiling warmly.

I want to believe his glowing eyes, though at the core they are hollow.

# Machiavelli

In 1444, Cosimo de' Medici predicted that Medici rule would end in fifty years. In 1494, exactly fifty years after his prediction, Piero the Unfortunate—a title afforded him, for good reason--fled Florence by night, fearing for his life, which, in that moment of time, had little value to the citizens who wanted him dead. Though he carried away as many of his family's valued treasures as he could, he departed bankrupt in mind and soul, reflecting a fitting end to a young man who lived and ruled without a clue. More interested in hunting and jousting in lieu of learning and employing the skills of governance through hard work, he managed to offend and alienate those to whom he should have received love and allegiance. When he did make a decision, other than what fine silks to wear, it was often ill considered and ill timed. While his father, in his twenty-three years, had used his diplomatic skills, balancing his needs with the needs of Florence and all the states of Italy to solidify peace, Piero, in less than two years, destroyed everything his father had achieved, leading Florence to the brink of destruction and bringing shame to the Medici name. "The peace of Italy is at an end," Pope Innocent VIII said in reference to Lorenzo's passing. Though hardly a man of insight, the pope assessed the impact of Lorenzo's death correctly.

Allow me this brief historical interlude, which had great bearing on the state of Italy and, in particular, on Lorenzo's son, Piero: Lodovico Sforza, the untitled ruler of Milan, opened the floodgates of war. Not the rightful Duke of Milan, he acted as *de facto* ruler for his nephew, the young Gian Galeazzo Sforza, who had succeeded his assassinated father at the age of eight. In 1488, at the age of nineteen, he married his cousin Isabella of Naples, the granddaughter of King Ferrante. Ludovico had no interest in surrendering his title to his nephew. He sent the young married couple to live out of the public and political eye in a villa south of Milan, at Pavia. Though Gian Galeazzo acceded to his uncle, Isabella voiced her discontent. She appealed to her father, Alfonso, the heir to the throne in Naples, to persuade King Ferrante to order the instatement of her husband as the rightful duke. Alfonso promised that when he ascended to the throne he would assert Gian Galeazzo's claim to power. Ludovico had no intention of surrendering his position. He aspired to fight, if necessary, to keep his title, and to that end he sought outside assistance, knowing that Rome and Venice would offer none. I do not mention Florence, for without a military what kind of assistance could it provide, other than cultural and artistic?

Enter King Charles VIII of France, one of the main shakers and movers of this story, who would, beginning in 1494, shape the political landscape of Italy for years to come. In an egregious act of betrayal to all Italians, who wished to take care of their own business in their own cockeyed way, Ludovico reached outside the bounds of Italy and courted King Charles for assistance, promising, in return, to support Charles if he decided to claim his ancestral right to Naples by way of his paternal grandmother. The thought of an expanded kingdom appealed to Charles, for he was not unlike any man who rules an empire. He equated his self-worth with how much he could possess. In January 1494, when King Ferrante died, Charles contested Alfonso being named heir to the throne of Naples. Alfonso refused to accede to Charles, at which time the king of France decided to invade Italy.

If he were alive, Lorenzo would have checked Ludovico's ambitions. He would have negotiated a truce between Milan and Naples. He would have persuaded the young king of France that it wasn't in his best interests to invade Italy. He would have used his wits, charm and intelligence to thwart the impending war. His son, Piero, however, possessed only a name, lacking personality, experience and brains. To be fair to Piero, he faced a damned-if-I-do, damned-if-I-don't-do conflict much greater than his skill set could handle.

How could he not back Naples? He married into the Orsini clan, who were powerful lords there. And what of Rome? He needed its goodwill for two reasons: his brother's cardinalship depended on the pope's benevolence and Florentine bankers depended on papal business. If he backed Naples, surely the pope would lend support, wouldn't he? Yet if he didn't, Florence might be left on its own. Yet if he chose not to back Alfonso, and the pope then sided with Naples, with the Venetians joining the alliance, Florence might once again stand in peril, this time from its Italian neighbors.

After much indecision and uncertainty, he backed Naples, believing he could resist the mighty French army. Even now, writing this, many years after the fact, I smile a smile that knows no joy, only cynicism, for how does a small republic, such as Florence, resist a foreign army made up of 40,000 cavalry and infantrymen, with a highly developed artillery train, complete with guns mounted on carriages with trunions, the likes of which Italy had not seen? The French army, comprised of men schooled in the northern European manner of warfare, actually killed their enemies. Contrast that with soldiers in Italy, hired mercenaries, who avoided bloodshed at all costs. The French had weaponry that could destroy the walls of any city or fortress that stood in its path. Florence possessed little to defend itself, unless you consider men wielding brushes and chisels intimidating.

Piero failed to understand history—a sin for any mortal man, no less a ruler--for Florence had traditionally been an ally of France. Did he not know his father had always sent envoys to the French court to maintain friendly relations with King Louis, Charles' father? How could Piero have not known that Lorenzo offered much advice and assistance to King Louis on matters cultural and ecclesiastical, and in return, the king supported his son's ascendancy to become a cardinal? If nothing else, Piero should have been aware that his brother Giovanni relied on French benefices for a sizeable part of his income. How does one rule without having an understanding of history, unless he is, of course, too arrogant to believe history has any relevance?

Piero had to know this: King Charles felt betrayed by Florence. Everyone knew it, and it caused no small amount of apprehension among we citizens. The Signoria, fearing retribution from the French, wanted Piero to abandon his alliance with Naples and form one with King Charles. Piero, keeping true to his perverse personality, stubbornly opposed popular opinion, believing in his undeveloped mind that he alone was right, saying without actually saying it: *I am the ruler. Thus I can do what I want, even if the course of action I propose is irrational, if not altogether insane.*

Piero's cousins, Lorenzo di Pierfrancesco and his brother Giovanni, more wealthy and popular among the citizens of Florence, secretly courted King Charles, writing to him and promising they would give financial assistance to him and his army in their passage across Tuscany. Piero accused his cousins of treason and had them imprisoned in the Palazzo del Bargello. When four ambassadors from France came to Florence, requesting safe passage across Florentine territory on its way to Naples, Piero refused their request, sealing his fate as one who would soon through bad decisions and failure earn the ignominious title *Unfortunate.*

# Savonarola

I am not advancing the overthrow of Piero in my sermons, as some have suggested. I am simply reporting what God Himself tells me: that a new Cyrus is coming from over the mountains. I am saying that the scourge of God is soon to arrive and cleanse Italy of all that stains it. I have not mentioned Piero's name, nor do I intend to. It is for others to infer the meaning of my messages. It is for me to deliver them. I will say this: many laughed when I made these prophecies nearly two years ago. I do not see anyone laughing now. I see fear, panic and rage. People, finally, are beginning to listen, for the time has come for all sinners to face their comeuppance. The words I speak--and the truth inherent in them--have suddenly become the hope of the city as it faces the dreaded siege by the French. People now turn to me and say, "Fra Savonarola, can you help us?" It is God's will, I say. He alone decides who will be saved and whether our city must fall under the wrath of His sword. This prophecy was given to you not by me, but by the word of God, and now it is being fulfilled.

I see myself standing before my congregation, which grows larger every day. I see the pulpit rising. From this height, I have a great vantage point to see clearly. I see the scared faces of the people, as they should be scared, with good reason. I feel empowered by their fear as I speak, still rising high above them, just as heaven rises high above earth:

"O Italy, because of your lust, your avarice, your pride, your envy, your thieving, your extortion, you will suffer all manner of afflictions and many scourges. O Florence, for your sins, your brutality, your avarice, your lust, many trials and tribulations will be heaped upon you. O Clergy, who are the principal cause of so many evils, woe unto you!"

# Machiavelli

Piero received word of the French soldiers' advance in northern Italy, through Genoa and down into Rapallo, Mordano, and Fivizanno, leaving a bloody trail of slaughtered citizens along the way who tried to resist them. Realizing he did not have the backing of his own people-- what took him so long to realize this?--or the other states in Italy, he retreated in his position. By then Charles and his army had successfully entered Pisa, a Florentine province. Fearing the French army would invade Florence next, Piero, believing money to be the root of resolution, sent a messenger to Charles, offering 300,000 francs to forestall any further advancement. Charles rejected Piero's bribe. Piero then made a decision that attempted to recall his father's glory fourteen years earlier, of which I will detail later, when Lorenzo saved Florence from further war and sure disaster, convincing King Ferrante to sign a peace treaty, and thus bringing him the respect of all Florentine citizens. Piero rode to Sarzanello, outside Pisa, to meet with Charles, probably thinking he could employ the same kind of charm and diplomacy his father had used many times with foreign leaders to secure peace. Unfortunately for him and the citizens of Florence, Piero possessed neither skill.

Charles met Piero with the knowledge that his own people did not back him and would not be displeased to see him overthrown. Charles had, in fact, already received assurances from leading men in Florence, such as Piero Capponi, former ambassador to France—a man he knew well, for he had lived in his court—that Florence supported the French advancing through Florentine territory. He knew, therefore, that he could demand whatever he wanted from Piero. If Piero believed he was meeting a friend in the French king, he was quickly disheartened to learn the truth: Charles, still stung by feelings of betrayal, had nothing but disdain for Lorenzo's eldest son. He treated Piero as one would a defeated enemy who had shown initial disloyalty. The king demanded an enormous loan and the right to occupy many Tuscan towns until he successfully concluded his enterprise in Naples. Piero acceded to each of Charles' demands. He handed over Sarzana and Pietrasanta, two Florentine fortresses, which would leave Florence defenseless on its northern border. Worst of all, he surrendered Pisa because Charles had promised to help the Pisan citizens rebel against their overlord, Florence. In addition, Charles wanted 200,000 florins to help contribute to his conquering of Naples. Piero not only capitulated to the money, he even offered the king use of the Palazzo Medici while he stayed in Florence.

Good grief, I'm surprised Piero didn't surrender to the king his wife and children as well. Am I saying the price was heavy? Yes I am. It had taken Florence years of bitter strife and fight to acquire Pisa, the seaport city that helped develop our trade with Europe and elsewhere. Aside from economic loss, losing Pisa meant losing status and pride. These dual losses did not settle well with Florentines, and they still don't.

As Secretary of War, I have devoted much time and thought into the re-conquest of Pisa. Tired of hiring outside mercenaries, who possess neither loyalty nor love for our Republic, I have created an army made up solely of Florentine citizens. Much of our citizens' blood has been spilled and untold treasures have been lost. I digress to the present for a reason: to point out the far-reaching consequence of Piero's decision to sell out his city to save his own skin.

What's equally maddening about Piero's capitulation to Charles is his surrendering so quickly and easily without realizing he had some strong negotiating cards if he but knew how to play them. The French, after all, living from camp to camp did not—if I am allowed the extravagance of a metaphor--lie on beds of roses, eating peaches and cream. The fortresses at Sarzano and Sarzanello had refused to surrender, despite the best efforts of the invading army. As winter approached, Charles' army would never last through its cold, unforgiving weather. Quartered along the cold, drafty coastal area, his army would be subject to sickness and disease. Surely he had no enthusiasm to bring these men into Florence to fight in narrow streets unbeknownst to them. Why Piero failed to consider the cards he held is further testament to his incompetence. He threw down his hand before the king's resolve could be tested, sacrificing his city and the little love that remained for him. Lorenzo, if alive, would have played that hand and won. Of that I am certain.

Not only did Piero accede everything to Charles, he also overstepped his bounds when he left to meet the king without first consulting with the Signoria. He did so knowing they would have thwarted his intent, understanding his visit to the king, with the limited skills and experience he possessed, would further damage the city's fortunes. When he wrote to the Signoria after the fact it was to appeal to them and all Florentine citizens to remain loyal to his father's memory. I still smell the stink of irony, for in recalling his father's memory he made it all the more impossible, because of their contrast, to be loyal to him.

The city, at that time, had come to a stop, as if holding its collective breath, waiting for the inevitable invasion of the French. I remember that for days on end the shops remained closed. Rubbish littered the streets, where only men and boys wandered in forlorn states. Women and girls had already left to seek shelter in convents. I must confess that I, unlike others, did not fear for my life. I feared instead for the city: the architecture, the culture, the soul and spirit where so much learning and achievement had taken place. I would have surrendered my life if it meant saving the treasure that was our republic. I must also confess that despite the danger to the city, I was a little more than curious to see for myself, firsthand, the might and power of the French army. I wanted to know, with certainty, if its strength was mythic or real.

When news of Piero's deal with Charles reached Florence, I heard Piero Capponi tell a crowd of listeners on the square—it remains one of my favorite quotes in Florentine history--"It is time we stopped being ruled by children." The end of an era had come. It remained to be seen if the end of Florence had come, as well. To prevent further disaster, Capponi suggested sending ambassadors to meet with Charles in Pisa. He recommended Savonarola, not only because he was aware of his increasing power, but also because he was "a man of holy life, courageous and intelligent, of high ability and renown." It was a defining moment in Savonarola's *de facto* rise to power, which none could dispute. When the Florentine mission set out, Savonarola insisted on walking the fifty miles, while the others rode behind him.

# Savonarola

I should have been sent alone to meet with King Charles, for none but me could stop him from ransacking and burning down every Tuscan town and city, including Florence. I did not possess charm and diplomacy, like Lorenzo de' Medici, now deceased. I possessed something greater: the word of God. He spoke through me, and I spoke for Him, giving me powers equal to any man. Even the king of France, an illiterate, vulgar man, who relied on the language of violence to form his personal identity, was no match for God, as my meeting with him would prove.

I entered his tent. A small man, with large limbs and disproportioned features, he sat on a throne made for a man twice his size, giving him a comical appearance, as if he were a monkey with a crown. Surrounding him were counselors and many of the trappings of his court, such as silk tapestries, fine linens and tables of food and wine.

"At last you have arrived, O King," I said.

He smiled, clasping me with a large hand. I marveled at the strength of that hand, connected, as it was, to a man dwarfish in size.

"I have heard of your gift of prophecy," he said. His speech sounded garbled and slurred, as if he spoke a language not fully developed.

"And I have heard of your deep religious beliefs."

"I am a man of God," he said.

"You are, in fact, His Minister."

He smiled, though his eyes belied any comprehension of my words.

"What do you mean?" he asked.

"You are the Scourge of God."

"The Scourge of God?"

"You have been sent by God to chastise the tyrants of Italy, and nothing will be able to resist you or defend itself against you."

"You are indeed a prophet."

"Which is why you should listen to what I have to say."

"You speak through God. You have my ear."

"Though Florence may have unintentionally given you offence, you should forgive the city and do no harm to its citizens."

"I expected the support of your city in my campaign against Naples."

"And you shall have that support."

"But why now after so many months of indecisiveness by your ruler?"

"He is no longer our ruler."

"The Medici ruler is gone?"

"Yes."

"Then who is to rule your city?"

"God shall rule."

He laughed. "If that were only possible, my friend."

"It shall happen, and you, as king of France, should not doubt that."

"I doubt nothing that God intends."

"Then do not doubt this: though you were sent by God as an instrument to chastise the tyrants of Italy, you must not harm the city of Florence."

"Is not Florence part of Italy?"

"It is."

"Then why should it be spared?"

"It is God's will."

He winced and looked around him, at his counselors and guards and the vast wealth of his possessions. He repositioned his body, trying to fill the throne with his small, awkward shape.

"I have come with an army of 40,000 men. We have not come all this way to merely parade ourselves. We have come to conquer."

I glared at his unsavory face and eyes.

"Heaven is capable of wreaking a terrible revenge even upon its own instrument should you allow your army to harm Florence."

He nodded, swallowing hard. I thanked him for receiving me in his tent and for allowing me to voice my concerns. He remained silent as I exited.

# Machiavelli

When Piero heard that the Florentine delegation was about to arrive at the French camp, he at once set off back to Florence to resume his leadership. He appeared at the closed doors of the Palazzo della Signoria, accompanied by a small band of armed guards. When they tried to force their way into the government palace, those inside called out "Popolo e liberta" (The People and Liberty), the ancient clarion call of revolution. The bell atop the tower tolled, signaling the traditional call to all citizens in time of danger or emergency. I arrived to see a mob already assembled in the square, calling out insults to Piero as he stood uncertainly on the raised pavement outside the door of the Palazzo.

"You have betrayed your people."

"You have shamed the name of Medici."

"Death to traitors of the republic."

Many threw stones and blocks of wood. Piero's armed guards surrounded him, deflecting the objects, as they rushed along the Via Largo, toward the Palazzo Medici. The mob followed, continuing to hurl insults and objects, until their group safely barricaded themselves behind the high walls of the palace.

Piero packed as many of his father's jewels, plates and precious objects as he could, until, under the cover of night, he fled with his wife and children, accompanied by his armed guards, toward Venice. The next day, I stood with a mob outside the palace gates and saw in an open window Giovanni, attired in his full cardinal garments, kneeling with his hands joined, his head and eyes looking upward, as if to heaven, to grant him mercy.

"Why is he praying near the window?" someone asked.

"Shouldn't he pray in the chapel?" another said.

"He wants to be seen," I said.

I explained what I believed: he was praying for the preservation of the Medici regime, which had always been popular, starting with Cosimo and ending with Lorenzo. He wanted sympathy for any wrongdoings Piero might have done. I was surprised and pleased that none in the crowd hurled insults at him. We let him pray in his time of distress. After all, it wasn't his fault his brother had made a mess of things for their family. Someone said something that caused everyone nearby to nod in agreement.

"It's a good thing Lorenzo is not around to see this."

We learned the following day Giovanni escaped that night disguised as a Dominican monk. He took various statuettes, gold and silver medallions, valuable and rare manuscripts and 200,000 ducats, among the last remaining assets of the Medici bank in Florence. Afterwards, citizens pillaged the palace, seeking whatever treasures remained and set fires. The Signoria seized the remaining funds in the Medici bank, effectively marking the end of the Medici banking empire. Rebels burned and razed to the ground the San Gallo monastery, one of Lorenzo's favorite architectural buildings.

On November 17, 1494, Savonarola's "apocalyptic flood, his Cyrus from across the mountains" reached the city. Though his main army had marched to Siena, King Charles brought 9,000 soldiers with him, with one glaring absence: their myth-making cannons. I very much wanted to see firsthand these advanced weapons of destruction. To my dismay, they had gone to Siena with the rest of the army. Still, for more than two hours, the invading army paraded, weaving through the narrow Florentine streets, past the cheering crowds, to reach the cathedral. I stood, enthralled by the sight of infantrymen with lances and shields and the many crossbowmen, pikemen, and archers, all richly costumed and decorated men at arms. The king arrived with a lance on his hip and a canopy over his head. Though he was outfitted magnificently, he appeared grotesque. This man who had been equated with Cyrus and Charlemagne hardly fit the image of former conquering heroes. Small in stature, he had monstrous features: large, hunched shoulders, over-sized, webbed hands and a nose more suitable for a Toucan bird.

Of course the citizens of Florence cheered. This army from across the mountains had might and power and made each of us in the streets aware of how comparatively small we were. We cheered because we knew if we didn't this army could crush us like ants. I cheered as loudly as anyone, though secretly I hated the French army. We all hated it. We hated its audacity, its arrogance, and its superiority. Mostly we hated it because we were forced to show it respect, as was evident by our cheers. Meanwhile, we hoped--some, excluding me, prayed--amid our cheering, that this invading army from across the mountains would leave us in peace after a short visit.

Florence had always succeeded in guarding its freedom, and now the people and its freedom had been brought to its knees, like helpless beggars. What I remember most was French soldiers marking crosses in chalk on houses that had belonged to Florentine nobility; that would now be used to house them. That was the worst insult of all: that King Charles of France was allowed to conquer Italy with chalk!

I wrote these words in an attempt to express my anguish:

*Italy faced hard times . . .*
*beneath stars hostile to her good.*
*So many mountain passes,*
*and so many marshes,*
*filled with blood and dead men . . .*
*When Italy in turmoil opened her gates*
*to the Gauls (the French)*
*and the barbarians rushed in . . .*
*So all Tuscany was in confusion.*

# Savonarola

When the French entered Florence, Charles and his advisors, along with his finest soldiers, occupied the vacated Palazzo Medici, and I quietly celebrated the end of Medici tyranny. His remaining soldiers ransacked and kidnapped homes, though this news I did not celebrate. Charles demanded 200,000 florins from the Signoria. In return, he promised to leave the city. The Signoria negotiated, bringing the total down to 120,000 florins. Even after Charles signed the treaty, he and his army stayed in the city, creating rising tensions, with each day bringing violence in the form of stabbings and killings. I waited expectantly for the Signoria to call for me, for I as well as every leading citizen knew none but me could influence King Charles to leave the city.

I went to the Palazzo Medici. Guards barred my way from entering. I told them my business, invoking God's wrath upon them if they refused my entrance, and pushed past them. I found Charles in full armor, ready to lead his men in a sack of the city. I stood before him. I did not speak. I raised my brass crucifix to his eyes, whereupon his manner changed almost instantly, referring to me as "most respected friar."

"It is not to me you should pay respect," I said. "You should show your respect to him who is King of Kings."

I saw his eyes roll, as he turned away from the cross.

"I have a duty to my soldiers," he said.

"And what of your duty to God?"

"I promised the soldiers they would be allowed to sack the city."

"God grants victory to the kings of this world only in accordance with his will and his justice, but punishes those who are unjust."

"Be assured, most revered friar, I wish to respect God."

"Then respect God by doing what is just. You and all your men will be destroyed by Him unless you cease at once your cruel treatment of the citizens of our poor city."

He again looked at the cross I held unwaveringly before him with both my hands. His eyes turned red as he groaned indecipherably.

"The longer you stay in Florence, the greater chance you lessen your true campaign, which is to march on Naples. Am I not right?"

"You are right. It is Naples we wish to win."

"Then you should be on your way, the sooner the better."

"Your people cheated us. We were supposed to receive 200,000 florins, not 120,000 florins."

"Is not 120,000 florins enough? You have already stolen more than the poor people of Florence can afford to give. If you take any more you shall feel God's wrath!"

"Stop speaking to me of God's wrath. Am I not his minister, his servant, as you have said?"

"I speak of God's wrath as a deterrence to your unjust acts."

"God made me king. Did he not?"

"To serve Him and do His work."

"Must I not also serve my country and my people by bringing home victory in Florence, as well as elsewhere?"

"What is more important to you: victory now or victory later, with God?"

He walked to a window, looking out at the city below. I followed him, standing behind him, still holding up the cross. He lifted his hand, as if to shield him against it.

"Listen to the voice of God's servant," I said. "Continue on your journey without any more delay. Don't try to ruin this city, or you'll bring God's anger down on your head."

"Say no more, please," he said.

He removed his sword from his sheath.

"I shall remove my armor if you agree to put down your cross."

I put the cross in the pocket of my robe. He removed his armor.

The next day Charles and his army left Florence.

# Lorenzo

How does a man know the right decision until he has lived that decision? Only then, in the aftermath, does he know whether the decision was right. In the meantime, it's a crapshoot, a roll of the dice. You win, you lose, and sometimes you lose when you win and win when you lose. Decisions are a gamble, but they have to be made. I have made many decisions regarding states of affair, but those are not what I think of now, lying as I am at death's door. I think of my decision to pursue knowledge, at the cost of faith.

I am not alone. My friends who once comprised our inner circle of intellectual and artistic ideas and endeavors face, as well, the decisions they have made and question now if in their pursuit of learning, in their opening exciting, though dangerous doors (I choose not to mention the indulgence of the flesh), they offended God. This question is not the result of accident or chance. It comes from Savonarola. He has great influence on them, and each day I see them walk a more traditional path and hear them sing a more traditional song.

I am bothered to see them change so easily. I cannot lie. Is it not natural to live on the dividing line, questioning the source and nature of our gifts? Do we not in our questioning honor, not disrespect, God? I do not know for certain. Only in the aftermath of death will God give us the answer to the questions we seek. I cannot change what has already happened. Nor do I want to change it, though I have lived with doubts. Of this I am certain: learning can never be wrong, nor can it ever be wrong to pursue the gifts of life. Is it not natural to think, feel, act and love? How then are these pursuits disrespectful to God?

If I could meet him before I die, I would say to God:

*Have I not tried to talk to you many times? Yet you have not given me proper evidence that you have heard me. All I have ever asked for is a sign.*

In the absence of this sign, I have used my words, in poetry, to communicate what has been for me my inner anguish:

*When the spirit escapes from the sea of storm*
*and strife that is our life, and finds refuge in*
*some tranquil haven of calm, we find ourselves*
*beset with doubts which we seek to resolve.*

*If a man is incapable of striving ceaselessly*
*for eternal happiness unless he is blessed by*
*God, and that blessing can only be given to*
*those who are ready to receive it,*

*What must come first?*
*God's blessing, or his readiness?*

# Savonarola

My congregation grows larger by the day, and it is not just the poor who come to listen. I have converted men who once belonged to Lorenzo's inner circle of intellectuals and humanists: Poliziano, the poet; Pico, the philosopher; Botticelli, the painter, even the young sculptor Michelangelo, who walks in the cloister, looking for me, waiting to hear the words of God. How, some wonder, did I do this? By sorcery or something bewitching? Here's the truth: when one, such as I, speaks the word of God, which is the only true word, he needs not the occult to refashion people's minds, no matter how great those minds, for men of high intelligence are no different than commoners in regards to the salvation of their souls. Thus, to answer my critics, I say this: I did nothing other than invoke in them the spirit of the Lord.

I first met Giovanni Pico in Reggio when he was a boy of nineteen. How could I not notice him? His auburn hair sprang from his head in long waves, flowing over his shoulders, and his face, petite and almost feminine in its delicacy, conveyed an exotic creature more peacock than man, especially given the colorful clothes in which he arrayed himself. He had already mastered many notable languages, such as Latin, Greek, Arabic and Hebrew, in his search to understand the religions from which Christianity originated. Though we shared different views about Christianity and God, I accepted him as an anomaly, an intellectual equal. Even I, though critical of men bred by humanism, recognized his genius. Appreciating my admiration, he sought me out, often visiting with me at the monastery to reveal the secrets of his heart, of which there were many, though none as great as his pressing need to synthesize (*syncretism* is the name he gave it) the ideas of various ages and religions into a creative unison, an imaginative vision, that all men would accept as a universal truth.

Though I refuted his philosophy (if such a view had come from anyone but him I would have condemned him, avoiding all further contact), I tolerated his unorthodox views for one reason: I perceived, despite his intellectual searches, he was, at his core, a deeply religious Christian. Though he sought to fuse the many to find the one, it was clear from our early meetings that the one for him was God, no matter what kind of intellectual spin he put on his search. Yet he steadfastly refused to surrender to what is true: that God is the only certainty in a universe of uncertainties. It would take time and the urgency to save himself from himself to learn how to follow the Christian faith.

# Machiavelli

Savonarola's influence begs this question: Why do men bend their wills to him? I do not mean lesser men. I mean men of great intellectual and artistic talents. Is the fear of God's wrath enough to trigger a reversal in one's intellect and reason—that same intellect and reason that takes a lifetime to plant and harvest? How does one surrender what was his livelihood, his core and essence, his means to an end? I, fortunately, have never believed in God's wrath, just as I have never believed in tooth fairies or monsters and goblins of mythic lore. I am a man of much sophistication and civility and understand the necessity, above all else, of staying sane, all the more necessary when surrounded by the insane. I refer, in particular, to those who fear the unknown and are thus susceptible to believing there's such a thing as God's wrath, in which case they will do anything, including sacrifice their minds, to avoid it. I will have none of that. What is unknown, such as eternity—and, yes, even God himself (strike me down if I lie)--is simply unknown. Why bother with it? More pressing matters concern me, such as the function of state, the essence of war, and the treachery of men, especially those with ambition.

I count Savonarola among those. He, like other men who crave power, is a publicity seeker, a chameleon who can make others believe he is a saint and prophet, while the truth is his prophecies are no more than hallucinations, the result of self-deprivation, living on water and prayer in a dim-lit cave—or is it a cell, as in *prison*? That he gets away with his wild, imaginative ravings is a testament to his skill as a performer and his astute understanding of the weaknesses of men. Make no mistake: if he has his way, the city of Florence will become his private monastery, wherein the only meal available will be the host and the only drink the blood of Christ. I will have none of that either.

All the more reason to stay sane, I say.

# Lorenzo

I hear Pico in the next room, speaking with doctors and servants. He does not enter, for my doctors have mistakenly told him I am asleep and should not be bothered. I want to yell that I am awake, but I can barely breathe, let alone talk at this moment. I am left to picture him in my mind. He has changed greatly. His hair has grayed, and his eyes have lost their shine, though he lives still with much enthusiasm, wishing to speak of his transformation. Many have wondered how a scholar many call the greatest of our age can surrender his scholarship full of questioning uncertainties so quickly in favor of what he had always challenged: the certainty of a single God who forms and shapes the universe. I do not wonder. I know the reason. He does not wish to die a heretic, burned at the stake, and his soul damned for eternity. The threat of such punishment can make a man alter his life's work and turn all his doubt to certainty.

He had earlier written his *900 theses*, a system of belief that fused philosophy, theology and ancient texts, illuminating man's condition, while incorporating hermetic and mystical thinking into the search for divine truth in an original style as fresh as the age in which we lived. I remember still his words: "Because no one's opinions are quite what he wills them to be, no one's beliefs are quite what he wills them to be." When he went to Rome to publish and debate his arguments, the Vatican clergy called his material "heretical, rash and likely to give scandal to the faithful." Pope Innocent VIII on August 4, 1487 drew up a Brief, condemning his work. Undeterred, he wrote another work called *On the Dignity of Man*, dedicating it to me. His words, written in the voice of God, rang out and became the anthem to those of us who clung to their truth:

"We have given thee, oh Adam, no fixed abode, no formed inner nature, nor any talent that is peculiarly thine. We have done this so that thou mayest take unto thyself whatever abode, form or talents thou desirest for thyself. Other creatures are confined within the laws of nature

91

which We have laid down. In order that thou may exercise the freedom We have given thee, thou are confined to no such limits; and thou shall fix the limits of thy nature for thyself. I have placed thee at the centre of the world, so that thou mayest the better look around thee and see whatsoever is in the world. Being neither mortal nor immortal thou mayest sculpt thyself into whatever shape thou choosest. Thou canst grow downwards and take on the base nature of brutes, or thy soul canst grow upwards by means of reason towards the higher realms of the divine."

He had given us freedom with his words, and we naively believed in that freedom, turning our backs as we did to the prior age, when thoughts of freedom were anathema to the Church and God. His critics cried out: What use was prayer if the human condition allowed humanity to create itself in whatever images it chose? Where lay the authority of the Church? Pico became a marked man, and he knew it. Charged with heresy, he left Italy, moving to France, though even there he could not escape the wrath of the Vatican. When the French, on the orders of Pope Innocent VIII, arrested and imprisoned him, I could not stand by idly. He had dedicated his book to me, and it was the intellectual circle surrounding me that had inspired him, for we, collectively, embodied his ideas and ideals. I interceded, persuading the pope to release Pico from prison. The pope agreed, though he refused to drop the charge of heresy. Pico returned to Florence, living in a villa in Fiesole, under my jurisdiction. The charge of heresy and his subsequent imprisonment had changed my friend. It was clear in his eyes, where the wonder of man and his beliefs had been replaced by the fear of his burning body and his soul's damnation. He vowed to devote himself to a more orthodox pursuit of the truth, hoping that if he did so Pope Innocent VIII would drop the charge of heresy.

On behalf of Pico, I wrote a letter to the Florentine ambassador in Rome, expecting it to be forwarded to the pope. "The Count della Mirandola is here leading a most saintly life, like a monk. He observes all fasts and absolute chastity: has but a small retinue and lives quite simply with only what is necessary. To me he appears an example to other men. He is anxious to be absolved from what little contumacy is still attributed to him by the Holy Father and to have a Brief by which His Holiness accepts him as a son and as a good Christian. Do all you can to obtain this Brief in such a form that it may content his conscience."

Pope Innocent VIII did not relent, and this caused my friend's spirits to further sink. He lives now as a broken man, the life draining from him, no matter how much he professes to follow Savonarola's ways and live with God. I will tell him when he enters that his writings from a former time are no less true because he has undergone a personal change. What he wrote he created with a clear conscience. What he believes now is only for the benefit and protection of his immortal soul.

# Savonarola

I received a visit from Giovanni Pico. His hair no longer fell to his shoulders in waves, and gone were the colorful clothes and the strut that had given him the appearance of a peacock come from an exotic island. Whatever feathers he had once possessed to signal his pride and firm standing in the world had fallen from him. His eyes that had once looked so bright and eager in their quest to hold within them the universe were now red and bleary. A charge of heresy and the threat of burning, both now and ever after, can do that to a man.

"When I hear you speak from the pulpit," he said, "I quake with fear and my hair stands on end."

"It is not I who makes you quake with fear," I responded, "it is God."

"I wish to know your God."

"I have waited for you to say that."

"I am a changed man," he said, refusing the meager bread and water I offered him.

"Change is necessary to your salvation," I responded.

"I have given my estate and villa to my nephew. I want to become a monk and follow in the footsteps of Saint Francis. What is your opinion?"

"I am a Dominican, not a Franciscan."

"Nonetheless, I want to travel barefoot through the towns of Italy. What do you think?"

"I believe your feet are too tender."

"I can learn, as you have, to endure the hardship."

"Are you ready to abandon your belief that one must synthesize all faiths into one divine truth?"

"I have already abandoned that belief."

"And are you ready to devote your life to Christianity and the one true God?"

"I am, yes."

"Is your conviction sincere?"

He grew silent and looked away. I sensed in the taut muscles in his neck that he spoke more from fear than sincerity.

"I am ready," he whispered.

"I do not believe that," I said.

He dared not look me in the eye. He knew that I knew of his lifestyle. Though it was true he lived simply, he, nonetheless, continued to share his bed with a concubine.

"To live as God, you must first denounce the world, as His Son, Jesus Christ."

"It is not easy to do."

"And why should it be?"

He wanted to know if I had ever had desires of the flesh. I proudly told him of my dream years earlier, being doused in icy water, forever cooling the fires of my flesh, and afterwards awakening to thank God for answering my wish to have the desires of my body removed, so that I could dedicate my life to Him without distraction.

"You are extraordinary," he said.

"I am a man like any other," I said, "capable, through faith in God, of extraordinary feats."

"When it comes to fighting the demands of the flesh, I am, and have always been, ordinary."

"It is because you listen to yourself instead of God."

"Neither God nor the charge of heresy can cool the desires of my flesh."

"You will never be free until you succeed."

"Why should I succeed? It is against nature, is it not, to deny the flesh?"

"All the more impressive in the eyes of God."

"I am not a saint, only a man."

"I will help guide you."

"And I shall give myself to your guidance."

"You must make this sacrifice."

"I cannot surrender the desires of my flesh."

"You do not have to surrender the desires. But you must stop acting upon them."

"Is it not enough that I no longer write?"

"God does not ask you to stop writing."

"Hasn't my writing been the cause of my downfall?"

"It can, as well, begin your ascent."

"I know not what you mean."

"You have a calling to write."

"I cannot and will not respond to that call ever again."

"You will write as a protector of the faith, not as a desecrator of it, and in doing so you shall no longer live as a scorned man."

"And the charge of heresy?"

"I am certain the pope, once he knows of your transformation and reads your defense of Christianity, will have mercy and drop the charge."

"I will do my best."

"And I will do my best, once you are reformed, to see that you live among us, as a brethren to the Christian faith and to God who serves us."

# Machiavelli

"When the soul acts, it can be certain of nothing but itself." I have often recited those words in the administration of my life's many challenges, believing they state concisely what I had always known: that man, not God, is the center of the universe. Man's existence—and the certainty of his existence—is the only truth worth worshipping. All else is fantasy and illusion. Pico had written those words in his book *900 theses*, labeled as heresy by the hypocrites in the Vatican who have always laid claim to ethics and morality without actually practicing them.

Sadly, the words, and the thought inherent in them, belong to the former Giovanni Pico, the man who once championed freedom of expression through the intellect, long before his conversion to Savonarola's religion. What a waste of intellect. His philosophical works were at their beginning. Who knows what his mind, unimpeded by charges of heresy and eternal suffering, could have achieved if he had not been first destroyed by Pope Innocent—far from innocent in his desecration of what was fair and just—and next by the rigid beliefs of Savonarola? Was it not the preacher himself who said Pico's mind was greater than St. Augustine's. Though I have never read the lives of saints, I know enough of Augustine to know he was an analytical genius. The same is true of Pico; that is until he became enmeshed in Savonarola's spidery web. That once great mind now writes only what the preacher tells him. Consider his latest work: *Disputations Against Astrological Prediction*. Though intended for a Christian audience, I confess to having enjoyed this work since, as Pico adroitly points out astrologers, far from being able to prophesy great events, are not even able to forecast the weather. Thus, astrology is nothing more than the death of sensible thought. I do not follow any such nonsense that disallows the mind of man to choose its own destiny, whether it is heaven, hell, purgatory, or none of the above. I will behave as I please, thank you very much.

# Savonarola

I am pleased with Pico's book, which makes clear that astrology is not and never has been compatible with Christian doctrine. And yet these astrologers profess to believe in and love God. How is that possible when the belief in astrology is, in fact, antithetical to the tenets of Christianity? Does not Pico deftly explain that astrologers rely upon the movements of zodiacal signs and planets named after secular images and pagan deities? How then is their worship of false gods who operate outside the realm of the true and only God a viable and accepted religion? What do the movements of stars and planets have to do with Christian orthodoxy, which is laid out authoritatively in the Ten Commandments of the Old Testament and in the teachings of Jesus Christ in the Sermon on the Mount? Have these astrologers bothered to read these works? I think not, for if they had they would know that the universe is not mechanical, wound like a clock. It moves only by virtue of God's love. Morality does not change with the seasons.

I had hoped his book would help release Pico from the charge of heresy. I could not have imagined it would cement the charge further. The new pope, Alexander VI, holds deep superstitious beliefs about astrology and will not accept any criticism of its basic tenets and value. How a Christian man, no less a pope, can believe in two contrary viewpoints belies sense. Of course, no one has ever said that sense is a requirement for one to sit on the papal throne. Power, deceit and lechery are more common attributes for someone who owns that position. If Pope Alexander had actually read Pico's book on astrology, and if he possessed accurate knowledge of the Christian faith, as found in its most reliable source, the Bible, he would know clearly that one is not compatible with the other. His ignorance is one more reason why there must be a scourge of the Church and a renewal wherein God, not a man dressed in fine silks and a miter hat, directs our actions.

# Lorenzo

Angelo walks away. He is overcome with grief and does not wish me to see it manifest in tears. He has been by my side since I came to Careggi, more than a week ago, unaware as I was at the time that I would never leave. It will be, as it was for my grandfather and father, my final stop before the end comes. Of this I am certain. I am certain he believes this as well, though he does not speak of it, wishing instead, in the silence of the subject, to keep alive the illusion--for that is what it is--of my recovery.

Here is the truth about my relationship with Angelo Poliziano: he has been by my side, in mind and spirit, if not always in the flesh, for more than twenty-two years. He has been for me more than a friend. I love him as much as any man or woman I have ever loved. A poet and scholar, he is, in fact, my soul incarnate, a man I esteem as much as the breath I once breathed in health and freedom.

He returns from the kitchen and offers me a sweet cake and water from the kitchen. He wants me to eat and drink. I cannot imagine the taste of food. He insists I give an effort. I suppose it is to show that I have not given up hope, that I will miraculously, sometime soon, spring from the bed which entombs me and go off riding and hunting with him and others of our circle. I look at his sad eyes. How can I refuse such eyes? I bite into the cake and chew the way a baby without teeth might chew. I can't swallow. The blisters in my throat are too painful to bear. I do not say this to Angelo. I do not want to disappoint him. He wants to believe this morsel of cake is what I need most at this moment. I oblige him as best I can. I swallow, wincing as I do. The pain sears my eyeballs. I hand the remaining cake to Angelo.

"How do you like it?" he asks.

"I like it as well as a dying man can like anything."

He stands up and walks to the window. I know I shouldn't have said that. I should have said the cake is delicious, for he served it to me with good intention. I tell myself I will pretend to be well, for his sake.

99

"There is a bright star in the sky," he says, turning back to me.

"There are many stars in the sky. Are there not?"

"None like this one. It is the largest and brightest star I have ever seen."

"You must write a poem for this star."

"Yes, I will do that when the time is right."

"Not now?"

He sits by me again and takes my hand. "I wish only to be by your side, to receive and worship your greatness of spirit while I can."

What he says is further declaration that my end is near. I know he did not intend it that way, though in my state of mind what else can he mean by "while I can"? There is no disputing its inherent truth.

"The Muses may not wait upon you," I say.

"You are my Muse and have always been."

"Likewise for me, my friend."

"How can I have been your Muse? I was not born to greatness as you. I have never been the champion of men, in all feats, both in body and mind. You are Il Magnifico. I am but a man of letters and scholarship."

"You are a genius, both to me and to the world."

"Someday I will be but a footnote in your story."

"You are the ink that writes the words."

He dips a cloth in the water basin and wipes my forehead. He keeps the cloth there. I reach and touch his hand. It is cool and refreshing. I am lucky to have his hand to touch and hold. I tell him this. He smiles and whispers lines familiar to my ears:

*And you, well-born Laurel, under whose shelter*
*happy Florence rests in peace, fearing neither*
*winds nor threat of heaven.*

I squeeze his hand and thank him for the kind words. I ask him to recall the background of how we first met, even though I know the details well. He satisfies my request. He had come to Florence at ten years old, from Montepulciano, where his father, the governor, had been

100

slain by conspirators who wanted to oust anyone associated with the Medici. My grandfather, a friend of his father's, rescued Angelo from orphanage and poverty. Even at a young age, he had remarkable ability with languages and learning. As a teenage boy, he strove to set Homer into Latin meter and wished me to receive this gift, saying in a letter he desired no other muse or God but me. Soon after, I brought him to the Palazzo Medici, inviting him there to live and work on his studies and poetry and to join the circle of artists and philosophers who daily engaged in discussions that were as exciting as they were dangerous.

Hearing sounds outside my room, he goes to the hall and returns to tell me Giovanni Pico has arrived and wishes to read a sacred passage to me. I am eager for his presence and whatever words he has to offer. I will not mention his recent affiliation with Savonarola. I shall allow him the freedom he deserves. He is a changed man. That much is evident as I see him walk in the room. He had always been handsomely attired. Now his clothes look worn and disheveled, as does the expression on his face. I worry for him. He has lost his good looks and his easy manner. The charge of heresy has infiltrated his body and mind. It is only a matter of time before he himself becomes ill. I am sad that I will not be around to comfort him, as he now comforts me. I am lucky to be the first of my inner circle of friends to die. Who will be there for them when I am no longer around? I don't say this aloud, of course. The point is this: I wish with whatever's left of my heart that they shall be kept safe. It pains me to think they will meet hardships. I refer mostly to Pico. He is the one with the charge of heresy upon him. Who will protect him? Savonarola will only further damage his cause with the pope, for the pope despises the friar. I have tried my best to help him. I have written letters on his behalf. If only the pope saw him now as I do. He is truly a repentant man. One might even say holy, if he were so inclined.

"You honor me with your presence," I say.

"The honor is mine, Il Magnifico," he responds.

"I hope my illness hasn't caused you annoyance."

"How can anything you do cause me annoyance? You are, and have always been, the center of my universe. You saved me from prison and in doing so gave me new life. I am indebted to you and desire to serve the rest of my days in blessing you."

"I wish you to live the rest of your days serving the mind with which God has blessed you."

"God has blessed me in other ways now."

He is living proof of what fear can do to a man. I look at Angelo. What does he think of his friend's sad transformation? He once wrote of Pico: "He is a man, or rather a hero, on whom nature has lavished all the endowments both of body and mind." He says nothing now, though his silence is revealing. He knows in the end we all must die, and at such a time what is left other than God's blessing.

"Shall I read to you from the Gospel?" Pico says.

"Do you wish to give me last rites?" I joke.

"Of course not, only reassuring words."

"To have my friends close by is what's most reassuring to me."

"And yet you shall receive words as well." Angelo says, rising, doing his best to bring levity and life to the room.

"Recite to me, Angelo," I whisper. He obliges me.

*Blest is your genius, your capacious mind*
*Not to one science or one theme confined*
*By grateful interchange fatigue beguiles*
*In private studies and in public toils.*

I feel suddenly nostalgic, desiring to sit up and hold discussions with my friends, and afterwards to drink wine and sing, as we did always on summer nights that held us gentle in their sway, seeming never to end with so much surprise and delight. We lived well. I take comfort in that thought.

"Angelo always recited your words better than you did," Pico says.

"My master's words give inspiration to my voice," Angelo replies.

Angelo is being modest. In truth, he was my inspiration to write, and I know with certainty that his poetry inspired Botticelli's great paintings. Sandro has not visited me. I know, of course, the reason. He spends his days and nights visiting the friar in his cell, desiring to abandon his former way of life, which, sadly, includes his former friends. He is convinced we celebrated the wrong God in art, literature and philosophy.

"I miss Botticelli," I say.

"We miss him, too," Angelo says.

"He no longer paints," I say.

"He paints religious scenes," Pico says. "For the friar."

"Without inspiration," Angelo adds.

"It is a waste of talent," I say. "God forgive him."

"What he does now *is* for God," Pico says.

Hadn't he always painted for God, even when his subject wasn't God? I see his *Primavera* before my eyes and believe that God was with him when he painted it. Though his subject was pagan classical mythology, I believe, nonetheless, that our Christian God guided his hand. I know what I say sounds contradictory, but I will believe to my last breath that God in heaven gave him such a gift. Savonarola has taken it from him. I cannot say that to Pico. He believes, I'm sure, that Botticelli is now on the course for which he was always meant: scribbling colorless drawings of man's torment on earth. Is this really what God wants him to do? Or is he merely satisfying the wishes of Savonarola? What I ask is rhetorical, I realize. It does no good to ask, anyhow, since Botticelli's fate as an artist is now sealed. Still, I can remember, and I do. I strain to lift myself, enough to give my lungs more air. I recite from Angelo's poem, "Rusticus," which celebrates springtime, in a classical, mythological setting:

*Nourishing Venus comes, companion to her sister, and is followed by the little loves; Flora offers welcome kisses to her eager husband (Zephyr); and in their midst with hair unbound and bared breasts dances Grace, tapping the ground with rhythmic step.*

"Thank you," Angelo says, squeezing my hand, smiling warmly.

"Your words were Botticelli's inspiration."

"The thanks go to Ovid, not me."

"Yes, Ovid, as well."

"Let's not forget the greatest philosopher of our time," Pico adds.

"Marsilio Ficino," Angelo says.

"My tutor as a boy, and my mentor," I reply.

"His Platonic views on love and beauty deserve more credit than my poetry for inspiring Botticelli's greatest works of art," Angelo says.

"Who knew that Botticelli's great art would turn out to be the source of his demise," Pico says. "He lives with the awful responsibility of having created the first painting devoid of religious overtones, in an obvious non-Christian setting, with innuendos of love, sex and licentious behavior."

"And yet it embodied all we believed and thought: Platonic idealism in all its sensuality and poetry," Angelo says. "Wasn't it Ficino who cried out for all the world to hear: 'This is an age of gold, which has brought back to life the almost extinguished liberal disciplines of poetry, eloquence, painting, architecture, sculpture, music, and singing to the Orphic Lyre. And all this at Florence!'"

I see Angelo rejoice in remembrance of an earlier time, when he and I and all of us possessed a zest for life unparalleled in the lives of those who had lived before us. Where is that happy state now? Was it only an illusion of time and place and space, never to be seen again? Will Florence live to see this age again, "where every Grace delights, where Beauty weaves a garland of flowers about her hair, where lascivious Zephyr flies behind Flora and decks the green grass with flowers"? I wonder at my ability to remember Angelo's verse more than my own.

I do not want to stop. I want to keep reciting, believing if I do so I will live forever, if not here, then perhaps in the Garden of the Hesperides, the blessed isle inhabited by nymphs at the western edge of the world. I want to be one of the Graces—Joy, Beauty and Creativity--fixed forever in Botticelli's art: standing beside Venus, dancing in a diaphanous robe, while above my head Cupid is pulling back his bow, about to pierce me with his arrow. I welcome his arrow, be it for love or lust. It matters little as long as I am immortal, along with Mercury, the messenger of the gods, with his phallic sword at his waist, and Flora, the goddess of spring, resplendent in her flowered dress, in the act of scattering flowers that blend into the flowers amongst the grass at her feet. I close my eyes. If I believe enough, with the force of my will, it can happen. After all, I am Lorenzo Il Magnifico.

I laugh to myself when I think how ridiculous this sounds.

# Savonarola

When I first saw Botticelli's *Adoration of the Magi* hanging in the chapel at Santa Maria Novella, I knew the Medici had overstepped the boundaries between man and the divine, placing themselves audaciously with the latter. One only has to look at the painting to notice the arrogance of this wealthy family, as they, the faces of Cosimo and his two sons, Piero and Giovanni, and not the Biblical Magi, are seen presenting gifts to the Christ child, making clear to all who see the painting that those with wealth and power can buy their way into the heavenly kingdom. Is it not enough that the Medici has for many years ruled Florence? Must they also make claim to heaven?

Their presence in the painting blasphemes the nature and virtue of the Epiphany, that holiest of days which belongs to a sacred realm, where man is not allowed. How dare they dishonor it? It pleases me little that Botticelli is now ashamed of that painting. I do not hold him at fault. Commissioned by Gaspare Lami, the Florentine banker, he had no choice but to honor his patron and, more importantly, those (the Medici) whom his patron honored.

I see Botticelli often now. He wishes to redeem himself of his past indiscretions. I have not seen his so-called masterpieces, reflecting humanistic ideals, and why would I? I have heard they are contrary to fundamental Christian virtues; that they celebrate the coarse qualities of man, with little naked pagan gods flying around, shooting arrows at humans, infecting them with lechery and lust. I will not desecrate my holy eyes with such a sight. I mean no disrespect to his talent. It is his former subject matter, influenced by men who followed false gods, I criticize.

He knows now that pagan figures or settings are not suitable subjects for his art. He has returned to painting religious scenes: the Madonna and Child, the Crucifixion, and the Last Judgment. More importantly, when he is not painting, he is on his knees, praying to God and asking for His forgiveness and blessing.

# Machiavelli

I knew of Botticelli's art through the reputation he had garnered in Florence. As for his person, I knew of him only from a distance, as a forlorn figure meandering along the Via Largo, while people, wonderingly, pointed at him.

"Look, it's Sandro Botticelli," I would often hear. "Is he not the greatest painter of his era?"

"Yet he no longer paints," would be the certain reply. "Savonarola forbids the practice."

"Is it not in penance for his former sins?"

I would walk away, thinking to myself: Is it not unreasonable that Savonarola should ask forgiveness from the city of Florence for taking from it one of its greatest men of genius? Sadly, I never saw Boticelli during the height of that genius. The man I saw walking the streets did not smile or talk. I cannot say his eyes appeared joyless, for, in truth, I did not see his eyes. They were downcast, always, as he hurried past, on his way to Savonarola's cell, where he imprisoned himself in denial of every natural desire. Though I met him only once--an encounter I will shortly reveal--what I report of him comes from reliable sources, for I had by then developed quite an impressive network of spies.

Botticelli did, despite the rumors on the street, continue to paint. What he painted, however, pales in comparison to the work he created during the heyday of Lorenzo's inner circle of artists, poets and philosophers, of which he was an integral member. As you well know, I am a man of public service, not an artist. Thus, my understanding of art is, at best, rudimentary. I do know this, though: men create best when they are free to create, when their minds are active, when they surround themselves with the passion of others equal in temperament and intellectual curiosity. Living and working at the Palazzo Medici, listening daily to brilliant thinkers and writers, Botticelli had no shortage of inspiration for his art.

He, like many, however, fell prey to the snake lurking in the garden of paradise. This snake takes the shape of a little monk. Do not be fooled by his size, though, for his sting is large, and once his poison enters the mind of his victim, it spreads to every organ in the body, until the person shrinks in stature. It matters not the pedigree or social standing of the person. Each man falls, one right after the other, begging the question: What is left of Florence if the greatest among us fall so easily?

As concerns Botticelli, another question must be asked: Where did his ideas of love and beauty go? I heard he painted scenes from Dante's *Divine Comedy*, creating vivid renderings of the ring of hell inhabited by those tortured souls condemned for eternity to inhabit the Inferno for having indulged in perverse vices that damage and corrupt the natural powers of the body. I refer specifically to the sodomites, of whom Savonarola wished to condemn and burn. Why would Botticelli paint such nonsense, unless he himself identified with the sinful sodomites and through his painting sought atonement? I offer only conjecture, not fact, since none of us knows what lurks in the hidden self of each man. I wonder, still, how the same man who once celebrated and painted the birth of the love child Venus, carried on a conch shell, wafted to shore by playful zephyrs, in a colorful array of abundant rejoicing, could become the man who painted naked bodies writing and staggering in pitiful agony across burning sands as falling flakes of fire fall upon them. How quickly Botticelli transformed the Garden of Hesperides into a biblical—you shall feel God's wrath—Sodom and Gomorrah.

This conjunction of opposites becomes more demonstrable in another of his paintings during his period of decline: *The Lamentation of the Dead Christ*. While I have never been drawn to paintings of religious scenes, I find this one remarkable, as it stands as testament to the divided man Botticelli became. To most, I'm sure, it is a depiction which includes the traditional grieving figures around Christ's prostrate body. If one is to investigate further, however—I, of course, have trained myself to investigate further all matters pertaining to human behavior—he makes a startling discovery about Botticelli's intentions, which may be conscious, unconscious or subconscious. I believe he himself is unsure.

I refer to the two women in the painting. One of them presses her cheek to the dying Christ's cheek. Her face, though now pale and white, is the same face as Venus in his earlier masterpiece. The other woman, who tends to the wounds in Christ's feet, is recognizable as one of the dancing goddesses in his *Primavera* painting. While I should not leap to a point of knowing as concerns the painter's motives, I am, admittedly, too seduced to resist. His once beautiful women had, as well, succumbed to grief, as he himself assuredly had. If their faces are not proof enough, one only needs to look at the face of Christ, hanging low in pain and resignation. It is Botticelli's face. No one can tell me otherwise. More than fifty years of age at this time, he understood suffering and sacrifice as never before. Thus, he painted himself on the cross, believing he had sinned and deserved his just punishment. His self-inflicted crucifixion leaves me to wonder: did he really save his soul by killing his life? I have great doubts. It is more likely he sacrificed his life and his art in vain, on a false promise, an illusion of salvation, on a dream that can never be realized as long as we live.

His story becomes worse. For a long time--it had by now been many years since Savonarola's death--I heard little of his whereabouts, knowing only that as an artist he could no longer support himself in Florence, as the days of patronage had long passed. I knew only that I stopped seeing him on the streets. The result was I no longer thought about him.

One night, as I strolled along the Via Largo, returning from a place of ill-repute, I am not ashamed to say, an old man appeared on the pavement, covered in rags, crouched low, supporting himself by two sticks. Decrepit and emaciated, he asked me for money, saying he was hungry. Though not my custom to stop for beggars--for if you stop for one a dozen others will notice and you will soon have a legion of undesirable followers on your heels--something familiar in his eyes, etched somewhere in my brain, drew me closer to him. I asked him his name.

"Allesandro di Mariano di Vanni Filipepi," he said.

"Botticelli?" I responded.

He nodded.

I knew then where I had seen his eyes: on the painting, *The Lamentation of the Dead Christ*. I took some coins from my pocket and placed them in his hand. His joints were too arthritic to grasp them, so I closed his hand around the coins to make sure they wouldn't fall. His face remained expressionless, as if the muscles needed to smile no longer moved for him.

"Thank you," he mumbled through broken teeth.

I told him I was a great admirer of his art.

He didn't respond. He turned and hobbled away on the two sticks. I stood watching him. People hurried passed him. I did not hear anyone say, "Look, it's Sandro Botticelli," and I didn't think it was my place to say, "He was the greatest painter of his era."

# Lorenzo

"Ficino read Plato to my grandfather on his deathbed," I say, awakening from a brief respite of pain.

"Ficino read Plato in his sleep," Angelo remarks.

"It has been his life's work to translate Plato from Greek to Latin," I add, aware that what I say is as common as air to these men standing before me.

"As Angelo has made it his objective to translate Homer from Greek to Latin," Pico states appreciatively to the friend he and I respect greatly.

"Yet none can translate into Latin from Greek, Hebrew and Arabic, such as you, Pico," Angelo replies, with equal admiration.

"We have been fortunate to have such great minds here in Florence," I say.

"You are the one who planted the seeds, Lorenzo," Angelo states.

"And then nurtured the growth of the flowering of ideas," Pico adds.

"I cannot take credit for men's natural genius," I declare.

"You are the fountainhead from which springs that genius," Angelo says.

"It takes much more than a fountain to spring the genius of man," I reply. "It takes, at the very least, a river, cascading into a waterfall."

Angelo will not be deterred. He wants to elevate me to a plane that no man deserves. I marvel at his voice and how freely words form from his mind and lips.

*Whilst Arno, winding through the mild domain,*
*Leads in repeated folds his lengthen'd train;*
*Nor thou thy poet's grateful strain refuse,*
*Lorenzo! sure resource of every muse;*
*Whose praise, so thou his leisure hour prolong,*
*Shall claim the tribute of a nobler song.*

I deflect a smile because the muscles in my face cannot bear any contortion. I shake my head instead, closing my eyes, knowing Angelo wishes to flatter and amuse me, to distract me from the wrenching pain in my bones and my impending mortality. I cannot take exclusive credit for what has taken place in Florence. My grandfather deserves most of the credit. It was he who brought so many ancient manuscripts, along with sculptures, to Florence. He is the true fountainhead. It's not an arguable point. When I was a boy, Ficino, my tutor, told me, "As God created Cosimo as a model of the universe, mold yourself on the model of Cosimo." I tried my best to do that, while at the same time become my own person, stepping from the large shadow my grandfather left. I am but one man among many who have helped shape the culture of Florence.

"Ficino has been my spiritual and intellectual father," I say.

"He has been that to all of us," Pico replies.

"We could not hold a discussion without the bust of Plato looking down on us," Angelo adds.

"He was the one who encouraged me to write in the Tuscan dialect," I say.

"And you have honored our language well," Angelo counters.

"Where is he?" I ask. "Will he come before it's too late?"

"He is on his way from Pisa," Angelo informs me.

"He would often chide me for wasting my time in the countryside," I say. "For once, I believe he is right."

"A man can never waste his time in the countryside," Pico assures me.

"Unless he is dying," I say.

Angelo recites again, in that lyrical voice of his, recalling words familiar to my younger brain:

*I've fled, a while, those vexing public cares*
*in order to refresh my soul by pondering*
*the pastoral way of life, a life I envy.*

"You, Angelo, are the true poet," I say. "My work is a dull light seen against the brightness of your literary landscape."

"You are ill, my friend, and know not what you say," Angelo replies.

"A man speaks more true when he is dying," I say.

"Further proof that you are lying," Angelo counters.

"Do not patronize me, dear friend," I respond. "You know very well that I am dying. Why else have you been here round the clock?"

"To experience the grace of your presence," he says.

I say no more about the subject. It is best to leave Angelo to his dreams. It is, in fact, what makes him such a great poet. He has always lived in dreams, where language and beauty enfold him in their long-reaching arms. I envy him. He has not had to be the leader of a state, where dreams are a deterrent to action. I have had little time to dream, except for my forays into the country.

"We shall chide the old master for being late," Pico says, in reference to Ficino.

"He will come," says Angelo, "and he will bring with him volumes of Plato. That is a certainty."

"Perhaps you, like your grandfather before you, will prefer a reading from Plato instead of the Gospel," Pico adds.

"My brain has shrunk in size," I say. "Plato is much too big for it now."

"Nonsense, you and Plato are compatriots. You are both immortal," Angelo reminds me.

"That is true of Plato," I respond, "That is certain."

"And Lorenzo Il Magnifico," Angelo adds.

"How can you be so sure?"

"I can see into the seeds of time."

"You are but one man."

"I am a poet."

"He is right, Lorenzo," Pico adds. "Though you are ill, your mind is as sound as ever and will continue to send reverberations far into the future."

"I am not Plato," I say.

"But you have known love even greater than him," Pico counters.

"And love in its attraction to the form of beauty, leads us in our philosophical quest for wisdom," Angelo states.

"That was Botticelli's reason for painting the *Primavera*," I add.

"And your reason for the many loves you pursued," says Pico.

"It is true perhaps that man is only happy when he loves," Angelo says.

"And yet what constitutes this abstraction?" I ask.

"If only Ficino were here, he would set us straight," Pico says.

"His book *De Amore* is on my shelf," I say.

"No need, I know it well, word for word," Angelo says.

"I have no doubt of that," I respond.

Angelo recites:

*Life is created by love, the world is sustained by*
*love, and creation attains its highest wisdom*
*and returns to its ideal by means of love and beauty.*

Pico takes up the mantle of recitation:

*Physical love is the first step on the staircase of love.*

"That is true," I respond, knowing he expects a reaction.

"Of course it is, you wrote it," chimes Angelo.

Pico continues the thought he began:

*And naturally the most imperfect, since Platonism*
*holds that corporeal beauty is a sort of shadow*
*of true beauty or the idea of true beauty . . .*

I conclude the line:

*Which in the body is seen only under a veil.*

"You see, Il Magnifico, you have not forgotten your Plato," Pico declares.

I take sudden comfort in my thoughts, realizing why my grandfather asked Ficino to read him Plato at his deathbed. After all, the material world to which I still cling, as apprehended by the senses, exists on the lowest rung in the universe's hierarchal structure. This Platonic belief relieves my mind. It is the soul, captivated by beauty, that ascends finally, through higher and higher spheres of reality until it, at last, approaches the eternal realm of the Divine. Love is the force that impels the soul upward toward the heavenly realm. Physical love, of which I have had plenty, is only a steppingstone. The soul wishes for the ultimate aim: consummation in the love of God.

I see that Angelo is ready to recite again. I surprise him, beating him to the starting line, recalling the words I wrote in "The Supreme Good," elucidating my understanding of Plato's views on love and immortality.

*For while the soul is bound in carnal bonds,*
*confined within this prison's gloom, it will*
*always be governed by desire and doubt.*
*The soul is so wrapped up in error when*
*it's body-bound, that it won't know itself*
*until its liberation is complete.*

"Bravo," Angelo says, clapping his hands together.
"My soul's liberation is almost complete," I say.

# Savonarola

To see and hear Marsilio Ficino, a short, limping hunchback who speaks with a stutter, one would think he was little more than one of God's misbegotten souls. It is a wonder that inside that fragile, broken frame sits a mind vast (though wholly unconvincing to me) in its knowledge and wisdom. Recently made Canon in the Church of Florence, he and I confer on theological issues, though we rarely agree. He seeks to reconcile Plato's idealism with Christian notions of the immortality of the soul. He is a deeply religious man, and I appreciate his eagerness to persuade me to incorporate the philosophical tradition of Plato into my faith. I have told him, however, that as Plato has inspired humanism, it is, therefore, antithetical to Christianity. He tells me I am shortsighted to think of Plato's ideals in terms of being a label associated with anti-Christianity. It should be seen, according to him, as an intellectual backbone to my theology. He should know (have I not made it abundantly clear to him through my repeated refutations?) he would have more success moving a stone mountain with his hands than convincing me of his argument. I am not one who possesses flexible beliefs. God did not set down his laws believing they were movable parts, subject to the whims of men's impulsive ideas. They are in place for a reason. They are our foundation. To move this foundation even the slightest would cause a spiritual disturbance, bringing the kingdom of heaven to its knees. I do not wish to see that. As the caretaker to the foundation, I must be rigid and steady, not allowing myself to be caught off guard. It is, after all, my life's mission to make sure I keep the devil off my shoulder. I am not saying Ficino is the devil. I mean that if the slightest crack appears the devil can slip through and into our lives.

"Plato is much like a Christian saint," Ficino said to me on a recent visit to my cell.

"How so?" I asked, bemusedly.

"His ideas prepared the ground prior to the arrival of Christ."

"Perhaps it was his ideas that made more necessary the arrival of Christ."

"How so?"

His mimicry of my question did not go unnoticed.

"Did he not, as you do, believe in homoerotic love?" I asked.

He conceded, saying, "Plato believed the relationships between young men and their older mentors to be the most exalted form of love."

"There is no place for the practice of sodomy in the Christian faith," I declared, making sure he did not misunderstand my serious tone.

"I never mentioned the word sodomy."

"You implied it clearly."

"An implication by its nature is not clear."

"And by its nature, sodomy is unnatural whether clear or implied."

"It is beneath you, Savonarola, as a theologian and philosopher, to limit your scope of vision because of an act of physical love."

"We are not talking about an act of physical love. We are talking about a degenerate act, which God clearly forbids in the Bible."

"Then let us not talk about homoerotic beliefs and instead talk about Plato as Christ's intellectual forerunner."

"I prefer not to associate Plato with Christ at all."

"Does it matter little to you that such an association would give Christianity a philosophical foundation and thus bring more believers to the faith?"

"If you mean by believers more humanists, it is not an inclusion I seek to make."

"It would bring together, not separate, Platonism and Christianity."

"For the sanctity of God and all He stands for they must remain separate."

"If you understood Platonism as I do, you would understand that it is just a different part of Christianity."

"It is antithetical."

"How can love and beauty be antithetical to God?"

"The ultimate aim of man is beatitude."

"Yes, and to honor God's blessing we must first obey the physical laws of nature."

"Beatitude has nothing to do with the physical laws of nature. It is the pure vision of God."

"You must first climb the stairs to see that vision."

I knew in that moment my relationship with him could not continue. He appeared in his true light: as a heretic and a sodomite. I know with certainty that physical love has no place in the love one needs to share with God. Physical love is not a steppingstone. It is an obstruction, a stone over which one trips and falls, and once that happens he can never again stand, for on the ground he finds all kinds of base vices, which keeps him slithering along on a plane far beneath God's kingdom. Physical love leads to lust and lust leads to sodomy and sodomy leads to hell. I would never allow the joining of Plato and Christ, and God would never allow Ficino into heaven for believing viewpoints contrary to sacred scripture.

"If you have true Christian faith, you are lifted up, without need of stairs," I say, my voice rising to a preaching pitch.

"In any case, we both believe that the final aim is the love of God." he states, believing we are closer in thought than is true.

"On that we agree," I say, "though I warn you, Ficino. If you take the stairs they will collapse, and you will find yourself forever on the ground, looking up at your lost opportunity."

# Machiavelli

I hold no particular fondness for Platonism or Christianity. Both depend on speculation, and I see little value in anything speculative, whether it's called philosophy or religion. I prefer not to spend my time floating in an abstract, ethereal space, with my head in the clouds, grasping at unknowns, seeking worlds that are nothing more than figments of men's imaginations. While I commend their imaginations, I find their quests for God and the nature of beauty and love just flights of fancy. I know nothing of God, other than what I've been told. It's not enough, frankly, to make me lose my mind. As for love and beauty, I care not for them in the abstract. A night spent with my favorite courtesan suffices for me. It does my mind well, to say nothing of what it does for my body.

Ficino's mysticism is, for me, no different than dreaming, and a man does not survive on dreams. He dies because of them. He must awake from his dreams if he hopes to survive in this world, where every day, it seems, foreign invaders want to cut our throats and take our lands, and in the process our liberty. How does Plato or God help me fend off these invaders? Thus, I concern myself with politics, not philosophy or theology, for I live in a world of men who scheme and deceive and are ready to pounce. Who has time for sleep or dreams in such a world?

Lorenzo did bring peace and stability to the state, and for that I give him credit, though perhaps in our peaceful, stable state we had been lulled to sleep, believing that peace and stability would last forever. Nothing lasts forever, not even an age of gold. For is not gold known to rust? We are not as great as we think. I fault Plato and God, as well as their emissaries of metaphysical existence, Savonarola and Ficino, for instilling in us false beliefs in regard to what we are capable of achieving. We are human, after all, and without our diligence and awareness to the necessary task of preserving the state at all times, we will—and usually do--fail.

I laugh at my contemporaries, who debate endlessly the merits of the contemplative life, replete with their philosophy and religion, living quietly in the countryside, versus the necessity of the active life in the city. What is there to debate, really? A man's duty is to his state, to serve the needs of the citizens. How will he accomplish this by grooming horses all day? I do not, nor did I ever, desire the quiet of the countryside. I am a man of the city. I thrive on sociability and stimulation from lively conversation and the observations of the human animal, even if it means bitter wrangling and clever gamesmanship. I find nothing of interest in the beasts of the fields, with their empty headed stares or in the languid leaves that stupidly fall from the slightest shake or breeze.

Though I hold the highest regard for Lorenzo Il Magnifico, I wish he had had more backbone for politics and the corruption of city life. Time and again, he expressed his disillusionment, as is evident, when he sings the paeans to the virtues of the countryside in his poetry, which I must admit I find, at times, disarming in its simplicity. Here is an example, of which I have memorized for the sake of my point:

> Lured on, escorted by the sweetest thoughts
> I fled the bitter storms of civic life
> to lead my soul back to a calmer port . . .
> and having reached a pleasant, shady glen . . .
> where a verdant laurel cast some shade
> below that lovely peak, I found a seat,
> my heart untrammeled by a single care.

Lorenzo's company of artists and writers retreated to a world of dreams, believing the countryside was an antidote to the poisonous atmosphere of Florentine politics. With deepest apologies to Lorenzo's soul, I say this: a man cannot address politics by retreating from it. He must look it square in the eye and stare it down. Only by fighting its poison with his own can a man live in peace "untrammeled by a single care." Lorenzo, as much as anyone, was aware of this stratagem. He wouldn't have become Il Magnifico if he hadn't realized it. In later life, however, he became increasingly guiltier of retreating to the countryside, believing that the hard work was behind him. Unfortunately for a ruler, the work is never behind him. It is always in front of him, waiting for his decisions and actions. Admittedly, I have never been a ruler and do not, therefore, understand its wearisome effect. Still, I do know a thing or two about the art of effective politics.

I say this to anyone wise enough to listen: philosophy and theology do not save the world. As much as I enjoy reading, I know one does not survive with a book in his hand. He needs to hold a sword, and he must keep his eyes open and ahead of him. If he looks up to the sky, he will soon be dead, having foolishly believed in false dreams.

Where did Ficino's dreams land him in the end? He retired to the countryside at Careggi, before famine drove him back to the city, where he had lost his former friends either to death, destitution or irreconcilable differences. Savonarola had proclaimed him a heretic. Such a label sticks with a man. Even Plato became for him irrelevant, as a survival tool, in his daily discourse with the ugly world wherein he lived. He wrote a diatribe against Savonarola, calling it the "Apology of Marsilio Ficino on behalf of the many Florentine people, who have been deceived by the antichrist Hieronymus of Ferrara, greatest of all hypocrites." He used his biblical scholarship, quoting St. Paul: "For such boasters are false prophets, deceitful workers, disguising themselves as apostles of Christ. And no wonder! Even Satan disguises himself as the angel of light. Thus, it is not strange if his ministers also disguise themselves as ministers of righteousness. Their end will match their deeds."

Here is language I can wrap my head around: men of vast learning and civil sophistication, making war with each other, realizing that it is deception that stands out most in human behavior. That's not something God or Plato teaches. It is the language of men, stripped of their scholastic abstractions. Thus, in the grand scheme of what really matters, it is as essential to survival as breath itself.

# Lorenzo

Pico has gone to meet the friar, whom I had requested at my bedside. I do not know what to expect of such an encounter. I know only that his presence is necessary for reasons I cannot consciously explain since he has been to me more foe than friend. It matters little, since I no longer possess pride. I have, in fact, been stripped of my former self and those characteristics that once made me proud. I can no longer rule as a leader or love as a man. My voice can no longer sing; my hands cannot write. I cannot sit and ride on my beloved horse and race across the fields, believing myself a god, such as Mars or Apollo, with the ability to command all of life to suit my whims and needs.

Angelo is still nearby, standing near the window, staring up at the lone bright star in the sky. I hope for his sake the star continues to shine. I am leaving him my manuscripts, of which I have over ten thousand, at least half of them written in ancient Greek. Without his help I would have never realized the treasures in them. He is a great man and a great poet. How did God make such an attractive man, with all the requisite gifts of a genius? He made me ugly; though I cannot complain with all the gifts I have been given. It in no way deterred me in my development as a man. The woman I have loved cared little about my ill-proportioned facial features. They loved my wit, my intelligence, my charm, and most of all, my fierce passion. I have known the love, beauty and tenderness of women. This thought consoles me. At the same time, it tortures me to know I will never realize those womanly blessings ever again. But I must not think like this. I must console myself in gratitude, not torture myself in regret. I must be positive for the sake of my character and legacy and for whatever was best and most dignified about me. I must do this not only for myself, but for my forebears as well. The Medici name means little if I cannot endure with grace my final hours.

I see Angelo sit at the desk. He writes something on a paper. I assume he writes words that will form a poem, perhaps ruminations about the lone star in the sky. He brings me the paper. I read the words:

*Le tems revient.*

"The time returns," I say.

He reminds me that those were the words I had inscribed in pearls on my shield during the joust at Santa Croce in 1469; the words that have been my motto ever since, in my attempt to bring a revival to Florence of all things classical in art, literature and architecture.

"Yes, the time has returned," I say, "but have we created something lasting, or has it been only for now? Can you look into the seeds of time, Angelo, and tell me?"

"The revival seen here in Florence under your rule is for now and always."

"How can you be so sure?"

"I am a poet."

He always gives me that answer when I ask him something of which there is no answer. He fashions himself a seer as well as a poet. I do not doubt his claim. I wish it to be true.

"Will people some day look back on Florence as we look back on ancient Athens or during the age of gold in Rome? If this is so, then we have succeeded mightily. If not, it has all been in vain, has it not?"

"How can the genius of our age ever be in vain?"

I tell him I must think beyond the now, for in death what does a man have other than what people will think of him later. This, then, is what gives me peace of mind, to know that my legacy and the legacy of Florence have gained the ultimate aim of man: immortality. Above all else, our art and culture, if nothing else, must survive.

"I can assure you of that," he says. "Is it not the reason you have loaned our artists and craftsmen to all the foreign courts of Italy and Europe?"

"Achieving through the dazzle of art what we cannot hope to win through strength of arms."

"The politics of art."

"And religion."

"Inextricably bound to each other."

"Though, at its core, the art exists for its own sake."

"As is evident in your palace and many villas and gardens."

"I wish to see my sculpture garden one last time."

"At San Marco."

"Yes, at San Marco, too see my good friend Bertoldo and the talented young men under his guidance. Yet never again will I see him or them."

"Bertoldi is gone."

"I miss him. No one can replace his wit."

"But the talented young men remain."

"The young Michelangelo."

"Is he not your favorite?"

"He will sculpt masterpieces never before seen."

"Thanks to your patronage."

"His talent owes no allegiance to me."

"And yet you discovered him and gave him a place to live and work."

Angelo is right. I did discover the young man, and even now the memory makes me smile and want to laugh, if it were physically possible for me to do so. I passed him once in the garden, studying an ancient sculpture I had purchased called *The Head of a Faun*. I saw nothing remarkable about him in that first observation. He was like any young man studying art. When I next saw him he was busy at work, copying the Faun in marble. Finally, I saw him polishing his completed work, alongside the original. The young artist had added what he believed was missing in the original. He gave to his Faun an open mouth, as of a man laughing, so that the hollow of the mouth and all the teeth inside it could be seen. I praised the piece and asked the boy his age. "Fifteen," he answered. I laid a hand on his shoulder and joked: "Oh, you have made this Faun old and left him all his teeth. Don't you know that old men of that age are always missing a few?"

He didn't respond. He turned away and gathered his sculpting tools, leaving quickly, as if embarrassed by my comment.

A short time later, I saw him again in the garden, standing next to his Faun. He had removed an upper tooth from his old man, drilling the gum, as if it had come out with the root. I was amazed at its excellence and perfection. I could see clearly he was a boy who possessed genius, just as I knew Angelo had possessed it. I knew then I would take him into my household, so he could live peacefully and securely, needing only to dedicate his life to his developing genius. I said to him, "Inform your father that I would like to speak to him."

"What is the news of him now?" I ask Angelo.

"He sculpts from morning to night at your palace, hardly breaking for food and wine."

"That does not surprise me."

"He wishes to see you, but does not want to interfere."

"Interfere with what--my death? Tell him I beg for his interference."

"He will do anything for you."

"I would like him to sculpt me some other pieces."

"I will summon him, and he will come."

"You have a great influence with him."

"I have given him books and ideas. He loves the ancient myths."

"I suspect he loves you even more."

"He has a superior spirit; I love him very much and wish to see him develop his mind in literature, as well as art."

"See to it that Piero treats him well. My son doesn't always have respect for artists as I have had and my grandfather before me had. Did you know Cosimo had invited Filippo Lippi to live with him?"

"I am aware of that."

I confess that much of what I have done in my life is a reflection of my grandfather's presence, which even in his death has not diminished. In fact, it has grown larger, reminding me always of my life's mission: to outshine him. It is my nature to be the best, not second to anyone. In this contest, sadly, my grandfather has a great advantage. He lived to the age of seventy-seven. I am barely forty-three and already dying.

I think of what Giovanni Rucellai once wrote: "There are two principal things that men do in this world. The first is to procreate, the second is to build." I have done both, but have I done enough? My grandfather said that a man's political legacy would eventually crumble, but the monuments in brick and stone would remain as a reminder of what he had done for his homeland. He had spent lavishly on the reconstruction of San Lorenzo and San Marco and had made sure Santa Croce was given a new chapel. It is believed he was attempting to buy his way into heaven, but that is a cynical, outsider's view. He was a deeply religious man and had, in fact, a cell at San Marco for meditation and prayer.

He built, as well, the palace on the Via Larga, as well as several villas, notably in Trebbio, Cafaggiolo and Fiesole, filling all of them with priceless works of art. I have inherited all of them, and for that I am grateful. I have also been anguished, knowing that, as Rucellai alludes, it is as a builder a great man's legacy will be measured.

"We have enjoyed the fruits of my grandfather's labors."

"And you have planted the seeds of that fruit."

"My grandfather built more."

"You built better."

He goes to the bookshelf, takes a book and holds it up. It is Leon Battista Alberti's book *On Architecture*.

"Is this not a book you have studied often?"

"Why do you ask me what is rhetorical?"

"Your skill in architecture is known the world over. Kings and dukes ask for your opinion, for you have adorned and perfected the theory of architecture with the highest reasons of geometry."

"And yet I am not Augustus."

"And Augustus is not Lorenzo de' Medici, Il Magnifico."

"He found a Rome built of brick and left it in marble."

"And you have created for Florence an age of gold."

"I have fallen short of my goals. You know I have."

"The genius of man lies in his reach, not in what he grasps."

"Did I reach far enough?"

"You reached as high as heaven, and in doing so you allowed us to glimpse paradise."

"Seeing paradise and living in it are not the same."

"If you mean by falling short of your goals that you have not delivered us the Garden of Eden, then, yes, you have fallen short of becoming God."

"If only I had more time."

"To become God?"

"To finish what I started."

"No man could have done more than you in forty three years."

"Forty three years is not enough. I will never see the completion of the façade at the cathedral."

"And yet with your doing we now have Verrocchio's bronze ball crowning the cupola."

"It is not enough. The façade was designed without any architectural rhyme or reason. Just a scattering of late Gothic figures at its base while above them hovers empty spaces begging to be filled. You, as much as anyone, know our duty, as men of God, to honor and magnificently enhance the divine cult, as represented in our largest church."

"You have planted the seed for its completion. In time it will grow and bring many artisans and sculptors to the city to see it sanctified forever in marble, glory and magnificence."

"Not during my lifetime."

"Still, you will be known as the greatest citizen that ever lived in Florence, a reincarnation of Maecenas, who was culture minister to Caesar and patron to Horace and Virgil, a true and living God among men."

"How can you say that with such certainty?"

"You asked me to look into the seeds of time. I did."

"And can you tell me if my marble library at the Palazzo Medici, with its ten thousand manuscripts, in Greek and Latin, will ever be completed?"

"The world will know of your collection, for it is the greatest in all of Europe."

"I wanted to accomplish what my forebears before me hadn't even dreamed of doing. Do you understand, Angelo, how I feel? I wanted a glory and renown for myself, apart from my grandfather."

He tells me I am named Il Magnifico for a reason. He reminds me that at forty-three-years old, my grandfather had only begun to build and renovate Florence. He wants me to know, as if I have forgotten, what I have done for my beloved city: the rebuilding of the female convent of Le Murate, the building of the churches and convents at San Gallo, at Agnano in Val di Calci and at the Angeli in Florence, my commissioning Verrocchio to build a tomb—"one of the wonders of the world"--for my forebears to house their bones, my establishing a university at Pisa for humanistic learning.

"I am aware of what I have done. It is what I have not done that consumes me with unrest and leaves me wanting more."

"Great men always want more. That want is the core of your greatness."

"I wish to see the progress of the palace I am having built at Poggio a Caiano."

"I have been there, as you instructed, and can report that everywhere the air is full of that holiest of sounds: master builders hammering stone and a horde of sculptors working at marble, and on all sides one hears shouting for more stone and more mortar."

"Have the water masters completed the embankments, dikes and canals?"

"The hydraulic work has no precedent, unless one looks to the mighty achievements of the builders of ancient Roman villas."

"Will it be as great as the palace at Maecenas in Rome?"

"To see it is to understand it is the work of magnificence."

"I wanted to create something not only admirable and beautiful but a thing apart from what has been created before me."

"I can assure you, it is already a thing apart, as are your other villas."

He mentions Agnanao, where I have planted fields of grain and thousands of olive and mulberry trees; where I have gardens and fishponds; where the pasturelands and farmlands stretch to eternity; where he and I and Pico and Ficino discussed Plato as the moon rose high above the cypress trees, lighting the world at our feet as our brains reached high to conceptualize the eternal goodness that is God.

He mentions Spedaletto, the hunting villa, where I went, upon my mother's recommendation, for my gout's sake, to drink the thermal waters at Bagno a Morba and soak in its mineral baths; where, in the villa's loggia, Lippi and Botticelli frescoed a great mythological cycle that included the story of Vulcan, in which many nude figures are at work with hammers, making thunderbolts for Jove. I ask him if Filippino Lippi has finished the frescoes at Poggio a Caiano. He tells me he is at work on a fresco in the palace's loggia. It saddens me deeply to know I will never see it.

"Why did I not go to my villa in Poggio a Caiano--my Ambra--instead of coming here at Careggi?"

"Your doctor advised that the air is better here."

"But he was wrong. The air is the same here or there, as is evident by the rapid decline in my health since arriving here. I wish now I had chosen Ambra rather than Careggi as my final resting place. Do you not agree it is a more suitable place to die?"

"Your Ambra is a suitable place to live, high on a hill, with a view of Florence."

"The best of both worlds: to breathe the air of the country and see our beloved city below."

"It lacks only Adam and Eve to make it an earthly paradise."

"I did not want my villas built like my grandfather's, such as those at Trebbio and Cafaggiolo. I spent much of my youth in those villas, and have great appreciation for them. Still, they were more like medieval fortresses, with their turrets and crenallations. They made a man feel he

129

would soon be under siege. A man should have peace and serenity at his own residence."

"A place more likely to invite the visitation of the Muses."

"Yes, at Ambra the Muses come to bathe in the pools and sleep on the leaves."

"While keeping a keen ear to the nymphs and dryads rustling in the trees and at our feet."

"I wish now to be at Ambra."

"You named the villa in honor of the nymph Ambra."

"In honor of her perpetual escape from the river god Ombrone's unwanted attentions."

"Are you not like Ambra, the nymph of your poem?"

He recites to me from a memory in his mind I have never possessed. I marvel at his memory and his voice.

*Fled is the time of year that turned the flowers*
*Into ripe apples, long since gathered in.*
*The leaves, no longer cleaving to the boughs,*
*Lie strewn throughout the woods, now much less dense,*
*And rustle should a hunter pass that way,*
*A few of whom will sound like many more.*
*Though the wild beast conceals her wandering tracks,*
*She cannot cross those brittle leaves unheard.*

I cannot imagine writing verse such as that now.

"Did I really write those words?" I ask.

"Written, as you told, while sitting beneath Bertoldo's terra-cotta frieze evoking Virgil's Golden Age."

"The openness of Ambra's architecture offered no physical protection. I wanted it to be seen from the road. I wanted people to marvel at it."

"And they did."

"I wanted to create an earthly paradise where the only protection a ruler needs is the love that people bring and bear."

"You did create that paradise, both at Ambra and in Florence."

"I cannot imagine now, in my current state of helplessness, that my mind was once active and alive."

"Your mind belongs to the annuls of time."

I will miss Angelo Poliziano. He is my muse, my inspiration, and now my nurse. He will be with me till the end. I can ask no more of a friend. I ask him to recite more, for as much as I want to remember, I cannot recall the words I once wrote. He complies:

> *Wretched is he who, stung by sweet desire*
> *That longed-for day has promised to fulfill,*
> *Lies sleepless through the long-enduring night*
> *And ardently awaits for day to come!*
> *And though in wakefulness or even sleep*
> *He may exclude sad thoughts and welcome glad,*
> *And though he shuts his eyes to cheat the time,*
> *Yet night will seem to him a hundred years.*

I enjoy his voice, but it is not enough for me to lie passively. I have an urge to speak, as well—to die with words on my lips. I suddenly remember. Yes, the words fill my brain. It feels good to speak them while Angelo is nearby to hear them. I know I have few opportunities like this left. I recite, with full understanding of the river god Ombrone, who has lost everything that has ever mattered to him:

> *How did I lose her, whom I never had,*
> *I who can never lose the life I have?*
> *My fate in this is too severe, to be*
> *A god—immortal and in misery!*
> *Whereas, if I could die at least, this great*
> *And everlasting grief would also cease.*

Angelo praises my recititation.

"Ambra," I whisper.

"Ambra," he repeats.

"My life is about to turn to stone."

"Yet the memory of it will flow like the Arno itself, for the good citizens of Florence to see for many years to come."

"As Cosimo's memory has flowed?"

131

"As much, if not more."

"How can that be? He was the wisest of men: the most famous man I have known, endowed with many and singular virtues."

"In you, he has met his rival, and is most appreciative that he has."

"He left the city peaceful within and without, with grain in great abundance and happier than it had ever been."

"Have you not heard that history repeats itself?"

"And yet my grandfather will never know."

"You are wrong, my friend. He will know, as he already knows."

I want to believe Angelo, and there is good reason why I should. He is a poet and scholar of no ordinary means. Given perspicacity at birth, he lives high above the fray. He is a thing apart.

"Tell me what he already knows."

"You spearheaded patriotic projects," he says, "turning the cathedral into a pantheon of Florentine greats; you commissioned a portrait bust of Giotto, and have succeeded in having the remains of Dante returned to his native city. Some day the Tuscan dialect will be the native language of all of Italy, replacing Latin, because of you.. Even Cosimo, as great as he was, cannot make such claims."

I mention the Via Laura project. It is my greatest regret that I will never see its implementation and subsequent completion. It is my most ambitious architectural plan, with the building of a vast palace and gardens, much bigger than Pitti's palace, the likes of which Florence has not seen, with colonnades encircling the church of Ss. Annunziata and the surrounding piazza. I see it as a place of retreat in the heart of the city.

"I go not alone to my death and resting place," I say. "I take my dreams with me, and they are many."

# Savonarola

Though I am a man of God, I am not immune to human conflict. I walk a fine line between the spiritual and the political. I want to incite change in Florence, where men of wealth build monuments for their pride and selfish satisfactions. I wish for the time when God's wrath will tumble these monuments and men will lie in fire, smoke and ash. I know, as well, that as long as I live at San Marco I live as a hypocrite because our monastery is in many ways no different than the very monuments I detest. When I entered the Dominican Order in Bologna, I saw everywhere on the walls the words written by St. Dominic: *Have charity, maintain humility, observe voluntary poverty: may my malediction and that of God fall upon whosoever shall bring possessions into this Order.*

At San Marco, there is no such inscription on the walls. An appendage had been added to the monastery's constitution, expressly exempting the community of San Marco from the Dominican ban on possessions, thus allowing we friars to own the various gifts that had been lavished upon us by our benefactors, Cosimo de Medici and his heirs. I recently stood outside a young friar's cell and observed as he talked with a man who wore fine tailored clothing. Inside the cell on a table I saw meats, cheeses, eggs, fruit and wine. The friar and his benefactor sat on opulent, wood-carved chairs, enveloped on all sides by brilliantly colored frescoes. I saw in the young friar's hand a bejeweled crucifix and gold pieces upon the floor. His feet rested in the finest leather, and his robes seemed custom tailored and washed. He wore a smile on his pink cheeks that one should never see on a devotee of St. Dominic. I did not say anything, for fear of embarrassing him in front of his patron. I walked away, though the incident stayed with me, the way a plague affixes itself to a sick body.

I thought of little but changing the habits at San Marco. I had a dream that gave credence to my conviction. I saw living in the afterlife the twenty-eight friars of San Marco who had died during the previous years. They lay naked, surrounded on all sides by flames, damned to spend all eternity in hell for breaking their monastic vows, especially with regard to poverty. They begged in unison, asking forgiveness to the Heavenly Father, for having fallen prey to the desires for luxuries and comfort during their life at San Marco.

I awoke knowing my fellow monks and I could no longer reside at San Marco. I desire to relocate to the countryside, to build a monastery from scratch, where we can live a life of sanctity, upon erecting a poor and simple place of worship, wearing woolen habits that are old and patched, eating and drinking sparingly in the sober manner of the saints, living in poor cells without anything but the bare necessities, maintaining silent contemplation and solitude, cut off from the world. It must be built in a remote and solitary spot, which would express in every part of its design the spirit of poverty and holy life, evident in its simplicity. The structure should have only one level, close to the ground, and be completely unadorned. Each small cell should be separated by partitions made of wattle. We do not need stone, for stone is costly. We shall build everything with wood. We shall no more have doors with iron bolts or keys. Most important of all, we will not allow visitors (patronage of our monks and monastery will not exist) who bring material possessions and unnecessary extravagance. I myself shall stand at the gate and ask everyone who wishes to enter: Are you a simple person, interested only in serving God and the poor who need our help? I shall turn aside anyone who does not answer this question the right way: yes, I am a simple person and wish to respect the holy life of your order.

This then is my desire for my fellow monks and me: to achieve salvation living a simple, remote monastic life. Yet how do I choose to turn away from the repentant, downtrodden souls throughout Florence, those willing to follow me onto the Ark, toward a New Jerusalem? Can I forsake their salvation for the sake of my own? I have asked God what is best: to turn inward and protect myself and my fellow friars from the luxuries of the world, or to take the bull by the horn and live not in utopian simplicity but in the storm of revolution, to destroy man's pride and strip him of his vanities?

I know only that God wants me to be both spiritual and political. Therefore, while I wait upon this new vision to relocate, I shall impart the ways of St. Dominic and create sweeping reforms, the likes of which my fellow friars have yet to see. I will emphasize, in everything we do, complete austerity. The friars under my jurisdiction shall wear plain cloth robes and partake in fasting and prayer vigils. All meals will now be communal, consisting of plain food and pure water. Private dining in cells with influential secular friends on sumptuous repasts accompanied by fine wines will no longer be permitted. The cells themselves will be stripped of all unnecessary ornamentation, possessions and opulent furnishings. Most importantly, all friars will be expected to work, in order to contribute to the cost of their bed and board as well as to the maintenance of the monastery. They must develop their intellectual skills and learn new crafts, such as woodcarving and transcribing sacred manuscripts. Finally, they must learn ancient languages: Hebrew, Greek and Turkish. I will persuade Pico to teach them, for who knows these languages better than him? Only then will they better understand the Bible and the messages I preach.

The monastery at San Marco will not become a monument of pride and selfish satisfactions, like the many buildings that line the streets of Florence. I will rant and rave, speaking through God, to assure that won't happen. The sanctity of salvation and eternity must be preserved at all costs. Those who tax and rob the poor to build their villas and palaces will be destroyed because they build not for God but for themselves. Even now I hear God tell me, "The revolution of destruction must begin before we can build our New Jerusalem."

# Machiavelli

Savonarola is a builder of lies. He creates a following by telling people he speaks in the voice of God and through him conveys prophetic events. What he creates, in truth, are fantasies and delusions of airy nothingness, from which his imagination can claim to know worlds that no man can ever know because they are beyond the senses and thus common sense; yet his followers are eager to hear of these worlds, to surrender their physical and mental lives to one man's illusion. This collusion can only occur when both parties, the communicator and the receiver, share a mutual craziness. In fact, the only thing crazier than someone claiming to speak through God is the craziness of the follower who questions not the sanity of a man who makes such claims.

I do not believe God speaks to anyone. I am not saying God doesn't exist. I believe he does. I just think he doesn't care as one might wish to believe he does. Here's what I believe, though I recognize it may as well be as much my fantasy as the one Savonarola holds; nonetheless, since a fantasy is as hard to disprove as it is to prove, I offer mine for inspection to those who share reasonable convictions: God did indeed make us, as is believed. Soon after he created man and saw the result of his creation--his mistake, if you will--he turned a blind eye, realizing it was too late to abort his project. Though he had made a creature beautiful on the outside, he failed to cover the blemish of his insides: his deceptive, greedy and murderous nature. At this time, cleaning his hands of his project, abandoning his creation forever, God decided to give man free reign to choose his own heaven or hell.

Savonarola's delusions are the result of his living in self-denial: starvation and sleep deprivation. I have heard it said that he takes only the minimum food required to live, such as bread and soup, and he sleeps little, if at all. It is no wonder he has hallucinations of talking to God and through him. Here's the truth: he is not immune to God's curse. He is as guilty as anyone, evident in his greed and deception. Though he hasn't literally murdered anyone, he is guilty of the attempted murder of man's mind. Can there be a more egregious, violent crime? Even still, despite Savonarola's crimes, God disregards him, as he disregards all of us.

# Lorenzo

It seems like only yesterday I was standing where others now stand, in this very room at Careggi, looking down at my grandfather, in this very bed, as he lay dying from the same disease that now afflicts me. While I still retain from my earliest days memories of his jocular spirit and engaging mind, as he conversed about great books and ideas and played on musical instruments, entertaining those of us lucky enough to be blessed by his genius and generosity, what stands out more are the vivid images of his crippling illness, watching as servants carried him from room to room in the palace he built in 1458. I was nine years old, and by then he had become a mostly silent man, too depressed by infirmity to find continued pleasure in life. His unhappiness would only increase given the tragic events that occurred in the ensuing years: the death of my little cousin, Cosimo, followed by the loss of uncle Giovanni, my grandfather's second son, with whom he had entrusted most of his hope for the future, since my father, Piero, had been sickly all his life and was presumed to not have much longevity as a ruler. After these deaths, my grandfather spiraled down, often murmuring, "Too large a house now for so small a family." Despite my grandmother's repeated jibes to get him to talk, he preferred silence to conversation. One day I asked him why he sat so long in silence with his eyes shut.

"I am practicing for death," he said.

Not long before he died, he desired to visit the Prior at San Lorenzo. I walked behind while a litter carried my father and grandfather to the church. My grandfather said the creed word for word and received the Holy Sacrament, with perfect devotion, having first asked pardon of everyone for any wrongs he had done them. I think often of his pardon. How could he not have wronged anyone? A ruler must wrong people if he is to maintain his power and wealth. He must banish rivals; he must ruin families and businesses that appear to threaten his own. He must give profitable and honorable appointments to his loyal friends and deny advancement to those who are not his friends. He must travel a road fraught with risk and danger, and if the head of an adversary is lying in the way, he must crush it with the wheels of his cart or his horse's hooves.

The very next day, the litter carried him through the gates of the city and up the hills to Careggi. He knew and all those who watched, including family, friends and the citizens of Florence, knew that he would never return to the city. He did not complain, as I did when I was similarly carried here, railing at fortune and fate, for stealing from me the many more years of life I wished to have. My grandfather, unlike me, was an old man; he had lived seventy-seven years, well beyond the age any man could expect. Thus, he could readily say to those walking beside him, "Nicodemo mio (I can bear no more). I feel myself failing and ready to go." He said little else as the litter carried him, preferring to keep his mouth and eyes closed, practicing, as he earlier said, for death.

He broke his silence on his deathbed, with an eagerness I hadn't witnessed in several years. I wondered how he could will himself to talk so much with death's stranglehold around his throat. I no longer wonder such things. I know now how death can make a man talk much, knowing he will have no further opportunity to talk once the ends comes. He talked with my father about the business of government and politics. He talked with Ficino about Plato and the immortality of the soul. It was with me, however, he most desired to talk.

"Do not be sad for my passing," he said, after I entered his room upon his request to see me alone.

"I and the rest of Florence feel a great loss," I responded.

"I am grateful to rid myself of constant fevers and unremitting pain in my joints and limbs," he said.

"Can I help you in any way?" I asked.

He nodded and said it was for the future he was worried. He did not believe my father, because of his illness, could effectively carry out the duties of his position. I would need to help him. Though I was only fifteen years old, the circumstance dictated more than nature that I become a man. I had no desire to be a man just yet. I was enjoying my youth and all the recklessness of being a carefree spirit that comes with it. I enjoyed boasting and carrying on, following the whims of my many desires, both in flesh and mind. The world of men seemed too trying and unfulfilling, immersed in business, foreign policy and arbitration, with little regard for freedom and leisure. Why would I want to abandon that which was most important to me to become a man? The price seemed high. I did not say that to my grandfather. I listened obediently, out of respect for the man who in less than two days would have inscribed on his tomb the words *Pater Patriae* (Father of our Country).

"Make up your mind to be a man," he said.

"My mind is made," I responded.

"The future of the Medici family rests on your shoulders."

The weight on my shoulders felt heavy. I knew that we, the Medici, made our fortune in banking. I remembered my grandfather once telling me that he loved business so much that even if it were possible to procure money and possessions with a magic wand, he would still continue to work as a banker. I felt ashamed of what I was thinking: that I was bereft of banking skills and had little desire to acquire them. I would have preferred a magic wand to make money, and would have been content to do so.

As a young married man in his early twenties, he lived away from home for five years, living in Germany, France and Rome, overseeing his banking branches, ensuring their expansion and growth across continents. I never saw myself as one immersed in counting numbers on paper or managing the affairs of an office. I believed in letting those who loved that work do it. I hoped that what rested on my shoulders was not a life of business.

Fortunately, he made no direct mention of business. He must have assumed I would learn on the job and do what was necessary to preserve the family fortune. It is a singular regret of mine that I squandered much of what was left me. Though the Medici name and legacy are stronger now, our accounts are weaker. It has been, admittedly, a failing of mine. For that, I beg the forgiveness of my forebears.

He said he was sorry to have to bestow so much responsibility on me, given me age. My inheritance should have come much later, if not for the untimely death of Giovanni, his second son. He was the one Cosimo had assumed would take leadership in the event, as inevitable as it was, of my father's death. He was an altogether more able, shrewd and cheerful man than my father. Thus, despite his order of birth, he was seen as the Medici torchbearer. Anyone who met both he and my father, side by side, could clearly see that my grandfather was right. I had heard often as a boy that I resembled my uncle much more than my father. Some had joked, in fact, that he was, indeed, my real father. I never believed that, though I realized I shared more of his features and behaviors than I did with my own father. Like me, Giovanni was not blessed with good looks. He had my large nose—I should say I possessed his--and we had the same swelling lump between our eyebrows and the same square, lantern jaw. Where we differed was in physique. He was a fat man, though it was not a natural shape for him. It was primarily the result of his excessive diet. His corpulence, however, in no way deterred him from being a conscientious citizen and a capable, if not overtly talented, businessman. He could charm anyone with his wit and impress anyone with his understanding of art and music. No reason existed why Cosimo wouldn't have expected him to run the family business and, in addition, the city of Florence. He had already held important positions, such as Priore in the Signoria and as ambassador to the Curia, where he spent a large part of his time eating and drinking with the more worldly cardinals, until in 1463 he died of a heart attack, at age forty-three, the same age as me, as I lay dying.

I have secretly wished, more than once, in the previous days, during my most unendurable pain, for a heart attack to take me as well: to save me from the torturous suppression of my urine and the feverous attacks that invariably follow.

141

"You are like my son, Giovanni," he said, "possessed of great wit, charm and intelligence." His eyes became teary at the remembrance and mention of Giovanni. I thanked him for the compliment, hoping to distract him from his suffering. He recovered quickly because he had not called me to his room to express his personal anguish. As long as he still had breath, he wanted to conduct what was to him the most critical business of his final hours.

"Make sure you dress quietly and are happy to walk in the shadows, as much as in the bright sunshine," he stated, more as a directive than as friendly, grandfatherly advice.

I did not wish to walk in shadows. I wanted my face to be seen; I wanted my voice to be heard. I wanted to ring the alarum bell to announce my arrival. I let my grandfather give his advice, however, for he had earned that right.

"Be wary of going to the Palazzo della Signoria; wait to be summoned, do what you are asked to do and never display any pride should you receive a lot of votes; avoid litigation and political controversy, and always keep out of the public eye. There's always someone who wants the power that you possess. Don't parade yourself ostentatiously. Envy is a weed that should not be watered."

He admitted to me those were the words his father, Giovanni, had given to him as a youth my age. It should be apparent that advice giving is something the Medici have passed down to one another, though in relation to the terminal gout we have given each, this curse is, at its worst, only comically annoying. He saw no reason why those words shouldn't be as relevant to me as they were to him. I did not say that times change, nor did I express my darkest thought: that I could never duplicate another's life, even one so great as Cosimo de' Medici. Even at fifteen years of age, I knew that I would follow no path not shaped first by me. "As you know," he said, "I rode a mule, not a horse."

I knew he was trying to tell me indiscreetly that my love of horses and my riding them through the city was an ostentatious display. I did not agree. Even men of modest means rode horses. A mule is a beast of burden, made for those tasks associated with labor. A horse can gallop fast and make a man of any age feel like he is flying and ascending to the gods, living on a heightened plane. I liked that feeling and would never relinquish it, even if it meant I watered the weed of envy.

# Savonarola

I had a vision or dream. I cannot tell which. I have not slept nor eaten in nearly three days. I have made it my purpose to deny myself in order to bring myself closer to the values set down by St. Dominic. Otherwise why am I here, serving God, unless it is to do his work the right way? I spend my nights deep in prayer, in a cell without embellishments: no frescoes, no candles, and no windows for air. I am not afraid to suffer. I am a disciple of Christ.

My episode occurred after I heard what sounded to my ears like a man scraping his sandals across the corridor floors, moaning in pain as he did. I followed the sound and entered the large cell that once belonged to the man the citizens of Florence called *Pater Patriae*. It is the largest cell at San Marco, and it has remained unoccupied since his death in 1464, long before I came here to reside. On this night, a man occupied the cell, standing before the frescoed *Adoration of the Magi*. He wore sandals and a simple robe over a body that sloped downward under the weight of a heavy torso. The man labored to breathe and mumbled in whispers through his open mouth. Without seeing his face, I knew the man was Cosimo de' Medici. I cannot explain how I knew this, nor could I explain the reason for his appearance, other than it was God himself who had granted me this visitation. I knew only that I was glad finally to meet and confront the benefactor of the San Marco monastery.

I had heard much of his meditations in this cell. Monks who knew well my predecessor, Antonio Pierozzi, who was good friends with Cosimo, have passed down his stories. As much as I respect the saintly friar, I have always believed he sold himself out to Cosimo's wealth and contributions to the monastery. Both men are responsible for adorning the monastery the way one would adorn a palace or a museum, failing to understand that the best place to worship God is in a simple room, void of art and statuary. I know many of my brethren do not agree with me. They see the art and statuary as embodiments of God's beauty. They confuse God's beauty with their own sense of beauty, which, in fact, is nothing but vanity. They, as monks, should know better. As Prior, it is my responsibility to teach and guide them to a more complete understanding of what it means to live and worship in a Dominican monastery.

Cosimo appeared to be in an earnest devotional state, staring at the fresco, mumbling what sounded like a prayer. Unsure of how long his visitation would last, I interrupted him.

"What is it about that painting that so engages you that stand before it, as a child before a gift?"

He turned to me. His face was ashen gray; his cheeks hollow, his lips dry and chapped, his eyes like small stones, flaked and full of dust.

"The image of the Magi laying down their crowns at the manger guided me as a ruler."

"It is a humbling act for men of wealth to lay down their crowns. Yet you did no such thing. You kept your crowns and offered crumbs to the poor."

He said he didn't recognize me. I told him I was the new Prior. He said the old Prior would not have confronted him as I had.

"I gave generously," he said. "The evidence exists in this monastery."

Yes, he gave generously. No one can dispute that. The motive for his giving carries more revelation. He had a midlife crisis of conscience. He asked Pope Eugenius IV how he might earn God's pardon for his sins. The pope told him he should spend 10,000 florins on alterations to the convent at San Marco. When the alterations were complete, the pope issued a bull of expiation. Cosimo had the text of the bull inscribed over the door of the church sacristy.

At San Marco, the frescoes on the walls and the library, with philosophical and theological texts, are among the finest anywhere and make everyone who visits, as well as the friars who live here, aware that these treasures are the gifts of the Medici. Cosimo, with his imprint on San

Marco, had made this monastery his theological playground.

"What you gave was for spiritual profit and the salvation of your soul."

"And what is wrong with a man saving his own soul, if his wealth can also bring virtue and redemption to others?"

He asked me if I knew the former Prior, Antonio Pierozzi. I said I did not, though I knew of him.

"Did you not speak with Prior Pierozzi about the sin of usury and how that sin in a banker's life might be expiated?"

"What we spoke about is of no concern of yours."

"The expiation of sin under false pretense is a concern of mine."

He smiled, believing his charm, like that of his grandson's, could ameliorate my judgment of him. He asked me if I had seen the many frescoes painted on the walls of the cells. I said I had. He wanted me to know he had commissioned Fra Angelico to paint everything I saw, excepting *The Adoration of the Magi* in the present cell. His assistant Benozzo Gozzoli had painted that one. I told him I had little interest in frescoes.

"Yet you must have interest in Fra Angelico."

"He was a man of simplicity, modesty and holiness."

"He was an artist."

"He was a saintly friar, more than an artist."

"Is it so terrible he could be equally adept at both?"

"A friar's primary task is to worship God."

"And do you believe this man failed to worship God because he painted? I knew him well, and allow me to say no one could have shown more reverence and devotion to God than him. Each morning before he worked on his frescoes, he knelt down and prayed. He painted many variations of the crucifixion, and each time he did tears streamed down his face."

"And even still the tears on his face paled in comparison to those on Christ's face.

"Every painter paints himself."

"He was a man of God, and every man of God sees himself on that cross. When I walk the halls and look in the

146

cells and see the frescoes of Christ dying on the cross, in dripping blood, I know whatever suffering I endure in fasting, prayer and self-denial cannot measure the suffering he endured. I wish nothing less than to divert his blood and pain onto my own flesh and conscience. I want to take his suffering, if only I can."

"We all suffer, not just you and Christ."

"And some make others suffer as well."

This time he did not smile and try to charm me. He shrugged and turned to face the fresco on the wall. Undeterred by his insolence, I continued to speak.

"The Church's ruling has been that the usurer might obtain forgiveness only by restoring during his lifetime, or at his death, all that he had gained unrighteously."

He rubbed his tired face. I heard him moan. When he turned, his face had darkened and his eyes were unclear. "I restored the monastery and subscribed money to be endowed to it after its restoration. I presented the friars with vestments, chalices and illustrated missals, and I bequeathed Niccolo Niccoli's library of sacred books. I believe I have atoned for the sins I may have committed."

"Overtaxing the poor and charging them higher interests that they can afford are sins not easily atoned. Only God can give expiation for those."

"I went out of my way to live my life in an understated way, not to draw attention to my wealth and position. I rode a mule; I dressed in moderate garments."

"And yet you built a palace which throws even the Colosseum at Rome into the shade. The builders tore down twenty buildings to put up your one building. Who would not build magnificently if he could do so with other people's money?"

"A man should be able to receive restitution from his investments."

"The Church is not a bank."

"And a man of God is not God."

"The friars never wanted your gifts, or the gifts of your grandson. Though they may seem to benefit us they, in truth, hurt us the more."

"The sacred mysteries more easily yield their secrets to those who have comfort. I speak from experience."

"The more comfort he has, the more he relies on that comfort."

"How can one with proper sense complain of patronage?"

"That patronage becomes a curse when we cannot live without it."

"I know not what you mean."

"We receive less lay donations because of your patronage."

"As you should receive less since you need less."

"Lay donors give to Santa Maria Novella, not San Marco."

"Because it is at San Marco, not Santa Maria Novella, that the monks eat the bread of the Medici."

"Worse of all, becoming more dependent on the Medici has made us more compliant."

"You argue without redeemable cause."

"You have given without virtuous cause."

"Never shall I be able to give God enough to set him down in my books as a debtor."

"The distribution of charity is insufficient."

"What else can I do? I cannot die on the cross."

"And even if you could, would you?"

"I am not you. I have no desire for self-desecration."

"Then you are unworthy to be seen among the Magi."

"I am among the Magi. Look there in the painting. Do you not see me?"

"Commissioned by you."

"Art fixes one's life forever."

"Art can be destroyed."

I looked at the painting. The figure in it bore a striking resemblance to Cosimo. When I turned my eyes to face him, he was no longer in the room. I fell to the floor. When I next opened my eyes, a young monk cradled me in his arms, presenting water to my lips.

"Do not give me that water," I said.

"You will die without it."

"I am already dead," I said.

# Lorenzo

I did not want to hear about the responsibilities required of me as a future leader, and I especially did not want to face my grandfather's demise. I wanted him to spring from his bed and discuss theology, philosophy and architecture. I wanted him to play on his musical instruments and tell stories about the artists he patronized. I wanted to see him smile and laugh because I desired the same for myself. It had been raining for two weeks, as if the sky mirrored the mourning that had taken hold of my family. I wanted the sun to shine, as it once did in Florence. If only I could command the heavens and ride the chariot like Apollo, dragging the sun across the sky at my whim. To be a god, that's what I really wanted in my youth, for gods do not die.

I wanted to say to my grandfather: Tell me about Lippi, Donatello and Brunelleschi; tell me about the *Rinascimento* and the life of a true gentleman, who pursues art and learning. That was, after all, the only life I wanted: to spend my days in cultivated idleness, consumed in the practice of research and artful fabrication. I never wanted to be a ruler of men, embroiled in political machinery and all the embittered ambitions of bloodthirsty men.

My grandfather had neither the will nor the inclination to return to the past. What was left of his mind rested on the future. I did not fully comprehend his feelings, as I do now, as I was fifteen years old. I now know the sum total of a man's worth, made greater by his wealth and power, is tied, bound, and connected to his legacy in irrefutable knots.

"My library is yours," he said. "It is of no use to your father, for he does not read as you do. I know you will cherish them."

I told him I would be honored to receive his collection, which he claimed was the single greatest treasure of books in Europe, containing ten thousand Latin and Greek authors, hundreds of priceless manuscripts from the time of Dante and Petrarch as well as others from Florence's remoter past. I knew many of the books appeared in his library as a result of the Great Council he hosted in Florence, bringing together leaders of the Greek Orthodox Church and the Roman Catholic Church, aiming to unify these churches into a single body of theology. He told me the city, at that time, was filled with Greek scholars, who became an important influence on what was already being spoken of as the *Rinascimento*. The presence of these scholars in the city stimulated interest in classical texts and history, in classical art and philosophy and in particular the study of Plato, who would become the great hero of my grandfather, his fellow humanists, and those of my inner circle. My grandfather said it was during a lecture given by Gemistos Plethon, a Greek scholar and the greatest authority on Plato, he met a young student named Marsilio Ficino, who had developed great skill at translating Greek to Latin. My grandfather became his patron, providing him a place to live and study, where he could develop his scholarship on Plato and later communicate his learning to those of us eager to receive sensory and cerebral satisfactions which led, as my grandfather liked to say, to "the road of happiness."

If this road existed for him, it lay in the country, not the city. This villa at Careggi meant much more to him than just a place to die. It was a place for him to read in peace, and to go out and do his chores: pruning his vines, tending his olives, planting mulberry and almond trees, and talking to the country people to learn of proverbs and fables that he used in his daily discourses with people back in the city. In the country he could talk to friends without interruption, and when he wasn't discussing Plato with Ficino, the two of them played chess, which was the only game I ever saw either play.

He built Careggi, Cafaggiolo and Trebbio as working farms. Fiesole is the exception. It is neither a working farm nor one of my grandfather's designs. His son Giovanni had it built solely for pleasure. The land around it is steep and stony and useless for farming. My grandfather could never understand his son's decision to build a villa that could not be farmed. Giovanni told his father that that was his point:

to have a place where one didn't need to work. He could simply sit and relax and enjoy the view, free of the burdens of labor. My grandfather saw no value in sitting on a shaded terrace on a summer evening and looking down upon the roofs of Florence. He preferred to look out a window and see the land that belonged to him, the land he himself worked. To him, the pursuit of pleasure unsupported by a steady return on investment was frivolous. He wanted me to agree with him, though I must confess I agreed with my uncle Giovanni in this matter, believing that the pursuit of pleasure for pleasure's sake gave savor to life. Angelo, as well, has always favored the villa at Fiesole, finding the solitude gratifying to his disposition. He said once, "What is there not to like about it? It has water in abundance, moderate winds, and is surrounded by trees, and yet these trees leave enough space between for a great view of the city below." I have always believed the difference between the fortresses at Trebbio and Cafaggiolo and the serene villa at Fiesole is the difference between the past and present: the medieval mind and the current humanism.

Though my grandfather made reference to his library, he did not mention the art he had amassed. It was understood that we, my father and I, would become the caretakers of the treasures seen especially through the archway in the courtyard of the palace on the Via Larga: the classical busts, statues, columns, inscriptions and Roman sarcophagi and, in particular, Donatello's masterpieces, *Judith Slaying Holofernes* and *David,* the first free standing figure cast in bronze since classical times. Never before had anyone in Italy portrayed the young male form so lovingly, realistically and sensuously, paying homage to Greek ideals.

My grandfather treated Donatello like a son, providing a home for the sculptor at his palace and doing everything in his power to improve the artist's appearance, such as buying him new clothes. Donatello, though, insisted on wearing old rags and had little regard for money, choosing to share what he had with others. The artist cared for only one thing: making his patron happy with the art he sculpted. The same loyalty and dedication could not be said about Filippo Lippi, who was at the palace at the same time as Donatello. He cared most about his own needs, not those of his patron's. I wanted my grandfather to transcend his pain and sadness and tell me once more about the artist he could not control. I wanted this to happen for selfish reasons. My grandfather always laughed good-naturedly whenever he told the story. I wanted to see that laugh manifest again before he took his final breath.

I understand now how impossible and unfair that wish of mine was, for a dying man cannot laugh so easily when he is faced with worries about his legacy and the equally worrisome thought of his soul's status in terms of his fortune, good, bad or indifferent, to live in eternal peace.

I recall being nine years old, before my grandfather's spiral downward into a despair he would never leave, when he told me about the painter Filippo Lippi, enlightening me about a subject of great interest to me, especially as I had grown up around it: the patronage of talented artists.

"The virtues of rare minds are celestial beings, not slavish hacks," he said.

I confessed to not understanding what he meant. After his initial reservation, believing I was too young to hear of such things, he told me about Lippi's preoccupation with lust. He had commissioned Lippi to paint *The Coronation of the Virgin*. The artist, however, had a difficult time fulfilling his responsibilities. Though he possessed great passion for creating art, he possessed equal, if not greater, passion for chasing and seducing young girls.

Could this be the reason his early attempt to become a monk failed?

"He is not Fra Angelico," my grandfather said, laughing. "He does not appreciate the cloistered life."

He said in the evenings Lippi found it impossible to concentrate on his work. He repeatedly slipped away from his studio in the palace, hurried through the courtyard, and disappeared down the Via Larga in search of a woman to satisfy his desires.

"It was my practice to obtain an artist's agreement to finish a work for a settled price on an agreed date," my grandfather said.

He told me the agreed date for the completion of *The Coronation of the Virgin* had long passed, at which time he did something he had never done before as a patron: he locked Lippi up in his room, telling the artist he would not be let out again until he completed the painting and met his mentor's approval.

I can still see my grandfather shaking his head and laughing as he told the story. He must have known, as was clear to me in my life as a patron, that artists could not be imprisoned. They are wild colts and need thus the freedom to roam, as they so desire. Lippi would not and could not be deterred from following his passions. He got hold of a pair of scissors, cut up the coverings of his bed into strips, tied them together, and, using them as a rope, climbed down into the street and ran away.

"I found him the next day on the streets, sniffing like a dog, following the scent that drove him mad," my grandfather said. "He refused to return to the studio, even if it meant the loss of his commission and my patronage."

He had to promise Lippi that he could come and go as he pleased. In the future, my grandfather resolved to keep a hold on his wild, artistic colt by using affection and kindness, not authority.

"An artist must, above all else, be treated with respect," he said.

Lippi completed *The Coronation of the Virgin* in time, producing a work of such beauty that could have only come from a man who obeyed no rules of custom other than his own.

"Discernment in matters of art is the mark of a true gentleman," my grandfather said. "The beauty and grace of objects, both natural ones and those made by man's art, are things it is proper for men of distinction to be able to discuss with each other and appreciate."

Thus, at a very young age, I learned that the knowledge and administration of art were as vital to men in our position as breath, exercise and nutrition. Politics and art were, in fact, two sides of a coin, for art could be used to level out the playing field against cities and countries stronger in military might than our small republic of Florence.

He referred, finally, to his illness, hoping I might be spared the gout and arthritis that had afflicted every male member of the family going back nearly a hundred years. For years I had seen my grandfather, father and uncle carried about the palace in chairs borne aloft by servants. I had even seen all three together in the same bed, verifying that misery does indeed love company. They lived and worked on the ground floor of the palace, moving about painfully in and among the four large rooms where management of the banking business took place, as scores of secretaries, clerks and assistants scurried to and fro all day. I chose to turn my back on the banking business and the terrible affliction I saw in my elders. I preferred the airy courtyard, with its statues and sculptures, and the garden with exotic fruit trees. If I stayed away from the place where my forebears perpetuated sickness, perhaps I would be spared. In truth, despite what I saw, becoming infirm like them did not consume my young mind. What fifteen-year-old does not believe he will remain strong forever? It would take another dozen years for my illness to manifest to such a progression to make me fully realize the severity of our family's curse passed from generation to generation.

My grandfather did not leave this world without a note of levity. He told a story I had never heard. Though it was about the severity of his gout, it was nevertheless a welcomed anecdote, for I did get to see something resembling a smile crease his lips. The one and only time Pope Pius II visited Florence, my grandfather tried to kiss his feet, though his gout rendered him unable to bend. He said to the pope: "Two Florentines named Papa and Lupo returning from the country met in the Piazza and offered each other their hands and a kiss. But they were both very fat that they could only touch their stomachs. Gout now denies me what corpulence refused them."

Pope Pius II said to Cosimo: "Mourning accords not with your age; it is contrary to your health, and we ourselves, your native city, and all Italy, require that your life be as far as possible prolonged."

My grandfather replied: "I strive to the best of my power, and so far as my weak spirit will permit, to bear this great calamity with calmness."

Before I left his room, expressing my love and admiration for him, he whispered into my ear: "You inherit much. Make up your mind to become a man and lift the Medici banner high."

I cried outside his room, vowing to myself to become the man he wanted me to be, albeit while still a boy in years.

# Machiavelli

I want to say to Savonarola: Do you like having a dome over your head in the great Florence Cathedral? I'm sure he thinks little of the wonders, to say nothing of the necessity, of art and architecture, choosing instead to condemn those who have built the everlasting monuments in the city. If he read more of history, as I have, instead of chasing dreams, he might appreciate the Medici legacy and realize that without this family's contribution to Florence he would have nowhere to preach and spread his verbal venom.

Does he even know that Cosimo de' Medici gave us the dome? Yes, I know it was Brunelleschi who designed and built it, but without the patronage of Cosimo, Brunelleschi would have been confined to a cellar that housed madmen. Cosimo, to his credit, saw in this madman the seeds of genius, and we, the citizens of Florence, are now the recipients of an architectural miracle never before seen in western Europe. I would like the little friar of San Marco to know the facts. Thus, I present them to him personally: Above your head in the cathedral, dearest friar, while you speak of mysteries we can never know, is the embodiment of man's greatest achievement, created by a gifted mind, communicating to all of us below that during this time period, the *Rinascimento*, man can accomplish the impossible. I do not mean impossible in terms of seeing God. That is not only impossible, but also little more than a dream conjured by men, such as yourself, too weak to look life in the face and own up to the task of living it the only way one can: with courage and ingenuity.

If you study the facts, you will learn that the dome above your head was made with four million bricks, carried and lifted by men. Those bricks did not descend from the heavens one fine day in the month of May, as an act of benevolence from God, for he had nothing to do with it being built. He is not a laborer, sculptor or architect, as are men. He is, instead, invisible and indifferent to men's aspirations. When a man aspires to build a dome weighing 37,000 tons and have it stand upright without it collapsing under its own weight, I can say with certainty that man, not God, stands at the center of the universe as the most glorious of creatures.

The dome took sixteen years to complete, and now sixty years later it still stands. Show some appreciation for the work of Brunelleschi and the patron who allowed him to build when others thought him mad. The dome brought Cosimo glory, as it should have. Not every rich man can promote his image to the rest of the world through the building of architectural wonders.

The next time you preach, look up and consider the facts: men build with bricks that stand the test of time. Sermons, written on dreams, wash like water.

# Lorenzo

After my grandfather died, my father wrote, "I record that on the 1st of August, 1464, Cosimo di Giovanni de' Medici passed from this life, having suffered greatly from pains in his joints. He was seventy-seven years old. A tall and handsome man, he was possessed of great wisdom and kindness, and for that reason was trusted and loved by the people."

Having believed Medici power was most effective when least visible--the reason he rode a mule rather than a horse--he wished to be buried without pomp or show in the family's private crypt in San Lorenzo, wishing neither more nor less wax torches than were used at an ordinary funeral. Though he had never wanted to water the weed of envy, had he been to his own funeral he would have seen that the weeds had already grown tall, needing no further water. In the days leading up to my grandfather's death, complaints began to surface about my father's inability to inherit leadership. Leading citizens could see with their own eyes on the day of the funeral servants carrying my father by litter to the San Lorenzo chapel. My father could not have noticed, ill and grieving as he was, as I did, the many ambiguous expressions of grief on the faces of the men who were once my grandfather's friends: the same men who in two years time would plan, with the help of mercenary rebels, to ambush and then murder my father on the road leading from Careggi to Florence.

While innumerable candles glittered during the solemn ceremony, I saw the faces of Luca Pitti, Agnolo Acciaiuoli, Dietisalvi Neroni and Niccolo Soderini: men who looked on with the eyes of vultures, circling around a corpse, believing they had paid their dues under my grandfather's leadership and thus saw themselves as more capable leaders than my father. Such is the ambition of wealthy men. Has there been a time in history when this has not been true?

With my grandfather's death, they saw a crack in the door that had long been closed to them. They planned to open it, to walk in and take their rightful seats.

I wonder still why I thought more of those men on that day than the death of my grandfather. I believe now that my grandfather's spirit had passed into mine, ending my boyhood for good, while ushering my body, mind and soul into the world of men and politics. My grandfather's wish for me to become a man had manifested itself. Thus, I saw everything with a new set of eyes and sensed for the first time an understanding of life, void of innocence: men of ambition possessed no compunction when it came to killing and usurping those in power.

# Savonarola

Lorenzo died naïve. Allow me to explain. First, he saw himself as a Platonic philosopher-king, a benign despot who ruled selflessly on behalf of his people. The fantasy of himself as the idealized ruler evident is in his own words:

> *The majesty of our imperial throne*
> *Is built upon the emperor's good name.*
> *He is no private person on his own,*
> *But stands for all his subjects by acclaim.*

This image of his elevated self is nothing but the mindset of an egocentric man, reaching for stars, believing the sky rests above his head, unaware that the stars are spears, alight with fire, in the realm of hell. Secondly, he held out hope that his son Piero would succeed in carrying out the usual business of peace and prosperity for Florence and all of Italy. That did not happen. Piero failed miserably. I have already mentioned that if it weren't for my persuasiveness with King Charles of France this wondrous small republic, known as Florence, would be a city of ruins. Thirdly, he must have believed his inner circle of friends would further develop his and their humanistic ideals, solidifying Florence's place as a second Athens and the rebirth of all that was once glorious in ancient Rome. That also did not happen. Ficino lives an ignoble life: friendless, in poverty, left alone with useless volumes of Plato by his side. Angelo Poliziano and Pico della Mirandola, sadly, have passed to the other side, where, with God's mercy, they may some day see the light of heaven, though not before suffering the pangs of purgatory, or worse. I had become close with both men, once they aligned their better selves with Christian doctrine. They died, as young men, seven weeks from each other. How does one explain the sudden and unexpected passing of young men other than believing that God had punished them for being sodomites? I knew of their love for one another. To what extent that love manifested I cannot say. I do know that both men expressed remorse for

160

their former lifestyles and beliefs. I accepted their remorse and embraced them as brethren in the community of God. I would like to believe that God accepted their remorse as well, and in exchange for their former lifestyles and beliefs he took them from this earth to be with Him. God, after all, despite what his critics say, is as compassionate as He is vengeful.

Angelo Poliziano died first at the age of forty, after having been overcome with raging fevers. According to Pico, his friend had never suffered more than a minor cold before his sudden, rapid demise. Pico told me, much to our lasting satisfactions, that the poet denounced humanism in his final breath, hoping God would hear his denunciation. Less than two months later, while the French army marched into Florence, Pico lay on his deathbed, consumed with the same fevers as his friend. (I remember the time well because aside from having to appease Charles and dampen the fire of his potential rage, I had also to contend with the death of my mother in Ferrara.) Thirty-one-years young, Pico never fulfilled his calling to become a monk. He lived instead in a villa outside Florence with his concubine, unable to surrender his worldly appetites. Till the end, he apologized to me for having been just a man. He wished he could have been able to deflect life's temptations wholly and completely. He said only an extraordinary man, such as myself, could live on a higher plane, above beasts and men. Despite his weakness and failing, he begged me, with his final breaths, to be allowed into the Dominican order. He had already bequeathed all his possessions to San Marco and could do no more other than offer his soul. I could, of course, not allow such a request, given the circumstances of his life.

"I beg you, Girolamo Savonarola," he pleaded, holding my hand in his. The young friars in the room cried and begged me as well, on his behalf, to make an exception for him. After all, he had visited there daily, praying with them while fasting on water only, reading the Bible to them in Hebrew, teaching them the Greek and Turkish languages. He had, for all intents and purposes, become one of them.

Was his request then not reasonable, O God?

I looked deeply into his eyes as his breathing slowed, reflecting his imminent expiration. He tried to speak, though other than moving his lips no sound escaped them. I saw then in that moment a glow above his head, as if a halo had appeared. I knew God had sent it as a sign, telling me I could, if I wanted, make an exception for this dying man, for he was indeed holy and had always been from the beginning, even though, at first, he defied Christian theology with his unorthodox beliefs.

Had I not watched him burn his early, un-Christian, books, as evidence of his redemption from sins committed?

The glow above his head brightened. His eyes looked heavenward as the grip of his hand in mine softened and released itself. With my hands now free, I laid a Dominican robe over his body. His lips moved one last time, trembling to speak. He took his final breath and died.

With much weeping and great exhortations of sadness, the young monks placed him in his coffin wearing this robe. We prayed to St. Dominic and then to God, asking that our fellow monk be shown mercy in the life to come. That night, Pico appeared to me in a dream, saying that he was expiating his sins in purgatory. This remission had been granted on account of his alms giving to San Marco and the fervent prayers of the Dominican monks who had come to regard him as one of their brethren. Before he departed, he moved his lips and sounded his words clearly:

"Thank you, Fra Girolamo Savonarola."

# Machiavelli

To say it is God's will that young men, with no apparent history of illness, die suddenly, weeks apart, felled by the same fevers and fatal symptoms, is to dwell in dreams, for such a claim cannot be further from the truth. Pico and Poliziano were poisoned. Do I have proof for such an allegation? Of course not. Our science is not yet that advanced. Give us a few years. The mind of man has no boundaries, as long as it follows a course of study based on what's real and observable. If Savonarola and his followers have their way, we will, all of us, retreat back into the bygone dark ages. Count me as one among many who steadfastly refuses to return there.

My conjecture is founded on what I know of the history of men, both here in Italy and abroad. What felled Socrates, Cleopatra and Demosthenes so suddenly? What caused the early demise of Drusus, son of Tiberius, as well as Claudius, Brittanicus, Germanicus, and Domitia? Poison, my friend—though I do not mean that poison *is* my friend. I offer, as well, an example from recent history, not far from where I stand: the sudden death of Gian Galeazzo Sforza, the rightful heir in Milan. Does anyone in possession of sense believe he died of natural causes at age twenty-five? Was that a smile on his uncle Ludovico's face, to learn of his nephew's death, knowing he could rule, though illegally, unimpeded? I could, if I wanted, drag up through the annals of time many more names of political and social standing. Good grief, Nero attempted to poison the entire Roman senate! But I wish not to bore you with excessive detail, for I believe I have made my point. Poison has been around for centuries, and since it cannot be detected it is the most convenient way for people with evil hearts to dispose of a person. Keep in mind that most people are not fortunate enough, as rulers, popes and kings are, to employ a slave as a taster of food and drink.

Assuming my assertion is correct, the next question is, who poisoned them? I suspect Piero de' Medici. Living in exile--many believe he had gone to Venice to seek support

163

and, more importantly, an army, for he harbored thoughts of returning to Florence to reclaim his leadership--he felt betrayed by Lorenzo's inner circle of friends for having formed alliances with Savonarola who, by this time, had become the unofficial ruler of many people who once supported the Medici. He had nothing to gain, of course, by poisoning the poet and philosopher of Florentine renown other than acquiring the satisfaction of vengeance. To such a small-minded person as Piero this act of cowardice to murder without a plan seems consistent with his unfortunate nature. Am I saying or implying that to murder someone--two in this case--is an excusable act if the act has the foundation of a sound plan? If murder is necessary for the survival of the state, then, yes, without question, it is justifiable. I do not wish to conjecture, however, about generalized murders. I wish to address these cowardly acts of murder by poison. If Piero's jealousy of Savonarola is taken out of the equation, with what are we left other than Piero's immaturity and spite, knowing he did not possess the loyalty of friends as did his father?

It is best that Lorenzo is no longer around to hear of such sadness coupled with madness. One can only imagine his reaction to learning that his son murdered his beloved friends, whom he loved, especially Poliziano, as much as family and blood. It is not beyond the unreasonable passion inherent in men to believe his rage at his son--he was known for having a temper when provoked--would result in an act of filicide.

Here I go again with my conjectures. I apologize for my rambling in excess. The point is Lorenzo is better off where he is, even if it's hell, though I believe in no such place as an afterlife. If there is such a place, we live it in the here and now because when men poison each other here on earth, it is as much a hell as can be believed.

# Lorenzo

My grandfather and father died while their wives kept vigil near their beds. I have no wife to comfort me. Clarice died five years ago. I have had many mistresses, but a man cannot ask a mistress to care for him when he is ill. A mistress is for love. A wife is for death.

Clarice died of long-suffering consumption. I did not attend her funeral, and for that I received many reproaches from leading citizens. I was at the time away from Florence, taking mineral baths in Filetta. My physician considered the treatment imperative to my health. I had no way of knowing the imminence of Clarice's death. I regret that I could not be by her side at her time of need. Though she had never been the center of my life, I remained close to her, respecting that she had given me seven healthy children. In truth, we shared few interests other than the children. While she came from the distinguished Orsini family in Rome, her mind reflected a simple narrowness, especially in regard to the love of my life: the artistic, intellectual and cultural vibrancy of Florence. Yet now I desire, as much as anything, to have her simple nature near me to console me in my final days.

My mother and father had a more devoted relationship than I had with Clarice. I often wondered if their shared Florentine blood afforded them that mutual devotion. I recall their writing to each other when one or the other was away from home. "Every day seems a year until I return for your and my consolation," I once read in a letter my mother wrote my father. He typically replied, sometimes saying aloud, that he awaited her return "with infinite longing." Perhaps if Clarice had been a Florentine girl I would have felt the same toward her. None of my forebears before me had married into a family outside of Florence. Why my parents had sought a foreign bride for me I understood. Did I not do the same for my eldest son, Piero? They wanted the Medici to be greater than any Florentine family, and having me marry into a family that included Cardinal Latino Orsini, as well as powerful political leaders, we could expand our ambitions in far more reaching ways. We could not only control the banking world, we could make cardinals and popes and thus become the leading dynastic family in Italy.

I met Clarice on my first trip to Rome, when I was seventeen, at a banquet the Orsini family hosted for Pope Paul II. I noticed her height, though she was only thirteen, and her long red hair. I greeted her; she smiled. That was all. I had no knowledge then that in two years I would become engaged to her. I could see in her manner, especially in the way her eyes darted downward when I said "Hello, pleased to meet you" that she conveyed a shy, modest nature, much unlike the girls in Florence, who held their heads high, as in evidence of their confidence and worldliness. Our encounter lasted but a moment and in no way captured my imagination or excited my passions.

Nonetheless, my parents decided that Clarice, with her aristocratic connections, best suited me for a wife. Because my father's poor health made it even more pertinent that I marry sooner than later, my mother traveled to Rome for the express purpose to observe my future bride. I recall reading amusedly the letter she sent my father, providing him with specific details of Clarice's body, as if my mother were there to buy a prized cow.

"She is of good height and has a nice complexion; her hair is reddish and abundant, her face rather round, but it does not displease me. Her throat is fairly elegant, but it seems to me a little meager, or to speak better, slight. Her bosom I could not see, as here the women are entirely covered up, but it appeared to me of good proportions. She does not carry her head proudly like our girls, but pokes it a little forward; I think she is shy; indeed I see no fault in her save shyness. Her hands are long and delicate. In short, I think the girl is much above the common, though she cannot compare with our daughters, Maria, Lucrezia and Bianca."

When my mother returned I listened as she and my father spoke about the matter of my marriage.

"Your report of the girl was less than enthusiastic," he said.

"I did not want to raise your hopes too high."

"You did not raise my hopes at all."

"The girl is handsome, despite all I wrote."

"Though not beautiful?"

"It is not necessary for her to be beautiful. She must give our son healthy heirs. That is most important."

"In addition to the political and financial standing of her family."

"She is a malleable girl and will thus easily adapt herself to our ways."

"Let us celebrate this match, then."

I understood at an early age that men in my position did not marry for love. I received Clarice as I would a gift. I accepted her as someone who would bear and manage my children. I could expect, as was the custom for men of wealth and status, to find emotional and sexual fulfillment outside the matrimonial bed.

Though I married Clarice to fulfill a duty to my family and its continuing legacy, my mother, not Clarice, would remain the most important woman in my life. She possessed great intelligence and social sophistication, and in the short time my father ruled, she made up for whatever shortcomings he possessed. She, in fact, took care of political business, maintaining the loyalty of the literally thousands of clients whose support was necessary to maintain our power. On an almost daily basis, I saw her correspond with nobles and dignitaries from near and far. Many times she went on important missions because my father couldn't travel. Ahead of her time as a woman, she appreciated the new trends in literature, embracing the pagan appetites of those who surrounded her, becoming herself a literary patroness and fine poet. I have kept a note that resides in the drawer near my bedside, as a testament of my pride. Gentile Becchi, one of the most renowned tutors in all of Florence, wrote to my mother, lauding her talents:

"You are well read, your bureau full of books, you have understood how to comment on the epistles of St. Paul, you have, throughout your life kept company with men of honor."

She suffered fevers and eczema, and frequented mineral baths looking for cures. She made the spa at Bagno a Morba in the Apennine foothills into a thriving business. When she died in 1482, the canon of San Lorenzo, Francesco da Castiglione, wrote to me:

"What part of the state did the wisdom of Lucrezia not see, take care of, or confirm! Sometimes your mother's actions from the political point of view were more prudent than yours, for you attended only to the great things and forgot the less. She knew how to manage the most important affairs with wise counsel, and to succor the citizens in time of calamity."

I had lost not only a mother, whose emotional love and support I received without condition or negotiation, I lost, as well, a social and political confidante, for she possessed much savvy and wisdom in matters of state. I could not have ruled the city for so many years without her guidance. Clarice, for all her devotion and patience, lacked an understanding of the ways of the world, and she never showed much interest to learn them. She arrived in Florence a simple Roman girl and stayed that way, turning a blind, indifferent eye to the cultural vibrancy surrounding her. Never was her narrowness more evident than in the feud she had with Angelo over how best to educate our children when Clarice, the children and Angelo, their tutor, lived under the same roof at Caffagiolo, while I remained in Florence. Clarice did not like the texts Angelo used to instruct the children in Latin, drawn from pagan authors of antiquity. Clarice, traditional-minded, wanted the Book of Psalms instead of Seneca and Cicero. She worried that pagan literature would distract, if not infect, Giovanni, who was already being groomed for the church.

"She has taken Giovanni away from us," Angelo complained.

"She is the wife of my children," I said.

"Nonetheless, she cannot thwart the development of their minds with narrow-minded learning."

"I will do what I can to speak with her."

"I do not mean to disrespect your wife, Lorenzo. It's just that we are now living in the dawn of a new day. We cannot go back to archaic learning."

Clarice became infuriated with Angelo and demanded nothing less than his dismissal as the children's tutor. Though I sided with Angelo's views, I bowed to the wishes of Clarice. As the mother and caretaker of our children, she had earned her position. I, as had always been my diplomatic nature, attempted to appease both. I sent Angelo away to stay at the villa at Fiesole and appointed new tutors for my wife's satisfaction, believing the problem between Clarice and Angelo personal and thus irreconcilable. It helped little that Clarice had always been jealous of my relationship with Angelo, evident in a brief conversation on the subject.

"You love your friend more than me. That I know."

"I love him as a friend, and you as a wife."

"And it is with your friend your love resides most."

To that, I grew silent, not wishing to discuss the depth and breadth of my various loves. I found it especially curious why she never expressed jealousy over my many mistresses: why only Angelo's presence in my life bothered her so. I soon learned, much to my dissatisfaction, that even this new arrangement did not mollify Clarice. She felt my sending Angelo to stay at Fiesole rewarded more than punished him, for at Fiesole he could rest in cultivated idleness, writing poetry and entertaining friends, while staying in my best room. Meanwhile, she remained subjugated, staying at Cafaggiolo, an ancient fortress, full of dampness and drafts in the fall and winter. She became further displeased to find I had instructed the new tutors, explicitly, in fact, to teach my children in the new literature from the Greek and pagan writers recently discovered in Florence. I shouldn't have been surprised to learn that it was during this period she first contracted consumption, the illness that would consume her for the next five years until her death.

When Clarice died, I experienced a cumulative grief, having lost the last of the three most important women in my life. My grandmother, Contessina, had been the emotional glue in the Medici household, the woman who, though not educated and cultured, managed hearth and home, making sure everyone experienced joy and safety. I had been lucky to have her during my early years as ruler. When she died, I still had my mother to give me continued love and guidance. When my mother died, I had Clarice and my daughters. With the death of the woman who had borne me seven healthy children and had been a devoted presence in my life, I felt the air in my breath begin to thin.

I wished to have another chance to express words to Clarice. I had been remiss in my absence from her. I had relegated correspondence to her to Angelo and other companions with whom I traveled, having them update my whereabouts and general health and respond accordingly to her letters. If I had been more like my parents, I would have written my own words. I would have expressed deep longings of missing her and the children. I would have done so much more. Not only did I miss her death and funeral, I did not go to Rome and then escort her to Florence when we became legally wed. I sent my brother, Giuliano, and other delegates. I was then in the process of planning a jousting tournament in Santa Croce, in honor of my mistress, Lucrezia Donati, whom I can now call my greatest love. Poor young Clarice: though she came from the great city of Rome, she arrived a provincial, sheltered girl. What anxiety she must have experienced coming into the gates of Florence, seeing and sensing the vibrancy of so much culture and sophistication. I did not try to understand her feelings: what it must have been like for her to uproot herself and live in a foreign land with strangers and, in particular, with a man who sympathized little with her situation. To her credit, she remained stoic and accepting of the world that she would soon learn revolved exclusively around me.

I take these feelings--hardly comforting to know I disappointed my wife--to my grave. I wish, even now, that she had seen the letter I wrote to Pope Innocent VIII days after her death. I hold that letter in my hands now and read it yet again, hoping it will suffice as a testament for what she meant to me.

"Too often I am obliged to trouble and worry Your Beatitude with accidents sent by fortune and divine interposition, which as they are not to be resisted must be borne with patience. But the death of Clarice, which has just occurred, my most dear and beloved wife, has been and is so prejudicial, so great a loss, and such a grief to me for many reasons, that it has exhausted my patience and my power of enduring anguish, and the persecution of fortune, which I did not think would have made me suffer thus. The deprivation of such habitual and such sweet company has filled my cup and has made me so miserable that I can find no peace, and I have faith that in His infinite love He will alleviate my sorrow and not overwhelm me with so many disasters as I have endured during these last years."

While I appreciate my friends and doctors and the many dignitaries who come daily to see me, I desire most the women I have lost. I would even welcome their ghosts, if they were to appear, though I have as yet given in to such superstition. What hurts most is I do not even see my sweet Maddalena, my daughter, whom I had bequeathed to Pope Innocent's bastard son, Franceschetto Cibo, the same year as Clarice's death, for the express purpose of gaining greater glory for the Medici family. If I wanted Giovanni, my second son, to ascend the ranks and become considered some day to become a cardinal, I had to make a sacrifice of some kind. Maddalena, fifteen years old at the time, became that sacrifice. The truth is hard to bear: I gave her to a fat, hard-drinking, gambling, good-for-nothing, forty-year-old man. I have had to live since with the pain of knowing my beloved daughter will never know happiness, living as she is with this horrid man, the pope's bastard son, in Rome, the sink of all iniquities. Many times, as I do now, I whisper the words, "Your father is dying, Maddalena. He begs your forgiveness."

# Savonarola

I have seen my own death many times. I am not hanging on a cross, nailed and bleeding, like our Savior, Jesus Christ. If I had my way, though, I would emulate him and walk in his path to die like a martyr. No greater glory than that could I wish. I often walk the dark corridors, holding a taper in my hands, looking at the many frescoes Fra Angelico painted of the crucifixion. As the candle wax drips and burns my skin, I wish only that I can place my face, body and blood on the cross and free Jesus from his suffering. Take me instead, I say to God. I offer you my body, for I am not worthy. None of us are. How many times I have blown out the candle and have fallen to the floor; how many times I have wept until the breaking dawn; how many times I have wished for the only outcome that matters to me: to die and be with God. I must be patient He tells me. I have work here on earth, where men must be made to see His truth. I have tried, I tell God, though I might have more success converting mules.

I pick myself off the floor each day and do my best, though I am not Jesus, our Savior. I am a poor friar, a humble servant of God. The death I see for myself is not as dignified and will not be recorded in the annals of history. Still, my pain and humiliation will be great. Men will torture and tear me limb from limb, and then cut my body into pieces. They will burn what is left of me, cheering as they do. I know this outcome to be true, for I have seen it as a vision late at night in my cell. I do not suppress it when it appears. I welcome it. I can bear the violence of man, for my body is little more than an empty vessel. Why should I care then to lose my limbs? Let them take them and all my bones and organs. It is my soul for which I care most. That they cannot have, for God alone is its caretaker. Why should I care then to die at the hands of man? I expect it. I always have, for it is what men do when they are afraid of God's truth. Jesus himself tried to tell them. If he didn't succeed, why would I? I accept my fate. It is God's will.

# Lorenzo

Though I was stronger and more athletic than my forebears, they lived longer lives. I have no right to complain. I could have died earlier, as my brother did, cut down by conspirators in his youth at age twenty-five. I should have died with him, at age twenty-nine, which was, after all, the conspirators' main objective, but fate or chance--do I dare say God?--intervened. I have lived to rule another fourteen years. They have been good years. I have loved; I have created and procreated; I have built a lasting legacy; I have not cheated myself. Perhaps time has cheated me, but I have done much in this world in the time afforded me. Though I have suffered illness and now impending death, I have not allowed my life to be distracted. I have been a patron of the arts; I have overseen architecture; I have brought beauty and learning to the city; some will say I have swindled, cheated, forged and embezzled. I can't deny that I have, though few understand the reason. I have built and created careers. I have given back to Florence, just as my grandfather had done. We Medici are not the tyrants others believe us to be. We are builders and creators. I hope people will consider that as the season's leaves turn not just for now, but also in the far, unseen future. We live imperfect lives in imperfect times and those of us who are fortunate or unfortunate to be wealthy must rule the city, if for no other reason than to maintain the wealth we have. If you are not one of us, you cannot understand our ordeals. I would have you ask my brother, Giuliano, if he were around, to verify what I say. He could, perhaps, explain better our crisis.

I hope those in heaven hold a place for him, for, in truth, they failed to protect him that fateful day, choosing instead to spare me. I didn't ask to be spared. I would have gladly given my life to see my brother live his, for in both looks and manner he appeared more god-like than me. The gods should have recognized that and saved the man more suitably carved in their image. I say what I do because mostly I have heard the opposite view expressed: sad as it was that he died, it was much better for the state that I survived, for I was the ruler, not him. Yes, and if I weren't the ruler, a conspiracy would not have existed, and he would have lived. Keep the tragedy of our family in mind before you condemn us. Conspirators do not conspire to kill common men. They want to kill and replace the rich and mighty. My grandfather had warned me--had he not?-- about the weeds of envy. Still, who would have thought the cathedral, of all places, not the safest of places to be in Florence? Why would God condone such an act of violence in his house? I have often asked that of him, though I have never received his answer.

I have trained my mind not to revisit the details of my brother's murder. I leave that to history. I have worked hard instead to preserve the memory of his gifts that earned him the title *The Prince of Youth.* He did not possess my introspective, melancholic nature. He had an easy grace, a winning personality and an infectious smile. Who did not love Giuliano? Men and women alike gravitated to him, for good reason. He symbolized all that Florence stood for: youth, vitality and dynamism. If there were any consolation to his dying young, it would be his being spared what I now endure: the rapid decline of my organs and the eating away of flesh from my bones. It is a sight unbearable to my own eyes. I am glad Giuliano does not see me this way. I am glad, too, that I can recall the image of his beauty and athletic prowess untarnished by age and illness. I see him as he appeared at twenty-five: tall and sturdy, with a large chest, his arms rounded and muscular, his joints strong and big, his stomach flat, his thighs powerful, his calves full. I see his bright lively eyes and his olive-skinned face free of blemish, his thick, rich black hair worn long and combed straight back from the forehead. I see him doing what he did best: riding, hunting and loving; making all who met him speak in reverence of the gods who had endowed him.

The day I staged a joust for him at Santa Croce--was it 1475?--he rode into the square resplendent in armor, carrying the banner Botticelli painted, depicting Simonetta Vespucci as a helmeted Pallas Athene. As was the custom,

Giuliano dedicated his joust to the woman he loved. I had asked Angelo to immortalize Giuliano's day, for as well as Angelo being the finest poet of his age, he and my brother were inseparable friends. He wrote, though never finished, *Stanzas Begun for the Joust of the Magnificent Giuliano de' Medici*. His narrative bears little resemblance to the winter weather in Florence. It instead moves as a soft breeze that wafts in the Greek mountains of Arcadia, in a world of myth, pastoral and harmonious: a world filled with fragrant blossoms and populated by wood nymphs, most assuredly conjured while Angelo dreamed of Ovid and the gods and goddesses of pagan mythology. And why shouldn't he have placed Giuliano with the gods? It was where he belonged. It takes little effort for me to recall some of the narrative's lines:

*Cupid tells the assembled gods,*
*And you know what his arms and shoulders are.*
*How powerful he is on horseback: even now*
*I saw him so ferocious in the hunt that the*
*woods seemed afraid of him; his comely face*
*had become all harsh, irate, and fiery. Such were*
*you, Mars, when I saw you riding along the*
*Thermodon, not as you are now.*

It should be of no surprisse that Giuliano received the prize trophy that day and handed it to Simonetta, the most beautiful woman in all of Florence. That assessment comes not from me solely. It was widely known and acknowledged by all. Though married to Marco Vespucci, her fidelity to him in no way discouraged Giuliano, Botticelli or any other man in Florence from making her his romantic ideal. A year after the joust, Simonetta died of consumption at twenty-two years of age. Angelo remarked that the gods in realizing they had made her image too much like theirs, took her from us in the flowering of her youth. On the day of her funeral, thousands followed her coffin as it was paraded around the city, speaking not her name but rather the titles she had earned: *The Queen of Beauty* and *The Unparalleled One*. Her beauty had made her more than a woman. She had become a myth, the incarnation of a real-life goddess.

Never had I seen such outpouring of grief. Giuliano did not eat or ride or hunt for days. He sat in a darkened room, holding the many dresses her father-in-law had given him for keepsake. Botticelli requested, upon his death, to be buried at her feet in the Church of Ognissanti. One only needs to look at his most famous paintings, depicting Flora and Venus, to see her face and to authenticate the words he once spoke to me.

"Beauty like that can never die. It must live for prosperity."

She died April 26, 1476. Two years later, on this same date, Giuliano died at the hands of conspirators. Coincidence? To those of us who followed the loves and losses of gods and the mythology of death, the dates of their dying did not go unnoticed without some reference to love being reunited on a higher plane, in a distant place. Angelo wrote the most memorable lines of his unfinished poem after Simonetta's untimely death, though, without knowing it at the time, he foretold Giuliano's fate as well. The words, even now, have remained etched in my brain. Perhaps only in my own death can I escape them.

*The air seems to turn dark and the*
*depths of the abyss to tremble,*
*the heavens and the moon seemed*
*to turn bloody, and the stars seemed to*
*fall into the deep. Then he sees his nymph rise*
*again, happy in the form of Fortune and the*
*world grows beautiful again: he sees her govern*
*his life, and make them both eternal through fame.*

*In these confused signs the youth was shown*
*the changing course of his fate: too happy, if*
*early death were not placing its cruel bit on his*
*delight. But what can be gainsaid to Fortune*
*who slackens and pulls the reins of our affairs?*

176

# Machiavelli

One of the conspirators, Giovanni Battista, Count of Montesecco, backed out at the last moment when he learned the killings would take place in the Florence Cathedral. He did not want to commit murder in church, where, to use his own words, "God would see him." I have always had a good laugh about that. Didn't he know God would have seen him just as easily on a street or in a palace or villa? I should defer to Savonarola on such matters, but isn't God, after all, omniscient? Why should it have mattered that the killings took place in church? It didn't matter to the two priests who stood behind Lorenzo with their knives poised and ready to pierce his flesh with mortal wounds. Fortunately for Lorenzo, the priests were amateur murderers. Giuliano, standing more than twenty yards from Lorenzo, was not as fortunate to have amateur killers behind him.

The choir sang, and the organist played. As the priest saying Mass elevated the Host, as the congregation quieted and the bell chimed, the priest chanted to begin the ritual: *Accepit panem in sanctas ac venerabiles manus suas* (He took bread into his holy hands.) At that moment four men unsheathed their blades, unconcerned that their murderous intent took place in the house of God. Bernardo Bandini struck first, stabbing Giuliano in the chest, saying "Here traitor!" Francesco de' Pazzi, the lead conspirator, didn't say anything. He let his sword speak for him, as he stabbed Giuliano more than a dozen times. Twenty yards away, where Lorenzo stood, the priests first grabbed their target's shoulder to steady themselves before advancing with their blades. That ill-advised action gave Lorenzo enough time to react and thwart the knives coming at him. Chaos ensued, as the congregation pushed and shoved each other stumbling toward the exits. Someone shouted, "The dome is collapsing," for people still believed the dome was supported more by black magic than sound engineering. Lorenzo's friends quickly ushered him into the New Sacristy and bolted shut the doors. He had received a superficial wound to his neck and nothing more. One of his friends, Antonio Ridolfi, fearing that the priest's blade had been poisoned, sucked out the wound and spat the blood on the pavement. The conspirators fled, their job incomplete. Soon after a loud banging on the New Sacristy door and the sound of familiar voices signaled the arrival of friends. The door was unbolted. Surrounded by a cordon of armed men, shielding him from seeing his brother's fallen, bloodied body, Lorenzo made his way out of the church, into the street, where the great bell in the piazza had already begun to toll, alerting citizens that their government faced grave danger. Though grief-stricken and bloodied, Lorenzo, nonetheless, conducted business to fortify his palace and secure his regime. He wrote to the Duchess of Milan: "My Most Illustrious Lords. My brother has just been killed and my government is in the gravest danger. Thus, My Lords, the time is now that you can come to the aid of your servant Lorenzo. Send as many men as you can with all speed, as you are, always, the shield of my state and the guarantee of her health."

Just a boy at the time, I stayed close to my father's side. He, in his wisdom, believed that the kind of civil unrest we were about to witness rivaled any education I could receive from school or books. I am grateful to him for the knowledge I learned in a few short days, having seen violence of the kind that informed my sensibilities and imprinted on my consciousness how men defended liberty and meted out justice. We stood beneath the gates of the Medici palace, which had become a fortress after the well-stocked armories had been emptied. We saw armed men everywhere. The palace roof rang and resounded with the din of weapons above the cries of supporters below. Citizens of every classification and age, both young and old, came armed with homemade weapons made of sticks and metals. Even clergy and laymen stood among us, ready to defend the Medici house as they would the public welfare. I understood then what it meant to be a Florentine. My feelings of love and pride for the city of my birth were born that day and on subsequent days as the real-life dangers of living among men who killed each other out of senselessness supplanted the innocence of my youth.

I saw Lorenzo de' Medici for the first time. He appeared at his window with a bandage on his throat. We cheered for him, not caring that he had imposed upon us high taxes and had fixed elections. We cheered because he was the symbol of everything great about Florence: the cultural center of the world, where learning and civilization outshone every other place on earth. That's what I had been raised to believe, though I would learn in the following days that civilization often takes a backseat to vengeance and coldhearted murder. He spoke briefly to those of us standing below. "I commend myself to you. Control yourselves and let justice take its course. Do not harm the innocent. My wound is not serious."

His words held no influence over the mob. People demanded blood for the killing of Giuliano and for the audacity of attempting to kill their leader and thus rob them of their liberty. My father and I followed the mob to the Piazza, where I saw a man's body quartered and his head cut off. My father told me he was one of the priests who had tried to kill Lorenzo. What I heard mostly were the words "Death to traitors" spoken repeatedly, followed by cheers from the mob as the man's head was stuck on top of a lance and carried about the square and then all the way to the palace, beneath Lorenzo's window. By then I noticed other ghastly trophies of dismembered body parts as well. Florence had been known for its colorful festivities, but I had never seen a spectacle like this one. I suppose I should have been disturbed by it. However, the reverse is true. I shouted and cheered along with the mob, believing that by doing so I was participating in an important patriotic function. Even my father, normally mild-mannered, expressed primordial satisfaction, telling me he had never seen such violence in his lifetime. He had heard about bloodbaths in Florence in the centuries preceding ours. A temple dedicated to Mars, the Roman god of war, stood at the foot of the Ponte Vecchio for more than a thousand years before it was washed away in a flood in 1333. This god had a malevolent influence on Florentines, seeing to it that the streets were red with blood and the sky dark with ash from the many fires torching the city, day after day, night after night, and year after year. Times of peace are an anomaly. Man lives for war. The spirit of Mars walks not in the shadow of man. The spirit of Mars is man: even during this era many called the *Rinascimeto*. My father told me he felt both thrilled and ashamed at the same time. I shared his feelings.

The violence lasted for several days and reached its pinnacle in the piazza. We had heard that two of the main conspirators had been captured. We stood underneath the Palace of the Priors, waiting to see Florentine justice manifest and rear its ugly, though necessary, head. We were not disappointed. Francesco de' Pazzi, who had been found and dragged, bleeding and naked, from the Pazzi palace, appeared in an upper window. Still naked, his hands were bound behind his back and a noose placed around his neck. In a moment that brought a deafening roar from the mob that watched, his executioner shoved him from the upper window, whereupon his naked body twitched and dangled in the air. While the mob cheered and relished the sight of his limp, dead body, there appeared in the same window a man dressed in clerical vestments. My father informed me he was the archbishop of Pisa and a native son of Florence, Francesco Salviati, who had been brought into the conspiracy through the influence of the Pazzi family. We watched as an executioner secured a noose around his neck and shoved him from the window. His body, still alive, hung above the deceased Pazzi. As the rope lowered slightly, I saw him sink his teeth into the corpse beside him. I thought I had only imagined seeing this gruesome sight. It soon became evident that others saw it as well. A man shouted, "Look, he is biting the naked traitor!" Even after the rope had choked away his final breath, the archbishop's teeth remained fixed in Francesco Pazzi's breast, while his eyes stared madly at the mob below.

I can't recall with certainty how many executions I witnessed. I know only that at one time in the Piazza I could see the bodies of more than two dozen men hanging limply, in various positions of height and depth, as if they were ornaments in the sky. Lorenzo took no direct part while the executions were carried out. He also did not intervene or stop anything. Though he was a prince who slept and ate with greater luxury than other men and surrounded himself with many sensual delights, including the viewing of art, the reading of literature, and the writing of poetry, his blood boiled with vengeance like any other man. He acted swiftly and decisively to mete out punishment on his own terms, seeing to it that the Pazzi family's assets and properties were liquidated and laws passed penalizing anyone who married into the disgraced clan, obliterating the name from public consciousness.

Jacopo Pazzi, the patriarch of the family, received the worst punishment of all. After he was executed by hanging, city officials--his family members had either been exiled or murdered--laid his body to rest in the family crypt at Santa Croce. Soon after the weather turned cold and rainy, destroying crops and making life miserable. People blamed the burial, saying it was divine retribution for the sin of burying a traitor in consecrated ground. Citizens dug up his body and buried it near the city wall, with other common criminals. The weather improved after that. Afterwards, a group of young boys dug up his body a second time and paraded the stench of his remains around the public square, singing songs, while the noose remained around his neck. When they tired, they threw what was left of him in the Arno river.

How does a city that created so much art resort to such violence, you may ask? Consider that art and violence are sometimes strange bedfellows. Leading citizens, Lorenzo among them, commissioned Botticelli to paint mug shots of the condemned men on the walls of the chief magistrate's palace. Under the portrait of Bernardo Bandini, who had yet to be found, Lorenzo wrote the following verse:

*I am Bernardo Bandini, a new Judas.*
*A Traitor and killer in a church was I.*
*A rebel awaiting a more cruel death.*

181

# Savonarola

I paid no attention to the crisis in Florence in April 1478. I had left the world of men, in all its sordid wickedness, two years earlier, entering the monastery in Bologna. Nothing surprised me about men's machinations and murderous ambitions. Death was the price tyrants paid for believing themselves above others, for believing that power and honor belonged to them alone. To that end, I say this: Life at the top of a mountain is precarious. Sometimes volcanoes erupt.

To live in their world was death; to die in Christ was life. I chose life, and I had never been happier than in those early years, far from the cares of political strife and shameful violence. Men live lives of illusion, believing their murderous deeds necessary installments in their manhood. They do not know they are false satisfactions because in the end they will suffer for their sins.

I gave myself freely and openly to the ascetic life, where I found liberty and salvation, believing I had passed from the dark of the world to the light of Christ. On my first night, I visited the tomb of Saint Catherine of Bologna. Her body, intact and fragrant with the odor of sanctity, was on view for the veneration of the faithful. I wrote in praise of her:

> *Virgin, thus with hope I come*
> *With hands pressed together and knees bent*
> *Though I am but a worm and mere mud*
> *Your lofty, singular virtues*
> *Will bear some fruit in me, I know.*

I did all I was told, though in secret I disagreed with much I saw and heard. Many in the order lobbied for the right of monks to own communal property. I held to the austere view that monks should live in poverty and eat and drink only when necessary. St. Dominic had written, "I invoke God's curse and mine upon the introduction of possessions into this order," believing all monks should observe chastity, humility and voluntary poverty. I did not voice my view, for as a novice monk I felt it best to weep and be silent. I cleaned and served meals and performed menial tasks, listening to preachers preoccupied with humanistic philosophy and learning, giving evidence to what I had already believed: that Christians, even the practitioners, had become too earthbound. I believed we should learn the books of Jesus Christ, for they more than any contained the truth of God's message to his followers. I therefore studied the Bible day and night, learning it word for word, paying homage to the Chaste Virgin, the uncorrupted Church of ancient times, lamenting the passing of the early saints, the great preachers and contemplatives, the holy virgins, clerics and saintly bishops who, armed with the Old and New Testaments, once vanquished the Church's enemies.

I learned to perform *the discipline:* the mortification of the flesh through self-administered whippings. I did not want to deny myself in moderation, as I saw others do. I wanted to emulate St. Dominic and Christ and all the saints who paved the path before me. I wanted to inflict my body with as much adversity as I could, knowing that if I did I would deliver it to perfect purity of the soul. St. Francis wrote, "I have no greater enemy than my body. We should feel hatred towards our body for its vices and sins." I taped his words to the skin of my arm to remind myself at all times. St. Dominic walked barefoot for miles over rocks and rubble. I did the same. He whipped himself three times a night with an iron chain: once for himself, once for sinners in the world, and once for the sinners suffering in purgatory. I did the same. Wilbirg of St. Florian chastised himself with an iron girdle that he wore under his clothing. I did the same, inflaming my skin, believing as he did, that such affliction would bring eternal rewards. I imitated Christ's suffering on the cross, whipping and scourging myself, then standing for hours with my arms stretched to either side. I found my justification for depriving myself of sleep in the Scripture of Luke 6:12: Jesus, before choosing his twelve Apostles, kept a vigil on a mountainside, praying all night to God. I stayed awake, praying till the break of dawn. I bathed my eyes in vinegar, feeling them burn and sting, making it impossible for me to sleep. I did not eat. I wanted to fill myself only with the love of God. I drank water, for I had heard St. Catherine of Siena died of thirst. She was, in fact, a hard act to follow. She forced herself to regurgitate by inserting plant stems or branches down her throat to her stomach, saying as she did, "And now we will deliver retribution to this most wretched sinner."

While I surrendered my body to God, I rejoiced in theological scholarship. I discovered St. Thomas Aquinas. His Aristotelian approach to God's existence proved to me that the belief in God is a science. It is not as many fools believe a construct of voodoo or magic. The laws of logic and faith, in conjunction, support His existence. One only needs to study Aquinas' *Quinquae Viae* (Five Proofs). I had, of course, already received the benefit of knowing his existence. I received it from the most reliable source: from God himself, when he spoke to me in church. Nonetheless, Aquinas proved *A Priori* (through reason alone) that God's existence was true and real, and anyone wishing to deny it would have to dispute the study of the greatest scholastic and theological philosopher the Christian world has known. I know of no one capable of such a feat.

Of no surprise, Aristotelian logic is not something Florentines understand. They are more inclined to that which is voodoo and magic, as is evident in their study and adulation of Plato. It is no wonder that many murders, deaths and tragedies have befallen them when they cannot distinguish what is true from what is not.

# Lorenzo

I understood life's fleeting passage. I saw it every day in the country, in nature, when I was a boy, observing the warm summer days become the chill winter nights. The passing of time to me became the passing of life, as was evident in the animals we housed and those we hunted. I wrote verse, even then, wishing to make the most of the gifts I possessed, both materially and spiritually.

*Autumn returns. The sweet ripe fruit is picked.*
*The days of warmth and sunshine pass away.*
*The trees, of flowers, fruit and leaves, are stripped.*
*Gather the rose, oh nymph, now while you may.*

I had no idea then I foretold the fates of Giuliano and Simonetta and the end of the golden era in Florence. Seven years before he was assassinated, I had campaigned for Giuliano to become a cardinal. I had hoped, at eighteen years of age, he would exchange his tailored clothes and the carefree life he lived for scarlet robes and a red zucchetto in the holy seat of Rome. His ascendancy would assure our family's elevation from bankers to nobility. Such plans for him and all we Medici became the root cause of his demise, for they brought me on a collision course with Pope Sixtus IV, who controlled all spiritual realms.

My brother, though generally complicit, wanted to make his way in the world far beyond the shadow the Medici name cast over him.

"I have little aptitude or interest in the church," he said.

"We will read scripture together," I responded.

"I prefer fast horses over scripture."

"You can have both."

I explained how it was not uncommon for a man of the world to become a man of the cloth. Wealthy men who rode fast horses and enjoyed the sensual pleasures of life, in fact, governed the Church.

"I am currently a student," he said, "engaged in studies that you yourself have directed for me, under the tutelage of Angelo Poliziano. Am I to surrender learning philosophy and literature for the reading of scripture?"

"Yes, if it means the addition of prestige and power to our family."

"Who will assist you, as I do now, entertaining dignitaries and deputizing at state functions in your absence?"

"I respect and honor the help you provide me now. But if you are a cardinal, you will be able to help in more valuable and immeasurable ways."

"I am your servant, brother, and will do as you believe is best for you and our family, yet in doing so I will become the most unhappy man in all of Italy."

"You will have greater power than me."

"No one can have greater power than you, for you are loved everywhere."

As I would soon learn, being loved was not the same as having my desires met. I visited Rome, bearing, as was the custom, ample gifts for the new pontiff: four hundred pounds of silver plates, vases and saucers. I kissed his feet, and he told me he would appoint someone "close to the heart of all the citizens of Florence." The newly appointed pope, despite his promise to me, was in no hurry to nominate a Florentine as cardinal. He treated the Holy Church like a family-run business, nominating instead two of his nephews, Pietro Riario and Giuliano della Rovere, making the former, to the shock of all Florentines, archbishop of Florence, which meant he drew income from our city without actually setting foot in it. It was one of the many corruptions afforded to prelates.

The pope's motives soon became evident. The Rovere clan, of which he was a descendant, had been impoverished for many years while less deserving clans lorded over vast feudal estates and surrounded themselves in unimaginable luxury. Thus, Pope Sixtus had a chip on his shoulder and made it his mission to advance his family name by buying up properties. One such property was the town of Imola, north of Florence, which at the time was owned by Duke

Galeazzo of Milan. Florence had always desired to add Imola to our empire. At the very least it was important that we keep it out of unfriendly hands. Therefore, when we learned of the pope's intent to purchase Imola for his nephew, Girolamo Riario, as a wedding present, we paid 100,000 ducats to the Duke in return for the contested city. Enraged by the transaction, Pope Sixtus threatened Milan with excommunication, wherein the city would suffer economic collapse. Thus, the Duke tore up the agreement he had made with us and offered Imola to the pope for the discounted price of 40,000 ducats. Shortly after, the pope asked me for a loan to make the purchase. I knew if my brother had any hope of becoming a cardinal I would have to grant the loan to the pope and in the process lose territory important to our city. My critics have always condemned me for placing self-interest ahead of civic responsibility. Where were those critics then when my patriotism for my city recoiled at the prospect of a powerful papal enclave on Florence's northern border? Not wanting to provoke the wrath of my fellow citizens, I refused the pope's request for a loan.

# Machiavelli

Though Lorenzo should have known that relations with the pope would not end well, how could he have known the course he embarked upon would encourage conspiracy and murder? He had hoped that by refusing the pope a loan the deal would fall through, especially if the Pazzi bank in Rome also complied in refusing to offer the loan. Lorenzo corresponded with Francesco de' Pazzi, requesting that he not loan the pope money, if asked. Lorenzo assumed that Francesco, as a native Florentine, would comply with his wish, understanding how important Imola was to Florence. What Lorenzo failed to perceive was the depth of Francesco's hatred toward him. To this end, you can either credit Francesco's masterful deception or Lorenzo's naivety. In Lorenzo's defense, I say this: it takes someone of equal deceptive, if not evil, ability to see beyond a man's smile or his nod of the head or his seemingly kind words and complicit manner. Lorenzo, in his infinite innocence, trusted people. How could he have known Francesco's reason for leaving Florence to live and work in Rome was due to him and, in particular, the larger-than-life shadow he cast over the Pazzi family, depriving it of honor? Lorenzo, due to fortune, inherited honor. Thus, he never understood it to be the scarce commodity it was to others. It is, in fact, the most heralded word in all of Florence to men of wealth and status. I have on many occasions heard a man say, "Life without honor is a living death." To men of prestige and power, Aristotle's words are etched in their brain: "People of superior refinement and of active disposition identify happiness with honor: for this is, roughly speaking, the goal of political life."

Florentine government denied the Pazzi the political life they sought. While Lorenzo allowed Francesco's uncle Jacopo to serve on occasion in honorable positions, he never gave him a central role in the government to which his wealth and status entitled him. Even outside of government, the Pazzi felt dishonored, as was evident in Lorenzo's famous jousting tournament in 1469. It was perhaps a defining moment in Francesco de' Pazzi's future as a conspirator and later as a man hanging from a noose, naked and limp. In the joust, Francesco knocked Lorenzo off his horse, yet the man he sent sprawling into the dust walked away with the trophy and, more importantly, with the honor afforded to the champion. Francesco said afterwards, "that fortune did him a thousand wrongs." He left for Rome, no longer able to live as a dim light in the galaxy where Lorenzo's star outshone him.

So is it any surprise that Francesco de' Pazzi not only gave the pope the loan he desired, but told the pope, as well, what Lorenzo had requested of him? It was the worst possible outcome for Lorenzo. Not only had he failed to block the sale, but he also inherited the pope's wrath and in doing so gave an advantage to his banking rivals. The Pazzi family saw Lorenzo's quarrel with the pope as a crack in the Medici foundation. They hoped to further weaken this foundation, seeking to profit from their rival's problems and to place themselves once again in their rightful place at the pinnacle of Florentine society.

Two further issues between the pope and Lorenzo made the Pazzi ascendancy an even likelier possibility. Pope Sixtus appointed Francesco Salviati Archbishop of Pisa, a city, at the time, still under the jurisdiction of Florence. Though Salviati was a native son of Florence, he was disliked because he had played a part in the Imola transaction, having conveyed the money borrowed from the Pazzi to the Duke of Milan, thus solidifying the deal. Prior to the nomination, Lorenzo had given the pope a list of candidates that he and the Signoria endorsed. After all, for centuries, Florence had chosen its own archbishops. The pope, however, disregarded the recommendations. Lorenzo fought vehemently to negate the nomination. The pope used his papal power in overstepping tradition. Lorenzo, with the backing of Florence's leading citizens, decreed that he would not allow Salviati to enter into Tuscany. Pope Sixtus called Lorenzo "a depraved and malignant spirit and a usurping tyrant."

Relations between the men grew worse. The Vatican wanting to seize the town of Citta di Castello on the border of Tuscany asked Lorenzo for military assistance. Already suffering from the loss of Imola, Lorenzo did not want to see further papal presence in the Tuscan region. Besides, he and the ruler of Castello had enjoyed an alliance. Once again, Lorenzo had to consider the feelings of the Florentine citizens. If he assisted the pope, his own people would revolt. Thus, again, he refused to assist the Vatican. Pope Sixtus, not surprisingly, became enraged. To punish Lorenzo, the pope withdrew the papal accounts from the Medici and gave them to the Pazzi as a reward for their role in the Imola purchase and their willingness to put the pope's interests ahead of those of their native country.

The Pazzi star had begun to rise, while Lorenzo's began to fall. Why, then, did the Pazzi star, in the end, crash and burn and disappear into nothingness? Here's where the Pazzi made a grievous mistake: Instead of conspiring to murder the Medici brothers and assume leadership of Florence, they should have waited patiently for Lorenzo's financial collapse, as was likely to happen given the loss of the papal accounts. If this collapse were to occur, Lorenzo would have inevitably lost power and status in the eyes of his citizens, rendering the Pazzi conspiracy and planned rebellion unnecessary. The Pazzi, for all their wealth and ancestral nobility, were not smart men, however. Driven by jealousy and past grievances, they allowed their emotions to color their better judgments. When men make that fatal error, they stand to lose every time. Their plot to overthrow Lorenzo, with the pope's blessing, and assume leadership, believing the citizens of Florence would follow them, was nothing short of delusional. Here's the truth: even if successful in their plot, the Florentine citizens would have never lain down their lives for them because their war against Lorenzo was personal and had nothing to do with freeing the state from tyranny. Though Lorenzo may have ruled like a monarch, the people of Florence loved him. No one loved the Pazzi. Thus, if they had gained power, they would have been condemned as traitors, intent on selling out their city to the interests of Rome. They would have been driven from power in no time at all. Here's what they should have done before they proceeded with their cockeyed plan: they should have polled the people of Florence and asked if they desired change. They would have received a resoundingly clear answer: NO ONE WANTED CHANGE! Equipped with that information, the Pazzi could have cancelled their assassination plot and thus would have saved themselves unimaginable pain, shame and destruction.

If only they had consulted with me, I would have told them the foolishness of their plan. Yes, even at nine years old, I would have known enough to distinguish for them what is real and what could only remain an unrealized dream.

# Lorenzo

All of Italy and the rest of the world knew the truth: Pope Sixtus, though not the originator of the plot, had sanctioned the murders of my brother and me. When the plot failed, he wrote me a letter.

Why was I not surprised when he didn't offer condolences for my brother's death? He instead hurled abuse at me, threatening the destruction of Florence if I didn't step down as ruler. He called Salviati's execution unlawful. As a member of the clergy, he deserved ecclesiastical rather than secular judgment. What really bothered him was the manner of his punishment.

"What kinds of monsters live in Florence?" He wrote. "It is an intolerable affront to the dignity of the Holy Church to hang a bishop in his clerical vestments—on a Sunday, no less."

The irony of his stinging criticism did not go unnoticed. Why is it okay with the Holy Church to murder two innocent men in a cathedral on a Sunday? Couldn't my enemies have waited till Monday and attack on a dark street, which is more conducive to the presence of evil? If Sunday is a good enough day to assassinate my brother and me, then it is equally good for the execution of traitors, whether they are naked or wear clerical vestments.

He wrote that I was a "son of iniquity and foster-child of perdition, with a heart harder than Pharoah's." My crimes were "kindled with madness, torn by diabolical suggestions disgracefully raged against ecclesiastical persons." Worst of all, he claimed I was one "who is not fit to rule—or live for that matter."

He punctuated his correspondence with a word written in capital letters:   EXCOMMUNICATION.

Again, I was not surprised by the threat of this word, given the history of papal behavior. Hadn't Pope Paul II told me when I was still a youth it worked "liked a charm?" Florence was now subject to incur spiritual and economic reprisals the likes of which it had never before seen.

# Machiavelli

The pope underestimated the citizens of Florence. We have never been people who can be bullied with threats. The Signoria issued a letter to the pope, declaring that they owed no obedience to one who had so brazenly abused his holy office. His patience tested, Pope Sixtus, in alliance with Naples, pulled his Ace of Spades from his already stacked deck of cards, declaring war on Florence "until such time as Lorenzo de' Medici is ousted from office."

I imagine the pope speaking of his motives: I shall make the cost to Florentine citizens so high they will question whether continued loyalty to Lorenzo is worth the price! Let's see how they like the invasion of Neapolitan troops around their borders!

He was right about one thing: we did not like the invasion of Neapolitan troops in our surrounding Tuscan villages. Fortunately, the loss of lives was minimal. The reason for this has everything to do with the history of warfare in Italy. The Neapolitan troops were comprised of mercenaries, as were those defending Florence, and these men--do not confuse them with the French--had an aversion to bloodshed. The rule for them has always been this: "You pillage there, and we will pillage here; there is no need for us to approach too close to one another."

Wars such as these are not fought to kill people. They are fought to kill spirits, and this killing of the Florentine spirit is exactly what Pope Sixtus counted on happening. Though the advancing armies killed few, they destroyed farms, fields and orchards, killing people's livelihoods. The price of food skyrocketed, and many starved. It didn't help that a plague ravished Florence at the very same time, bringing sickness, disease, further famine and many deaths. This plague, along with the threat of excommunication and the terror of war, took its toll on citizens in terms of physical, economic and emotional hardships.

I imagine the pope thinking: how long will the people of Florence stand by Lorenzo while their fortunes dwindle and their families starve? Is this not the war of attrition Pope Sixtus had hoped for all along, without much cost in lives to the papal armies?

Meanwhile, the Medici banking business suffered because Rome and Naples had repudiated their massive debts. This financial loss resulted in Lorenzo resorting to two practices that tarnished his reputation. He embezzled money from his cousins' inheritance, of which he was the executor of their father's will; and he diverted funds for his private use from the state-run dowry fund (*Monte delle Doti*) of which citizens paid money. I still hear the cry of many, using the word "unscrupulous." I am not among the many who condemn his so-called immorality, and I shall discourse on the ambiguity of morality at a later time. Suffice it to say the situation was such that his collapse would inevitably have damaged the public interest. Here then is the truth: his borrowing the money, without the sanction of any law and without authority, was a necessary evil. The circumstance dictated his action, and anyone who doesn't understand that knows little of political expediency.

# Lorenzo

I saw the rising costs of bread and grain and the shutting down of trades and the growing poverty that resulted. I saw people begging in the street, victims of famine and disease. The citizens of my city bore many hardships. It is a mistake to believe I didn't, as well, feel pain and misery, for the war belonged to me alone, and I wished for nothing else but to have it done and over, especially in light of my citizens' continued support. How do I express what it meant to me to have their love at this time, knowing the security it brought me was the only saving grace of this otherwise hellish time?

I had to forgo all pleasures of visiting the country to groom and ride my horses, to entertain friends and engage in discussions of philosophy and literature. My family members, since the assassination attempt on my life, had been living in one villa or another, shuttling back and forth, observant of the threatening winds that blew in their direction. Angelo traveled with them. I have already spoken of the rift between him and my wife, have I not? It helped little that I was unable to visit them, despite Clarice's pleading words to do just that.

I contracted a serious illness and remained bedridden for weeks. I believed I suffered from the plague that had ravished so many others. Daily, I received correspondence from Clarice, the children, and Angelo. Their well wishes and updates of their lives, kept me hopeful. I did not express my worst fears to them, telling them only that I had contracted a cold that stubbornly refused to leave my body. My mother, servants and doctors kept vigil until, mercifully, it was ascertained I had malarial fever, not the dreaded plague. I informed my family that I would be recovered and on my feet shortly.

My illness gave me--ironic, I should say--some respite from my responsibilities as ruler, and this time in bed afforded me well, for when I did recover I reconciled to remedy the sorry circumstance I had created. The war and the suffering I witnessed had to end both for the sake of my people and my regime, which had been mostly favorable in my lifetime. I had to do all I could to avert it from ending ignominiously. I wracked my brain for days, finally deciding on a course of action that would either save us all or kill me in the process. In secret, I headed to Pisa, stopping halfway in the town of San Miniato, where I wrote a letter to the Signoria, laying out the steps I proposed to bring the war to a speedy conclusion.

# Machiavelli

On December 7, 1479, while his city faced threats of famine, disease, plague, excommunication and war, Lorenzo de' Medici wrote a historic letter to the government of Florence, hoping to quell the dissatisfaction that had grown like weeds in a beautiful garden. I share his letter in its entirety.

*Most Illustrious My Lords,*
*If I have not already informed Your Illustrious Excellencies of the reason for my departure it is not out of presumption but because it seems to me that the troubled state of our city demands deeds, not words. Since it appears to me that the city longs for and demands peace, and seeing no one else willing to undertake it, it seemed better to place myself in some peril than to further endanger the city. And so I have decided that with the blessing of Your Illustrious Lordships I will travel openly to Naples. Because I am the one most persecuted by our enemies, I believe that by placing myself in their hands I can be the means necessary to restore peace to our city. If His Majesty the King intends to take from us our liberties, it seems to me better to know it as soon as possible, and that only one should suffer and not the rest. And I am most glad to take that role myself for two reasons: first because since I am the chief target of our enemies' hatred I can more easily discover the King's intention, since it may well be that they seek nothing but to harm me; the other is that having received more honors and benefits from our city—not only more than I deserve but, perhaps, more than any other citizen in our day—I owe a greater debt than any other man to my country, even if I should have to sacrifice my life. It is thus with a good heart that I depart, knowing that perhaps it is God's will that this war that began with the blood of my brother and myself should be brought to an end by my own hand. My greatest wish is that by my life or by my death, by my misfortune or my prosperity, I should make a contribution to the*

*good of the city. I shall therefore follow the course I have set out, and if it succeeds as I wish and hope it shall, I shall have served my country and saved myself. Should, on the other hand, evil befall me, I will not mourn if it benefits our city, as it certainly must; for if our adversaries wish nothing but to seize me I shall already be in their hands, and if they want something else we shall soon know it. It is certain that our citizens will unite to protect their liberty, so that by the grace of God they will come to its defense as our fathers always did. I go full of hope, and with no other goal in mind than the good of the city, and I pray God to give me grace to perform what is the duty of every man towards his country. I commend myself humbly to Your Most Excellent Lordships.*

*Your Excellencies' Servant,*
*Lorenzo de' Medici*

# Lorenzo

I looked deeply at myself the night before I decided to leave Florence and travel to Naples. What I found convinced me that only by taking this mission could I bring redemption to my city and me. I had failed as a banker, and I possessed neither astuteness nor skill in military strategy. What I owned was the ability to charm people and make them love me. Though it may seem like a minor skill to own in life-and-death circumstances, it is, in truth, the most necessary skill to possess. Had it not served me well thirteen years earlier when I was still a boy, taking my first mission, and then later in Florence, among my people, both with leading citizens and the poor?

I had rehearsed what I needed to do: face King Ferrante eye to eye and make him see I held no threat; that I had only good intentions for my city and for the country. If Florence fell to the papal states it would be Naples' loss as much as ours, for the more powerful the pope became the weaker Naples would become, making the prospect for peace as beneficial for Naples as for Florence.

The perils of my trip revealed themselves to me. I could be detained as a prisoner of war. I could be killed, stuffed and propped at King Ferrante's table of notable enemies. How would such an ignominious end affect my chance for eternal salvation? Nonetheless, I needed to set aside any personal peril and proceed for these reasons: if I stayed home and did nothing, Florence--and I in terms of legacy--would lose. The Republic was dying from slow strangulation: financial, economic and spiritual. Peace would never come from Pope Sixtus, for he hated me with passionate irrationality. Besides, was he not winning the war of attrition?. King Ferrante had less emotional engagement in the affair, and had he not praised me thirteen years earlier for having, with courage, averted the coup against my father, saying, "our affection to you has grown remarkably"? Would not our history together trump recent controversies, which had resulted in Neapolitan troops camping on and destroying our lands?

I had charmed the snake before. I could do it again.

I am not naïve, though many have called me that. As I wrote the letter to the Signoria, I heard the collective voice of my critics: *His willingness to sacrifice himself and thus become a martyr is nothing more than his attempt to save his image, which has become, because of the war and the embezzlement of public funds, more negative.*

How could anyone believe anything other than the truth? I acted in the name of patriotism, for my love of Florence. I knew, for certain, that only a successful mission could quell talk of criticism.

When I arrived, ambassadors and members of the King's court greeted me warmly, though the King was not present. He had gone hunting a day earlier and still had not returned. I rode out a mile from the city to meet and greet him, hoping he would receive my gesture in good graces. He met my presence most graciously, using many kind words and assurances that he had only affection for our great city and wished to resolve whatever issues created a chasm between us. As the days passed, however, he seemed either too busy or reluctant to broach the subject of peace. I grew impatient with the slow pace of negotiations and walked in his room one day to address the urgency of the issue.

"I did not summon you, Lorenzo de' Medici."

"My deepest apologies, your Majesty."

"Where are those Florentine manners we barbarians here in the south hear so much about?"

"We are as impatient for peace as we are well-mannered."

He assured me again he wanted to end hostilities with Florence. At the same time, he did not want to jeopardize his relations with the pope. He had already been receiving displeasure from the pope because of my unexpected appearance in Naples.

"How can I make both you and the pope happy at the same time?"

"Peace, in the end, will make us all happy."

"How will defying the pope bring me peace? I will receive his wrath and vengeance. His bite is worse than yours. The Count of Urbino, Montefeltro, fights for him. He is the greatest soldier in all of Italy. I do not want to bring his enmity to our shores."

"I do not wish to bring you hardship, only peace."

"Do you know that only yesterday I received a correspondence from the pope? Do you know what he desires?"

"It cannot be good."

"The Holy Father wishes me to imprison you."

"I never knew you to be a man who lived under the spell of the pope."

"Nonetheless, he is the pope and thus holds jurisdiction over our souls. Does he not?"

"I would not entrust my soul to his care."

"Nor your life."

"Nor my life."

"And yet you entrust your life to me? I am a cruel and violent man to all my enemies. You must know that."

"I am not your enemy. I am your friend."

"And yet we are at war."

"It is the pope's war, not yours."

"I must honor my alliance with the Vatican."

"Have you considered who receives the greater gain in this war?"

"I do not follow your argument."

"If Florence falls to papal forces and the Vatican strengthens itself in the north, what will stop it from strengthening itself in the south?"

"And if Florence does not fall?"

"Then the balance of power remains, meaning peace for everyone."

"What you really mean is peace for you."

"And for you, as well."

"Why would a cruel and violent man such as myself desire peace?"

"Peace in Italy is most critical, now more than ever. The Ottomans are advancing as we speak. They will be on Italian shores, just south of here. Unless Italy unites against them instead of wasting our time on our own wars, the invasion of the Turks will eventually come to Naples.

That is the war, against the infidels, we must all fight. Why should Christian men fight each other and waste our resources? Even the pope, if he were a reasonable man, would agree with what I say."

"I like you, Lorenzo de' Medici, but that is not the reason I do not imprison you. My daughter-in-law is the reason. She is fond of you, and every day she champions your cause."

"I am fond of her as well."

"Do you know what I call her? Lorenzo's confederate."

"I am honored to have such a great friend."

Ippolita Sforza's loyalty to me had a foundation. After having met and befriended her in Milan when I was seventeen, I had since loaned her money on more than one occasion. Outside of my mother, she was the woman I admired most for her intellectual gifts. She was conversant with the great Italian poets and could quote Cicero at length. Even more impressive, she could read Plato in his native language. When I wasn't trying to convince the king to sign a peace treaty, I spent time with her at her castle at Capuano or along the Bay of Naples at the Riveria di Chiaja, indulging in talk about art and literature, far from the cares of politics and state affairs. I told her I wished only to return home to peace, to once again regain my friendships and to sit and discuss philosophy in my gardens at Fiesole beneath the bust of Plato. Time spent with her was the perfect antidote to everything that pained my mind, though as pleasant as it was I could not disassociate myself from the nagging discomfort of my purpose for being in Naples. I desired the king's signature above all else. She promised me she would do all she could to ensure it would happen. He loved her as a daughter. Thus, she was allowed inside places of his heart others could not know.

I continued to wait as days turned into weeks. I spent freely in Naples the money I had borrowed from Florentine public funds. Yes, I use the word *borrowed*, for I had every intention of returning the money I took, as I did, did I not? Borrowing the money, with the blessing of leading citizens, I point out, could not be avoided. I could not visit Naples without spending money as a prince, for without first giving generously I could not hope to receive anything in return. Such is the nature of politics.

I gave money to the daughters of the poor. I wined and dined the local nobility. I purchased the freedom of one hundred Christians enslaved by pirates. I bought innumerable gifts for King Ferrante and the members of his court. I spent lavishly, and to my critics I say this: I did not use the money I borrowed for my own personal satisfaction. I used it in the name of my city, Florence, to preserve its peace and solidarity, and if that is a crime of immorality to man and God--if he is present to hear my words--I plead guilty, though I know of no one in my circumstance who would have acted differently.

# Machiavelli

Do not speak to me about the nature of morality, for it limits, restricts and confines. Speak to me about the nature of freedom and the preservation of one's country, by whatever means necessary, and I will listen. When news came that King Ferrante had signed the peace treaty, the citizens of Florence greeted Lorenzo, who had been gone two months, like a conquering hero when he entered the city gates. Some of the same people celebrating his return were those who had condemned him for embezzlement of the city's exchequer and for diversion of funds from the public dowry.

Where was their morality then? It had taken the high road, for good reason: the people, old and young, rich and poor, stood to gain by what Lorenzo had achieved. Isn't the reward of prosperity for the state and all its citizens a testament that the ends justify the means? Let us cease talking about virtue and righteousness. They are useless to a ruler. He must, by all and any means, hold to power and act accordingly. Lorenzo committed no crime. He robbed Peter to pay Paul, understanding what we must all understand: that necessity determines our behavior, and the person, ruler or not, who does not adapt to circumstances, or, as I like to say, act in harmony with the times, is doomed to failure.

I stood in the crowd and listened to the cheers when only days earlier I had heard only criticism about Lorenzo's motives and absence from the city. One man standing close to my father and me said Lorenzo was lucky he wasn't killed and stuffed by the mad ruler of Naples. My father had an interesting response. He said, "Powerful men make their own luck." The other man had no reply, for he must have known my father spoke the truth.

Throughout the city, bonfires accompanied the ringing of bells, as people rejoiced with cries of "Liberty." No one seemed to care now that Lorenzo had lied about the money he had taken. I commend him for having lied. I would have lied as well, for a lie convincingly told is among the most powerful weapons in a ruler's arsenal. The only important fact was the outcome. Lorenzo had ended the war that had done so much damage to the republic, and he had done so without compromising our sense of honor. I took my cue from my father, who stood with tears in his eyes, watching Lorenzo ride past on a white horse, waving to the people who shouted--the first time I had heard it--*Il Magnifico*. He had earned our love and admiration—and his title—for having returned safely and bringing us safety through a diplomatic feat hailed as the greatest of our Florentine lifetimes.

No one cared that in the days that followed Pope Sixtus issued to our city another bull of excommunication. Had he known that the people of Florence, in regard to religion, responded more with sense than sentiment he could have saved the ink used to write his declaration. We knew that without the armies of Naples to support his cause he could not hurt us. From that time forward, in the early months of 1480, Lorenzo's reputation as a diplomat and peacemaker grew in great measure. He became a sage on the world stage and could thus focus more on what mattered to him most: bringing to Florence a golden age of art, literature and learning.

# Savonarola

I believe God sent me to Florence to expose the golden era as a fraud. If there is any gold, it is exclusive to only the few, sitting in their villas, celebrating Bacchanal rites, as the sun rises and sets on them alone. Ask the poor person, living knee-deep in mud, if the streets he walks are paved in gold or if the sun ever rises or sets on him. He would say the dark cloud of tyranny keeps him from seeing anything but the sorry state of his own affairs, namely famine and disease.

The Medici justifies their taxes and embezzlements, believing they give back what they take, as is evident in the art and architecture they contribute to the city. Should the poor person be appeased by these false charities? He cannot eat a building or a sculpted marble. The *Rinascimento* I hear about in the exalted places where men live in cultivated idleness is nothing but the rarefied air that those of means breathe. It does not exist in the streets where the poor live in squalor, spreading tuberculosis and the sweating sickness, leading inevitably to death for so many. Yet these deaths are footnotes, if even that, to the main story the Medici writes on gold parchment.

I walk into the back street tenements and narrow lanes of the slums. Some people tug at my sleeves and beg for money or food. I tell them to come to my sermons. I will feed them God, for the only thing worse than hunger of the stomach is starvation of the soul. No man should suffer without a cause. Jesus had a cause, and I have followed his cause, suffering in self-denial for God. A man spits at me and curses the Dominican order, believing his taxes pay for our fine linens and comforts. I tell him it is not I to whom he should vent his rage. I do not over tax him and subjugate him to a life of poverty.

I wish, at times, to return to Ferrara, where the poor treat the Dominican monks as friends. Here in Florence we are their enemy. I blame the Medici for that. The people in the streets know well the story of how the monks at San Marco sheltered Cosimo's money before he went into exile.

When he returned to the city, he expanded the monastery, bestowing it with art, sculptures and amenities never before seen in a church. It matters little that I tell people I am a poor friar. They are convinced I am on the Medici payroll. As much as I am hurt by their perception of me, I understand their feelings. After all, why should a friar be honest when the Church in Rome is the very seat of sin and corruption?

One needs to look no further than Florence for evidence of the extent of the corruption. How is it that Lorenzo can have a son, a mere boy, who is made cardinal? Only through corruption and the worst form of simony is that possible. It is no secret that (call it mismanagement by our esteemed leader) many of the Medici banks have closed throughout Europe and Italy. How do I know this? I am a learned man, and I have my sources. I know, as well, that his financial advisor, Antonio Miniati, uses sleight-of-hand tricks to make money appear to Lorenzo. The source of this money is the city's exchequer, which Lorenzo treats as his private account. He pilfers money from the people of Florence to pay for his lavish lifestyle, and to pay the pope for his son's candidacy. Even the people in the streets know of his embezzlement of state funds, yet they are powerless to oppose it. Besides, Lorenzo appeases them with daily festivals and entertainments, also paid from the exchequer, making them believe all is well in Florence.

Thus, a child, with no formal theological education, becomes a cardinal. Only here in Italy can a man in no possession of holiness become a holy man. Let those who enter the holy order do as I have done. I am not a pirate, a drunkard, a whoremonger, a liar and a thief. I did not buy my holiness. I earned it through self-denial, through teaching and preaching, through living without vice and sin. Let them travel as I did, barefoot in sandals, walking over mountains, coming to towns and villages, with no possession other than the holy bible. I fasted, slept little and prayed through the night, weeping for the crucifixion of Jesus and the wickedness of man.

Those were my happiest days. I did not ask to come to Florence. Lorenzo requested my service. He had heard about my preaching reputation and my honest respect for the teachings of God. He had an ulterior motive: to make Florence appear more religious and to use my presence as a bargaining chip to convince the pope to make his son a cardinal. He will learn, in time, that I am no man's pawn.

I am not a tyrant's son.

I am a man of God. I work for Him and Him alone.

As for the wealthy men in Florence and the pope in Rome who know not the will of God, they can expect from me to rail against them, condemning their evil ways. I will, with the blessing of God, plague their minds and souls by prophesying how the wrath of God's sword will fall upon their heads, killing forever their greedy dreams. I will do such until the day they murder me. I have much work to do before that happens. I must save this city and lead those who follow me to the New Jerusalem, for I have a destiny, given to me by God, to fulfill. I will not let Him down.

# Machiavelli

Lorenzo correctly foretold the Ottoman invasion. They reached Italian shores, with 14,000 infantry, capturing the port of Otranto in the heel of Italy. More than ten thousand Italians died fighting the Turks. Those who survived were sold into slavery. The invasion got the pope's attention, diverting his thoughts about Florence and Naples' betrayal. He directed his energy instead into defeating the infidels, as evident in his message to all Christians: "If the faithful, especially the Italians, wish to preserve their lands, their houses, their wives, their children, their liberty, and their lives, if they wish to maintain that Faith into which we have been baptized and through which we are regenerated, let them at last trust in our word, let them take up their arms and fight."

Lorenzo, happy the pope had larger concerns than pursuing his vendetta against his city, chose to defer the fighting of that war to Vatican and Neapolitan troops. Though his standing at home and abroad had never been higher, he knew that since the Pazzi conspiracy he lived as under a spotlight of vulnerability; he, therefore, focused on strengthening his own position in lieu of worrying about the invading Turks in the south of Italy. He reformed his government, creating the Council of Seventy, making sure only his men could be elected and have a voice, concentrating power in fewer, more reliable hands, and removing the illusion of democracy wherein every citizen felt he had a share in state affairs. Lorenzo would now have a say in everything, and he wanted everybody to acknowledge himself his debtor in almost every particular. Thus, his security supplanted civil liberties. He created a network of spies and informers called the Eight of the Watch, a group which had unrestrained power when it came to anything that reflected criticism or threat to the state. One did not see Lorenzo walking alone ever again through the streets, conversing, as he always had, with common citizens. He now had a twelve-man bodyguard accompany him everywhere. This behavior went against the principles of Cosimo de' Medici, who believed men of wealth and power should keep out of the public eye and not call attention to themselves and should always avoid offending the sensibilities of their fellow citizens. In fairness to Lorenzo, I say this: the threat of death changes a man. He had every right to create an authoritarian state. I, for one, applauded it. Is it not much preferred to the chaos that ensued after his death?

Some call Lorenzo's behaviors and actions tyrannical. That is erroneous. Lorenzo was not a tyrant. Those who believe he was do not understand the meaning of the word. They should study history, as I have, for a better understanding of what constitutes a tyrant. Yes, Lorenzo meted out just punishments to his enemies, embezzled funds and fixed elections, controlling every aspect of government. None of these examples exclusively point to tyrannical behavior. I call what he did "acting with political savvy." It is what men of wealth and status do to protect their wealth and status. It is neither fair nor accurate to label a man a tyrant for possessing power and exercising that power authoritatively. If he administrates well, he is a good leader. A tyrant, in addition to possessing power and exercising that power authoritatively, is cruel, murderous, paranoid, bloodthirsty and delusional. I offer this brief lesson in history as proof:

I begin with Tiberius, an emperor who, in his old age, made men avoid the senate for he killed his senators—the noblest men in Rome--for so much as twitching their noses or blinking their eyes. Such was the developed state of his paranoia that he believed most people, including family and friends, suspicious of wanting to kill him. Is it any surprise that his people refused for him a divine burial and instead shouted: "To the Tiber with Tiberius"?

Nero did not kill to appease suspicion and paranoia. He killed because of his predilection for blood and cruelty: he poisoned his stepbrother, murdered his mother, and kicked to death his pregnant lover. He did, however, continue to shower love for his favorite monkey. I'm certain the people of Rome appreciated that display of magnanimity to a pet. Should it be a surprise that a conspiracy formed to kill him? When he failed to discover the specific conspirators, he suspected hundreds and forced them, including his tutor, Seneca, and another poet, Lucan, to kill themselves: opening their veins in warm baths. Whether he allowed the writers to recite verse as they died is not known.

And now for the crème de la crème: Enter Gaius, known to the world as Caligula. I offer for starters one of his famous lines: "Why would I have an heir? He will kill me when he grows up" Here's another, even better: "Although I have taken the form of Gaius Caligula, I am all men as I am no man and therefore I am God." Afterwards, he forced his senate to confirm that he indeed was God. What could they say, out of fear of retribution, other than "Aye"? To further prove himself as a god, he waged war against the sea god Neptune, ordering his soldiers to attack the waves with their swords. How do these words and acts make him a tyrant more so than a lunatic, you ask? I was about to get to that. He executed men, such as his half-brother Gemellus and his most important soldiers, the way one swats flies on a summer night.

These rulers deserve the title of tyrant because—this characteristic is what separates a tyrant from someone who merely rules authoritatively--they inflicted terror on their subjects during their reigns. Who, I ask, did Lorenzo terrorize? Who among his own family or friends did he poison or murder? Who among his closest advisors did he execute on suspicion of treason? Most citizens of Florence loved him. Love as a word, feeling or concept is antithetical to the tyrants aforementioned. They ruled by hate and fear. If Lorenzo had a fault it was that he, as a man, no less a ruler, had faults, and who among us has not faults? These faults, however, do not qualify him to be called a tyrant.

It is to Savonarola I should be addressing this lecture, for he is most guilty of referring to Lorenzo as a tyrant. Though he professes to be a learned man, he needs to further his education before he jumps so quickly to use a word he doesn't understand. He knows well scripture and the lives of the saints. I give him that. I also credit his knowledge of science and logic, given his innumerable references to Aristotle and St. Thomas Aquinas. Still, it is evident he has not studied Roman history. If he had he would not call Lorenzo a tyrant. He would instead associate him with the great Roman emperors: those I like to call the five good emperors, who ruled consecutively during the period between 96 AD and 180 AD, bringing peace, stability and prosperity to the Roman Empire for nearly a hundred years. In case you are not aware, here are the five, in order of their rule: Nerva, Trajan, Hadrian, Antonius Pius, and Marcus Aurelius. These leaders, like Lorenzo, prided themselves in diplomacy with foreign states and negotiation with their senates and people, making virtuous and wise decisions, and encouraging arts and culture and the building of lasting monuments. Is it any surprise that this period is referred to as the golden age of Rome? And did not Lorenzo deliver to us the golden age of Florence, further proving his worthiness to be placed among the immortal leaders in our rich heritage?

I offer further proof to those not yet convinced: He brought peace to our small republic, which had neither economic nor military assets, through his prestige and reputation. After his daring and successful exploits in Naples, who would dare label him an inexperienced politician, a banker's son, someone who merely inherited his status and position? Hadn't he proved himself as a statesman, almost single-handedly leading his nation through its darkest moment and emerging triumphantly? And who, if not he, could be "the needle of the Italian compass" through the wisdom of his learning and advice, seeking to maintain the affairs of Italy in such a balance when one or another state attempted to increase its power, causing a threat to the Florentine Republic? Here is one such case in point, regarding the brief war in 1482, when papal and Venetian forces, in alignment, threatened Florence, in alignment with Milan and Naples. Leaders came together in Cremona. Lorenzo not only attended; he was the force behind the settlement of peace, honorably received as a man of merit. A foreign ambassador wrote, "Various were the opinions, diverse the remedies, and the debates were long and ill-tempered. But finally Lorenzo, with great wisdom, laid out the state of affairs in Italy, and spoke with such eloquence and with such seriousness of purpose that all came to share his point of view."

Soon after the peace settlement, Pope Sixtus died, wherein a popular couplet circulated:

*Nothing could daunt the ferocious Sixtus,*
*but as soon as he heard the word of peace, he died.*

All of Italy rejoiced, and Lorenzo's star rose higher.

# Lorenzo

*Sixtus, at last you're dead: unjust, untrue, you rest now,*
*you who hated peace so much, in eternal peace.*
*Sixtus, at last you're dead: and Rome is happy,*
*for when you reigned, so did famine, slaughter and sin.*
*Sixtus, at last you're dead, eternal engine of discord,*
*even against God himself, now go to dark Hell.*

I did not write those lines, though many believe I did. I
believe the writer is anonymous, most likely a member of
the clergy, who, for years, have expressed their disdain for
papal corruption.

Though I rejoiced in the pope's death, I would never
fully recover from the harm he had caused me. He had
been made pope the year I became the ruler of Florence,
upon my father's death. Over those thirteen years, I
suffered financial reverses, years of war, and the loss of my
beloved brother, Giuliano. The cumulative effect took its
toll on my body. When I returned from Naples a hero to my
people, I had excruciating pain in my lower joints and had
developed chronic eczema and asthma. Thus began—it has
lasted these past twelve years--my decline into physical
hell.

I do not wish to recall the numbers of bleedings and
purgings I endured, or the many applications of poultices.
Only the consumption of and immersion into various
mineral waters helped ease my pain and failing health. I
traveled often in search of these waters. It was my mother
who first suggested the waters at Bagno a Morba and
Spedaletto. I found others as well at Agnano, Poggio a
Caiano, Bagni di San Filippo, Careggi, and Loggia de' Pazzi.

My absence from Florence caused problems. When I
reformed the government, I made sure I controlled every
facet and every decision: economic, political and cultural.
Thus, wherever I traveled, people came looking for me, for
without my consent to any proposal or document the city
remained at a standstill. I did not make it easy for those
who interrupted my cures. I chastised them to no end and

made them leave me in peace. Yet the minute they departed, I pondered their motives and the continued security of the state. Here's the truth: whenever I traveled more than ten miles out of the city the love and loyalty of friends came to an end. Perhaps that paranoia had its roots in the trauma I experienced and continued to feel over the conspiracy that aimed to take my life and thus my title as leader. How could I ever again trust men's smiles and words of assurance, believing deceit lay hidden in them? Yet it has always been my nature to trust people and love my friends and advisors openly. Enmity and distrust are bitter fruits that keep a man awake at night, tossing and turning on a bed made of insecurity.

I did not wish to have such thoughts permeating my brain, for they caused me greater bodily discomfort. I wanted only to drink and bathe in the thermal waters, far from state affairs, and upon that completion I wanted to write poetry. I longed to discuss philosophy with my friends, Pico, Poliziano, and Ficino. Anything related to the business of the state or of foreign affairs I wanted to deflect or erase from my consciousness. Even correspondence with my family became a chore. My wife Clarice often criticized me for not writing. I finally dictated a note to one of my servants and had it sent to her:

"My having been ill these days with some leg pain means I have not written to you; though the feet and tongue are far apart, one can still get in the way of the other."

# Machiavelli

Lorenzo could not have imagined that in a little more than two years after his death, Savonarola, not his son Piero, would become the man guiding Florentine politics. Allow me to qualify this statement. I don't believe Lorenzo would have been shocked to learn that Piero had failed. After all, he, as his father, knew of his son's arrogance and incompetence and, in fact, had feared for his future because of those overt deficiencies. Still, he couldn't have foreseen Savonarola's star rise. He would have said what many said: A preacher's job is to preach, not speak on matters of government. Of course, Lorenzo had no way of knowing--even someone named Il Magnifico cannot see from the grave--how much had changed since his death.

Although no one assigned Savonarola a title, it was clear to everyone that amidst the rubble and chaos that ensued after Piero's departure and the near debacle of the French army's entrance into the city to lay siege, curtailed by the ingenuity of the preacher himself, Savonarola's voice, full of prophecies and visions, rang loudest. Give him credit. He exploited the terror that the French invasion brought. He saw the sorry affairs of a state where anarchy and ambition commingled and public business regressed from bad to worse. These problems served him well, giving credibility to his apocalyptic sermons, and thus giving rise to his career. Bring on chaos, ruin and disease, I can imagine him saying. The sooner the better, for once Italy is cleansed it can be reborn. It is not hard, after all, to step inside the mind of one so singular in his purpose.

Though I count myself among his greatest critics, I owe much to the little friar. Did he not establish the Great Council, where I have been employed as a government official for many years? "Government by one man can only end in tyranny," was his rallying cry. "The will of God is that the city of Florence be ruled by the people and not by tyrants." He wrote, "Treatise on the Constitution and Government of Florence," setting down his rationale for this Great Council, where a wide spectrum of citizens, from wealthy bankers and merchants to small shopkeepers and artisans, could decide important decisions. Florence, under his guidance, reconstituted itself as a true republic and became the forerunner for democratic assemblies, where a sizeable number of the population had a say in their government.

The problem with such thinking is that while "ruled by the people" sounds ideal, it is, in practice, doomed to fail. The more voices and opinions added to decision-making, the more complicated and ultimately unproductive the system of governing becomes. A state is better off with one leader: one definitive voice, assuming he has the interests of the state in mind, as opposed to his own. I have seen "ruled by the people," and it is a sure way to bring the political machinery of a state to a stop because, more often than not, when one man's opinion counters another we are left with a stalemate and nothing gets done.

If one looks further into Savonarola's idealism, he finds the stink of irony. Allow me to explain: He believed in a free government by the people and for the people, yet at the same time he insisted that a strict morality be imposed upon all of us, and if we did not follow his moral teachings we were condemned to hell. He may have believed the Great Council was the best safeguard to civil and social justice, yet under his direction those ideals became laughable when one considers the price. What good is freedom from political evil if it is accompanied by imprisonment of one's personal freedom to choose sin and vice, if he so pleases? Give me absolutist rule any day, if it means I alone decide what is best for my mind and body.

# Savonarola

I visited the Virgin Mary in heaven. It matters little how I saw her, whether it was in a vision or dream or by a miracle made real by God. What matters is that I did see her, and, in fact, conversed with her, reaffirming my long-held belief that she is indeed immaculate, having been conceived without sin or stain, to the contrary of many theologians who have argued she was born in sin like everyone else; that she was sanctified and rendered sinless only after she conceived the Son of God. If these same theologians can see what I did and hear her speak, they would know, with certainty, that this saint of heaven never knew sin.

Saint Joseph accompanied me on my journey to paradise. He spoke only to tell me he saw himself as a humble servant, a messenger and purveyor of truth. My adulation, he said, should be reserved for the Holy Virgin, placed on the seat of heaven by God. I thanked him for his humility and promised to him I would encourage all my followers to follow his humble path, in word and deed. Though he smiled, he said nothing else.

We climbed a staircase to the clouds until I saw only a glowing brightness, through which I saw embroidered walls filled with gems and jewels and flowery fields that stretched on as far as my eye could see, bringing the sweetest taste of fragrance to my nose and lips. The Holy Virgin appeared on her celestial throne, more resplendent than the sun, encased in clouds, in hues of purple-gold. I stood on these clouds, as if the firm earth were below me, though I could see no ground beneath my bare feet. She sat statuesque, dressed humbly in a plain-colored robe beneath a blue, unmoving mantle. She wore a white veil that covered her head. Her cheeks and lips were rosy and her eyes clear and blue. Her right hand held a scepter; her left hand extended outward, its palm up. Beneath one of her feet, she crushed the devil's serpent, its tongue hanging lifeless from its open jaws. Two angelic cherubs, suspended above her in a splash of illuminating light, held a canopy of flowers. She said my name.

"Girolamo Savonarola."

I knelt before her, holding out to her the crown I had brought from the people of Florence, in homage to her title as Queen of Heaven. Silently, and in perfect motion of her hands and arms, without the slightest turn of her neck, she placed the crown on her head.

"You are here by the holy bequest of the Lord, our Father," she said.

"I am your servant," I replied. "Tell me what I must do to serve you and your heavenly Father."

"You wish to establish a New Jerusalem in your city?"

"Yes, Holy Mother, to have my people live in praise of you and your Holy Father."

She displayed a sphere showing Florence bedecked with lilies and guarded by angels. I wept at the sight of such a promise of glory.

"The City of Florence shall become more glorious, more powerful and more wealthy than it has ever been. My heavenly minions will protect your city against its enemies and support its alliance with the French. In the New Jerusalem that is Florence peace and unity will reign. All the territory that it has lost shall be restored, and its borders will be extended further than ever before. With the guidance of the Holy Spirit, you have prophesied the conversion of the infidels, of the Turks and the Moors, and more, and this will all take place in good time, soon enough for it to be seen by many who are alive today."

"Thank you, Holy Mother."

"None of these changes will occur, however, without the suffering of many tribulations," she said, displaying yet another sphere, this one depicting a time of hardships for the citizens of Florence.

"Tell me, Holy Mother, what we must suffer."

"The good citizens of your city will be less afflicted, according to their conduct, and in particular according to how severely they pass laws against the blasphemers and gamblers and those who commit the unspeakable sin against nature."

I knew what she meant and felt ashamed that she, the holiest of the holy and the purest of the pure, had to bring up a reference to the most unspeakable of sins, that being sodomy.

"It shall be done, Holy Mother. I shall declare your Son, Jesus Christ, the King of Florence."

She raised her sceptered hand to bless me, and all at once I felt myself descending from the clouds, falling to the hard earth, once again among men who lived in sin and vice, until I realized I was lying on the stone floor of my darkened cell, the words "Jesus Christ shall be the King of Florence" still on my lips.

To those who would question the veracity of such an event happening, I say this: I did not go in body; I went in spirit. Why should that make it any less real? The spirit is a much greater vehicle of truth than the body and the senses. When one is inflamed by the sanctity of God, he has no need of his body. I know only this: I am an empty vessel. God fills my vessel. If I have these visions, these otherworld adventures of the spirit, it is because God wills me to have them. I go where He takes me. If he wishes me to see paradise and the Holy Virgin, then that is where I go, gladly, with a full heart open to receive love as only one enriched in the spirit of true faith can experience it. Men who doubt me are jealous, for they only see degradation, vice, and sin. I see beauty in its most heavenly form. For that I should be praised and admired, not admonished.

# Machiavelli

Carnival season had always been a time of unrestricted celebration, where the highest form of debauchery and vice, with gambling, drinking and whoring, took place on every street. Do I dare say it was my favorite time of the year? That is until the winter of 1495, when I first encountered the morality police, in the guise of young boys. I had heard that Savonarola and his fellow monks had recruited boys from the tenements, who in prior times roamed the streets, stealing from vendors and pedestrians and throwing rocks at houses to amuse themselves. Who knew these street urchins could be so easily indoctrinated and made into a sacred army, soldiers of Christ, waging war on immorality and any and all things considered fun by Florentines? Hearing about it and seeing it are two different things, as I soon learned.

I had just turned a corner, on my way to my local tavern and gaming table, and saw to my shock and outrage an altar, with crucifixes atop it, set up directly in my intended path. On either side of it, a parade of boys, ranging from children to teenagers, maybe a hundred or more, marched down the street to the sound of pipes and drums, carrying crucifixes and holy images, saying in unison, "Long live Christ and the Virgin, our queen." They were dressed identically in white robes, and when they weren't repeating their mechanical refrain, they were singing hymns, praising God and the holy heavens. Though curious, I must confess to feeling perturbed by their intrusion into what I believed was going to be an afternoon of sin and pleasure.

One young man--his eyes abnormally large in their eagerness--approached me, asking me to join him and his friends, even holding out a cross for me to hold. I told him he and his friends were blocking my passage in the street and thus prevented me from pursuing my pleasures.

"The streets belong to us," he said. "And your pleasures are now against the law and punishable by death."

"You are surely not serious," I said.

"If you are a sodomite or an adulterer," he continued, "you should repent now before it's too late."

I told him my business was mine alone. He said it was their business to make my business theirs as well. Others surrounded me, beating drums close to my ears, singing, "O splendor of God's glory bright."

"You know not what you say or sing," I told them. "You are brainwashed children."

"We are soldiers of Christ," one of them, a child no more than six-years-old, carrying a cross nearly as big as him, screamed.

"You are soldiers of Savonarola," I answered.

"We shall be saved," the boy said. "You shall go to hell if you don't repent."

"If I go to hell or heaven, it shall be my choice, not yours," I said amusedly, realizing I was speaking to a child only recently out of his diapers.

A woman passed, holding the hand of a small girl wearing a veil-holder. One of the older boys broke from his group and snatched the veil-holder from the girl. The mother cried out for the boy to return it. He refused, saying, "It is against the law for women of any age to wear unsuitable ornaments."

"To hell with the law," the mother said. "Give it back."

The boy rushed to another boy holding a candle. He placed the veil-holder under the lighted candle and then dropped it to the ground. His friends cheered as the ornament burned before their eyes. The mother and the girl rushed past the boys. The mother said, "Your laws are evil. Tell that to the friar."

Many of the boys rushed among the passers-by, imploring them to give money to the Poor Men of St. Martin. Many did, out of fear of retribution. When I was asked to give, I flatly refused. I told the boys I counted myself among the poor, though even if I were rich I wouldn't give my money to them. I watched as they knocked on doors, asking for donations of material objects. One boy passed me holding clothing, jewelry and books. I asked him why he extracted these items from those in their houses. He told me such items distract one from the important work of salvation.

"Whose salvation?" I asked.

"Yours," he said.

"What if I don't want salvation?"

"Everyone wants salvation," he answered.

"Not if the price is too high," I said.

"Your material possessions will last only the fifty years you live. Is not the eternity of your soul worth more to you?"

"I care not about the eternity of my soul. It is not something I can see and feel. Jewels and books and clothing have more value to me."

"You will sing a different tune later."

"What is later?"

"When you are dead."

"I care not for when I am dead. I care more for the life I live now, and I plan to enjoy that life while I can."

"I warn you, Almighty God desires justice; renounce your pleasures. This is a time for weeping, not rejoicing."

This boy was no more than fourteen years old; yet he talked like an old prophet. Clearly the words were not his; they belonged to the friar who force-fed them into his brain. I would have none of it.

"You do not understand," I said. "I wish to be a sinner, if it means I get to enjoy the gifts given to me in this life."

"It is against the law."

"To enjoy life?"

"To do anything that distracts you from God."

"You are distracting me from the God of my desires."

"As punishment for just one sinner, God vented his wrath upon the entire tribe of Israel. God would only be appeased by the death of this sinner."

He thrust his crucifix in my face and said, "Repent your sins!" Others surrounded me and took up the chant: "Repent your sins!"

I pushed my way through them and hurried to the next street. To my dismay I encountered another altar, set up with crucifixes, and a similar tribe of boys. This time their procession stretched on until I could no longer see where it ended. I had thought there were a hundred boys. I now realized their number counted more than a thousand. Some ran up close to my face and sang:

"Jesus, through grace, inflame our hearts with your love."

I shoved boy after boy out of my way, though I could see no clear path ahead of me. Everywhere I walked I encountered a crucifix thrust in my face and the continued voices of their singing:

"My Lord, summon up your might and come, show yourself as God."

A small child smacked my face with an olive branch, while one of his friends tried to pry open my moneybag tied to a rope on my pants. I smacked the child's hand away and took the olive branch from my face and threw it to the ground. More than once my hand brushed a burning candle, infuriating me. As their singing echoed in my ears and their bodies blocked my way, I began knocking over small and large boys in my desperation to free myself from their collective madness, until finally I turned down a vacated alley, where the sight of their haunting brainwashed eyes and the sound of their senseless song could be seen and heard no more.

# Savonarola

Mother Mary, I hope you watch and see our fortitude in the fight against luxury and vice. What we do is out of love for you and your heavenly Father. The day is coming soon when our city will become the New Jerusalem and only those who follow the ways of Christ shall live and thrive here. Already we have passed a law making sodomy, that most unspeakable of sins to which you referred, a crime punishable by death. My boys who parade the streets in your honor tell me of people's repentance and their willingness to surrender their minds, souls and possessions to our cause.

After visiting with you, Holy Mother, I knew the course I had to take. To win the people of Florence to our cause (and I do mean *our* cause, not mine) I needed the children of the streets to speak, as only children can in all their innocence and purity. Fra Silvestro Maruffi has organized the recruitment and education of these boys. We have more than five thousand under our tutelage. They are young boys between the ages of six and sixteen and almost all are from the poorer quarters of the city. Many of these boys are from troubled backgrounds; they possess innate fury and passion that need only to be harnessed into goodness. We promised them salvation, which is a great deal more than what they would receive from the tenements and their fathers, who do little more than introduce them to abominable vice. In such an environment they could only hope for further degradation and a life leading them to hell. Now they are soldiers of Christ, willing to fight the war we wage to save Florence from itself. As part of their education, they are required to attend religion classes, where they learn and memorize the questions and answers from the catechism as part of their graduation into being soldiers for Jesus Christ, your Son and Savior.

It is not such a marvel as some think to see their transformation from hardened street boys to warriors for the cause of your Holy Family. We are filling a need they always had: to live in righteousness and in the nourishment of their souls. We give them shelter and clothing and feed them little, expecting them to fill themselves with the love and thought of your Heavenly Father. That should be enough to satisfy anyone.

Did you see, Holy Mother, the procession that passed the Piazza and crossed the Ponte Vecchio until it returned, after two hours, to the cathedral? The boys marched, three or five abreast, accompanied by drummers and pipers, bearing olive branches in their hands, singing the praises of God and heaven; some carried a banner with your painted figure on it: you and the Child in your arms, the Son of God. The citizens on the streets cried to look upon your image and the Child who would one day become the Savior, Jesus Christ.

Others carried with them a petition with an official seal, signed by thousands, to take to the Signoria, asking for authorization so that the boys may, like a moral police force, proceed against sodomites and remove prostitutes, gamblers, and drunkards and purge the whole city of vice, wherein we will fill it with the splendor of virtue, thus signifying that the will of Almighty God and his son, Jesus Christ, the King of Florence, and you, the Holy Mother, will show us the path to righteousness.

Did you notice the day, Ash Wednesday? Did you see that when the procession ended thousands of people packed the church? Surely you saw the boys sitting on steps along the walls. Before the sermon, you would have noticed (for we all felt your spirit that day) that the boys collected much money for charity and the poor. Gold florins and many copper and silver coins were tossed freely into collecting bowls. Some women gave their veil-holders, some their silver spoons, handkerchiefs and shawls. After collection, the boys sang to God, and when all of we in the clergy began singing the Litanies, the boys and the congregation joined. I heard a woman cry out, saying, "This is a thing of the Lord." You must have heard that as well. How could you not? Before long, every man, woman and child in the cathedral repeated the refrain, tears streaming down their faces, as the walls reverberated with that same line:

"This is a thing of the Lord."

I addressed the boys in my sermon, saying, "In you, young men, I place my hope and that of the Lord. You will govern the city of Florence, for you are not prone to the evil ways of your fathers, who did not know how to get rid of their tyrannical rulers or appreciate God's gift of liberty to his people."

When I speak, I am infused with your spirit and the spirit of your Heavenly Father and your Son, the Savior, Jesus Christ. Those who hear my words feel your spirits as well. No longer can anyone doubt the truth of what is happening in the city of Florence. We move closer each day to the throne where you sit. I shall deliver all my people there. You shall see; it is my promise to you. You will be proud when you see the multitudes I set before your eyes. The angels will herald our arrival with trumpets, and only those free of sin will hear their sound. We shall sing, *Glory to God in heaven.*

# Lorenzo

I am alone again, with only a burning candle to light the dark. I hear the voices of Angelo, Pico and the doctor in the next room. Though they speak softly, I would not be wrong to say the subject of their discussion is the imminence of my death. They know, as do I, the bell tolls for me. I prefer they speak frankly in place of offering me encouraging words when they have no basis of truth. I am not foolish enough to believe I can overcome what no man has ever been able to overcome: the grip of death. It slowly strangles me, teasing me with its starts and stops. Just when it feels I am about to expire, the grip releases and I breathe again. What am I to think during these relaxations? That I will again rise to my feet and resume the life I once knew? I believe no such thing. I know that death's slow grip will return. In the meantime, the mechanics of life continue. A young servant girl enters and empties my pan and gives me cool water to sip. She smiles apologetically, as if she should not be allowed to smile in the company of one who suffers. I want to tell her to smile all she wants, but at the moment I am having trouble breathing. Is it the grip again? She washes my feet. If I had enough breath I would tell her to lift her face and smile. I would say I am grateful for her presence. She is one of few women who have entered my room in the past two weeks. I miss women. I mean not only my wife and mother and daughters. I miss loving women with passion and desire. I understood early in life through poetic convention—and for this discovery I am grateful--that the delicate rose should be plucked before it becomes a heap of faded petals.

When I came to Careggi, I brought with me the small portrait of Lucrezia Donati I have treasured since my youth. It hangs on a wall convenient to my eyes when I am lying down, unable to twist or turn my head or body. If I have had a lasting love relationship in my life, it has been with her, for her beauty possessed me like no other. Her portrait, simply done from the neck up, conceals her nature and the poetry of her body. When I think of her I see her moving, dressed in black with her head veiled, stepping so gracefully that it was as if the very walls and stones should worship her as she passed. If I could have, I would have married her. Two impediments prevented that. First, my parents had greater dynastic plans for me, and, second, she was married to another man. Still, neither time nor bad health has cooled my desire, though fortune has placed me in this darkness, among such great shadows. I think of her often and will continue to see in the beauty of her movement amorous rays of light, where I hear her voice saying, "O Magnificent Lorenzo, mirror of youth."

The young servant girl does not speak. She is, nonetheless, a lovely woman, fair in feature and feminine in her breath and touch. Years earlier I could have loved her and written her a verse. I could do both with equal agility in mind and body. Now I can do neither. I can do nothing but piss into a pan and wait for the grip of death to tighten its hold around me, so that I may finally expire and be spared further pain and humiliation. The humiliation is, in fact, worse than the pain. I have only remembrances of being a great man or even a man who was once capable of walking, riding and loving.

I think of my last love, which lasted for more than a year after the death of Clarice. "Bartolomea," I form her name on my lips, though no sounds escapes. Not as beautiful as Lucrezia, Bartolomea de' Nasi, wife of Donato Benci, graced me with her charm and pleasing manner. I became enamored with her and was in such longing for her love that many times in the winter, while she stayed hours away in the country, I left Florence on horseback, with several companions, early in the evening to go see her. Where was her husband, you may ask? Often I visited her on his invitation, for he, old and invalid, knew of my love for her and wished, as he himself said, "to serve me in any way he can." In any case, I stayed these nights with her, and at dawn the following morning rode back to Florence to take care of matters of state. I kept that schedule for many months until my failing health made it impossible for me to ride any further.

I have heard it rumored--even now it makes me want to laugh, if I could--that my current state of decline is the result of my having indulged in amorous excesses since an early age. Is it not laughable to believe too much love kills a man? If anything, his death is more likely to occur from a lack of love. I know this to be true, for in my present condition, with only the remembrance of having once loved, I have lost my will and *joie de vie*. What is the point now, really? To lie like this, a shell of my former self, brings me only humiliation. I often wish for the grip of death to finish its job. I close my eyes and see words I once composed. I speak them to myself.

> *O sleep most tranquil, still you do not come*
> *to this troubled heart that desires you!*
> *Seal the perennial spring of my tears,*
> *O sweet oblivion, that pain me so!*
> *Come, peace, that alone can stanch*
> *the course of my desire! And to*
> *my sweet lady's company guide me,*
> *she with eyes so filled with kindness and serene.*

Many criticized my passion for writing poetry about affairs of the heart, saying it was a trivial occupation for someone engaged in affairs of the state. If I possessed poor judgment for preferring my passions to political skullduggery, I am proud of that poor judgment. Do not my critics understand that because I suffered in my youth much persecution by men and by fortune, I have needed comfort any way I could find it? If there is a greater comfort to a man than loving fervently and writing verse, I should very much like to experience it before I expire. Why should it have been of any concern to others how I spent my time, as long as I effectively addressed my affairs of state? Hadn't I sacrificed much for Florence's safety and goodwill? I had been raised to believe that a man of letters could, with pride, call himself a gentleman. I have held that title with as much esteem as I have that of statesman. When I die, I hope to ride out on a chariot driven by Apollo, who has guided my verse since my early years. I hope to die, in fact, with the language of verse affixed on my lips, believing if I do I will not only die happier but also take with me to the next world what is most important to me in this one. I watch the young servant girl gather the pans and rags and implements of a sick man's room, and I remember suddenly some of the first lines I ever wrote, in a carnival dance titled, "The Triumph of Bacchus and Ariadne."

*How lovely is youth in its allure,*
*Which ever swiftly flies away!*
*Let all who want to, now be gay:*
*About tomorrow no one's sure.*

*Those who love these pretty nymphs*
*Are little satyrs, free of cares,*
*Who in the grotto and the glades*
*Have laid for them a hundred snares.*
*By Bacchus warmed and now aroused*
*They skip and dance the time away.*
*Let all who want to, now be gay:*
*About tomorrow no one's sure.*

*Among you lasses and young lovers*
*Long live Bacchus and Desire!*
*Now let us pipe and dance and sing,*
*Our hearts consumed with sweetest fire!*
*Away with suffering and sorrow!*
*Let what is fated have its way.*
*Let all who want to, now be gay:*
*About tomorrow no one's sure.*

# Savonarola

I see her sitting in the front pew. Her hair long and dark, she wears a shirt that reveals the outline of the parts that incite lust and ought to be hidden. Her dress is slit on the sides, revealing the flesh of her legs. I speak to myself.

*Woman, reform yourself. Bring up your dress and cover your bosom. You are in a house of God, not a brothel.*

She stares at me. Her eyes shine and draw me to her. I must look elsewhere, for she is surely an instrument of the devil. Once the devil gets on a person's shoulder he is hard to shake, for his grip is strong. My voice, as I begin to preach, sounds hoarse and choked. The devil is trying to silence me. I must fight. I am a Christian, and fight is what Christians do.

"You, my Florentines, are like the man on the road from Jerusalem to Jericho. For your sins you have fallen into the hands of robbers and devils that have bruised your souls. Only Christ the Samaritan offers the healing oil of his mercy and the wine of repentance."

I hear myself speak, but I do not understand what I am saying, for it is hard to manage two voices at once. Her tongue touches her lips. It is the serpent's tongue. I know for certain.

*Be gone, devil. You are not allowed here, in a house of God. I forbid it.*

I begin to sweat. I am about to fall. I drink from a glass of water on the pulpit. It is not enough to quench me. I must submerge myself in icy water. It is the only way I know to rid myself of the devil.

She brushes back her hair. The nails on her fingers are painted red. It is a sacrilege to mock the blood of Christ in such audacious display.

*Leave me be, whore, daughter of Babylon! You cannot enter this church and attack the sanctity of this order.*

I continue to preach, though with my inner voice I call on God to help me.

"Do penance and pray and humble yourselves before God. Fight the devil by resisting his libidinous temptations."

I see her smile, flashing bright teeth. She nods her head. The devil, knowing many disguises, is good at what he does. I must be better. With a moist hand I wipe my forehead.

*God, help me through this ordeal.*

I close my eyes, and in my darkness I see the light of God. He returns to me my voice, cleared of hoarseness. The voice I preach is now the only voice I hear. Tears form in my eyes.

"Every path is befouled by vice. Maidens deck themselves out like whores; sodomites run free; everywhere astrology is being used to divine the future. Only one recourse remains: to take refuge in the spiritual Ark of Jesus Christ. The flood is coming. You want to know when? I can only say, *Cito, cito, cito.*"

I am grateful for the blindness. I feel the devil lose its grip. I do not take a chance, though. I keep my eyes closed.

# Machiavelli

Though the government has passed the harshest law against sodomy in Florentine history, I know of no one who has been put to death because of it. Our leading citizens have too much political wisdom to actually carry out this punishment for a crime that many--who would actually come forward and admit it?--find indulgence. To appease Savonarola, they have instituted a policy designed to punish repeat offenders. The first offense results in public pillory. I admit to having seen this on one occasion in the piazza. If it was meant as a punishment, it didn't work, for the man was fortunate to have been surrounded by friends and well wishers who provided him with much food and drink while his head and hands poked through holes in a wooden plank. If he suffered a humiliation, it would have been from having pissed himself, though even that could have been attributed to his laughing too hard with his followers. A second offense results in the person being branded on the forehead and paraded naked around the city. I have yet to see this firsthand, though a source— drunk he was and known for his artful fabrication--tells me it happened to him, though he was innocent of the charges. If convicted a third time, the guilty party is burned alive. Good grief, I can't imagine such a punishment for an act that many young men engage in routinely. The city would soon be depleted in a large number of its promising citizens, many of whom claim noble birth.

Savonarola's authorities have gone so far as to employ informers to catch people in the act and thus punish them. The truth is that even when caught the perpetrator usually is made to pay a small fine. Most reasonable people know that Savonarola uses the threat of the harshest form of punishment, as well as all his apocalyptic threats foretelling the end of time, to frighten people into reforming their ways. Though I have no intention of reforming anything I do, I concede that his scare tactics influence many of the people of Florence to lay down their

234

lives to join the growing campaign, declaring Christ the King of Florence.

Savonarola's annoying little boys loom large in this troubling revelation. Their numbers grow greatly; their singing grows louder; and their aggression grows more violent. If the word *violent* strikes one as too excessive, allow me to justify its use. Though, admittedly, they aren't burning people or hanging and quartering them, they attack in insidious ways, infiltrating people's minds with the threat of God's sword upon their heads as they sleep in their beds or eat at their tables, saying their blood will spill and fill the streets, unless they repent their sins and reform their ways.

I believe that qualifies as violence, wouldn't you say?

If one isn't strong enough to withstand these assaults, he surrenders himself to their cause, and in doing so surrenders, as well, his possessions and any and all principles he may have once held. The fear of God's wrath holds the people of Florence in its web, and it isn't about to let go anytime soon. Even hardened gamblers fear the boys, often crying out, "Here come the boys of the friar!" They gather their possessions and run. I no longer run, as I did on my first encounter with them. I now go out of my way to cross paths with them. They are harmless to me, though they promise at every chance to send my soul to eternal damnation. I have learned to view their crusade with detachment, believing that the candles they hold with such certainty will one day burn out.

In the meantime, they use their candles and, more specifically, the flames atop them in accordance with the beliefs they have inherited from Savonarola. They are clearly on a mission to seek and destroy, and never was this more evident than on the day of the great bonfire set up in the Piazza della Signoria. I looked on in awe as the boys erected an eight-sided pyramid, sixty feet high, with seven tiers and a forty-foot circumference at the base. When I asked one of the boys why there were seven tiers, he said, "There is one for each of the seven deadly sins." On each tier sat sacks of straw, piles of kindling wood and even small bags of dynamite. A wooden effigy of the devil, complete with hairy, cloven-hoofed goats' legs, pointed ears, horns and a little pointed beard, stood at the peak of the pyramid. I remember once seeing a Pan god atop a wooden structure in the square during a festival. Citizens danced and sang under its gleaming, welcoming presence, in celebration of sensual pleasure. Such was not the case during Savonarola's bonfire. A celebration of perverse proportions, it would have been unimaginable during Lorenzo's reign.

The boys had collected that day what they called "vanities" or distractions. They placed these vanities on the various seven tiers. I saw jewelry, wigs, mirrors, perfumes, dice, packs of cards, musical instruments, books by Ovid and Petrarch, statues of nudes and paintings of anything nonreligious. Trumpets sounded from the Palazzo, the boys sang hymns, the bells tolled, and the crowd surrounding the bonfire applauded as it was lit and its flames rose high in the sky, extinguishing what the boys believed represented the sin and vice of mankind. Many from the crowd brought additional possessions, such as silk cloths and tapestries and even coins and paper money, and added them to the fire. One of the boys took from a man a painting of the Blessed Virgin and threw it into the fire. I asked the boy, a freckle-faced lad no more than nine years old, why he burned a sacred painting. The boy looked at me as if he wanted to spit. He said the painting was not sacred. Whoever painted it made the Virgin look like a common whore.

"Long live Christ and the Virgin, our queen," the boys sang in unison as the fire roared, taking with it the best of man's labors. I should think this incident qualifies, as well, as another example of how their aggression grew more violent. Let us never again say that childhood is the sweetest, most innocent time of life. One needed only to observe these boys to understand their disingenuous acts of Christianity. As they screamed with glee as the fires rose higher, it took little stretch of imagination to envision them as devils in hell.

I wondered if the boys and Savonarola, in particular, would be satisfied with burning material objects. What would stop them from burning Florence, in addition, to the ground? After all, in establishing their City of God, their New Jerusalem, they acted without limitation. The more I watched the fire, though, the more I knew it was only a matter of time before the same flames that burned the vanities would some day consume Savonarola; wherein the boys could go back to being boys, throwing rocks through windows and stealing purses, in lieu of expressing themselves as mad prophets of doom.

# Lorenzo

Servants, daily, bring me precious objects and artifacts from the Palazzo Medici. Though my sickness has taken me to St. Peter's gates, I continue to hunger for beauty. What else is there, as I lay crippled with gout and failing organs, but to see and touch what has always been for me, since my earliest beginnings, a sacred affirmation of my mind and soul? As long as I have breath, I shall continue my hunger and worship.

I recall, as a boy, following my father around the palace during the worst of his infirmity, watching his servants carry him in a litter from room to room. First he entered his study to look at his books: gold leafed, inscribed in Greek and Latin, inherited from my grandfather. He had commissioned from a scribe, Neri Runuccini, a sumptuous manuscript called "The History of Augustus," with portraits of emperors and empresses. It is the same book that now lies within arm's reach of me. Sometimes he stopped to read one of his books. Usually it sufficed for him to look upon them and touch their fine leather. Always he stopped in the corridors to view the effigies of emperors, made in gold, bronze and marble, and the many portraits of noble men. From there he entered a room to gaze upon his jewels, stones, ancient vases and silver cups. Later, I followed him to a room where he kept fine tapestries and paintings from northern Europe done in oils by men named Jan Van Eyck and Rogier van der Weyden. His tour ended, suitably, in the chapel, where Bennozo Gozzoli and his assistants frescoed the ceiling, depicting the *Adoration of the Magi*. I did not understand then, though I do now, what my father told me.

"I have little else left in life but to see the completion of this fresco."

When I inquired why that was true, he answered, "We are the Magi. Do you not see yourself, as well as your brother, Giuliano, and your grandfather and me there among the holy men?"

I did see that, and took great pride in my family's acquired divinity. Mostly what I saw, though, was men of genius creating art, and with it glory, excellence, and magnificence. I knew then, in those mornings with my gravely sick father, that I wanted to collect and commission art as my forebears did: to surround myself with beauty in its many shapes and forms.

Though some say I have amassed art and objects to excess, I care not whether I have exceeded my wants and needs. I have had the means, and I have used those means for what I believe to be the greatest pursuit of human life: to gaze upon with delight, and feel and touch the dignity and mastery of man's creations. Though the fine objects of art do not bring with them health and long-lasting life, they bring, nonetheless, a permanence and continuity, an eternal union with an inevitably lost world, and this is the reason I inscribe my name-- LAU.R.MED.—on many of my artifacts and possessions. When I am gone, I hope to be remembered through my collection. I cannot lie. I wish to be remembered for a great deal more. I think of Augustus and Marcus Aurelius and envy their immortal fame.

My eyes fall on Botticelli's circular, "Madonna of the Magnificat." Servants brought it to me earlier today and hung it on a wall convenient to my eyes. He had painted it for my mother and father twenty years ago. The two angels kneeling before the Virgin and the Child represent my brother Giuliano and me. When the Pazzi murdered him, the brightest light went out of my life. I want that light back, even for a fleeting moment, in an illusion of time, in the genius of art, in beauty eternal and true.

My hands tremble at the thought of touching Verocchio's "Christ and St. Thomas." It sits on the bedside table. I had planned and directed the work, and its completion took years. No finer depiction of the Savior, done in bronze, exists. If it did, I would have possessed it. Such has been my quest to procure the greatest art in the world. On another table sits three beautiful little fauns on a small marble base, all three bound together by a great snake, which in my judgment are most beautiful, and even if they are silent they seem to breathe, to cry out, and defend themselves with certain wonderful gestures against the animosity of cruel death.

I view the Tazza Farnese cup, which has traveled through centuries, having been owned by popes and emperors. Around my neck, I wear a Roman carnelian necklace depicting Appolo, Marsyas and Olympus. I want to believe in its supposed magical and sacramental powers. Laid out on the bed sheet are hundreds of coins, medals, gemstones and cameos. I have thousands more at the palace. I see a marble sculpture of the Madonna and Child at the far end of the room. I thank my mother for passing on to me her love for the Virgin Mary. Adjacent to it hangs Squarcione's painting of San Sebastian. More than ever, I identify with the saint for enduring the shafts of arrows without so much as a word or cry. Leaning against a wall, waiting to be hung, are paintings by Fra Angelico, Paolo Uccello and Piero del Pollaiuolo. In my hand, I clutch the silver-figured Christ on a crucifix, superbly set in pearls and gems. I am aware that Christ did not die with jewels. Still, I am grateful that an artisan has adorned his memory. Why shouldn't suffering and death be as beautiful as life itself?

I am happy to have fine objects around me. They cannot alleviate my pain. Nothing can. Nonetheless, they please me in a simple way, just as they pleased my father and grandfather before me. The nights are terribly long and lonely. A man needs whatever help he can receive. Though I am fortunate for the company of my children, friends, doctors and servants, I cannot fool myself into believing they will accompany me to a place no man alive can say he knows. Before my final breath, I plan to clutch as many small, fine objects as I can, to keep me company on my journey to what I hope will be a kind and rewarding destination.

# Savonarola

I received another vision and visitation; this time from Jesus. He came to me in my cell, his wounds still fresh, leaving a trail of blood upon the stone floor. I reached to stop the blood from his wounds. My hand touched only air, though his image and his blood remained clear to my eyes. His voice when he spoke sounded as real as any man's I have heard.

"Jesus, it is I who should suffer for man's sins."

"To suffer for a cause is a noble feat."

"I hope to bring great suffering to this city, to cleanse it from sin."

"The fires that burn must spread further."

"I shall burn all of Italy if it is that you desire."

"Not all of Italy, just Rome, the seat of iniquity."

"The false, proud whore that is the Vatican."

"Fortune rewards the bold and repels the weak."

I had always believed Virgil wrote those lines, yet now I understood they came from Jesus. I should have known, for he is the true and only poet of mankind, able to see into the spirit and lift it up to a position high in the heavens, and is that not what all poets should do instead of writing verse about love of the flesh and worldly possessions?

"I will be bold."

"Purify our faith, in the name of God."

"I will purify our faith, though in doing so I will suffer a cruel death."

"To suffer for a cause is a noble feat."

"I will be bold and make you proud."

Both his image and his blood vanished. It was my blood now that appeared fresh on the stone floor. From where it came I did not know, for I had no open wounds, though I did notice engraved upon my chest the word "Jesu" together with the outline of the golden crucifix under it, illuminating my cell with the light of faith. I cried in the name of Jesus, his Holy Mother, and God, their Father.

"O kind Jesus, what love convinced you to wash me in your blood? You have gently pierced my ungrateful heart. You have shattered all hardness. Jesus, now make me die. Jesus, make me languish. Jesus, make me come to you."

The light enveloped me. I knew not whether I was lying on my back on the cold stone floor or whether I stood, my feet raised from the floor, suspended in the air. Such was the absorption of my spirit with Christ that I had no sense of my body. I can never remember being happier, for I know he was with me in that light, in the illumination of my cell, just the two of us, as I have always dreamed it would be. I experienced love as never before and used the power of my words, which cried from my heart:

"O Heavens, stand still for the passion of our Lord! Sun, give no more light! Earth, tremble! Rocks, break! Mountains, split apart! O man, here is your Lord, nailed and dead for you on this wood. O sweet love, o gentle scar, o honeyed wounding, how sweetly it leads to eternal life!"

# Machiavelli

To any sane mind not clouded over by his false visions and prophecies, it should be frighteningly clear that Savonarola is leading Florence to the precipice. His refusal to join the Holy League and the rest of Italy in their fight against France angers Pope Alexander VI and causes our city to suffer diplomatic isolation. In aligning himself and all of Florence to France, he holds to a delusional belief that King Charles--please, no more about his being the new Cyrus and scourge of God!--will soon arrive to cleanse all of Italy from sin and corruption. Hasn't anyone who follows Savonarola been paying attention? Hasn't Charles already waged war on Italy once before? He didn't succeed in purging the country of sin and corruption then. Why, in a second attempt, would he succeed this time? Why would he bother to travel again away from home for many months, if not a year, subjecting himself and his soldiers to plague and hardships? For what reason? To fulfill another man's destiny? Only a fool could believe it was the will of God. I want to cry out: His army is not going to bring the Holy League and the Vatican to their knees! The papacy is not going to crumble, along with all of Rome! The prophet Savonarola is not going to be the last man standing among the rubble! He is not Moses, and he is not going to lead his people and what is left of Italy to a New Jerusalem! Only a preacher on his personal death march--does he have to take the rest of Florence with him to the grave?--can believe such nonsense. Though he is more than willing to fall into the abyss, a growing number of Florentines, dismissing those under his spell, do not wish to follow him there.

If he gets his head out of the clouds, and stops talking to Jesus, Mary and the rest of his holy saints, he will see and hear the growing discontent in Florence, evident by the many developing divisions. It is yet another example of a man who will be destroyed because he is driven by dreams rather than what is real in front of him. I have said this before and will continue saying it until it is made law:

nothing is accomplished in dreams. Here's what's real: Florence is a small republic, a survivor of the Middle Age, pathetically overmatched by the rising nation-states that surround us. We do not have an army, depending entirely on mercenaries. Lorenzo understood our position. He used his diplomatic skills, solidifying important alliances, to ensure us peace. Savonarola possesses neither diplomatic skills nor political perspicacity. What he has are ill-used words that do nothing but inflame vengeance toward Florence. I offer the latest of his inflammatory comments, during a sermon: He called the Vatican "a false, proud whore, a whore of Babylon." Whether that is true or not is beside the point. What matters is whether it is effective and useful to the state in any way, and of course it isn't. While I credit his audacity, I deride his stupidity, for such an incendiary statement will only fall hard on the heads of Florentines, especially the bankers and merchants who rely on good relations with Rome for their profits. While many of these citizens are willing to gamble with their immortal souls, they are not willing to lose their worldly goods. It is only a matter of time before they rise up and eliminate the source of their troubles.

# Savonarola

I have absolutely never made any claim to be a prophet, though no man can deny I have foretold events that have already come to pass, such as the deaths of Lorenzo de' Medici and Pope Innocent VIII and the invasion of the French army. From where did these prophetic visions come from, if not from God himself? I have not asked for the danger of this gift (for is it not a danger for a man to possess what only God himself should know?). I do not pretend to be God, as some have accused me. I prophesy only what comes to me first from Scripture and then from God. I am not delusional. That word insults the efforts of my spirituality. I know what is real and what is false, and the truth is this: The Lord has bestowed me with gifts here on earth and has said to me, "I have placed thee as a watchman in the center of Italy that thou mayest hear my words and announce them."

The Holy See in Rome cares little about my relationship with God. A Brief, intended for the Signoria and all the citizens of Florence, appeared from the Vatican last month. I had secured it by means of espionage, for my survival depends on such enterprises. This example should suffice to show I do not live in illusion. I watch the world as a hawk watches its prey. Here are the words of Pope Alexander's Brief: "Savonarola has become so deranged by recent upheavals in Italy that he has begun to proclaim that he has been sent by God and even speaks with God, claiming that anyone who does not accept his prophecies cannot hope for salvation. Despite our patience he refuses to repent and absolve his sins by submitting to our will. Thus, Savonarola is suspended from all preaching. Anyone who does not comply with the requirements of this brief will suffer instant excommunication."

I had no intention of obeying this Brief. I not only continued preaching, I continued to attack the Church, as is evident in the following sermon I gave:

"The pope cannot command me to do something that contradicts the teaching of the Gospels. I obey God, not man, especially one whose lust, love of luxury and pride have been the ruin of the world. He and all the Roman Curia violate the world with their lasciviousness, turning men, women and children to sodomy and prostitution, spending their nights with concubines in drink and revelry. How can any believe the sacraments they conduct in the morning when they live in sordidness and sin every other hour of the day and night?

"The pope and all those who inhabit the iniquity of the Vatican must be prepared to suffer the fates of hell. They will be clapped in irons, hacked to pieces with swords, burned with fire and eaten up by the flames. The light will vanish and amidst the darkness the sky will rain fire and brimstone, while flames and great boulders will smite the earth because Rome has been polluted with an infernal mixture of scripture and all manner of vice.

"Friars have a proverb amongst themselves: 'He comes from Rome, do not trust him.' O hark unto my words, you wicked Church! At the court of Rome men are losing their souls all the time, they are all lost. Wretched people!

"O harlot Church, once you were ashamed of your pride and lust, but now you acknowledge this without the least show of remorse. In former times, priests would refer to their sons as nephews, but now they quite openly call them sons on every occasion.

"Thus saith the Lord God, Behold, I will stretch out mine hand against mine enemies, and I will execute great vengeance upon them with furious rebukes; and they shall know that I am the Lord, when I shall lay my vengeance upon them."

Soon after that sermon, the Vatican responded to what it called my act of insubordination. If I am insubordinate because I tell the truth, then I shall live and die in insubordination. Pope Alexander issued another Brief, saying the San Marco monastery would no longer be an independent Dominican church. We would now be under the jurisdiction of the Tusco-Roman Congregation. I would take my orders from this branch of church authority. I ignored this Brief, as well. Pope Alexander wanted to rein me in. I preferred to play the part of the wild colt.

A rumor persisted that Alexander (I shall from this time forward remove the title of pope from him), in hoping to buy my subservience, had offered me a cardinal hat. I quelled that rumor in my next sermon: "If I coveted such a thing would I be standing before you in this threadbare habit? It is not my habit to seek human glory. Away with that! I want no hats, no miters large or small. On the contrary, the only gift I seek is the one God gives to his saints: a crimson hat of blood, ending in death. That is all I wish for."

Here's the latest: Alexander has invited me to visit Rome, saying he believes my presence there will help ameliorate our differences. Does he think I'm a fool? I know his real reason for the invitation. He wishes to capture me and cut me into pieces: to shut my voice for good. He should know that whether he succeeds in killing me or not, I am just a man, doing God's work. God cannot be stopped, and His voice will ring loudly and his sword will fall mightily until the sinners in Rome and throughout Italy are destroyed.

I wrote to Alexander, offering an excuse for why I couldn't visit Rome. Though I left out the true reason, what I wrote was not without truth in that it made direct reference to the many spies and "ambassadors of goodwill" he had already sent to Florence "There are many enemies here who are thirsting after my blood," I wrote, "and have made several attempts upon my life, both by assassination and by poison. For this reason I am unable to venture out of doors in safety without endangering myself, unless I am accompanied by armed guards, even within the city, let alone abroad."

# Machiavelli

I happened to be on the Via Larga the day Savonarola left the cathedral, surrounded by his boys and his armed men. The boys marched in front, carrying crucifixes and singing hymns. Though they had been a curious novelty at first to the citizens of Florence, their act had become increasingly annoying, since they supported a man who might do the rest of Florence great harm if he persisted in his recalcitrance. Some had begun to believe his prophecies came not from God, but from the devil. The proof for them was in the inclement weather Florence had been enduring nonstop for nearly a year. Floods washed away the young crops planted in the fields, resulting in food stocks being as low as they had ever been. Neither corn nor grapes nor figs ripened. Having always been particularly fond of figs, this absence caused me no little amount of dismay. People, in hordes, left the countryside and came to the city, camping out in the streets and begging for food, bringing with them disease, plague and public health hazards.

"Where is the promise land you promised?" A woman shouted over the din of singing boys, while holding the bony flesh of a young child. "You who have referred to yourself as Moses."

Some threw stones at the boys and the monks who sheltered Savonarola. "This wretched priest has brought us bad luck and wishes to see us drown," a man yelled.

Neither stones nor words could stop the boys' singing or the procession as it made its way to San Marco. I was certain Savonarola saw the rain not as the devil's work or in relation to his insolence to the pope. He saw it as a sign from God. How many times had he told his followers "The flood will come and wash away the sins of the earth? Repent your sins and join the great Ark, toward the New Jerusalem." He would say as well that his promises to the citizens were not fulfilled because the city continued to live in impurity. What more could the people do? They had sacrificed their possessions to the bonfires; they had given up gambling and lewd vices; they had placed their faith in the Holy Spirit, giving the preacher their immortal souls. They wanted something palpable in return, such as food in their mouths, a thriving commerce and peace with Rome.

Savonarola had organized the monks and his boys to distribute free grain to the destitute in the Corn Market in the Piazza del Grano. I did not go. I knew what would happen: what always happens when a mob of poor people assemble to receive handouts. Many people, some of them mothers and young children, got trampled or suffocated. Savonarola and the monks received blame, in this case unjustifiably so. If nothing else, the little friar had to know he no longer dwelled in dreams. The growing famine and revolt in the streets of Florence were real events, not dreams that quickly pass in the night.

His most significant dream—am I not being benevolent in not calling it a delusion?--was his continued trust of the French and the likelihood of its impending invasion. This dream was, in fact, the reason, as well as the provider of false confidence, behind his insubordination toward the pope. If I were inside Savonarola's head, as unimaginable as it is, I might have had such thoughts as these: if the pope pushes me too hard, he risks raising the ire of the king. You, the pope, the Vatican, and all your Holy League, are no match for the French army. Have you seen their bronze cannons hauled by teams of thickset horses? Have you seen their gleaming array of firepower? Are you aware they fight to kill and will destroy all of Rome? This terror freezes you in its tracks, doesn't it? As long as this is true, I hold the all-important trump card, for as well as having the French in my corner, I have God. If you were holy and righteous, as one with your title should be, you would understand the power of his defense. It is too bad for you that you are not holy and righteous and know not the love of God, as I do.

I believe that is a fair imitation of Savonarola, wouldn't you say? I wish to say this to him, if I could, though it is much too late: beware the fickleness of fortune, for its smiling eyes often deceive the beholder.

# Lorenzo

I see Michelangelo enter with Angelo. He is a boy, only seventeen; yet his genius is as old as the stars and as deep as the earth that once belonged to the ancients. When he chisels, his eyes are guided by a light few, if any, can see, and his hands give the marble he touches a pulse, as if it lives and breathes like man himself. I know this, though I have seen only two of his reliefs: his *Madonna and Child* and his latest, *The Battle of the Lapiths and the Centaurs*. They are enough to inform me of this truth: he shall assume the mantle left by the great sculptors of the previous age, Donatello and Ghiberti. Even they, as great as they were, could not have produced the Madonna. Never before had I seen such audacity in sculpture, where Mary dominates the marble, larger than life and heroic in stature, with a force of intelligence and independence that speaks to anyone who looks and listens. I had never seen the Christ child so secondarily placed, with his back turned, as if to say, I must wait thirty years to become what I will become. It is my mother, rightfully so, who is the center of my life and this composition.

I can only imagine what this young sculptor will produce, if he is lucky enough to live a full life, without affliction of debilitating health. I have not been so lucky, though I am comforted to know I have had, at least, a part in planting a seed in the garden of his mind and thus encouraging the gift given to him by nature. What else is there, after all, than discovering genius and surrounding oneself with it in the hope that this genius will ripple through, seep into, and consume the person fortunate enough to be near it?

"I have brought the young Michelangelo to your bedside to cheer you up," Angelo says.

"I am much pleased," I say.

Michelangelo continues to stand near the door, looking at me with a frozen look. I do not blame him for not wanting to come near me. He has already seen the death of Bertoldo, his mentor. Now he must look at the death of his patron. I want to say, I know what it's like to see death at such a young age, but I much rather talk about life.

"Come here, my young friend," I say. "I wish to speak with you."

He approaches me and says, "How are you feeling, Lorenzo?"

"Much better now that you are here," I say, taking his hand in mine. "Angelo tells me you are well, though in search of inspiration."

"He is reading Ovid," says Angelo.

"Thanks to you, we can all read Ovid in our native language," I respond.

"It is a most wonderful translation," Michelangelo says.

"Have you considered Hercules?" I ask.

"I have, for your sake, Lorenzo," he answers.

"As half man and half god, sprung from Zeus and the mortal Alcmene, he is the perfect subject for marble," I say.

"I know that," he responds.

"Of course you do," I say.

Angelo approaches Michelangelo, placing an arm around the young man's shoulder. "Michelangelo has told me on more than one occasion that you are the living embodiment of the mythical character."

"If I were, I would be able to raise myself from this bed," I say. "I am afraid I am all man, not half god as him."

"There you are wrong, Lorenzo," Michelangelo says, releasing himself from Angelo's hold to kneel at my bedside, "for you are every bit a god as him."

"I act as him on symbol alone."

"You once told me if we use that which is half god in us, we can perform the twelve labors every day of our lives."

"You remember well."

"To me you are his incarnation. Have you not gone forth on twelve labors in your life?"

"He is right, Lorenzo," Angelo says, standing over the kneeling Michelangelo. "As a ruler, you have fought against every vice of the human heart, and you have prevailed."

"But now, facing death, I have met my match."

"You shall be the model for my Hercules," Michelangelo says.

"It is mankind itself that is the model," I reply.

"Nonetheless it is you as a poet, patron and statesman that will guide me in my work, for you, more than any man, have acted like the hero in every phase of his trials and tribulations."

"I regret only that I will not be around to see your work."

"Whatever I do is because of you."

"I wish one other work from you."

"Tell me what it is and it shall be done."

"It is much greater than Hercules."

"Then I shall have to be half god to do it."

"I believe, young Michelangelo, that you are all god."

"I wish to reach God through my work."

"Create for me twenty marble statues on the façade of San Lorenzo."

"Twenty marble statues?"

"If you do that you will not have to reach for God. He will reach his hand down to you."

Michelangelo squeezes my hand. His eyes remain firm. "For you I will create these twenty marble statues, even if it takes my lifetime to do it."

I believe him, for a man such as him, even at his young age, knows only his work. He forgets to eat and foregoes the desires of the flesh that always consumed me. It is for this reason I am certain he will be our greatest sculptor ever: a man willing to sacrifice himself on the cross of art.

"Thank you," I say.

"It is my pleasure, Lorenzo."

"No, my young friend, the pleasure is entirely mine."

"Michelangelo, why don't you read to Lorenzo from your collection of Ovid?" Angelo says.

"I shall, if it is what Lorenzo desires," he says.

"Read to me, Michelangelo, and make me dream."

"I shall read Hercules."

"Read of his death."

"By his death, you mean his birth."

"Yes, please."

The young sculptor reads. Angelo smiles. I drift in peace as I hear his voice, slow and deliberate:

*The snake sloughs its age and dullness*
*In a scurf of opaque tatters,*
*Emerging, new-made, in molten brilliance—*
*So the Tirynthian hero emerged*
*More glorious, greater, like a descended god.*
*Then his omnipotent father hoisted him*
*Through clouds, in a four-horse chariot,*
*And fixed him among the constellations.*

Men of genius surround me. I am lucky, even as my body writhes and struggles for breath. After all, how many men are fortunate enough to be in the same room with Michelangelo, Angelo Poliziano and Hercules?

## Savonarola

I received news today from France that King Charles' infant son has died. The king is so grieved he is backing out on his promise to invade Italy. I must write and tell him he can do no such thing. He is our only ally. Without his aid, the dragon in Rome will devour us.

*It is your duty to God. Have you forgotten? If you turn from us and fail to smite the dragon in Rome, you will betray God. I understand your grief, but this grief cannot distract you from your holy mission. Consider that the honors of this world, as well as its riches, vanish like the wind, and our time upon earth forever grows shorter. Suffering saves those who might otherwise be damned on account of their prosperity. Think of your son. Do not jeopardize his eternal salvation, risking the condemnation of God, by canceling the invasion of your army. If you act in defiance of God's will, your son's death will have been in vain and will suffer the pangs of purgatory. No infant should suffer such. You must listen to me for I speak not only as your spiritual advisor but also as God's emissary. What I write are the words of God Himself. It is He who wishes you to invade Italy because it is He who is most dismayed by the sins of man, most evident in the Vatican. Only an army such as yours can vanquish this sin and obliterate it forever. The pope is Satan manifest. God Himself has told me. You among men have been called by God to do His work. I am his messenger, his voice. You are His might and power. Take vengeance on those who oppose the will of God and those who have taken from France what is rightfully yours. We have given money to your cause, and in doing so we have surrendered our allies in Italy. You are our only friend and protector. Your armies will be such a welcome sight to our eyes, as they were years earlier. If we act together, we shall bring Italy to its knees and restore the Kingdom of God on earth. Heed my words, Majesty and friend. You have no choice if you care at all for your soul and the soul of your son.*

# Machiavelli

King Charles not only cancelled his invasion, he signed a treaty of peace with the Holy League. Savonarola's "Scourge of God" had betrayed him. Why was I not surprised? The preacher and Florence stood alone on the precipice of an abyss. Pope Alexander, no longer fearing a French reprisal, sent a Brief to every church in Florence, officially announcing Savonarola's excommunication, making it clear that he was banned from preaching and administering or taking Holy Communion. Anyone found assisting him in any way, either through speaking to him or approving of anything he did or said, would also be excommunicated.

I never gave much credence to talk of excommunication because it is a punishment for the life to come, not the one on earth. Why would I care if I can no longer receive the sacraments or be buried as a Christian? Does it make any difference once I'm dead? My fellow man believes it does. Thus, he will jump through hoops of fire or throw his children before him into the flames to avoid being excommunicated. The pope, as all popes before him, knows this well, and he uses it to maximum effect. I find it ludicrous, for it makes no sense to me how a man, albeit one with the title pope, believes he, among all men on earth, has the power to inflict such condemnation and punishment on his fellow humans. What's even more laughable is that people believe he possesses the aforementioned powers. Such a belief is only possible if a man lacks proper education. I, gratefully, am not one of those. The same was not true for many of Savonarola's supporters, who dropped from him like beads of sweat dripping from his temple. It is only understandable when viewed from a Christian perspective, such as this: What man of simple, unquestioning means would willingly bring about his excommunication and the presumed death of his immortal soul if he could help it?

Even Savonarola's boys disappeared from sight. Perhaps they continued to cling to his every word inside their cloister. The streets, though, had become for them dangerous. The last time I saw boys marching with crucifixes and candles, I witnessed young rebels from the crowds tearing off their robes, setting them on fire with the lighted candles, and throwing their crucifixes to the ground, whereupon the rebels stomped on them with fury, saying, "Death to the preacher!" I had heard from a reliable source that some of these same young rebels once broke into San Marco in the early morning to smear the pulpit in donkey excrement to prevent Savonarola from preaching.

On Ascension Day I walked over to the cathedral because I had heard a riot might be planned to disturb the service. I was at the time reporting to the ambassador in Rome and did not want to miss out on anything as exciting as a riot in church. Sadly, I missed most of it. As I approached, the cathedral's great doors swung open and men and women, with children, rushed down the steps, many saying, "Jesu!" Inside I saw swords drawn, though I saw no blood. Men pushed and shoved each other, some clanging their weapons near the pulpit, where Savonarola knelt in prayer, his head and eyes beseeching heaven. The young rebels rushed past me, content in having disturbed the service. I followed them out the door, for the armed men surrounding the preacher had made their way down the aisle, toward my direction. I stood on the street, inconspicuous in a doorway, long enough to see Savonarola's armed supporters hurry him back to San Marco up the Via del Cocomero.

# Savonarola

My faithful boys and devoted monks look to me for a response. I tell them I have no intention of accepting my excommunication. God will vouchsafe us from all danger and grant us a great victory, though the French have abandoned us. Now, more than ever we must prepare to fight, for make no mistake: this is a war we face. It is a war no different than those Christians have faced since time beginning, against any and all obstacles to the spirit and faith. I tell my followers that with Christ as our captain we will win, just as Joshua won, leading his followers through the obstacle of Jericho on his way to the Promised Land and as Gideon with an army of three hundred defeated the Midians, with their more than 135,000 soldiers. Did not David slay Goliath, who had mocked our faith and religion? How could such a young boy defeat one so formidable if not for his trust in God? We draw our strength from these examples, knowing that God is with us, and his defense is greater than any offense of man.

We can gain strength as well in knowing that what we follow is true, for the truth always wins out in the end. Those who label me a heretic cannot even tell me the meaning of the word. Thus, they are the hypocrites to the faith of our Lord. They are nothing but wolves that disguise themselves as sheep. We shall cut off their heads with the sword given to us by God.

We no longer speak of King Charles. He wrote, saying God had failed him in taking his infant son. He is a stupid and idle man. God does not fail anyone. It is man who fails God, and the king in signing his treaty of peace with the pope failed God. For that, he will suffer and die. I know not when or how, only that his death is imminent. I have prophesied the deaths of others, and all the prophecies came true. I know for certain this one will be true as well, for God ordains it, and no man can fight the will of God.

I have written to other theologians and learned authorities in defense of my wrongful excommunication. Here is my argument: I have only been accused of suspicion of heresy. Yet no proof or evidence has been given; no charge has been brought against me; there has been no trial; I have not been found guilty. Why should we of the clergy accept such charges when they are blatantly unlawful? Shouldn't we members of the clergy speak out for what is righteous and fair and defy wrongful excommunications? The pope cannot act as God, for he does not follow God's way. He, in fact, desecrates them. Why should I then accept a decision from one so fallible? I ask my fellow theologians for support in this matter. It is we who follow and live by scripture who should dictate the true tenants of spirituality and the laws of God. Let us not bend our wills to politics, for that is what the Vatican represents and cares about, not religion as set out by God.

To Alexander, I say this: It is you who are wrong. You are not the Church. You are simply a man and a sinner. This excommunication is a diabolical thing and was made by the devil in hell. You will rot and suffer for your sins, while I shall rest with God in heaven. That is the eternal truth. You may control the acts of men here on earth, but when you die your soul will suffer for your egregious sins. The sword of God will strike swiftly on your head, if not in this life, in the next. In time, all that will matter is the triumph of the cross. I don't expect you to know of such things, for you have not made theology and learning your calling, as I have. Instead you have sunk in iniquity, in all manner of vice and lasciviousness, blaspheming both the laws of nature and those of God. You may fool many with the miters you wear upon your head and the vestments with which you dress yourself. It is not, however, these outer trappings that make a man one with God and entitle him to enforce his laws. It is what lies in his heart and soul, made evident in his behavior and actions. I know what I say, for I have dedicated myself to my faith. I have shunned the appetite of the senses, choosing to douse myself in the icy waters to kill all desires of the flesh. I have suffered and sacrificed. I have earned my right to preach my sermons. You, as one who disrespects Jesus Christ, hold no authority to stop me.

# Machiavelli

I celebrated Savonarola's excommunication. My motives, unlike many, were not driven by personal animosity toward the preacher. I was just happy to see the taverns once again open and lively with bawdy songs and lewd conduct. I liked seeing people dance barefoot again in the Piazza, and most of all, I liked seeing prostitutes walk the streets, selling their wares without remorse. With one blow delivered by the pope--leave it to the pope, the king of the sensuous world--pleasure blossomed like a flower under a naked sun, and it shone for days on end.

It's not as if I didn't enjoy myself during the lean years of Savonarola's fundamentalism. I continued to meet my concubines, and neither the crazy, cross-carrying boys nor Savonarola's threats to execute those caught in adultery made me alter my ways. Though the threats got my attention, they made me all the more determined to circumvent the laws. Those who know me know I'm sly. Was I born that way? Perhaps. Then again, it could be my ability to adapt to the times. A man who is not sly gets caught, and I prefer to win.

I heard someone at the government office say, "Let's cheer the people up; should we all behave like monks?" The next day I attended the first horse race run in years. I set down my bet, for I have always enjoyed gambling. The jockeys arrayed themselves colorfully as their horses raced through the streets for a mile. I remember as a boy watching Lorenzo de' Medici race one of his prized horses. He raced only to win. Of course, as the prince of the city, no one questioned whether he cheated in his quest to win. If his horse galloped out before anyone else's, it did so with impunity.

I stood among a throng of wildly cheering people, reborn not in Savonarola's New Jerusalem, but in good old-fashioned civic entertainment. Suffice it to say I won my bet and afterwards spent my winnings on much drink and a fine woman.

# Savonarola

I sit in my cell, reliving the words I preached earlier in the day. God was with me then, as He is with me now. Is not this excommunication on all of us the same kind of burden of oppression laid on the children of Israel by the Pharaoh? And did not Moses lead his people from bondage? Do not leave me, people of Florence, as many have already in fear of being an accomplice in insubordination against the pope. I am like the good shepherd, ready to die to defend his flock. I will not leave you alone and abandoned in a sea of iniquity. Know that I will not stop preaching because I cannot stop preaching. My tongue will never stop talking as long as my head sits on my shoulder, for if I lie, Christ lies.

O Florence, do these four things to overcome the devil and his agents: love God, love the common good, forgive your enemies, and complete the reform God has given you. If you do these four things you will be richer, more glorious and more powerful than ever. You will become the City of God, O Florence, the wellspring of reform for the whole Church, and this renewed Church will lead the way to the Holy Land, where we will convert the Turk and other infidels. As new Christians, in a New Jerusalem, we will battle the Antichrist and win a glorious victory.

I saw for myself their hands raised to heaven. I heard for myself their weeping and their shouts for "Jesu." The City of God is alive. Christ still reigns supreme. As long as I have breath, I will speak the words of God, and I will speak against those who oppose Him. I whisper the words I said earlier: "A governor of the Church is a tool of God, but if he is not used like a tool, all of which are alike, he is no greater than any man. You may say to him, 'You do not do good, because you do not let yourself be guided by the supreme Lord.' And if he says, 'I have the power', you may say to him, 'That is not true, because there is no hand guiding you, and you are a broken tool."

My head throbs with pain. I have not slept, nor will I tonight. I have much to think about and write. Already I have bathed my eyes in vinegar to ensure my staying awake. I strike my bare chest with a stick. How many times I do not know. I cannot let go of the thoughts that punish me. I do not want to let go. What was the purpose of those who lied in order that I should be excommunicated? Once my excommunication was announced they once more abandoned themselves to excessive eating and drinking, to greed of all kinds, to consorting with concubines, to the sale of benefices, and to all manner of lies and wickedness. On whose side will thou be, O Christ? On the side of the truth or lies? Christ says, "I am the truth."

With burning eyes, I read St. Thomas of Aquinas. I have a need to channel his thoughts through my brain. Only then can I fully grasp his message. He wrote not for his times, but for posterity. I wish to do the same. I fear my words fall on deaf ears. Will they be better received in later centuries when the mind and spirit of man evolve accordingly? I have no answer at this time. I have only my words:

*We will not rely upon any authority, and will proceed as if we reject the teachings of any man in the world, no matter how wise he might be. Instead, we will rely solely on natural reason. Reason proceeds from the seen to the unseen in the following manner. All our knowledge is derived from the senses, which perceive the outer world; the intellect, on the other hand, perceives the substance of things. The knowledge of matter thus rises to the knowledge of the unseen and hence to God. Philosophers seek to find God in the marvels of visible nature. In the visible Church we seek and discover the invisible Church, whose supreme head is Jesus Christ. The mystic chariot of old passes across the heavens, bearing Christ the conqueror with his crown of thorns, and his bloodied wounds, illuminated by the celestial light from on high, shining like a triple sun, representing the Blessed Trinity.*

I strike myself again and again. I will not sleep. I will not rest until my work is complete; that is until my death. It is not my death I think about at this moment. I think of Alexander's death, for I am certain that before I die he must first die. At the very least he needs to be deposed. I must do something to expedite its occurrence. I decide to write a letter to many leaders in Europe, asking them to summon a Council of the Church, with the purpose of vanquishing Alexander. (I admit in this letter to referring to him as pope, for I do not want to offend my readers.) These men, Christian all, will understand the importance, and the urgency, of saving the Church from ruination. Even King Charles, I have learned, has reformed himself since his signing the treaty of peace with the Holy League. I hear he has since turned his thoughts to living according to God's commandments, asking for daily forgiveness for writing that God had failed him.

I see through the cell's tiny window dawn breaking. It is a sign from God. I ask Him to guide the words I write. It is, after all, for Him and His sacred, holy church I set about this task. I must save the church from ruination.

If not me, who then, O God?

"It is for you to do," He says.

I strike myself and wash my eyes with water. My head throbs and my hand shakes. Still, I write, as I must.

*The time to avenge our disgrace is at hand and the Lord commands me to expose new secrets, revealing to all the world the perilous waters into which the ship of St. Peter has sailed. Such circumstances are due to your lengthy neglect of these matters. The Church is filled with abominations, from the crown of her head to the soles of her feet, yet not only do you neglect to cure her of her ailments, but instead you pay homage to the very source of the evils which pollute her. Wherefore, the Lord is greatly angered and has for long left the Church without a shepherd. I now hereby testify in the word of the Lord, that Alexander is no pope, nor can he be regarded as one. Aside from the moral sin of simony by means of which he purchased the Papal Throne, and daily sells Church benefices to the highest bidder, as well as ignoring all the other vices which he so publicly flaunts—I declare that he is not a Christian, and does not believe in the existence of God, and thus far exceeds the limits of infidelity. Therefore, I invite all you princes of Christendom to summon a council as soon as possible. I cannot say where it should be held. That is for each of you to decide. I know only that it must take place. For the love of Christ, do not delay.*

I write a separate letter to King Charles, my first correspondence to him since he abandoned Florence. Knowing he is a changed man gives my words new confidence. He cannot disappoint God or me a second time.

*You surely cannot have forgotten the sacred role which the Lord has bestowed upon you, which means that should you fail to join this holy enterprise the punishment inflicted upon you will be far in excess of that meted out to the others. Be mindful that God has already given you the first sign of his wrath. You who bear the title of Most Christian King, you whom the Lord has chosen and armed with the sword of his vengeance, are you prepared to stand aside and witness the ruin of the Church? Are you willing to ignore the grave dangers that imperil her?*

I rush to have these letters dispatched at once. All of Christendom depends on their safe arrival to the various kings and emperors. My war against Alexander is official. It is a war none of us in the Christian world can stand to lose, even if it means I lose my life in the battle.

I am prepared for that.

I welcome it.

# Machiavelli

The Council of the Church never happened, for the letters Savonarola wrote failed to reach their intended destinations. Instead they reached Pope Alexander in Rome. Did Savonarola really think he could outfox the fox himself by slipping seditious letters past the borders into the hands of kings and emperors? Such an act insults Pope Alexander's greatest skill: sniffing out treason among the clergy, both near and far. Now the fox, with indisputable evidence of Savonarola's treachery, roared like a lion, pushing Florence further on the precipice, making life even more precarious for us as long as Savonarola held his title as Prior of San Marco and continued to preach his vitriolic sermons. The question that possessed every sane person--the insane still made up nearly half the population--was this: how can we curb Savonarola and thus eliminate the threat of citywide excommunication, which would spell the ruin of Florence economically as well as spiritually?

Enter Fra Francesco da Puglia, a Franciscan monk from Santa Croce. What he suggested brought a change in the tide that would never again revert back to the previous tide. He challenged Savonarola to an ordeal by fire. When the challenge reached the offices of government leaders, it was met initially with amusement. Florence was, after all, in need of serious solutions to a serious problem, namely excommunication. Such a barbaric ritual as ordeal by fire belonged to a cloistered Middle Age. I imagine a far off, remote, corner of the earth ruled by men with brains the size of walnuts, not to a city known for the *Rinascimento*, where evolved men from all of Europe came for its culture, art and learning. Would the people of this once great city witness a regressive act, wherein barefoot monks would walk along a passageway through fire, on red-hot coals to see who would burn and who, by some miracle, would survive, as people cheered for them, as one would cheer, I suppose, for a lion—is that Pope Alexander's roar I hear?--mauling a Christian?

How could this perversity be called anything but an entertainment? Yet it was exactly what the monk from Santa Croce proposed to reveal the fraudulence of Savonarola's sermons. Though his method for unmasking Savonarola was a desperate measure in accordance with the equally desperate time, who could argue against Fra Francesco's reasons? He did not believe Savonarola spoke with God, or that God spoke through him. He believed Savonarola was little more than a charlatan preacher, fooling people with false prophecies and visions; and if he weren't stopped he would lead the city to the brink of disaster with his holier-than-thou rhetoric and his insolence toward the pope.

"I believe that I shall burn," he told his fellow Franciscans, "but I am willing to do so for the sake of liberating the people of this city. If he does not burn, then you may believe that he is a prophet."

# Savonarola

Fra Domenico enters my cell. I have of late been writing my sermons for him to deliver. He has great oratorical skills. Someday, when I am gone, he will take my place and continue the work God has given us. He does not like such talk. He believes God will keep me safe forever, even into my old age. Can a man have a better protector than God? He says this whenever I question his optimism.

"You have heard of the challenge?" he says.

"I do not have time to walk through fire," I say.

"You do not have to do it. I will," he responds.

"You will do no such thing."

"I have delivered sermons for you."

"Delivering a sermon and walking through fire do not compare."

"It will not look good if we back down from the challenge."

"Let the Franciscans burn if they wish. We Dominicans have no time for foolish superstitions. It is the devil's work to walk through fire. He wishes to consume our souls in hell."

"Fra Francesco wishes to discredit that you are a prophet."

"Why should I indulge his jealousy of me?"

"You must prove him wrong."

"Do you really believe my followers require me to prove myself?"

"I am afraid we will lose credit with our followers if we don't do it. People will have reason to question our beliefs."

"I do not have to prove my doctrine comes from God. It is evident in all I have prophesied."

"And yet I worry about the risk to your reputation if we turn away from this challenge."

"Anyone who fails to accept my reputation does not understand the ordeals I have suffered at my own hands, in self-flagellation and fasting, in order to bring my soul closer to God's and to the truth He speaks and entrusts me to deliver."

He turns away, momentarily. I see in the droop of his shoulders a man in conflict with himself. I wait for him to turn back to me and reveal himself. He does again face me, though he looks not in my eyes.

"I have already accepted the challenge," he says.

I reach for his face and lift his eyes. "You must rescind the challenge."

"It is too late. I have signed and sealed a document, saying that I, not Fra Girolamo, will walk through the fire."

"You did not consult me."

"You were busy writing your letters to the Church Council."

"I cannot allow you to burn alive."

"God will guide and protect me."

He falls to his knees and prays to the crucifix on the wall. His eyes remain steely and determined. I cannot expect him to walk through fire in my place. I kneel beside him and begin a necessary communication with God. I ask Him to forgive Fra Domenico for his impulsive error, and afterwards, I say, in silence: I will enter the flames myself, Lord, if You tell me it is the right thing to do.

# Lorenzo

Angelo dampens the cloth in the water basin near my bed. He washes my hands and arms, continuing until he reaches my face, careful not to rub too hard on the open lesions and sores that mark it.

"I already have a servant girl hired to do what you do," I say.

"I am a servant as well," he responds.

"You are a poet."

"One who serves you."

"I marvel at how you are not offended by the sight of me."

"I see only your heart and mind."

"Does the world see my heart and mind, as you do?

"How does it not? Look at what you have done."

"Remind me."

I say this, I believe, with a wink of the eye. He smiles and indulges me.

"You are the world's greatest cultural ambassador. You sent Botticelli to Rome; Leonardo to Milan."

"The politics of art."

"Cultural imperialism."

"And yet Savonarola wishes to return us to the Dark Ages."

"That will never happen. The mind of man and his achievements are a wonder. Nothing will ever interfere with their continued growth."

"Let us not forget there was once a golden age of Greece, followed by Augustus and then the golden age of Rome."

"To which we now reap the benefits."

"And yet for more than a thousand years the doors of learning men had opened had closed."

"Until we opened them yet again."

"Yes, but is not a door as easily closed as it is opened?"

"Rest assured, the year is 1492, and the time returns. Do you not remember your motto?"

"*Le tems revient.*"

"These doors that are opened are forever. What has been created under your reign, and that of your family's, will reverberate through the ages. The darkness of the past has been replaced by the golden light of the future."

I do not want Angelo to leave my side. I want his face to be the last image of my eyes and his voice to be the final sound to my ears as I begin my journey to the other side. If I ask him, I know he will take that journey with me, if only he can. Such has been the depth and breadth of his service and friendship. His presence and words act as a balm on my mind and body.

"Recite to me the words of the dying Emperor Constantine."

"The play you wrote."

"Yes, *The Martyrdom of Saints John and Paul.*"

He draws closer to me and speaks. I marvel at how he can recite on memory alone. I take solace knowing that his mind and words will continue for the sake of Florence and beyond when I am gone.

> *With endless tribulations I have reigned*
> *And met the dangers offered by each day.*
> *Rest there, my sword, with victories ingrained;*
> *No more I'll challenge Fortune in the fray.*
> *Fickle is she: men lose what they have gained,*
> *And those who seek too much will go astray.*
> *The pain of rule, its anguish, sons, you'll learn*
> *When you control the state for which you yearn.*

"You will look after Piero?"

"I shall remain loyal to your family's name."

"I am afraid for his deficiencies."

"And yet his greatest asset is the Medici name he bears."

"A name is but a name, though it carries the greatness of its legacy. A man needs wit, charm and intelligence, as well. Those, I'm afraid he is lacking."

"He will maintain what you have left him, which is much: a solid state and peace throughout Italy."

"A solid state and peace can change with the tide. I know that well."

"The leading citizens have been united around your administration for the past twelve years. None have dared speak against it."

"Yet I know all too well how the death of a leader changes those who have served him. Men, by nature, are ambitious and vengeful."

"In bad times, perhaps, but the past years under your reign have seen good times, and there's no reason to believe they won't continue to be good. We have abundant supplies of food and crops. The trades are bringing great wealth to many. Men of intellect and talent are engaged in arts and letters and are being rewarded for their gifts. You have created strong foreign alliances with Rome, Naples and Milan. Why should any man be dissatisfied to live in such peace and prosperity?"

"You are a man of poetry and dreams, Angelo, and that is why I have always loved you."

"My poetry and dreams reflect yours."

"But you have not sat on the hot seat of politics as I have."

"From that I have been graciously spared."

"If you have sat on that seat, you would understand the fickleness of friendship and alliances. Thus, as much as I want to share your optimism, I am afraid for Piero and the future of Florence."

"What good is fear, my friend? It only serves to kill hope. Is it not better to hold fast to poetry and dreams?"

He squeezes my hand and kisses it. His eyes hold me in a warm embrace. I want to live inside them and never leave their wondrous world.

"Yes, you're right, as you always are," I say. "Give me more of your poetry and dreams and do not let go."

He smiles warmly, squeezing tighter. His eyes are moist with impending tears.

"Neither time nor death can separate or remove the love I and all of Florence has for you, Lorenzo de' Medici."

"Thank you, Angelo," I say, turning from the unbearable sight of his eyes. "Now give me words and soothe my mind, as only you can."

"Close your eyes and dream as I speak."

I do as he asks, clinging to the hand that holds mine, feeling its rush of life pass through me like the blood in my veins.

"I give you Ovid's world, far from the cares of this earthly life."

My eyes remain closed as he speaks. I picture a world made perfect by a blend of poetry and dreams.

> *When he, whoever of the gods it was, had thus arranged in order and resolved that chaotic mass, and reduced it, thus resolved, to cosmic parts, he first moulded the Earth into the form of a mighty ball so that it might be of like form on every side, and that no region might be without its own forms of animate life, the stars and divine forms occupied the floor of heaven, the sea fell to the shining fishes for their home, Earth received the beasts, and the mobile air the birds—then Man was born. Though all other animals are prone and fix their gaze upon the Earth, he gave to Man an uplifted face and bade him stand erect and turn his eyes to heaven.*

When he finishes, I open my eyes. I watch him walk to the window and draw the curtains, allowing inside the room a bright sun.

"Turn your eyes," he says.

# Machiavelli

No one in the city can remember a time when an ordeal by fire took place. According to history, it's been nearly two hundred years. As a young man, when I read about such a spectacle in previous centuries, I believed the stories only as mythology, something as unlikely and unreal as the god Zeus throwing thunderbolts in rage or his son Apollo racing a chariot across the sky, pining for love and adventure.

I'm sure the sane world, if such a world exists, begs to know how and why the leading citizens of Florence laid aside republican, humane values to approve a barbaric practice belonging to a bygone period. Hadn't they initially reacted to Fra Francesco's proposal with amusement? What happened for them to consider it seriously? Here's my explanation: Leaders who opposed Savonarola began to lick their chops after having evaluated Fra Francesco's challenge to Savonarola. I imagine them saying this:

What a perfect scenario! The little friar can't win, no matter what he chooses. If he enters the fire, he will burn. If he refuses the challenge, he will reveal himself as a fraud and a heretic, unwilling to put his doctrine to God's test. His followers will abandon him, and the city will riot against him, ending with his seizure and imprisonment. The city will rid itself of his presence once and for all and can then restore its alliances and economy, to say nothing of its freedom from religious oppression.

Seen from this angle, Florence has much to gain by staging a spectacle wherein monks from both the Dominican and Franciscan orders will burn alive. As a leading citizen said--I dare not write his name, for fear of retribution--"As far as I am concerned, if this trial restores harmony amongst our citizens, then let it go ahead. We should be worried about the city, not about a few friars getting burned."

Now that leaders have officially sanctioned medieval barbarism, we can no longer fool ourselves. Talk of Florence as an advanced culture and civilization shouldn't cloud the truth, and the truth is that men in Florence in 1498 are as barbaric as men a thousand years earlier, in places far and wide in dark corners of the earth, where conquerors split open the heads of men, women and children with blades of steel. Oh, sure, there are a few detractors, holding to some storybook ideal about how people in a republic should behave. One such person suggested a trial by water, saying if the friar could pass through the water without getting wet, he would certainly join in asking for his pardon. His suggestion was quickly laughed away, to the delight of the many. The citizens of Florence, at their core, are bloodthirsty. They talk of little else these days but the impending ordeal by fire. I hear it everywhere: in the market, taverns, palazzi, and streets.

"Is Savonarola capable of performing a miracle?"

Most know he's not and want to see him burn. Though it's an event about men walking through flames, I believe that more than bodies will burn. Their beliefs will go up in smoke as well, extinguishing the illusions, delusions, and conversations of miracles. In the end nothing will remain but the charred remains of a monk who believes himself greater than other men. No one should ever think that. We are just men, after all. We struggle for years to live, and in what takes only a moment, we die easily.

I haven't seen anyone place bets, though it won't surprise me if I do. People are excited, and who can blame them? It's not every day they get to see their fellow men, albeit monks, burn themselves to death on their own accord. I've seen carnivals, horse races, festivals and even executions, but I have never seen excitement such as this event has created among the citizens. Given the recent problems, who can blame anyone for their excitement? Our commerce is all but stagnant, our vanities consigned to flames, our leaders divided and embittered over the collective loss of civic pride. Does not this event then come at just the right time to distract people from their disappointments? Besides, everyone knows it's a once-in-a-lifetime occurrence, likely never to happen again.

# Savonarola

Is it possible that a miracle will occur, Lord? Give me a sign, for I know not what to think anymore. Fra Silvestro came to me to share a vision he had. He said he talked with two guardian angels; one was mine and the other was Fra Domenico's. Both guardian angels said Fra Domenico would walk through the flames unscathed. Did you send these angels to the friar? Can I trust him, Lord? He is old and given to hallucinations. Fra Domenico has such faith and enthusiasm, believing you will protect him from the flames. I fear the outcome unless you do indeed protect him. We will be exposed to the wrath of the people. I shall be exiled, or, worse, condemned to death, and if by some chance, the ordeal is cancelled, we shall be condemned as frauds. The people now are certain they want a miracle or they want death. Nothing else will suffice.

Can you give us this miracle, Lord? It is our only hope. I have locked the gates of the monastery. No one is permitted to enter or leave. I have asked each of my brethren to engage in continuous vigil. They pray now in the cloister as I speak to you. I have told them you will answer their prayers. You will guide our actions, as you always have, for we are beholden to you. Men know not what they do or say. They are blind and deaf without your guidance. I pray now for the salvation of the Dominican order. I pray now to justify all I have done as Prior of this monastery and as servant to you, Lord. If I must lay down my life, it is for your cause I do so.

I pray that tomorrow, the day of the ordeal, will be our day of reckoning, when all who witness our brethren walking through the flames unscathed will surrender themselves unequivocally to the one true belief that is you, my Lord. I have not asked for anything from you, for I am not worthy. I ask now, however, that you show your will and spirit tomorrow and lead us to victory, for the sake of our faith and our undying devotion to You, your Son and the Holy Mother.

# Machiavelli

The day is April 7, 1498, a Saturday. Only men fill the Piazza. Women and children, on order of the Signoria, are not permitted. It's too bad for the children. I was grateful to my father when he took me to see the executions twenty years earlier. I credit those human horrors for providing me a critical education about the nature of man. I do not understand why we protect children from such activities. Each day they see people dying in the streets from starvation. Why shouldn't they be allowed to see people die in flames? Where else but here in the Piazza della Signoria can they see such memorable theater? To see men from religious orders act upon crazed superstitions has great value in shaping one's mind. If nothing else, it will inform him to avoid becoming a monk.

I stand in front of the crowd, my view unimpeded. The man next to me says, "This will surely result in such a miracle that it will reflect upon the glory of God, as well as bring peace to our city." I do not respond to him. How can he see what I do and believe such nonsense? In front of us is the apparatus, the death machine. It should be clear to anyone looking at it that there will be no miracle, no glory of God, and no peace. It should be clear to him that there will be only death, followed by more death in the coming days and years, well past our lifetimes, and into the ensuing centuries. Men die horrible deaths at the hands of men. Get used to it, I want to say to him, but I don't, for I have better things to do, such as watch the festivity, because that's what it is, a spectacle on the grandest scale, and I don't want to miss it on account of senseless chatter.

I appreciate the effort of those who constructed the apparatus. It is an impressive work of engineering: more than seven feet high and perhaps as long as one hundred feet and easily wide enough to accommodate two or three monks, side by side. Logs, covered with brushwood and boughs, line a walkway, consisting of brick and rubble and covered with earth, on both sides. I can see the logs glisten with oils, and I can smell the resin on them. I wait eagerly to see them blaze like an inferno when they are lit.

I have been told what to expect. Each contestant will start simultaneously on opposite ends. Each will walk for the entire one hundred feet, through the flames, until he emerges at the other end unscathed or consumed by the flames. If Fra Domenico burns, Savonarola must leave Florentine territory within three hours. Though it has been agreed upon by the Signoria that he will be exiled forever, I do not believe the authorities, his enemies, will let him off so easily. I believe he will be captured and sent to Rome, where Pope Alexander salivates at the prospect of having his nemesis under lock and key.

It is now one o'clock. I watch as the Franciscans arrive in silence, dressed in plain brown robes tied with knotted white ropes. I estimate their number to be as many as two hundred. Much cheering greets them as they take their place on the side of the piazza designated for them. The Dominicans appear thirty minutes later. Their number is greater, as is their display. Hundreds of them walk in pairs, holding torches, candles and red crucifixes, chanting prayers and singing, "Let God rise up and dispel his enemies." Fra Domenico follows, dressed in a full-length cloak of fiery red velvet. He holds a large crucifix four feet high. Savonarola walks behind him, holding up an enlarged Host. When they take their designated place, separated from their opponents by a wooden barrier, they erect an altar and say a brief Latin mass. Meanwhile, the Franciscans keep their heads down, in silence and meditation.

The crowd grows impatient with the drawn-out preliminaries. "We are not here for mass," a man yells. "We are here to see you burn!"

Some throw rocks and sticks in their direction.

"If you are God's chosen one, let us see the evidence," another man says. Finally, the Signoria interrupt the Dominican mass and call forth the contestants. Fra Domenico steps forward to assume his position. The crowd cheers. Many yell, "Burn!" Fra Francesca also steps forward, but he does not take his position. The

276

Franciscans, collectively, voice an objection. They want Fra Domenico to remove his full-length cloak of fiery red velvet, believing the cloak will protect him from the flames.

"The color red may have demonic powers," I hear Fra Francesco say.

Fra Domenic claims that angels with pure white hands stitched his cloak.

"Remove the cloak," Fra Francesco demands.

The crowd by now has fast become a mob. Much pushing and shoving occurs behind me, as men take sides.

"Remove the cloak," one says, "He wants the devil's advantage."

Another says, "Let him wear his cloak. It is made by God in heaven."

After more conferring by both sides, with the government leaders acting as judges, Fra Domenico takes off his cloak and steps forward wearing only his undershirt. The Dominicans chant and pray. Still Fra Francesca does not take his position. He now says that Fra Domenico's undershirt may also be bewitched. "You will not be happy until he walks naked into the flames," Savonarola says. "But this we cannot allow."

"He must wear someone else's undershirt," says Fra Francesca. "We do not trust the authenticity of any of his garments."

"It is we who should not trust you," says Savonarola, "for you have tried to befoul our image."

"Your image needs no befouling from us," says Fra Francesco, "for it is already soiled with demagoguery and demonic intent."

The governing officials, who had been conferring, agree that Fra Domenico should change his undershirt. He leaves briefly with another monk and an official—who I assume goes with them to ensure the swap of undershirts actually occurs—to go inside the building.

Meanwhile, the crowd jeers and protests loudly. "We did not come for a fashion show," says one man, running from the guards towards the stage. "Give us what we want: the charred remains of evil monks."

Guards escort the man back to the crowd. Fra Domenico returns, wearing a different undershirt. Savonarola hands him the four-foot high crucifix. The Franciscans protest again. Fra Domenico should not be allowed to carry the crucifix into the flames. Since Fra Francesco does not carry a sacred object, seeking an advantage from Christ, it is unfair for Fra Domenico to be allowed this privilege. After a brief conference, out of my earshot, by the leaders from both sides with the Signoria, I see Savonarola take the crucifix from Fra Domenico. It appears the Franciscans have won yet another appeal and that with the grace of fickle fortune the event will now proceed. Such is not the case, however, for as Savonarola takes the crucifix away from Fra Domenico, he replaces it with the enlarged Host Savonarola had been carrying.

I hear Savonarola say, "He must be allowed to carry the Host."

The Franciscans, of course, disagree and voice a loud protest. They equate the Host with the crucifix, saying that he shouldn't be allowed to carry any sacred object. On this issue, Savonarola is less diplomatic. He insists that Fra Domenico be allowed to take the Host. He will not relent. The Franciscans do not back down either. They refuse to proceed with the event until Fra Domencio surrenders the Host. I care not at all that Fra Domenico carries a crucifix or a Host. I do not believe such superstitious tricks will help him, for I am not a holy man, as are the Franciscans. They understand the power of the crucifix and Host in ways I can never know. Frankly, I do not want to know, and neither do the people near me. They jeer both religious orders with equal dissatisfaction.

"We are not here to hear monks talk theology," someone says. "We are here to watch whether they will burn in the flames."

The officials confer again with leaders from both sides. I hear one say, "Fra Domenico can carry the Host as far as where the fire starts. Then he will have to relinquish it. He cannot enter the fire with it." Though the decision satisfies the Franciscans, Savonarola protests:

"I forbid his entering the flames without the Host."

"Light the fire!" someone yells, and these words are quickly repeated by others in the crowd, building with bloodthirsty fury. I find myself saying it as well. Today I am no different than anyone else. I have come for the ordeal by fire. I want to see monks burn, though my motive is not for the sake of its violence and abomination. I want proof that men who aspire to be higher than others because of their faith are, in the end, no more blessed than sinners, such as myself. Flesh burns, no matter what one believes. I want the illusion of faith to be put to rest. I detest men who dwell in dreams at the expense of what is real and true.

The sky turns dark, as the monks on stage appear motionless. A man breaks free from the crowd with a lighted torch. He runs to light the logs. Armed men intercept him.

"You have betrayed us all with your false promises," the man yells as he is taken away. The crowd jeers the armed men, which results in more armed men approaching the area where I stand. The armed men shove the crowd. The crowd shoves back. The "Light-the-fire" refrain continues; yet little is resolved among the judges and the religious leaders.

I hear a rumble in the sky. I look and see a streak of lightning.

"It will not happen," I say to the man next to me.

"What, the miracle?" he responds.

"The ordeal by fire will not happen," I say.

"It is God's will," he states.

As I move away from him, I hear repeated rolls of thunder. It starts to rain. No one moves. We are used to rain. The rain gives the Dominicans reason to speak foolish words:

"It is a sign from God."

"He is upset with this ordeal by fire."

"He will not allow those who serve Him to burn."

The Signoria confer with armed men and leading citizens. I watch the Franciscans and Dominicans separate. Fra Domenico places his cloak on his body once again.

I hear, "The ordeal by fire is cancelled."

The voice does not come from the crowd. It comes from the Signoria. They wave their hands and signal people to leave the piazza. Armed men begin moving the reluctant crowd. It is now raining heavily. I walk away and find shelter under the overhang of a building, continuing to watch and listen as people walk away angrily. I hear only anti-Savonarola sentiment.

"He is to blame for this."

"He never took on the challenge himself."

"Why is that?"

"He is not the prophet and messenger of God he says he is."

"Where are his miraculous powers now?"

"He is a fraud."

"A charlatan."

"The end is near for him."

I watch the Franciscans leave.

Is that a smile I see on Fra Francesca's face? I am not surprised. He had no intention of submitting himself to the flames. He never did. His only intention was to trick Savonarola into the ordeal by fire. He walks away a winner since he had nothing to prove to anyone. It is Savonarola who must prove his doctrine comes from God. Fra Francesca knew all along that people would turn on Savonarola if they came for miracle, and it didn't occur. He was right. No wonder he is smiling.

I suspect the Signoria, most of them enemies of Savonarola, are part of the *coup* to undermine the preacher's reputation. It is easier to rid one of power when his supporters turn from him. These are not stupid, idle men. They are men driven by ambition and vengeance. I imagine their voices: How dare Savonarola bring our beloved city to the precipice of an abyss? He will pay, in due time.

That due time is now.

I watch the Dominicans leave as they entered, walking in pairs, holding crucifixes and candles, still chanting prayers and singing hymns, as if they had just won a great victory. Though they continue to live in delusion, Savonarola, finally, knows what's real and true. I see him shrink in the rain, becoming smaller with each step. He is neither the messenger of God, the prophet, nor the holy man he had always believed himself to be. He is just a man, subject to the rain that dampens both his clothing and his spirit. He does not pray or sing along with the others. He is silent, alone in contemplation, for he knows what the cancellation of the ordeal by fire means. He knows he is the loser. He knows, as most of the people in the piazza know, that the end for him is near. I can see it in his eyes. They show not the fear of God.

They show the fear of men.

# Savonarola

I am dressed in my sacred vestments and hold a crucifix at all times. Many of my faithful brethren surround me in the choir of the church, where burning torches illuminate the room. It is a beautiful sight, though the sound of explosions, rioting and shouting in the monastery distracts my eyes and the spirit of God that is normally among us. Many leave the choir brandishing halberds in their hands, helmets on their heads, and breastplates donned over their Dominican robes. They move swiftly into the area outside where the fighting builds even greater with their shouts.

"Long live Christ!" I hear, followed by the firing of the halberds. We had been preparing for years for such a siege on our monastery, which explains the formidable array of weapons in our possession. Still, I know we cannot match the firepower of the Signoria and the mob of vigilantes. I am told there is a thousand ducats reward for anyone who captures me. I cannot allow the fight to continue much longer. Why should my friars die because of me?

Fra Domenico and Fra Silvestro have remained by my side. They shield me, promising to sacrifice their lives for me, saying I am more important than them; that they are replaceable, and I am not. I tell them I do not want anyone to die for me. I prefer to die alone.

"Let me go forth," I say, "since this storm has only arisen because of me."

"Do not leave us," Fra Domenico responds. "You will only be torn limb from limb; and what will become of us once you are gone?"

"You will continue to live according to scripture."

"You are our bridge to God. Without you the passage to Him becomes so much harder."

"Harder maybe, but possible just the same."

"You are our light. Without you we shall live in darkness."

The fighting outside the door grows louder, with more shots being fired and more determined cries of "Long live Christ." I imagine the sight of my courageous monks lying bloodied. I can take no more. I assemble the remaining monks in the choir and have them sit near my feet.

"Listen to me," I say.

"We are your servants," they respond in one communal voice.

"Every word that I have said came to me from God, and as He is my witness in heaven I do not lie. I am departing from you with deep sorrow and anguish, so that I can surrender myself into the hands of my enemies. I do not know whether they intend to kill me. However, you can be certain that if I die I shall be able the better to aid you from heaven than I have been able to do here on earth."

Many of them weep. I tell them to hold their tears and shed them for the Lord, our God, and for his Son, Jesus Christ, and his Holy Mother. They are more worthy to receive their tears, for they have sacrificed much for us. Fra Domenico asks what he can do for me. I tell him I wish to receive communion. He stands and offers me the Host, saying, "May the body of Christ be with you." I receive the Host gratefully and walk among my loyal friars, kissing each one of them. Each begs to go with me. I look at Fra Domenico, who was willing to walk through flames to prove his love both for God and me. I choose him to go with me, though I prefer to go alone.

"You will not go alone," he says. "If you must die, I prefer to die with you."

Fra Domenico opens the door. The fighting stops momentarily as I walk out. The enemy soldiers aim their weapons. The helmeted monks, with their halberds at the ready, make a move toward them. "Do not shoot," I shout. "No more blood and violence. It is over."

"Who are you?" a soldier I presume to be a mercenary from a province far from Florence asks.

I consider telling him I am Jesus Christ, for in this moment I imagine his capture by Temple guards in the Garden of Gethsemane.

"Who is it you want?" I ask.

"Fra Girolamo Savonarola."

"I am he."

"You are the wretched monk who has deceived the good people of Florence?"

"I have already said that I am he."

Several monks rush to shield me. The enemy soldiers cock their rifles.

"If you are looking for me," I say, "then let these men go."

A soldier places manacles on my wrists and ankles.

"I am with him," Fra Domenico says.

"We do not want you."

"I shall go just the same."

"As you wish."

Fra Domenico is also shackled.

Many of the monks protest our being chained. "It is the Lord's will," I say to them. "Pray for us and the glory that is Christ."

They weep as a soldier drags me by the arm. I cannot walk. The chains around my ankles dig deep into my flesh and bones. I move beyond the doors, into the street, which is illuminated by flickering torches held by those who hate me. A man spits in my face, and another throws a torch in my direction, saying, "Behold the true light!" The soldier dragging me deflects the torch and stamps out its flame with his foot. A young man rushes from the crowd and kicks my backside, yelling with laughter as he says, "Look, this is where his prophecies come from." I look down and notice a trail of blood beneath my feet.

I say nothing, for I am at one with Christ at last.

# Machiavelli

Here's an irony of historical relevance: Savonarola was locked away in the same tiny cell in the palazzo where Cosimo de' Medici had been imprisoned more than sixty years earlier. Cosimo, unlike the monk, had a network of wealthy supporters who helped him escape. Savonarola had no such network. He had only God and a contingency of poor monks, though I never knew God and monks to help a man stave off torture and execution. Only in man's mythology did that happen. In this earthly paradise of ours, an imprisoned man finds himself face to face with one tormenter after the other, and in most cases he breaks under the duress of physical pain. I know this not from having witnessed it from a distance. I know it from having lived it. I myself was imprisoned, years after Savonarola's demise, during the Medici return to power, when it was fashionable to label those of who had been loyal servants of Florence all our lives as traitors plotting to overthrow the new regime. Thus, I have experienced the Strappado, the torture most favored by our Florentine fathers for centuries, designed to tear a man's limbs and, even more so, his will.

I recall having my hands tied behind my back and hooked to a pulley, which was raised until my wrists suspended me in the air. When the pulley was released, my body dropped many feet before coming to a sudden stop above the ground, the fall broken by the rope tied around my wrists. I felt the pain most in my shoulders, which became dislocated after each drop. My tormenters were not entirely unsympathetic. They made sure to have a surgeon on hand to manipulate my shoulders back in place so the procedure could be repeated several more times, until I confessed to treason for betraying my government. I gave no such confession, of course, because I never betrayed my government or committed a treasonous act. I have been nothing but patriotic towards Florence in my lifetime. Why, then, should I confess my guilt to something of which I was innocent?

I viewed the Strappado as little more than a character-building exercise, believing that if I bore it with stoicism I would esteem myself the more for having done so. I have always believed, and will to the end of my days, that the first law of nature is self-preservation. The truth is the torture I received was not the most painful part of my imprisonment. Listening to prayers being said outside my window, for the salvation of my soul, was worse. I had not embraced religion during my lifetime. Why would I embrace it just because I was imprisoned and being tortured in my perceived weakest time? Why should I turn to God in my hour of need when I never turned to him during the good times? I am not a hypocrite, nor do I look for what is easy and comfortable, if it means surrendering my principles.

I mention my brief personal history--though, as should be clear, I am more interested in the history of others--only because this particular anecdote is relevant to Savonarola's experience, since he also received the Strappado. One might think that given his personal training as a monk wherein he tortured himself with self-deprivation, believing suffering an attribute, as well as a prerequisite to living with God in holy heaven, he could endure the Strappado with stoicism, as I had later done, and in doing so would have refused to give a confession that would damage the sanctity of his reputation as a genuine holy man.

Such was not the case, however. The little friar could not overcome having his limbs torn repeatedly. Perhaps if he had placed more faith in himself and less in God, as I had always done, he could have managed better. Perhaps if he had eaten well and taken better care of his body during his lifetime, his muscles and limbs could have withstood more punishment. Who's to say, really, why one can endure more pain than another? What's clear is that spiritual strength alone is deficient in helping a man at such times. He needs something stronger than a belief in God. He needs pride and a will the size of a continent. Those are not characteristics one gets from God. He gets them from himself. Savonarola thus was ill equipped to face the judicial commission set up to discover, through means dictated by men without fear of retribution from God, whichever laws he might have broken, and whether his claims to be a prophet and to have spoken with God were true.

Though I wasn't present at his interrogations—the first of which took place on Good Friday and the second on Easter Sunday--I learned from a reliable source that after many drops of the Strappado, Savonarola told his tormentors, while hanging suspended by his wrists, "I am not a prophet! Take me down, and I will tell you what you wish to know." Having been made an official civil servant at that time, I was invited to attend, several days later, the protocol, which was in effect the transcript of the preacher's confession, which included his signature. I did not believe he wrote anything, for a man with broken limbs cannot write. I know this to be true from my own experience. I believe rather that someone wrote the words for him, and he merely signed or had someone help him sign his name to this confessional. Such is the power of torture.

Here is what I heard read aloud:

"If you are not and never were a prophet, why then did you lie to the people of Florence?"

"Regarding my aim, I say, truly, that it lay in the glory of the world, in having credit and reputation; and to attain this end, I sought to keep myself in credit and good standing in the city of Florence, for the said city seemed to me a good instrument for increasing this glory, and also for giving me name and reputation abroad."

"Did you receive from God the words you preached?"

"I did not receive any words from God?"

"You lied about having receiving divine revelations?"

"Yes, I lied."

"Why did you lie?"

"For the sake of my standing with the people of Florence."

"None of your prophecies came from God?"

"They came from me alone."

"The New Jerusalem of which you spoke was also a lie."

"Yes, I never intended Florence to be a City of God. I created that lie to advance my position of power."

"So you are saying the City of God was a lie?"

"The City of God and the New Jerusalem were lies I told to deceive the good people of Florence."

"Christ was never the king of Florence, as you said?"

"Christ was never king. I was the only ruler of the people."

"What was your purpose for creating a new republic for Florence?"

"I created a new republic because it allowed me to reach my aims."

"Did you fix elections for the Signoria and the Great Council?"

A long pause is noted here. I imagine Savonarola's eventual response came after a threat of another Strappado.

"Yes, I did. I sought to shape it accordingly. I intended that those who called themselves my friends should rule more than others, and this is why I favored them best."

"Did you have an alliance with Piero de' Medici?"

"No, I strongly opposed him."

"You did not commit treason by conspiring with Piero de' Medici?"

"No, I did not."

The transcript continues two days later, after it is certain that Savonarola received more torture and dislocated limbs.

"Did you have an alliance with Piero de' Medici?"

"Yes, I did."

"For the purpose of conspiring against the republic of Florence?"

"Yes, if this is what you wish me to say."

"We wish to know the truth."

"I have told you the truth when I am not under torture."

"Do you wish further drops of the Strappado?"

"No, please, no more."

"Then what is the truth you wish to tell us?"

"That I was in alliance with he who you mentioned."

"Piero de' Medici?"

"I have already said."

"Say his name, then. Say 'I conspired with Piero de' Medici in an act of treason against the republic of Florence'?"

"I conspired with Piero de' Medici in an act of treason against the republic of Florence."

"And did you as well write to King Charles of France?"

"Yes, I did, for the benefit of Florence."

"Are you aware that news has just come from France that the king has died from a fall to his head?"

"I prophesied that he would die."

"You said earlier you were not a prophet."

"I am not."

"And yet you say you prophesied his death."

"Yes."

"And did this prophecy come from God?"

"It came only from me."

"Did you call for a Council of the Church?"

"Yes, I did, to rid the Church of the corruption in Rome."

"And what of the corruption of your own church?"

"I know not what you mean."

"Did you not corrupt the friars at San Marco?"

"No, I cannot confess to having done that."

"Shall I read to you what your friars wrote to the pope in defense of their own excommunication?"

"I wish not to know."

"I read verbatim what they wrote about you: 'Not only ourselves, but men of much greater wisdom, were persuaded by Fra Girolamo's cunning. The sheer power and quality of his preaching, his exemplary life, the holiness of his behavior, what appeared to us as his devotion, and he effect it had in purging the city of its immorality, usury and all manner of vices, as well as the events which appeared to confirm his prophecies in a way beyond any human power or imagining, and were so numerous and of such a nature that if he had not retracted his claims, and confessed that his words were not the words of God, we would never have been able to renounce our belief in him. For so great was our faith in him that all of us were ready to go through fire in order to support his doctrine.'"

"Men will write anything when their immortal souls are threatened."

"Does this letter not prove that you are as corrupt as those you accuse in Rome, including the Holy Father?"

"You know yourself the depth of corruption in Rome. All of Florence's citizens know."

"Did you wish to become pope yourself by laying such claims?"

"I wished to become greater, for the pope is a low man."

"And you see yourself as higher than any man?"

"No."

"You see yourself higher than the Signoria and all our judicial commission?"

"I am not and yet if I say I am not you will torture me. Thus, I say that I am to receive a reprieve from the pain you will surely render me."

It mattered not at all whether anyone present believed Savonarola had said or written any of what was revealed in the transcript. What did matter was that the officials conducting the inquiry receive his signature. To that end, credit the founding fathers of the Republic for creating a torture machine such as the Strappado that can make even a man of God and high intelligence into a lower form of animal, not much better than our beasts of burden.

No one took into account either that priests did not fall under the jurisdiction of the civil authorities and could only be tried by the Church courts. The pope in Rome, Alexander VI, least of all, didn't care. He wrote, applauding the Signoria:

"It gave us the greatest pleasure when your ambassador informed us of the timely measures you have taken in order to crush the mad vindictiveness of that son of iniquity, Fra Girolamo Savonarola, who has not only inspired such heresies amongst the people with his deluded and empty prophesies, but has also disobeyed both your commands and our orders by force of arms. At last he is safely imprisoned, which causes us to give praise to our beloved Savior, whose divine light sheds such truth upon our earthly state that He could not possibly have permitted your faithful city to have remained any longer in darkness."

Ironic words for sure from the pope, considering what had transpired in recent weeks: the ordeal by fire, the war at San Marco, and the torture and subsequent confession of Savonarola.

Evidently hell had opened beneath our feet.

# Savonarola

I lie in complete darkness on the stone floor, utterly broken; my arms have been destroyed, especially my left one, which is useless, dangling lifelessly by my side. My worst punishment is that I cannot write. Even if I possessed pen, paper and light, I would be unable to write, for my arms are so damaged that I have no feeling in my hands and fingers. I have only my voice, and I have never loved it as much as I do now, given it is the only instrument I have to transmit words. I am thinking of the Psalm *Miserere* as I speak aloud.

Unfortunate am I, abandoned by all, I who have offended heaven and earth, where am I to go? With whom can I seek refuge? Who will have pity on me? I dare not raise my eyes to heaven because I have sinned against heaven. On earth I can find no refuge, because here I have created a scandalous state of affairs. Thus to Thee, most merciful God, I return filled with melancholy and grief, for Thou alone art my hope, Thou alone my refuge. Have mercy upon me, O God, according to thy loving kindness.

Have mercy as Thou did to St. Peter, after Christ told him the night before his crucifixion, "Verily I say unto thee, That this day, even in this night, before the cock crow twice, thou shalt deny me thrice." And yet St. Peter only denied Christ when he was asked whether he knew him. What had I done in confessing I did not receive words from you, my God—in having lied about not having received your divine revelations? What would St. Peter have done if the Jews had come and threatened to beat him? He would have denied once more if he had seen them getting out the whips. If St. Peter, to whom Thou granted so many gifts and so many favors, failed so miserably in his test, what was I capable of, O Lord? What could I do?

O God, you know my aim was in loving you, not in attaining the glory of the world. What would a man not say under torture? Can you forgive me, O God? I have lived in self-denial and have practiced self-flagellation to understand better the suffering of your son and the love he had for all mankind. The torture I experienced, though, was nothing I had ever before known. I am a man, after all, not your son Jesus Christ. I bleed and break much easier. I hope you will forgive my transgressions, for I meant not what I said. Though St. Peter denied he knew Christ, he did not deny his faith, and I have not denied mine, O Lord. My faith is greater because of my suffering. You must know that. You who know and see everything must know that I suffer deeply in body and in spirit. Send me word that you have mercy upon me. I signed a paper; that is all. The words did not emanate from my heart and soul. They came from my torturers. My words are those I speak to you now. Do you hear them, O Lord? Send me a sign that you do, for I am alone in my agony and need to know that you have not forsaken me.

I shall be executed soon. That I know with certainty, for as well as denying you, O Lord, I confessed to treason. I am not sorry, God, if it means I see you sooner rather than later. My job here is finished. I acted in the name of social justice and moral reform. I acted in accordance with your laws. Now I await my job with you, as your eternal servant, in the Kingdom of heaven. I hope I have earned my way. Please tell me I have. I need the strength to face these final dark days. No man should be alone like this, in body and soul. It is the reason I speak to you. I cannot bear this punishment without you. You are my judge, not these men who act with ruthless power. I know they will suffer in the end for their cruelty. You who are just will make sure of that. That thought alone cannot comfort me, however. It is only the thought of your love that comforts me. I know you will receive me for the man I am, a true Christian, who lived to echo your words and die in your name. Though my cell is dark, I see the crucifixion before my eyes. Is it you who sent it to me? Thank you, Lord. Teach me how to suffer. Teach me how to die with grace and honor. I feel the nails driven through my flesh, crushing my bones. I see my blood rushing from my veins, washing and cleansing the sinful earth. I wish to die now, with this image. Help me if you can, O Lord.

# Lorenzo

Angelo holds a book of my poems in his hands. He reads aloud quietly. A friend can do no more than he has done in wishing to honor me. Has he not reminded me more than enough that I lived in glory and recognition, as few men have? I am grateful to him and hope I have expressed my gratitude sufficiently. Yet no man can give to another on his deathbed that which he desires most: *Le tems revient.*

The time returns to those who live in the ripeness of youth: each day recycling itself in renewal, offering, as if divine, a light made of gold, wherein the mind knows no bounds and the world is held in the palm of a hand. Time, for me now, shall never return. I can no longer engage and command it to stop. Even Angelo, endowed with gifts immortal, cannot stop it. He can only help me return to a time I formerly lived in achievement. Yet I am not appeased by what I have done. I am consumed by what I leave unfinished. I refer not only to my many building projects. I refer, as well, to my poems. As he speaks the words I once wrote, I think: have I written enough to make my poetry lasting?

He reads from one of my long, incomplete poems called "The Supreme Good." How old was I when I began it? Was I twenty-four? I can't recall. I remember only that it was during a time when I engaged and commanded time: when time recycled itself to me each day, energizing my passions. Was there a greater joy for me than writing verse and through it address what consumed my mind? And what was that, other than what my grandfather called "the road to happiness"? Was that not the basis of the poem I hear Angelo read? Was the knowledge of God essential to happiness? Or could this happiness be achieved through love alone? Or must the two be fused together? Could we through love achieve the knowledge of God and thus live in satisfaction of this divine goodness?

Even these thoughts remain unfinished. The truth is they are too big for my brain right now. If I didn't succeed in discovering their answers in the ripeness of my youth, how can I expect to now on the bed of my death? I give up thinking for the moment. I resign myself and listen to Angelo read.

> *That man who's pleased with what he has seems much*
> *more rich to me than he who values what*
> *he doesn't have above the things he owns.*

> *Oh light resplendent, pure, and true, through you,*
> *I pray to you to cleanse my clouded vision*
> *of haze and make it absolutely clear*
> *that I may see your pure and limpid light.*

> *And make us love your boundless beauty, free*
> *of any care that might the heart torment.*
> *Oh sovereign Good, inciting every mind,*
> *let us enjoy you always, avid yet content.*

I raise my hand in reach of the water glass on the bedside table. Angelo closes the book and lifts the glass for me, bringing it to my lips. I sip as well as a man lying down can sip. I wave the glass away from my mouth. He returns it to the table.

"I shall never receive fame as a poet, as you have and will for posterity."

"Your poetry will be read in future centuries."

"But I will not be known, primarily, as a poet."

"If that is true, it is only because you are renowned as a great statesman."

"And yet I am as much a writer as a statesman."

"You do not need to convince me."

"The world will need convincing."

"Your poetry will be read in future centuries. Of that I am certain."

"Even though many of my best remain unfinished?"

"Beauty resides in what is left incomplete."

"Your idea of poetic justification?"

"My idea of truth."

"Truth in what way?"

"Your unfinished poems will forever be in a state of becoming, and this is often more attractive than what is fixed. This state of becoming allows the reader to infer, to imagine, and to dream. What is fixed is sometimes limiting."

"And for this reason you never completed the poem about Giuliano?"

"I would like to say 'Yes, that is the reason,' but I cannot lie. The truth is my poetic well ran dry. I had no other excuse, such as you have had. I was not, at the time, the ruler of a city being pulled in myriad directions."

"Though, as you say, beauty resides in what is left incomplete, I believe my poems would be more beautiful in their completeness."

"That is perhaps true, but let me demonstrate my point."

He opens my book again, selects a page, and reads.

> *By now the east had turned completely red.*
> *The mountain peaks seemed fashioned out of gold.*
> *The peasant was returning to his work—*
> *You heard the fledgling sparrow squawk and scold.*
> *The stars had fled, and you could almost see*
> *The one who loved the laurel tree of old.*

"Why do you select such an early poem of mine? I wrote that while still a boy at my grandfather's villa at Caraffilo."

"It matters not what the poem or when you wrote it. Did you not notice that I left it incomplete?"

"You didn't even finish the stanza."

I speak the final two lines.

> *The horned owl, barn owl, and the night owl too,*
> *In quite a hurry to the woods withdrew.*

"I purposefully stopped at 'The one who loved the laurel tree of old.'"

"And your point?"

"It forces me to infer, imagine and dream. What you wrote at a young age was far beyond your years. It foretells the past, present and future. The laurel tree is synonymous with your Latin name, Laurentius. It is a tree that stands outside your window here at Careggi. Both you and the tree stand for regeneration, for continuity, for resilence: 'The one who loved the laurel tree of old.' The poem is already complete in its incompleteness. Beauty resides in the word "old" because it proclaims the magnificence of the Golden Age and makes clear the authority of the Medicean government before, now and hereafter."

"You are a master salesman. Perhaps you should finish my poems."

"I do not wish to finish them, but as long as I'm alive I will convince the world of their merit, as they currently exist, for they remain for posterity as the poems of a man who was so much more than a man or poet. He was a statesman and prince, a philosopher-king, a man of Plato, a man of God, a man for all ages and time eternal."

"And yet despite all that you are the superior poet."

"Nonsense. Look what you have done in your so-called unfinished poems, 'Corinto' and 'Ambra.' You give substance of the everyday in myth. You give us what is real: the language of peasants, nature in its intricate detail, human life in its earthly particulars, the pastoral life, the man in search of God and spirit and the very meaning of existence and our search for happiness. What more can a poet do?"

He turns the pages of the book, stopping when he finds the poem "Corinto," of which he reads the opening stanza. I listen and wish to sleep for now and always with the soft breath of his voice brushing gently to my ears.

*The moon, amid the lesser stars of night,*
*shines forth so full through heavens deep and still*
*the lustrous stars seem almost lost to sight;*
*and Sleep grants every living soul release*
*from all the toils of the daily round,*
*and shadows fill the world, and deepest peace.*

# Machiavelli

I was in the government office the day Bishop Francesco Remolino arrived in Florence from Rome to head the Papal Commission to determine the fate of Savonarola and two of his fellow monks, Fra Domenico and Fra Silvestro, who had been recently arrested, as well, for his professed prophetic visions and influence with those still supporting Savonarola's cause. Let's be clear here: the Papal commission was nothing but a formality. The Signoria and Pope Alexander had already pre-determined Savonarola had to die. Whether he had actually done anything deserving of execution was beside the point. His arrest and subsequent interrogation had already gone too far. As one of the Signoria said, "If we spare him and his two followers and they return to San Marco, the people of Florence will turn on us and stuff us into sacks and tear us to pieces. Can we allow that? Of course not. We must execute the monks to save our own skins." The commission simply needed to create enough evidence to damn the monks, and that is not difficult when those involved are equipped with the ability to lie and deceive. Men in power have always used these skills to great advantage, and who can say they are wrong if their lies and deceptions prove beneficial to the state? Give me benefit over morality any day of the week.

I must confess to feeling moved when Savonarola appeared before Bishop Remolino and his fellow commissioners. He appeared broken in every which way: his face, his eyes, his body, and his will. He had every reason to look terrified. Bishop Remolino had ordered the Strappado be placed in the room. I could see Savonarola, shaking his head, looking at it. The Bishop had been informed that Savonarola had retracted his signed confession. He had not come all the way from Rome to mince words.

"Do you deny what you have already confessed in writing?" he asked.

Savonarola dropped his head and refused to answer. I anticipated the Bishop's response, for it was a certainty. He ordered the Strappado.

Savonarola fell to his knees and cried out, imploring help from someone not present in the room. "Now hear me. God, Thou hast caught me. I confess that I have denied Christ. I have told lies. O you Florentine Lords, be my witness here. I have denied Him from fear of being tortured. If I have to suffer, I wish to suffer for the truth: what I said, I heard from God. O God, Thou art making me do penance for having denied Thee under fear of torture. I deserve it."

A guard tied his arms behind his back, in preparation for them to be yanked into the air. He yelled out in terror, "I have denied you, God, for fear of torture. Jesus, help me. This time you have caught me."

His hands were hooked to the pulley, which began to raise him into the air. "Don't tear me apart," he yelled. "Jesus, help me."

"Why do you call upon Jesus?" the Bishop asked.

"So I seem like a good man," Savonarola answered. "Please, Jesus."

"Why do you call on Jesus?" the Bishop repeated.

"Because I am mad," Savonarola cried.

I saw his small, frail body fall as the pulley was released. He screamed in terror as his body came to a sudden stop above the ground.

"Do not torture me any further," he screamed, "I will tell you the truth."

"Are you sure?" the Bishop said.

The pulley began to raise the friar once again.

"You have torn the limbs from my shoulders," the preacher yelled. "Do not torture me any further. In the name of Jesus!"

"Why did you deny what you had already confessed?" the Bishop said.

"Because I am a fool," Savonarola replied, heaving and gasping for air.

"Why did you deny what you had already confessed?" the Bishop asked again. "Are you not a man of your word, Girolamo Savonarola?"

"When I am faced with torture, I lose all mastery over myself," the preacher said.

"Have you ever preached that Jesus Christ was just a man?"

"Only a fool would ever think such a thing."

"Do you believe in magic charms?"

"I have always derided such nonsense."

"What did you know of the Council of the Church?"

"I authorized it."

The pulley was released again. The preacher screamed in agony, as he lay suspended by his wrists, his body writhing and swaying. It was my first exposure to seeing a man tortured, and I must confess to being both thrilled and horrified at the same time. The thrilling part was the game itself, where one man's power was set against another's will. Clearly the odds were in the favor of the one with power, but that's what made it so thrilling. If a man could withstand this kind of punishment it would reflect greatly on the testament of his will, on his ability to survive the worst kind of punishment without submitting his pride or will to another. I didn't know at the time that I would one day be such a man. I couldn't have foreseen it then, though now I am grateful for having played and won, for it does much for my esteem, and in the end, isn't my personal value of my esteem what counts most? Savonarola, for certain, didn't see it my way. To him, there was nothing in it that was thrilling. He experienced only the horror in unremitting pulls and releases of the rope. I assumed he dreamed of death at such moments to stop the pain.

Clearly, the Bishop held the power and the winning hand, and he would not stop until he received his desired satisfaction.

"Do you wish to depose the pope, the Holy Father?" he asked.

"The Holy Father resides in heaven," Savonarola yelled.

The pulley began to raise the friar up again.

"Do you deny the Holy Father in Rome?" the Bishop repeated.

"Do not torture me further. I will confess," the friar said.

The pulley was released again. Savonarola screamed.

"Do you deny the Holy Father in Rome?"

"You are killing me," the preacher yelled.

"Do you deny the Holy Father in Rome?" the Bishop kept persisting.

The pulley was released yet again.

"I do not deny him," Savonarola whispered. It was clear his voice was dying, along with whatever was left of his spirit.

"The Holy Father?"

"Yes."

"In Rome?"

"Yes."

"Say, 'I do not deny the Holy Father in Rome.'"

Savonarola didn't speak. He couldn't. The pulley pulled him up again, taking the air out of him.

"Say, 'I do not deny the Holy Father in Rome.'" the Bishop repeated.

"I do not deny the Holy Father in Rome," Savonarola managed to say, lifeless as he was.

"Do you deny that you are a prophet?"

"Yes."

"Do you deny that you speak with God?"

"Yes."

"Do you believe you have brought harm to the citizens of Florence?"

"Yes."

"Do you believe you have conspired with foreign leaders to bring about the demise of the Holy Father in Rome?"

"Yes."

"Will you sign your confession to these egregious acts?"

"Yes."

Officials made him sign yet another document, this time with the Papal Seal attached to it. Afterwards, a guard removed the crestfallen friar, returning him to his cell. Bishop Remolino dictated a report to the pope, stating the following: "He confesses to inciting citizens to revolt, to deliberately causing shortages of food which caused many of the poor to starve to death, and to murdering important citizens. He sent letters and communications to many Christian princes, urging them to defy your Holiness and to create a schism in the Church. Such was the depth of iniquity and evil in this dissimulating monster that all his outward appearance of goodness was nothing more than a charade. Of such a horrendous nature were his vile crimes that I cannot even bring myself to write them down, let alone pollute my mind with the thought of them."

# Savonarola

Is it possible that I am feeling happiness to be lying again on the stone cold floor of the cell? I think again. It is not happiness. Only God can bring me that. It is relief, nonetheless, that I am free from the presence of men who act with evil in their hearts, torturing me at their will, on a machine made to terrorize the heart, body and soul of man. I am nearly blind from pain, though I can see clearly each of my interrogators, especially Bishop Francesca Remolino, burning in hell.

I do not have to wait long for the words I have longed to hear since I arrived in this cell more than a month ago. I am on my knees, praying, as I see two men whom I do not recognize burst in my cell to tell me I am condemned to death for being a heretic and a traitor and for having used black magic in preaching the devil's words. I do not speak. I do not even ask the manner of my death. Does it matter? Soon I will be placed out of the hands of my tormenters and into the hands of God. This is all I think about, and it brings me the greatest relief imaginable. These men have no idea the favor they are giving me. I almost thank them for the news.

I am told Fra Domenico and Fra Silvestro are condemned to death as well. I see them for the first time since our separation, as we are given this last chance to speak with each other before our deaths. They enter my cell, chained and manacled as I am. They are little more than skin and bones. I feel sorry that they have been made to suffer for me. The guards stand some distance away, giving us our space to speak freely. I am grateful for this opportunity.

"We are to be degraded, stripped of our priesthood," Fra Silvestro says.

"Only God is authorized to do that," I respond.

"Do you not know the manner of our deaths?" he asks.

"How we die matters less than where we shall be delivered," I say.

"We shall be hung by the neck and burnt alive," he cries.

"We must accept willingly the fate which God has assigned for us," I say.

"I shall gladly cast myself in the fire," Fra Domenico says. "It is only my body they burn. My soul, and all of our souls, shall be preserved for God."

"You are a courageous man," I say to him.

Fra Silvestro weeps. He says, "We must be given a chance to proclaim our innocence before the people. They will not allow our unlawful deaths."

"I order you to put away all thought of this idea," I respond.

Fra Silvestro grows silent, though he continues to weep. I do not try to stop his tears. I do not blame him for not wanting to die, though I do not say this to him. I must give him hope. It is my job as Prior, and I aim to fulfill my role until the very end.

"We must now follow the example of Our Lord Jesus Christ, who refrained from protesting his innocence, even when he was on the cross. We must do likewise, because his is the example which we must follow."

"It is not dying that concerns me," Fra Domenico says.

"As it shouldn't," I respond.

"What does concern me is the preservation of your writings," he says.

"About that we can do nothing now," I say.

"I have already acted upon it," he says.

"You have?"

"During my first days of imprisonment, having anticipated that we would die at the hands of the authorities, I wrote a letter and had it smuggled out."

"And what is the content of this letter?"

"I wrote to our brethren at San Marco, telling them where they can find your writings."

"That is something only you know."

"Exactly. Now others know. I urged them to make your writings into books that should be read every day and night so that your teachings are preserved and taught."

"Your gift will be held in esteem by God."

"It is not for God I did this. I did it so the legacy of your words will live on in the minds of all who now hold the mantle of the holy order we have served."

"Bless you, Fra Domenico," I say. "Your words bring me joy."

I look at Fra Silvestro. He does not react to what Fra Domenico has said. I see and smell his fear. I do not like it.

"Do you not wish to bless Fra Domenico for his courageous act?" I ask.

"Bless you, Fra Domenico," he says. His response is disingenuous, but I do not push him to be more sincere. He is hurting. I reach for his hand, though I am too weak to grasp it.

"And bless you, as well, Fra Silvestro. You have been a loyal servant both to me and to God. You shall be rewarded for your suffering."

He is about to speak, but the guards interrupt us, saying our time together is over. I ask my brethren to kneel before me. They do. I hold an imaginary Host and offer it to them. "Take this, the body of Christ," I say. They reach with their hands to take what is there only in spirit. The guards lift the men to their feet and take them out. "Go with the Lord," I shout after them. "Let Him be your guide."

I lapse into a light sleep, though deep enough for me to see a vision or a dream. I can no longer tell one from the other. I don't care, since what I see is good and holy. I see God in heaven. I see the Holy Spirit. I see the Holy Mother and her Son, Jesus Christ. The Holy Mother speaks, telling me the angels above await me. In heaven I will not need my broken body. My soul will rest on clouds of glory made by the Holy Father.

# Machiavelli

Hell had opened six weeks earlier, swallowing much of Florence and its occupants. Never was this more evident than on the night workers built a scaffold in the middle of the Piazza della Signoria, in the same spot where the ordeal of fire had been due to take place. While many faithful still clung to the hope of a miracle—that the glory of God would manifest itself and save the monks, whereas the righteousness of life would prevail over vice and sin, bringing renovation to the Church—the majority of people gathered in anticipation of what they had been deprived of seeing six weeks earlier: monks burn to death and become ash.

People cheered the construction: a solid piece of wood many feet high, with a large circular platform around its base. Another piece of wood nailed horizontally near the top of the vertical piece made the scaffold look like a cross. This did not go unnoticed. "They are going to crucify him," a man shouted, "and when they do we will witness another resurrection sent from God." When word of the scaffold appearing as a cross reached the ears of the authorities, orders were quickly given to saw off part of the wood to remove any Christian symbolism. As one official said, "We do not want a crucifixion. We already had one, and we have been suffering ever since."

By the following morning, May 23, 1498, the execution date, the crowd had swelled in numbers far surpassing those of the ordeal by fire. Much cheering and crying accompanied the presence of the prisoners, who walked barefoot, robed in their clerical vestments. Their wrists were tied in ropes behind their backs as guards accompanied them along the lengthy raised walkway. At the end of the walkway was the circular platform with the gibbet, beneath which were heaped bundles of brushwood and kindling twigs in preparation for the bonfire. Someone yelled, "Long live Jesus Christ! Show us the miracle we have longed to see." Most, however, did not want to hear talk of a miracle. A man jeered in response, summing up the views of most who attended:

"Savonarola, the time to perform a miracle is past. Now you will burn and go to hell for deceiving the citizens of Florence."

Bishop Remolino presided over the first tribunal, which included the removal of their vestments, officially degrading them of their priesthood. The authorities moved from one to the other, and as each vestment was removed the Bishop said, "I separate you from the Church militant and from the Church triumphant, in heaven."

"Only from the Church militant, " Savonarola said, "the other is not within your jurisdiction."

In the second tribunal, as the prisoners stood in their undershirts, Bishop Remolino read a Brief, bestowing upon the three friars the pope's plenary indulgence, granting them a formal pardon for all sins committed in this world, absolving them from punishment in purgatory in the next world. Savonarola remained silent during the reading of the Brief. He gave no indication that his being absolved from punishment in purgatory pleased him. His faithful supporters among the crowd did not remain quiet, though.

"Savonarola is already blessed by God."

"You who are doubters will see the great miracle appear."

"Only the truly righteous shall survive in the end."

His detractors, who made up the majority, shouted down the remaining faithful Savonarola followers. They cared little for the pope's plenary indulgence.

"Hell is the only fitting place for such a one as he."

"I care not for purgatory, heaven and hell. Light the fires. Let us see the just punishments here on earth."

"Savonarola must die to rid Florence of all that ails it."

The majority won out, for in the third and final tribunal, members of the Signoria read the official decree that all three monks would be hanged and burned while still alive. This decree brought a raucous reaction from the crowd, and the chant that had been heard at the ordeal by fire began once again:

"Light the fire!"

# Savonarola

Why should a pope resolve a man of sin when he has none that has stained his soul? It is the pope, not me, who needs pardon for sins committed in this world. I have lived a righteous life. He has sinned in all manner of ways. I do not care that the vestment has been taken from my body. It is not, after all, the vestment that makes the priest. Proof of that is seen in Rome, where the clerics dress in ostentation, ornamenting themselves with religious robes while underneath these robes their souls are stained in black. I want to say this to the tribunal, but I don't, for I wish to follow the example of Jesus and die with grace, no matter the suffering I endure. I hear my faithful followers among the crowd. Some weep; some whisper loud enough for me to hear: "Speak to us. Give us word that a miracle will pass." I do not respond, for I do not believe a miracle will come to pass. If it does come to pass, it will be in the next life, not this one. It is eternal life with God that is the true miracle. I must endure much before that happens. I see the noose; I see the kindle and the wood; I smell the oils and the resin. I can only imagine the lick of the flames on my flesh. I must suffer in unbearable ways. I know that. God knows that, as well. He is with me now, as is Jesus Christ and his Holy Mother. I give myself to them. Let them be my judge, not these raving fools who know only hate, vengeance and personal ambition.

Fra Silvestro is first. He keeps his head down, his eyes closed. I hope he hears not the words of the crowd:

"Hang him."

"Burn him."

"Rot in hell."

I hope he hears the words of Jesus, as he suffered on the cross, nails driven through his feet and hands: "Father, into your hands I commend my spirit."

The noose is around his neck. He is sent downward, where he comes to a sudden stop, his legs kicking. The noose is not tight enough around his throat to kill him. It is intentional. The authorities do not want us to die by hanging. They want us to hang, while still alive, and burn us, fully conscious. Fra Silvestro chokes and manages to say, "Jesu!" intermittently, though his breath is choked. I hear many in the crowd cry out to me to bring the miracle to pass. Others mock me, saying it is proof finally that I have no such powers from God to prevent these executions. I agree. I do not have such powers. What I have is a belief in God and eternal joy that will come to me, making the unbearable suffering worth it in the end. I watch helplessly as Fra Silvestro dangles, saying "Jesu." I want to tell him his suffering is almost done. I want to say God in His glory awaits him.

Fra Domenico is next. He keeps his head up and his eyes open. The noose is placed around his neck. Someone says, "You are a sinner, not a priest." Another tells him, "You must pay now for your crimes against our city." I know he doesn't hear them. I know he is one with God and accepts his suffering, if not actually welcoming it. He is not afraid. He is sent downward and comes to a stop only feet from Fra Silvestro, who continues to dangle and choke, saying, "Jesu." Now both of them kick their feet and say "Jesu" in unison.

"God in heaven, help them!" a man yells.

"We shall all suffer for killing these innocent priests," another says.

He is right. The people of Florence will suffer. They had their chance to redeem themselves and find salvation through God's word. Now they will suffer a worse fate than the monks they see hanging. They will suffer for eternity. In the meantime, they wish to drink from the cup of vengeance and savor its every last drop. It is evident in their vitriolic words. While they are happy to see Fra Silvestro and Fra Domenico hang and writhe, ready to be burned, it is my punishment and death they really want, as is evident in their shouts.

"The wretched liar is next."

"He who consorts with the Devil."

"He who wanted all of us to be excommunicated with him."

"He who has caused the food shortages and starvation for so many."

"It is your turn now, Savonarola."

"Enjoy the fires. They are nothing compared to the fires of hell."

I feel the noose around my neck.

I am released.

# Machiavelli

I have been asked "Why not just burn them at the stake? Why hang them alive first, leaving them writhing in pain, crying out to Jesus?" These questions presume that the recipients of the punishment are the three friars. The truth is this: the recipients of the punishment are the citizens who watch, for the spectacle is performed for them. The reasons are twofold: the authorities wish them to be satisfied that the men who committed injustices against them are punished. More so, they wish these same spectators to be stupefied by what they're watching, and to remind them of the awesome power behind such an act. This power induces fear in the common man, and this fear is held by a dread of punishment that will never leave the beholder. Anyone seeing first the hanging and then the burning will never forget it, and he will never forget that the power behind such an act can commit the same act upon him as well. If this explanation is not a sufficient address of the questions, consider this: the friars' punishment is a testament to the reasonable certainty that God does not rule men on earth. He who prophecies that God, through fires and storms, will wreak vengeance on those who sin will, in the end, die in the same manner.

Thus, this is the reason the three friars hung from ropes around their necks, still alive, calling out to Jesus before their real execution—death by fire—began. The hangman did not start the fire, as planned. A man ran from the crowd with a lighted torch. He set the brushwood alight, saying, "Now at last I can burn the Friar who would have liked to burn me!" His action caused further vigilantism. Some people tossed gunpowder into the fire, causing small explosions and cascades of sparks. Just as the flames began to leap up into the air towards the hanging figures a sudden wind blew up, forcing the flames away from their bodies. People backed away, saying, "A miracle! A miracle!" In the next moment, the wind stopped, and the fires rose unimpeded, catching the hanging friars. Fra Silvestro and Fra Domenico continued to call "Jesu." Savonarola said nothing, even as the flames consumed him.

Those in the crowd who wept or called to Jesus or God for help were in the minority. Most of the people yelled and cheered, expressing a freedom from personal oppression they had experienced under Savonarola's rule.

"They burn as any ordinary men would burn."

"It is proof of their deception."

"Good riddance to the City of God."

The fire burned through the rope securing Savonarola's hands behind his back. His arms fell free. The upward current of the fire then caught his right arm, raising it into the air, his hand opening dramatically, as if from amidst the flames he was blessing those who stood gazing up at him. Women began to sob; some fell to their knees, believing the man they believed to be a saint was blessing them. Some fled in fright and panic.

"It is the devil's work," a man said. "Let us run from the fires of hell."

If it were only that easy to run from hell, for Florence had become the very denizen of the underworld. If there had been any doubt, there was none now. The fires blazed, darkening the sky, making clear to me the root and cause of the inferno: Savonarola had sowed so much disunity in the city that his prophetic light had to be extinguished by a still greater fire.

Young boys threw stones at the burning friars, and no one stopped them for fear of retribution. Many chanted "Burn, you ministers of Satan," and those who didn't chant, laughed and danced in the piazza until the charred body parts of the men fell to the ground, causing an even greater stir, for many wanted their ashes and bones for relics. Armed men, on order of the authorities, made sure that would not happen, for the last thing government leaders wanted was for people to own relics of the men they had just burned. They wanted everything about them erased. To ensure this end, their ashes were shoveled into a cart. Armed men pushed and followed the cart, while citizens and leaders followed behind. When the cart reached the Ponte Vecchio, it came to a stop. The armed men lifted the cart and dumped the friars' ashes into the waters of the Arno. I watched the current rush their ashes into oblivion, thinking to myself, *These are men who had dwelt in dreams, foregoing pleasures. What a shame for them if there is no heaven to acknowledge their sacrifice.*

Savonarola believed that redemption would come from the Almighty. He failed to understand the limitations, if not intentions of God: that he does not want to rob from us of our free will and the infamy that comes with it. He thus stays out of the affairs of men and allows us to fight it out till the end amongst ourselves, watching us make a mess of things. Where would be the fun in following a script written by a higher authority? What would be the point of all our deceptions and machinations?

Savonarola stupidly relied on Providence. That alone does not denigrate his talent. Yes, talent, for it takes much imagination and invention to hold people on a string, like a master puppeteer. He ascended the ranks and could have continued to ascend to stand alongside men of history who founded new states. Men such as Cyrus, Romulus and Theseus. I do not jest when I say this, though here is where he failed to live up to them: he was unarmed, and no one who has ever ruled or desired to rule has done so without might and firepower. Not in a world populated by men, where war and violence prevail to such an extreme that God himself would be brought to his knees in humble admiration. A ruler must fight envy—the most bitter of all human fruits—with violence. That is not conjecture. It is fact. Ask Moses or Brutus or any others who killed many of their opponents. Savonarola in time of need had only God instead of a necessary army. He could only crow, like a castrated rooster, failing to understand that only other castrated roosters, such as himself, heard his voice, and I have never read in history of roosters, castrated or not, defeating the power of men.

I wish to credit him, nonetheless. In fact, if he had only showed us how to go to the house of the devil, I may have followed him because I believe the true way to go to paradise is to learn the way of hell and thus avoid it.

# Lorenzo

Savonarola tells me my soul is damned. I do not, for all his supposed perspicacity, believe him. If my soul is damned, then his is as well, for we share the same human plight. He is but a man, as am I, and as such we are born damned, or born saved, depending on how one chooses to look because they are two sides of a coin that is easily flipped and likely to land on one or the other.

I say nothing more. It is futile to argue with such a one as he. I face death with the only truth I know: I have lived. I am secure with this truth because it is mine to own. If I am damned for having lived, I have no defense. Perhaps he is damned for not having lived. In any case, it is too late for either of us to change the course of our lives.

If I chose to speak further, which I do not, I would say this: my soul, damned or not, is a beautiful soul, for it is the soul of man. Neither of us exists as the reincarnation of God. We exist as His creation, and as such we have received the title of man. I, for one, am grateful for having had this opportunity to live during the *Rinascimento*. Though I die tonight, the future is bright, for this mind of mine is the mind of many, and it will shine under a golden light for years to come since the *Rinascimento* is not for now. It is for always.

You may leave now. You have given me more than I expected. You did not give me your blessing, and in failing to do so, I have come to bless myself, which, in the end, is much greater.

I watch you leave, becoming smaller in stature, until you fade, not only from my eyes, but also from my consciousness. My senses begin to wane. I am slipping, suddenly unsure. Is this Angelo now beside me? Are those my lips upon the cross?

I breathe my final breath.

Now falls the shadow.

I hear—or do I speak?

*Le tems revient.*

# Machiavelli

Though I am not a man given to superstition, I believe the dead have much to tell the living. Thus, I listen to the dead. I would, in fact, not be a writer if I didn't invite the visitation of ghosts. I like nothing better than to step inside the venerable courts of the ancients, where, solicitously received by them, I nourish myself on that food that alone is mine and for which I was born; where I am unashamed to converse with them and to question them about the motives for their actions, and they, out of their human kindness, answer me. And for many hours at a time I feel no boredom, I forget all my troubles, I do not dread poverty, and I am not terrified by death.

But enough of my ghosts and the habits of my craft! It is about Lorenzo where the time returns and forever shall, for his ghost has the most allure. Do not take my word. Take the word of Angelo Poliziano, who watched Lorenzo's final breath, clasping his crucifix set in pearls. Only a poet can take from the rubble shards of glass and make of it a window comprehensively clear about the death of a man he loved and revered:

> *Who from perennial streams shall bring*
> *Of gushing floods a ceaseless spring?*
> *That through the day, in hopeless woe*
> *And through the night my tears may flow.*
> *As the sad nightingale complains,*
> *I pour my anguish and my strains.*
> *Ah, wretched, wretched, past relief;*
> *Oh, grief beyond all other grief!*
> *Lightning flies from heaven down*
> *to rob us of our laurel crown,*
> *now silence rings us all around,*
> *Now we are deaf to all thy sound.*

On the night of Lorenzo's death, April 8, 1492, the brightest of stars fell from the sky and extinguished, as if the most golden light of the most golden age had ended.

The evidence appeared in the city below. Two of the lions on public display that served as the republic's mascots tore each other to death in their cages. A bolt of lightning struck the cathedral, sending marble blocks crashing to the street below. A woman in Santa Maria Novella cried out that a bull with horns of fire would burn down the entire city. Lorenzo's physician, Piero Leoni, committed suicide, throwing himself down a well. Many said the cause of the calamities could be traced to Lorenzo himself; that he had released a ghost he had long imprisoned in a ring on his finger, causing a disruption in the heavens.

It is senseless to conjecture about mystery. Invisible strings will always tug at us, making us believe something other than ourselves controls us. Do not believe it. A wise man alone alters the influence of the stars. These portents fail to shake the foundation of my core beliefs. I will continue to live on my own terms, believing will and determination forge my destiny. As for my death, I have had a recurring vision. In this vision, I see two columns of men. One consists of miserable wretches dressed in rags. When I ask who they are, they reply, "We are the saintly and the blessed; we are on our way to heaven." I spy another column, this one filled with men dressed in fine robes, deep in conversation. I approach and recognize many of them: Plato, Plutarch, and Tacitus, all discussing grave matters of state. When I ask what brings them here, they reply: "We are the damned of Hell." I say to them in response, "I wish to follow you, for it is among learned men, not pious fools, that I hope to spend eternity."

Perhaps after death I will receive my comeuppance and be slapped silly into believing in an unstable, fickle deity. Till then, I will shift and adapt to the winds of fortune, as the changing circumstances dictate, compelled by necessity to know the ways of evil and the path to hell, singing the praises of Pico's words: "O great and wonderful happiness of man! It is given to him to have that which he chooses and to be that which he wills." If by following this creed I am labeled a cynic and a fool, I wish only to say:

I love within me the soul that in defiance breathes.

# Notes

Piero the Unfortunate, Lorenzo's eldest son, remained in exile a broken man, residing mostly in Rome, where he lived off the collection of jewels and objects he had taken from his father's palace. He immersed himself in a life of drunkenness, gluttony and all manners of debauchery until in 1503 he drowned in a river near Naples, fleeing the Spanish troops at war with the French, with whom he was allied, for control of Naples.

Lorenzo's second son Giovanni fared better than his older brother. In 1512, with the backing of papal forces, he captured the city of Florence, restoring Medici power. The following year, he became Pope Leo X, wherein he famously said, "Since God has given us the papacy, let us enjoy it." Known for selling more indulgences than any other pope to pay for his lavish lifestyle, he inspired Luther's Protestant Reformation.

Machiavelli, suspected of being part of a conspiracy to oust the newly formed Medici government, was imprisoned and tortured for twenty-two days, though he never confessed to the charge of treason. He lived quietly in the countryside, away from the political maelstrom of which he had always been accustomed, and began dedicating himself to scholarship and writing, producing many books on political theory, which, in his lifetime, brought to him mostly sharp criticism from his contemporaries. In June 1527, he drank a homemade remedy for his ailing stomach and died. Many historians question the validity of his having received last rites, since he was never a conforming Christian. The Church, in 1559, officially banned his books.

In 1527, the year of Machiavelli's death, the corrupt Medici rule was overthrown in favor of a republic that recalled Savonarola in declaring itself the Republic of Christ. Though that republic lasted only a short time, it became evident that Savonarola's life and teachings would not die easily in the minds and hearts of his devotees. Beginning in the 16th Century, his writings have enjoyed many printings, and reverence for his saintliness has never waned, as is evident in the fact that talk of his beatification has been ongoing for five hundred years.

With Lorenzo de' Medici's death, the golden age of Florence ended, never to return. Never again would Florence receive the honor and esteem of kings and emperors on continents far and wide. Never again would it have as its lead statesman a Renaissance man of diplomatic genius, who could encourage the arts and learning through a belief that man's mind was the main star in a galaxy of possibilities. It is no wonder then that Lorenzo de' Medici, in the passage of time, has become more myth than man.

# Acknowledgments

I am indebted to the authors, scholars and historians alike, whose biographies and histories inspired the writing of my book. They provided me with facts, stories, dialogue and poetry. Any misrepresentation of historical detail in my book is due to my negligence, not theirs. I transformed in my own fashion what I read, creating a work that, though based on fact, is shaped by imagination and thus not to be taken as literal, as is evident in the truth that my narrators have been dead more than five hundred years.

I consulted or read in full more than a dozen books. For some of these books, I did more than read. I studied them, taking voluminous notes. Paul Strathern's *Death in Florence* is one such book, which provided me a detailed history of Lorenzo de' Medici, Savonarola and Florence during the final decades of the 15th Century. Another book significant to my research and writing is Miles Unger's biography titled *Magnifico*. Though I had consulted other sources about Lorenzo's life, I found his book the most accommodating in terms of language, style and storytelling. I owe much to Jon Thiem's translations of Lorenzo's poetry, as found in his book *Lorenzo de' Medici: Selected Poems and Prose*. F. W. Kent's book *Lorenzo de' Medici and the Art of Magnificence* provided me with all-important details of Lorenzo's involvement as an art patron, his many commissions of architectural projects, and his vast collection of jewels and objects, including ancient statuary. Donald Weinstein's book *Savonarola: The Rise and Fall of a Renaissance Prophet* provided me a comprehensive examination of Savonarola's beginning, middle and end, chronicling in rich, dense detail every facet of the preacher's beliefs, writings, sermons and dreams for a New Jerusalem. I returned to Miles Unger for his biography on Machiavelli, which gave me much more than facts and stories of interest. It helped me discover Machiavelli's cynical eye and biting tongue in regard to his beliefs and philosophy of men and political life.

# Bibliography

Hibbert, Christopher. The House of Medici: Its Rise and Fall. Harper Perennial, 1974

Hughes, Ted. Tales From Ovid. Farrar, Straus and Giroux, New York, 1997

Kent, F. W. Lorenzo de' Medici and the Art of Magnificence. Johns Hopkins University Press, 2004

King, Ross. Brunelleschi's Dome: How a Renaissance Genius Reinvented Architecture. Bloomsbury Publishing, 2000

Lloyd, Christopher. Fra Angelico. Phaidon, New York, 1979

Machiavelli, Niccolo, The Prince, New American Library

Machiavelli, Niccolo, History of Florence and Italy, W. Walter Dunne, 1901

Martines, Lauro, Fire in the City: Savonarola and the Struggle for the Soul of Renaissance Florence, Oxford University Press, 2006

Strathern, Paul. Death in Florence: The Medici, Savonarola, and the Battle for the Soul of a Renaissance City. Pegasus Books, 2015

Roscoe, William, The Life of Lorenzo De' Medici: Called the Magnificent. George Bell and Sons, London, 1902

Thiem, Jon, Editor. Lorenzo de' Medici, Selected Poems and Prose. Pennsylvania State University Press, 1991

Unger, Miles J. Magnifico: The Brilliant Life and Violent Times of Lorenzo De' Medici. Simon and Schuster, New York, 2008.

Unger, Miles, J. Machiavelli. Simon and Schuster, New York, 2011

Viroli, Maurizio, Niccolo's Smile: A Biography of Machiavelli. Farrar, Straus and Giroux, New York, 2000

Weinstein, Donald. Savonarola: The Rise and Fall of a Renaissance Prophet. Yale University Press, 2011

# About the Author

Thomas Crockett is a theater director and writer. His books include *The Hitchhiking Journals*; *Hope Beyond All Hope: New York Stories*; *Teaching Drama: Fundamentals and Beyond*, and two full-length plays, *A Tyrant for All Seasons* and *The Burrow People*. Born and bred in New York City, he currently resides in San Mateo, California.

68459093R00205

Made in the USA
San Bernardino, CA
04 February 2018